I0708527

BOOK 2

A LITRPG

BY AKASO

ISBN: 979-8-88993-032-7

Written by Akaso
Cover Art by David Haire

Published 2025 by MoonQuill
www.moonquill.com

Table of Contents

CHAPTER 1

LEVEL 15

Krahe awoke to a strange feeling in the back of her head and a hollowness in her gut which she could not physically place. It felt as though some organ that wasn't actually there had distended and now yawned with empty space. What had woken her was a sound, the knocking of a beak against her window, ringing and resonating with an unearthly tone.

She was deathly certain that she saw a raven with infernal coals for eyes sitting there upon first waking, but now that she had gotten her bearings, it was gone. In fact, the window didn't even face the outside, but a swirling, collapsing maelstrom as if the building hung perpendicular to the side of a cliff. This, combined with Casus' absence, made it more than obvious that this was a false awakening. She still felt a faint ache with each breath as her new ribcage settled in and drifted off to sleep once more within moments.

Thereafter, she dreamt of the data-plane which she had trawled in her past life, that virtualized pseudo-reality, which some had called things like the "matrix" or the "neo-astral." The semi-independent network programs which inhabited much of the data-plane were the closest thing to this world's eidolons that Krahe was familiar with. She wasn't sure why this unplace had shown up in her dreams, and of all times now, but then *it* made itself known; the Wound-like Grin, rendered in collage from garbled visual data and images of gore. It opened its fanged maw, the void filled by repeating, crudely tiled textures made from a cartel victim's skinless face bedecked by a scarf of his own intestines. From there, a simplistic icon of a crow emerged, slowly gaining definition until it became a fully realized high-fidelity model. It perched upon the Wound-like Grin's teeth, pecking at them. A moment later, Krahe awoke to the sound of pecking on a windowpane… But just as before, there was nothing there when she looked. Not even a feather.

With the dream only vaguely floating at the edge of her awareness, she blinked away the remnants of sleep and went about her morning. Casus was gone, but she found a tall glass of water on the table next to the box of Class 1 suppressants and a small ceramic dish. At first, she wasn't sure what was in it, being eight crescent shapes coated in brown sugar. The absence of one pill from the box followed by an appraisal using the Prospector's Eyes confirmed that the Banisher had prepared her pill in this way before he left.

Sighing, she ate one of them. Sticky. Aggressively sticky. The taste was strongly herbal, sour-sweet, and somewhat spicy, fitting nicely with the sugar. She finished the rest while reading a hefty tome on the pseudo-continent of Xaugeth, basking in the dawning sun.

As she read the book, *"Xaugeth Encyclopedia Vol. 1, Edition of 5201,"* she realized that Ronin had to have been one of the Herculeans listed as a civilized race of Xaugeth. Great big beetle-men, they were, who molted repeatedly as part of their life cycle, growing stronger and smarter with each molt, while each subsequent molt grew more difficult. Some chose to metamorphose into pseudo-adult grubs, called Eternity Larvae for their comparatively extreme longevity, while the beetles were Shieldbacks. The tome went on to detail that Eternity Larvae were subject to the same molting cycles as Shieldbacks, though theirs were far easier and only conferred growth in intelligence while the Herculean remained as an Eternity Larva.

"Some sources claim that at any time, an Eternity Larva may choose to initiate a metamorphosis into a Shieldback, while others claim that it must be initiated by consuming a special kind of jelly. It is possible that this differs between tribes, as the Herculean tribes are as varied as the species of their

animal cousins. Once an Eternity Larva metamorphoses, rather than becoming a juvenile Shieldback, it emerges at an advanced stage.

"There is a clear correlation between the number of molts an Eternity Larva has gone through and the Shieldback it becomes, though the ratio is not known, and once again, it likely varies from tribe to tribe. Eternity Larvae frequently remain as such for many years, and some simply live out their extremely lengthy lives without ever metamorphosing, acting as the scholars of the Herculean kingdom.

"A number of mighty Shieldbacks have come from Eternity Larvae, most notable among them the great unifier of the Herculean tribes, the Thousand-year Sapphire Monarch. As his name suggests, this Herculean remained an Eternity Larva for 1000 years, emerging as the Thousand-year Ruby Monarch. He went on to unify the Herculean tribes before molting into his current form, in which he has remained for the past century."

The tome went on to describe various known stages of Herculean development. They had a generally consistent appearance within their tribes, starting at dark earthy colors, moving into greens, yellows, oranges, and then reds. In the same way, the body shape changed and the size of a Shieldback's horns, mandibles, and other such extremities grew. Patterns and specific colors seemed to differ greatly between tribes. From the descriptions, Ronin had been effectively a juvenile, having only recently metamorphosed from a larva.

"It is known that Shieldbacks possess intelligence comparable to human adolescents from before their metamorphosis, but they do not develop the ability to speak until anywhere between the third and fifth molt. They commonly learn sign language to compensate."

There was a sudden tug at her mind's edge, pointing inward. After the third or perhaps fourth tug, she gave in and looked at her menu... She found there were some substantial changes.

[NAME: Brunhilde Krahe]
ARCHETYPE: Cherno Caster Lvl. 15
TITLE: Blackhand
RACE: Human
SEX: Female
AGE: 43/0
MIGHT: E1
CONTROL: D2
ATHLETICISM: E3
DURABILITY: E2
THAUMIC THROUGHPUT: D3+E3
ENTROPY TOLERANCE: D2+D1
ENTROPY DISSIPATION: E1+F2
BOONS
FLESHGRAFTS
EIDOLON VAULTS
THAUMATURGIES
STORAGE
OTHER

Before she could get a good look at her attributes, she already felt that same tugging sensation trying to bring her attention to her Boons.

[SNARE-SIGN OF BLACKEST PITCH]
Tags
Eidolon Vault
Outer God's Touch
Details
The holder gains two Lesser Eidolon Vaults and one True Eidolon Vault.

A raised eyebrow and a faint smirk were the only reactions the boon elicited from her; Krahe wasn't familiar enough with this side of the Seven Spokes System to evaluate the boon's true value, but having seen the effects of common Eidolon Vault applications, she was perfectly happy with it even if she just ended up adding Red Reapers to her arsenal. The growth of her actual attributes, though, was an indisputable benefit. She could feel that a fair bit of it was thanks to the Liminal Coil, but only a fraction. Taking a look at her attribute ratings again, she thought back to that first time in Jas'raba. Since then, her Control had jumped from E2 to D2, while athleticism and durability had both grown by a single numerical increment each. In stark contrast, her base thaumic throughput had gone from F1 to D3, her entropy tolerance had gone from E3 to D2, and entropy dissipation had grown from F3 to E1.

Krahe thought how convenient it would be if the system tracked growth changes, but since she had a habit of intermittently checking her attributes, she would need some way to record attribute snapshots. A memory slate would probably work, but she would have to always keep it in storage so to avoid it becoming a security issue.

It wasn't long before Casus returned from wherever he had gone, laying out an array of Mamon Couplers across the coffee table, including the non-functional coupler with the cracked core from before. He began polishing them.

"How do you feel?" he asked.

"Good, good. Seems I jumped to archetype level fifteen and got a new boon since I first got out of Jas'raba."

"What level were you then?"

"Five."

Casus continued meticulously checking his collection, furrowing his brow as he mentally reviewed recent events.

"An outlier, but not absurd progression for a late starter. Considering the Butchershop and Slaughterhouse 9, it's to be expected. What is the boon, if you do not mind me asking?"

Many would have said that he was downplaying, that her growth was absurdly fast, but Casus himself spoke from the perspective of an outlier, a man fully expected to become a powerful graft-saint. The very idea of being able to tame the Silberblut Coupler had been considered absurd before he set himself to the task. Favonia, his not-quite-sister, had gained a name for becoming strong at a similarly breakneck pace, and much like Krahe, she too had applied her own memory of her past life to that end. Within his frame of reference, Krahe's archetype-level progress was par for the course, and he thought nothing of it. No, it was everything else about her that stood out. If anything, her rapid progress in archetype leveling felt like a foregone conclusion, a mere side effect of this woman applying her pre-existing skill set to the Seven Spokes System.

"The holder gains two Lesser Eidolon Vaults and one empty True Eidolon Vault. Not sure why it only specifies that for the True Vault," she said. Even now, she continued leisurely reading her book.

"Two Lesser Vaults and one True Vault... One would expect a boon of this sort from a specialized occultist or a shamanist, but it is nonetheless well within plausible bounds. Misunderstand me not; this boon is certainly valuable, but you still have to fill those vaults before you can make use of them, and find some means to harness the spirits besides, which I cannot help you with."

"Your turn; tell me your boons," Krahe prompted. "Just the effects, no need to list the names."

"Surely, you have more than one boon."

"Of course, but I suspect you have already figured them out. My other boons grant me a Kenoma Pocket, play havoc with appraisal magic, and facilitate my unique abilities pertaining to harnessing anathema and tolerating Isotope," Krahe said, purposely leaving out most of the actual details and completely leaving out Chernobog's Mystic Wisdom.

"Isotope?" Casus asked, confused.

"Anathemic remnants. I found it easier to assign a one-word name to it."

"Ah. That is a good name for it. I've always found it strange that it is so often simply called anathema or anathemic remnants. Even the specific names it has are merely local slang. Bane Soot or just Soot is the most common one I've heard of."

"C'mon, your boons," she reiterated, continuing to read the Xaugeth Ecyclopedia. "I wager most of them have something to do with Mamon Couplers."

Casus nodded.

"As the Foreman mentioned, I possess a boon which forcibly raises my compatibility with any Mamon Coupler. Another guarantees the presence of an arm-mounted weapon, nearly always a long, slender blade, as you have seen. My Mamon Knight transformations are abnormally durable, scaling with my durability attribute, and I can push them to perform well beyond their normal specifications for short periods of time. I derive minor benefits from any Coupler I am wearing even if I am not transformed, and lastly, I can make use of catalysts that would normally only be usable by a specific person. However, there are... side effects. Surely, you noticed the change to my personality when I donned the mantle of Silberblut? That is the side effect. The "true" user's personality bleeds into mine."

"Can't say I'm even a bit surprised about those. Well, I guess I'll have to look into Eidolons before I can make any use of them. Does the Church have exclusive tomes on these subjects, or should I just visit a library?"

"I do not know. Apostles do gain access to some restricted sections of church libraries, however."

"Figured as much. I'll look in the Central Temple first, then..."

"You would want the Temple of Records, instead. It is not difficult to find; the building stands adjacent to the Central Temple."

Despite saying as much, Krahe remained as she was, on the sofa, for the next hour and a half, reading. Casus, true to his habits, also took to reading after ensuring his Mamon Couplers were in good condition and storing them away elsewhere in the safe house. Then, eventually, she rose up, and looking out the window, stretched in place. Casus beheld the gruesome manner in which the Liminal Coil protruded out of her back, creating an unsettling shape even through her biosuit. Despite having seen many grafts, something about that particular sight made a shiver run down the banisher's back.

He watched as she left, taking the Class 1 suppressant pills with her.

* * *

Krahe, first of all, bought a pair of tight leather pants and a button-up shirt, getting them adjusted on the spot to better fit her. She also bound her hair into a ponytail as a slight alteration to her appearance that may throw off anyone who may be looking for her. Even small changes such as these could have a tremendous effect.

Thereafter, she made her way to a place where she could have breakfast and listen in on people's morning conversations. She constantly kept an eye out and moved in such a way as to make less of a target out of herself; this didn't mean scurrying through side alleys alone, as she didn't know the city well enough to make that the optimal strategy, but rather using crowds and open spaces to vanish in plain sight. Even if an assassin were to see her, most professionals would try to avoid collateral damage. She was fairly confident that if she kept an eye out, she could dive or skim before an assassin's shot could reach her, even if it were the same man as before.

No attempt on her life was made, nor did she feel any hostile intent; all she felt were wandering eyes crawling upon her back, as her shirt was half-transparent, and her biosuit's color made it shine through all the more. She wagered, though, that it was more the gruesome shape of her spine than the biosuit. Eyes upon her left arm were, of course, a foregone conclusion. So long as she limited its movement, it wasn't too much of a stare-magnet.

The place she ended up at was neither seedy, nor squeaky clean. It was a happy medium between the two, with good food and drinks at a reasonable price, singled-off stalls, and staff that acted as invisible as the likes of Imraal. It was the sort of eatery she would have considered a great place to eat and ask about local goings-on back home. In Audunpoint, it was one among many, easily found if one knew how to look.

One of the first things she learned in the course of her investigation was that there was a standing order to all Hashem Family members in quite specific wording: Report her location and kill her if the opportunity presents itself but do not actively go out of your way. From what intel she managed to gather, the higher-ups were effectively treating her as an enemy gang member rather than a priority target.

She was perfectly content to reciprocate this treatment until she determined why an attempt had been made on her life. It was possible, likely even, that a higher-up in the Hashem Family had hired the killer. They were the only ones who had a motive.

Krahe had another coffee with her proper breakfast, finding this one to taste completely different from what Casus brewed; it was silky and buttery, without an iota of sugar, pushing notes of caramel into her nostrils. Her breakfast, rather than anything salty or meaty, was a nougat-like candy with whole pistachios inside, apparently a timeless classic eaten all throughout the Afshani Sultanate and beyond. She banished the cloying sweetness with a baked biscuit made with pork rinds that were ground up into the dough, with the rendered pork fat used as a leavener.

Later in the day, she went to the Temple of Records. They let her in without asking any questions. Unlike the Central Temple's receptionist, the librarian was a grizzled-looking human man, with burning metal spheres in place of eyeballs and thick cables coming out the back of his head to connect into spots on his back. He came across as friendlier than the Central Temple's receptionist.

"The High Grafter has made arrangements in your stead. You have access to Sections One through Sixteen, as well as special access to Section 38. Temporary supernormal access may be requested, though it may not be granted. Our public title archive includes a comprehensive inventory of all documents within the first thirty sections," the librarian explained.

Krahe easily found the documents she was looking for, or at least the general category. Everything was sorted by general topic, then by subtopic, and then alphabetically. Books on the basics of harnessing eidolons, known by other terms such as shamanism, demonology, occultism, or spiritualism, were found far from any restricted section. In fact, they were so out in the open that Krahe felt the need to take them and scurry into a secluded corner to read.

There, she first learned that Eidolons could be bound in a vast variety of ways, not necessarily requiring a pre-empowered vessel as she had been made to believe by Thaumshot. It was, rather, one of the easiest methods of harnessing eidolons, because the user didn't need to actually work with the eidolon; the vessel itself contained the instructions for the spirit alongside everything "extra" needed to make it achieve a specific result.

"Throughout history, such objects of power have ever found their place among the most common and most well-established conduits for eidolons, and for good reason. Sacrificial effigies, talismans and scrolls, arrows, and more recently, bullets. There is, however, a good reason why the mighty wizards of olden times were so famous for memorizing their mightiest magicks and wielding wands and staves..."

She split her attention to a notably thinner and trashier looking book, with a ghostly yellow snake winding its way around the Banishment Wheel with a representation of Zastreon in the center. Blocky, yellow lettering across the cover read *Secrets of the Atropal*.

Despite the sensationalist cover and foreword, claiming to have been written by a renegade from the group that first developed the Atropal line of Thaumshot, the book itself was factual and well put together. It went over the history of modern Thaumshot manufacturing, emphasizing on how the majority of new Thaumshot was refined and empowered by a vanishingly tiny few highly skilled craftsmen. It also openly admitted that their work targeted those who lack the skill, patience, understanding, or all of the above to make their own eidolon conduits and put together the instructions for the spirit.

"Imagine my shock, then, when I heard of well-respected wizards throwing around Citrine Atropals because they were, in their own words, good enough to get the job done."

The history of Atropals and their rivalry with Reapers apparently went back over 2000 years, with the two theurgies embedded in every conceivable form of conduit throughout the millennia. One interesting method that stood out was the usage of scrolls wrapped around high-grade casting catalysts, such as a staff, allowing the user to benefit from the flexibility of scrolls while empowering the catalyst's effects. The book went on to lament that unless a firearm was specifically engineered to enhance a certain type of Thaumshot, it was generally incompatible and underperformed compared to traditional methods. Dregshot apparently outperformed Thaumshot in terms of output and was easier to manufacture, but it had its own flaws, including lack of focus and no reusability.

When she reached the section that meticulously broke down how an Atropal worked, Krahe realized what this book really was—a craftsman's effort to procreate in the memetic sense, to pass his own discipline onto the next generation.

That section ended up swallowing her for several hours as she compulsively correlated everything with her own understanding of weapons systems. It was altogether occult and mind-bending, but by the time she tore her eyes away from the book, she felt like she had gained enough understanding to experiment with theurgy. She had also learned that "theurgy" was the most commonly used word for explicitly referring to the pattern by which the power of an eidolon was channeled into forming the likes of Reapers and Atropals.

Before any experimentation, however, she needed to figure out how to get herself an eidolon. She read and read and read, finding numerous different methods and rituals, but, eventually, she became frustrated and queried Chernobog's Mystic Wisdom regarding the Snare-sign of Blackest Pitch and how she might most easily catch herself an eidolon. It pointed her toward Section 38. So, she checked out a hefty stack of books, some scrolls, and a memslate, then made her way there.

Section 38 was well underground, in a cold, dry-aired chamber with heavy stone doors that used three keys, all of which the librarian had given her. The room was small, more of a large closet tucked away in the corner.

There, she found scrolls on Astro Diving and immediately knew why she had been given special access. Among them were texts penned by Barzai himself, significantly more legible than anything pertaining to the Liminal Coil.

In her exploration, Krahe discovered not just guidelines for executing a full dive but a rite for doing so safely, including precautions, the so-called "Rite of Dho-Hna." The prerequisites were only that one needs to be capable of performing a Partial Dive unassisted, leading Krahe to believe she could make use of this rite even without a Gulf Key. The many treasures of Section 38 numbered far more than merely four volumes. However, Krahe found that, for the time being, most everything beyond the fourth volume was incomprehensible to her or simply covered the same topics from a different perspective. So, she took with her the first four volumes of Barzai's work, *Dream-Quests Into the Astral Gulf: Of Ye Unguents and Angle-Webs Most Sublime, Of Ye Invocations and Words of Power, Of Passing Through the Veil Without Rending It,* and *Of Ye Rite Of Dho-Hna.*

The Dream-quest Scrolls were as bulky as they were strange. Though their construction was that of wood or bamboo-slip scrolls, they were made of dark chitin and bound by ligaments. Krahe added them to her bag alongside all the other books she'd decided to check out. The librarian, before even reviewing her selections, informed her, "Due to the conditions of your Special Access to Section 38, nothing you check out from there will be recorded, only the fact it was done. How many items did you take?"

"Four."

"Four items from Section 38…" He wrote it by hand, despite the presence of a typewriter-like terminal that projected a holographic screen from where the paper would normally sit. He jotted down other relevant information in the same manner, then proceeded to disappear the black-bound book into a drawer out of sight.

With a smile, he bid her farewell and offered his blessings. "May Zavesh and Igaria both bless your pursuits."

Before returning to the safe house, she visited a market where she bought the pincer of a "Great Spiny Land-crab," which was, as the name implied, from a giant, spike-covered crustacean. The pincer alone was sufficient for several meals. Preserved in a jar until purchase, the land-crab meat, as Krahe knew from her recipe collection, surpassed its water-dwelling cousins in terms of longevity without spoilage. It could be cured like mammalian meat, maintaining qualities similar to sea crabs, and was a valuable export for marshy regions that fed the "Calbian River Machine," the desalinator megastructure that fed Audunpoint's river. It was still dirt-cheap as far as Krahe was concerned, only a touch more expensive than poultry.

It would take a few hours to cook in the manner she had picked out, but she had no trouble waiting. Three hours and some spare change later, Casus came by to drop off a message and a memslate.

"It holds a series of keywords. Hand it over to the receptionist at the Central Temple when you wish to claim your share of the payout for the entire Slaughterhouse 9 incident. There is no information about you on it or in the system, merely contextless data pertaining to the incident and payments due."

Decontextualization. A reasonable infosec tactic.

The banisher stuck his head in further, sniffing a few times.

"Are you cooking land crab?"

Krahe nodded. "Yeah, it's been in there for... three hours? About an hour left, I reckon. I'll have more than I can eat, if you want some."

"Outstanding! I've always liked land crab!"

Since Casus was now there to act on the kitchen timer's ringing, she took the opportunity to do two things: claim her payout and visit Garvesh to shop for some necessary materials.

The former went without issue. Krahe managed to remain inconspicuous as she slipped into the temple. The bulging of her spine was not so conspicuous, thanks to her hair naturally covering the upper half of her back, where it was most obvious.

She passed a handful of faces she vaguely remembered from earlier, in particular, the stitch-trail-covered, musclebound woman who had gotten blacklisted from the Silversword Agency for calling out favoritism in their ranks. She was still just as massive, but she had a new weapon, a huge shotgun with a long axe blade on the end. It had a four-chambered revolving cylinder with eight or perhaps even six-gauge shells. What drew attention, though, was the subject of conversation. As before, it was the musclewoman talking and another contractor listening, and this go round, the subject was Krahe... or rather, some unknown third party involved in Casus Aristedes destroying Slaughterhouse 9. Supposedly, a mad Anathemist that single-handedly obliterated a graft-beast of Hashem construction.

Close enough.

The lack of extra stares in her direction was proof enough that her appearance hadn't been leaked.

She reached the receptionist after a short wait in line and a man throwing a tantrum over not being given the medication he wanted. He was summarily picked up like a ragdoll and carried out of the temple by an extremely chiseled, bearded man wearing nothing but a turban, a loincloth, and many bracelets on his wrists and ankles.

Krahe simply handed over the memslate. Seeing its subtly different design, the receptionist immediately looked at one of its sides and took out an eyebox with no visible projector lens. A few moments passed. Squinting, looking back and forth between the eyebox and a document from a lower drawer. Then the eyebox went away and the receptionist said, "Come with me, please."

And so she did, being escorted a short distance into the Central Temple complex. From there, another clergy member took over, checking the memslate and leading Krahe deeper. He neither spoke nor asked questions and was clothed similarly to Fidelia, though much less ornately and with a simple flat mask.

She walked out of the Central Temple with several hundred thousand dregs to her name, most of it stored on her dregstones, while one-third was in a variety of Calbian Rings. It was then that she learned their common denominations went up to 10,000 DD rings, each made of dark-purple thaumstone and shod with glowing runes that spoke of the power in the ring. The 5,000 DD ring was made of the same stone, but it was thinner and had five small gems in shades of purplish-blue. 1,000 DDs meant a golden, silver-inlaid ring with a single small purple-blue gem, while 500 DD and 100 DD rings were both set with orange gems; 500s were silver, with a large gem. 100s were bronze with a small gem, while fifty and tens were two different sizes of plain bronze, these three being the rings with which she was already familiar.

In good spirits, she made her way to Garvesh's pawnshop.

Little did she expect it to be closed, and even less so for the lizard to come out pointing a double barrel loaded with reapers in her face.

CHAPTER 2

CASE THREE: THE TALISMAN ASSASSIN

"You..." he hissed. A dejected sigh. The gun went down. He waved her into his flat, and she followed. As he closed the door behind her, he continued muttering, "Of course you'd show up. It was only a matter of time. I'll have to disappoint you; I don't know shit about the incident. Just that my cousin's dead and the Hashems probably did it."

Krahe was more than familiar with people she knew personally meeting unfortunate ends. Even without the hazard factor of associating with her, abrupt and unceremonious death was a part of life in Megacity Gamma. But... such an incident struck a bit differently without the relative amelioration of a world where it was the norm. It was a familiar feeling. A numb pressure in her chest, spreading like a parasite unfurling its tendrils, burning and seething, gripping her stomach. A faint shiver went down her back, and murder flared behind her eyes.

Before she could say anything, Garvesh noticed her brief dissociative stare into the middle-distance, realizing the truth.

"Hol' on, you didn't know? Why're you here, then?"

"I..." she started, then took a moment to collect herself, blinking a few times and sighing. "I need these."

She handed over a paper listing several reagents and materials for the Rite of Dho-Hna.

"Occultism, huh? Some of these are a bit out there, stuff from the Beyond Frontier, but I can source that. There's just one problem: I'm a bit shook up what with the incident..."

"You don't have to leverage me. I was already planning on finding out whoever is behind this—and then who is behind *them*."

"You'd better. I won't blame you for anything, but it couldn't be more obvious that this whole mess is some brainfuck with too much influence trying to take revenge for what you and Casus did at Slaughterhouse 9. I gotta wonder, though. Why'd you decide to do it of your own volition? Y'liked Imraal's street food that much?"

"I'll tell you. Mind if I take a seat?"

"Sure. Want… Well, I'd offer you coffee, but I don't have any. Ever had homemade machine crab juice?"

"I've had it a few times, but only from a street cart," she said, curiously looking around as she sat down.

"Yeah, I know that guy. Mine's better; at least, I'd like to think so!"

The lizard returned, having already disappeared into his kitchen. Krahe heard pouring, mixing, chopping and grinding.

A few minutes later, Garvesh returned with two bulbous glasses that at first looked like ornamental, colored glass, but Krahe felt a faint magical aura from them, and they felt heavier than they should've been. This version of the drink was purplish rather than blue, and tasted of banana and ekarone, though it was a different kind of banana than she was used to. Overall, she found it to be sweeter and somewhat stronger than the alternative, and undeniably better, but better in the way that something made by hand was better than something bought for cheap from a street cart.

After drinking one-third of her glass, Krahe explained herself. "Imraal wasn't the only one they came after. I almost got turned into mincemeat myself. Someone shot a thaumshot through the warded, solid thaumstone window of a church safe house. If I remember correctly, it was a bladestorm-type. It came from a rooftop around two hundred meters away. So if you've got any leads, I would appreciate those, and if you want to pay me for this in some way, feel free. For starters, besides those ingredients, I'm looking for a very special kind of voidkey."

"Even more special than the Twin Serpents?" Garvesh smirked. The expression vanished nearly instantly.

"C'mon. It's a third-order key. It's not that special. But that's not what I mean. A fourth-order key would be nice, but what I want is a Gulf Key."

"So instead of something hard to get due to restrictions and hoarding, you're looking for something that's hard to get for those same reasons... plus sheer obscurity."

"More or less."

"I'll look into it. No promises. As for the occultism supplies, I'll have them within a week. I'll even throw in some Red Reapers and a Howdah pistol for when you get your eidolons, just something to get you started. No charge, so long as you promise to get even for Imraal. His place is on lockdown; you won't get in there on the down-low, but... I knew what had happened the moment it did, so I was able to take a look around before the lawmen arrived. He had a Bloody Reaper that I'd given him, so I knew he was in deep shit the moment it went off and burned out one of my eidolons."

He took out a yellow talisman paper, curled inward and charred at the edges.

"Here. There was a shell of these things there in the shape of half a man. I'll bet a horn that it was some kinda protective artifact. It grieves me to know that the filthy rat probably crawled away to live another day, but hopefully, the tail he left behind will lead the cat to his burrow. Wait here for a touch. I'll bring the gun and bullets."

With that, he stomped off.

She finished another third of her drink in the time he was gone. The pistol was a chunky, crude thing with two triggers and barrels twice the diameter of her Pattner.

"Finish the drink and leave. I wish to be alone. And close the door on the way out," he said, taking his glass and leaving for another room.

* * *

For the next two weeks and four days, Krahe balanced obsessive study against obsessive investigation. Like a lascivious rumor, she made her way across the city, from reputable markets to small agencies and seedy bars and everywhere in between, and much like a rumor, she took a different form each time. A different hairstyle, a different coat, a jacket or other top, different trousers and footwear, skirts and heels on a few occasions. On two occasions, she even used a wig. None of this was cheap by any means, but that wasn't a problem; a small wardrobe of disguises didn't make too much of a dent in the funds she received for the Slaughterhouse 9 incident.

Bit by bit, she found grains of info on the influx of strange, yellow-paper talismans of abnormally high quality. It wasn't long before she bought herself a corkboard and started working things out using it and an array of memslates and documents. By the end of the first week, she'd gotten her hands on a device that could take notes onto a memslate directly from her thoughts merely by funneling a hair-thin strand of thauma into it.

There were multiple threads to follow, and, in her pursuit, she pulled on all of them.

First was the source of the talismans: a foreign woman known only as the "Talisman Mistress." Supposedly, she contacted prospective clients rather than the other way around, and she has yet to actually meet with any, using remote communication talismans to discuss orders, even to deliver goods and receive payment in the same act.

Second and third were the assassins. The first was both well-known and considered utterly unreachable: A wizard known by a variety of nicknames, the most common among them "Crescent Jezail," for his rifle-staff, which was nearly as renowned as himself. He was known to be difficult to contact and expensive, charging not for results but for his effort.

"One shot costs a hundred thousand dregs, against any random individual. The price doubles for "direct hit insurance." Double the price for the bastard to make sure he actually hit his target. Can you believe that? He must be one hell of a killer if he still gets work. Tracking and shooting someone that might be a troublesome target for any reason. Every bit of extra effort is another charge. If I could afford it, I would sooner hire him than, say, Hassan Asadi."

As for her studies into eidolons and the Astral Gulf, she progressed in a significantly less concrete manner. She couldn't exactly quantify how much closer she felt to getting results, but she did feel she was getting closer.

Then, on the seventeenth day, she broke through.

Krahe sat in the living room, wearing only her biosuit. The table was pushed against the wall, out of the way. There, using thaumine-based ink that had cost way too fucking much, she drew out a so-called "angle-web" across the floorboards, a strange pattern that both detailed a series of movements, guided Kenomaic energies, and subtly weakened the Banishment Veil, merely widening one of its eyes rather than trying to tear at the net.

In accordance with Barzai's instructions, she held out her most potent casting catalyst—her left arm—and began chanting, stepping onto the angle-web from the Gate of the North. Barzai's texts had specified a general structure and what each incantation should contain and mean but demanded the practitioner to construct their own.

Krahe called on key-holders and lock-openers, breakers-down of walls and locked gates.

She invoked the pseudonyms of hackers and jailbreakers, of those who had torn down the meticulous protections wrought by almighty megacorporations out of petty spite or for their own amusement.

Reaching the South-most Pinnacle, she initiated a partial dive. The void tore in, the world fell away, and the angle-web now sprawled across untold eons. Barzai had foretold this.

With a breathless hiss, she invoked digital daemons and dataphagic AI, whose names had been plundered from the names of ancient gods.

Proceeding to the Angle of the North-east, she recalled words and thoughts which she had dredged up days prior. It had been a mere query as she worked away on the incantation, and the answer she had gotten was a deluge—a vision of what she was certain to have been her entry into this world, nothing but fragments of light dancing over that chamber of the words by which it had been carried out. These words of power, alongside others, the Wound-like Grin gave unto her; or rather, it spoke them in pieces, rearranged and twisted, in a soundless voice that blasted through her head and made her nose run bloody.

Even now, as she repeated them, she couldn't quite comprehend many of the words coming out of her mouth. Zasas. Zasas. Nasatanda. Amrakas.

Crossing the Penultimate Angle to the Pinnacle of the West, she once more invoked: "Eternal darkness now surrounds me, Sunken One be my guide!"

At once, the final, eastward path became as a burning road of coals, and, as she walked across it, she traced with her left arm's fingers Barzai's Sigil of Transformation and chanted: "Stepping past the precipice, into the howling vortex, let the Black One's yawning maw carve my chosen path! Trespassing the boundaries of mortality, I embody the key, ancient and immortal! *ZENOXESE, PIOTH, OXAS ZAEGOS, MAVOC NIGORSUS, BAYAR!*"

At the Ultimate Angle, on the angle-web's south-eastmost corner, the world rippled and tore open. Krahe stepped through, finding herself now wholly submerged within the Astral Gulf. She no longer felt the urge to breathe, and she plunged deep into the cosmic depths, feeling drawn in a particular direction. In accordance with the Rite of Dho-Hna, the angle-web would collapse and draw her back to realspace should she stray outside the Astral Gulf or remain submerged for too long, giving her a limited time to find herself an eidolon, or hopefully, three.

* * *

Casus returned merely for a change of clothes, as his shirt was drenched in gore, blood, and other vital fluids, but found himself perplexed at the state of the living room. He found a complex, eldritch sigil drawn on the ground, shining so brightly it projected a cage of unlight all the way to the ceiling.

It took his Third Eye to peer through and see Lady Blackhand slumped down near the south-easternmost corner of the sigil, her body constantly billowing with ghostly smoke, as did her hair, back and forth in all directions. He turned his gaze to the pushed-aside coffee table and instantly knew what was happening when his eyes fell upon the manuscript. There was nothing he could do at this point but watch, and so, after quickly changing his clothes, he did just that. His butcher's work for the night was done regardless.

* * *

There, in the depths, she found them. Atop a vast, blackened spire, something that her mind interpreted as a volcanic funnel, surrounded by fathomless astral depths, she found a gnarled tree of coral and a pool filled with a swirling, writhing mass of formless serpents, indistinguishably blending into one another. The Wound-like Grin gaped wide upon the tree, affirming that these were eidolons. Specifically, Grade Three Lesser Eidolons; eidolons comparable to those which had empowered Shiva's Red Reapers and Yellow Atropals. The deeper she delved into the well, the greater and more powerful the eidolons would grow. That was the knowledge which made itself known to her before the Wound-like Grin vanished.

Through the mass, she pushed, further and further still, feeling these Kenomaic spirits rubbing against her, yet also passing through her as if she weren't there. The mass of astral bodies gave way to a bottomless well, eidolons of increasingly greater magnitude hidden within recesses in its walls like eels. There, she went down, and what felt like an eternity passed before one of them shot out of the wall and entered her ribcage, vanishing within. A second one followed, and what yawning emptiness she had felt upon awakening was suddenly filled, though only most of the way. Curious still, she pushed a bit deeper, only to find each and every eidolon drawing back from her, no longer interested. The way above, too, had cleared, and as she exited this strange un-place, she found the writhing mass of astral eels splitting in her wake.

At the shore of the brine pool, upon a branch of the coral-tree, a raven made of smoke awaited, with eyes like burning coals.

It opened its beak and said, "Gwah. Gwah. Gwah... Wawawawa."

Then, upon closing and opening again, came a horrible, distorted woman's voice. No, not just a voice, but an atrociously compressed recording of *I Love Beijing, Tiananmen.* That song had a somewhat macabre connotation, as Goujian II had erased Beijing from the map in his Reconquista of the mainland, with the first of his fusion bombs having been detonated in the middle of a parade in Tiananmen Square by a CCP official who had been brainjacked and had the bomb implanted in his chest cavity. How that official actually met his unfortunate fate was still a topic of heated discussion in Krahe's time.

Again, it closed its beak. Were the situation any different, she would have dismissed it, but she felt it would be exceedingly foolish to dismiss something so explicitly foretold to her in a dream. So, she approached the bird, and, turning its head to stare at her with a single burning eye, it once more made a noise. This time, it was the ticking of a geiger counter, followed by the clatter of something to the ground, and the slamming of two heavy metal objects together. The ticking instantly turned into a scream, and the noise was drowned out by buzzing.

The Raven fell silent, and just as Krahe realized what that sequence of sounds meant, it flew off its perch and dove headfirst into her chest, and no more did she feel an iota of that strange, intangible emptiness. She still felt a strange pull, a call to another place deeper in the Gulf, but she knew better. Barzai had warned of this time and again, and so, she focused her will and carried out the Sign of Return. In an instant, the Astral Gulf fell away, and she found herself in the center of the angle-web, disoriented and gasping for breath.

* * *

Casus had been watching for hours now, cautiously looking for signs of the angle-web's failure. Then, when he least expected it, the web collapsed. Unnatural darkness engulfed the room, and as light flooded back in, there came a high-pitch screech. If he didn't know any better, he would have panicked, thinking that Krahe had just triggered a full-blown Archon Flash. Compared to the tsunami of such an event, this was a wave lapping at the shore, and with it, Krahe washed up. In the middle of the floor, her astral form collected itself, and into it, three indistinct shapes of blackest blackness entered. One was an oblong spheroid, while the two others were long and narrow, like serpents or perhaps eels. Then, she snapped into physicality, drawing in a desperate breath and glancing about.

Before he could express his relief, however, something else began to take place. A distortion made itself known under her biosuit, right in the center of her chest, like something trying to pull it apart. The viscous material tore, and beneath, a fanged maw into cosmic nothingness yawned open, running the whole length of her chest from the sternum to her waist. Out from the black flew a black bird, made of smoke and with coals for eyes, and the maw snapped shut, vanishing in an instant. The only evidence it had been there—the ragged tear in Krahe's suit. She stood, seemingly unaware of Casus' presence, the smokey raven landing on her shoulder.

* * *

It was at this point that Krahe fully regained her bearings and realized Casus was sitting there.

"Thank Zavesh," he said. "When the clock struck the third hour, I began considering whether to collapse the angle-web myself. I hope you've succeeded in... whatever was your reason to dive into the Gulf?"

"Three hours?" she asked, glancing at the clock. It had been over six hours. "I've been down there for six. Christ."

"Christ?"

"Don't worry about it," she sighed, struggling to her feet. The raven hopped off of her shoulder, tilting its head side to side. It moved as if to crow, and the sound of a geiger counter spiking came out, mimicking the sound pattern of a raven's caw.

"Yeah, I did succeed. Got myself some eidolons to work with."

"You... carried out a full dive ritual and spent several hours in the Astral Gulf in order to capture eidolons? Forgive me for casting doubt on your choices, but I must admit that even I, lackluster as my knowledge of occultism is, must wonder what led you to such a choice in favor of a simpler spirit-calling rite."

She would've thought anyone else was mocking her with such a question, but nothing in Casus' tone or demeanor suggested that his question was anything other than wholly genuine.

"It's 'cause of these. Got special access to their section of the library," she gestured to the coffee table, over which all four of Barzai's scrolls were rolled out. "There was another text noting that one could find eidolons that would otherwise be exceedingly rare to obtain from a spirit-calling rite."

It was a half-lie. She had, indeed, read that the results of most spirit-calling rites were unevenly distributed, with weaker eidolons of a given class being more common. It just so happened that by then, she had already decided to get her eidolons by diving directly into the Gulf.

Turning to the raven, she held out her hand. It was a strange thing, as she felt a place in her mind connected to it, and when she looked there, she saw a window through the raven's eyes. Its vision was in a different aspect ratio, but it saw in full color, largely unlike a real bird would see. Within Krahe and Casus, the bird spirit saw glowing flames, centered in the stomach and brain, coursing throughout their bodies.

"Now, what do I call you, huh?"

She considered several names. From one of the ravens of Odin, to the names of several nuclear scientists, to something as trite as Nevermore. Quickly, she decided to name the spirit in honor of the man who had facilitated her ability to capture it in the first place.

She shrugged. "Barzai won't mind if I borrow his name."

The response she got was another bit-crushed sound clip, this time the instrumental opening to *Red Sun in the Sky*. It wasn't funny, yet it caught her off-guard, and Krahe laughed.

"Alright, that's enough. Get back in."

And it did. As before, Barzai dove straight into her chest and disappeared in a burst of smoke.

"I have never seen a True Eidolon, yet I feel this one is somehow aberrant. It erupted from a great maw that split your chest down the middle."

"It... did, did it? Interesting. I didn't realize until now."

She furrowed her brow in focus.

"Oh, yeah. I can feel it pushing right here when I try to call it out again," she commented, offhandedly rubbing up and down her sternum.

Moving on from that unsettling fact as if it weren't anything to worry about, she looked around. The angle-web had burned out, leaving only ash and crusty residue. Her eyes went wide after she crossed and uncrossed her arms, and long threads of slimy residue were pulled between them. Instantly deciding that cleaning the floor was a lower priority than this, she made her way into the bathroom.

Casus, struck by curiosity, turned his attention to Barzai's writings and found himself unable to parse anything past the halfway point of the first scroll. Moving onto "Occultic Practices of Ashametan," he quickly skimmed over the fundamentals of occultism and theurgy, then moved on to the manners in which an eidolon might be called forth. It even included a tiering system for Eidolons, breaking up the greater system classes into a wide variety of sub-tiers. Amusingly, of the top three eidolon rating systems, the Reaper Standard and Atropal Standard were numbers two and three. The number 1 was, of course, the Seven Spoke System's own method of classification, though the book described it as imprecise, breaking each greater eidolon class into only three sub-tiers. In this same section, he learned of the diverse methods for achieving what Krahe had just done and realized that what she had said was wholly correct; compared to the uncertain rod fishing of these rites, she had simply decided to do it herself.

Wet feet on tile. Frantic. Then, the noise was gone. Krahe's astral form strode through the flat, into the kitchen. Rustling of paper. Water being poured. Then came the unmistakable sound of someone trying to swallow a Class-1 rejection suppressant all at once. A full minute later, she once more passed through the living room in astral form. Casus continued his reading, unperturbed.

Meanwhile, in the shower, Krahe took time to look inward.

[EIDOLONS]
[LESSER EIDOLON VAULT NO. 1]
[Astral Morphology]
Three-eyed Chthonian Eel
Developed through consumption of astral matter sloughed off from humanoid souls traversing Kenoma and residence within the astral brine pool.
[Eidolon Status]
Tier 1
Fully Nourished
Unbound

[LESSER EIDOLON VAULT NO. 2]
[Astral Morphology]
Three-eyed Chthonian Eel

Developed through consumption of astral matter sloughed off from humanoid souls traversing Kenoma and residence within the astral brine pool.

[Eidolon Status]
Tier 1
Fully Nourished
Unbound

[TRUE EIDOLON VAULT NO. 1]
[Astral Morphology]
Raven of Ruinous Eyes "Barzai"

Developed via retroactive cogniphagy of the host upon bonding.

[Morphological Archetype]
Scout/Skirmisher

[Eidolon Status]

Boon Symbiosis: Deathsmoke Blessing

When manifested in its natural form, this eidolon is difficult to notice for those not intended to notice it and may appear as a mundane raven.

Boon Symbiosis: Phase of Earthen Jade

This eidolon benefits from the reinforcing properties of this boon.

Fully Nourished
Unbound

By all accounts, it couldn't have been more of a success. Her Lesser Eidolons fell well into the highest tier of their class, though she couldn't quite grasp how she might achieve the Demon Core or whether a True Eidolon could even be stretched that far. Perhaps one of her Lesser

Eidolons might suffice for a smaller version of it, if they turned out powerful enough; after all, a Bloody Reaper demanded only a Tier 2 Lesser Eidolon to empower it. Who was to say that her Demon Core couldn't be made to work with a Tier 1?

While she mulled these thoughts over, she meticulously scrubbed away the film of slime that had formed on her skin. It was among the listed side effects of the rite, supposedly "benign astral condensate." Then, as she reread Barzai's listing, a new boon symbiosis appeared.

Boon Symbiosis: Chernobog's Mystic Wisdom

This eidolon wishes to become a Daemon Core.

The second to last word continuously flickered back and forth between "Demon" and "Daemon." It looked more like Daemon than Demon, so Daemon Core it was. It fit, Krahe supposed, if this spirit—this daemon, by any other name—was to fuel her magical atrocity.

When she looked into the place inside herself where Barzai made its nest, she found the raven spirit gorging itself on… something. She wasn't sure what. Vague, smoky wisps floating in the void. It ate the last wisp and turned the burning coals it had for eyes directly into her mind's eye, staring at her from nowhere. Looking at the raven and knowing its wishes, she reconsidered her original concept for the Daemon Core thaumaturgy. At that instant, more wisps of smoky substance appeared around it, and it began its feast anew.

Not quite sure what was taking place, Krahe honed in on the fundamental concept of the Daemon Core and tried to fine-tune its specific elements. In particular, the possibility of altering the instability of its core so that, if necessary, it could be enclosed only most of the way to direct its ruinous energies in a particular direction. Before she was even done showering, Barzai had already fallen asleep. At least, that's what Krahe interpreted from the spirit losing all cohesion and reverting to a vaguely spherical ball of smoke.

CHAPTER 3

IT'S A RESEARCH AND DEVELOPMENT MONTAGE

A short time later, as she sat in the window, smoking Arrha and looking out over the docks, she found that she couldn't call Barzai out. Looking at its system readout, the spirit's status had gone from *"Fully Nourished,"* to, *"Exhausted—Cogniphagic Metamorphosis in Progress."*

Barzai became available again the next day, making itself known to Krahe as she was cooking lunch while casually reading through Secrets of the Atropal. When she looked inward towards the raven spirit, its natural form shifted to a poorly defined image of how she had imagined the Daemon Core. It then sent her a mental demand to be fed, and so, she did.

Time continued to pass. Krahe furthered her investigation by day while studying and practicing theurgy by night. It quickly became a habit of Casus' to stop by for dinner. The man often returned exhausted and covered in blood, and as it turned out, it was due to the fact he was going out of his way to hunt down Hashem Family members—a direct investigation style that by its very nature often turned violent.

"Many of them have done nothing to deserve death, but I shan't spare traffickers and drug pushers. Not in a million turns of the Wheel," he said.

Meanwhile, in her own investigations, Barzai became a second pair of eyes for Krahe. It gradually built up an understanding of the Daemon Core, and only when she was already four days into the process did Krahe read deeply enough to learn that this was a common practice for allowing a True Eidolon to manifest in more than its natural form. It seemed that the longer a True Eidolon was attached to someone, the stronger it grew and the more forms it could take. While Barzai's growth was merely a matter of time, conceiving of her own Theurgy was something wholly contingent on active effort.

At first, she experimented with simply attempting to translate her keystone thaumaturgies directly to an eidolon level of power output and found that it just didn't work that way. All the disparate actions of carrying out the thaumaturgy were muscle memory by now; by comparison, finagling an eidolon into carrying out the task was as difficult as programming a robot to do a summersault versus simply doing a one herself. Krahe had done something of the sort before, and she could do so again, given enough time. Theurgy wasn't by any means analogous to programming, but that was just her closest point of comparison.

Several more days passed, and Krahe gained a stronger grasp on the intricacies of Theurgy, allowing her to translate some of her own skills. She reached ever closer to achieving what she had said she would do back in the underground gymnasium. Eidolons, as it turned out, very much liked to act through vessels rather than directly. Instead of an absurdly powerful beam, a short-lived construct would be given form to deliver that power. The power of an Eidolon was produced neither by thauma burning nor thaumic fusion, but by some vaguely understood third process; the only part that mattered, however, was that Anathemists were known for achieving eidolon-like levels of output, and that, in turn, occultists were known for replicating the feats of Anathemists in a safe manner using eidolons. From these writings, combined with various well known theurgies, Krahe concluded that what she wanted to do was perfectly achievable.

After yet more days of effort, she arrived at a hybrid application that would benefit from her left arm's unique properties as a living casting conduit as well as the advantages of dregshot. This meant that she had to source dregshot bullets, that was true, but Garvesh made that a non-issue and even gave her a discount in his vengeance-stricken state. Her delivery method would be a construct-missile partially formed through her own power, adding an entropy and effort cost to the theurgy in exchange for allowing it to be even more powerful and efficient. It would be purposely less powerful than a Bloody Reaper, due to the single-target design, allowing her to get more shots out of one eidolon. She wasn't sure how many, but she hoped for three per Chthonian Eel, so that she could have a full six-round clip.

With her nascent understanding of occultism, Krahe ended up using a crude method of refining her dregshot, embedding the occult pattern in writing. She would roll up the talisman so it rested against the walls of the casing and partly protruded outward around the bullet, crimping it inward and gluing it in place with an occult glue made of her own blood, the so-called "Unguent of Nug-Soth." Leaving a baking dish full of the stuff overnight in the moonlight had the whole safe house filled with its stench, but such was the procedure laid out by Ibn Ghazi Barzai. She filled all the remaining free space inside the bullet with thaumine powder that she had ground down into ultra-fine grains.

Out of this whole process, the talisman would be the hardest part. She started with a stack of talisman papers and began the rite for embedding eidolon instructions into writing, focusing her mind on particular aspects of what the eidolon was to do as she meditated according to the guidelines, trying to commune with one of her eidolons. A hard-to-perceive visual element would float by the edge of her awareness, ephemeral like the memory of a dream, and she would try to replicate it on the paper before it vanished from thought. Sometimes, even when she successfully drew the sigil, looking at it made her realize that the eidolon had misunderstood her, and so she would have to try again. She dug deep not only into her own objective understanding, but, according to the guidelines of the texts, she also dug up emotions to better communicate with the spirit.

As Krahe understood it, it was infinitely easier to make an eidolon understand hatred and murderous intent for an individual than to convey how a guided missile found its target through trigonometry. It was equally unsurprising and inconvenient that occult spirits worked on occult rules.

And so, with the glassing of Oasis being fresh in her mind, she dug into that hatred and found the guidance portion coming out with remarkable ease.

There were supposedly more direct, faster methods, but they were, unsurprisingly, both advanced and kept closely guarded by those who knew them.

It took several hours, dozens of talisman papers, and an eye-watering sum in magical ink to work out the full pattern, but it was done. Casus returned as Krahe was finishing the third copy, with the first and second framed up above the writing desk for reference, one for each side.

* * *

It was done, and it made Casus grimace in apprehension when he first saw it.

He'd seen grisly talisman designs before, sure, but there was something malicious about this one. The central image was a disembodied forearm, clawed and with gnarled skin-like cooling magma—a more monstrous version of Krahe's own arm, clearly—with smoke billowing from its back and rays of crimson killing light shooting from its palm. Around it swirled ominous patterns that dragged the eyes, resembling at once the legs of a centipede and the bones of a ribcage, but the back of the talisman paper gave him pause. In the center, a three-cornered eye with three pupils fused into one shape, and around it, letters which he could not read, alongside the typical occult patterns seen on all talismans.

Killing intent. Malice. Hate. Hate beyond hate. Hate so virulent, so vitriolic, that it alone could teach an eidolon, a thoughtless spirit that knew neither death nor emotion, what it was to deeply desire another's demise.

Casus had read that the exposed theurgic patterns of a Reaper exuded a ceaseless, furious forward drive, and those of an Atropal did the same with the impression of a coiled snake, locked onto prey, ready to pounce. He had even examined archival examples of old scrolls just to get a feeling for it, part out of curiosity and part out of a desire to understand Lady

Blackhand's capabilities, thinking it only fair since she had shown an interest in the workings of Mamon Couplers. This was, nonetheless, fundamentally different compared to a mass-manufactured pattern; not merely more intense, but more profound, in the same way that the feeling of transforming into Silberblut was more profound than transforming into Omniphage.

Keeping quiet, stilling himself utterly, the Banisher looked on as Lady Blackhand completed the third talisman and began on a fourth. Horrible, murderous malice poured out of her, smoke of blackest pitch, filling the room with the smell of sulfur and stinging fumes, only to gather at the tip of her brush as she raised it from the inkwell. She rendered the clawed hand's outline with a small handful of strokes and filled it in.

"How long do you intend to wait?" came a deadpan statement as she dipped her brush. From the windowsill, a horrible noise followed. Once more, that distorted section of music, like alarm trumpets coming out of a speaker made of scrap metal reading off of a broken and glued-together memslate. He hadn't noticed it at all, but now, he could see that infernal crow perched next to the window as clear as day.

"I merely did not wish to disturb you, and at the same time, I was curious."

"If you want to watch, just watch. It disturbs me more if I know you're trying to avoid my notice."

As if to punctuate her point, she clicked her tongue and tossed the talisman paper into a nearby baking pan of odorous liquid. Coming closer, Casus saw half a dozen more similar papers floating in the dish in various stages of having the ink leached from them. He wanted to comment on how Blackhand would have saved a great deal of money if she had learned of this solution earlier, but she had already started over.

For a solid half hour, Casus looked on, watching three of the malicious talismans being completed and a fourth started, only for his stomach to rumble and cause Lady Blackhand to make the tiniest of errors. It was a deviation he himself with his vastly superior vision barely noticed, but she nonetheless tossed the paper—and shot him in the head. A single beam of burning wrath, searing away at his wards and briefly glaring his vision like a bright flash of light. It was much weaker than he had expected.

"Next time, it will be a real one. There's some leftover stew in the fridge. Heat up the whole pot, and don't call me over."

"Very well," he acquiesced, already starting to mend his wards as he left Blackhand to her devices.

Later that day, Krahe tested her prototype dregshot. Well out of sight, in a subterranean gymnasium of the Grafting Church. She also sicced Barzai upon several dummies to ascertain the eidolon's natural combative abilities. She found herself satisfied with learning that it could ram into foes as a potent kinetic attack, as well as create seemingly instantaneous explosions with flashes of its eyes. The range of this "Blast Flash" was limited to only around ten meters within Barzai, required line of sight of the bird, and, from testing against artificial wards and barriers, Krahe ascertained that it was of an arcane nature.

Nonetheless, both Barzai's natural capabilities and the performance of her new theurgy were anything but disappointing. Casus had expressed that he wished to come along but couldn't due to apostolic duties.

Yet later, they met again, and as was his nature, the Banisher immediately opened with, "By your demeanor, I presume that you are not dissatisfied with the fruits of your work. What do you intend to call the theurgy? Another alien play on words?"

"Of course," she said. Then, purposely speaking actual German, she intoned: "Wandrei Faust."

"That must be in a language from your world, I presume. What a strange sound. It will eat at me if I do not know what absurdly stretched play on words this one is."

Krahe chuckled.

"Nothing so far-fetched as Six Trees Killer. Wandrei is the surname of an author who wrote of creatures called Fire Vampires. Thus the connection to my element, and it sounds somewhat like the word for wandering. Faust was the name of a fictitious man who made a deal with an otherworldly entity. It also translates to fist, and there was a long line of directed-blast missile weapons with that same word in the name. Though it's not the exact same operating principle. My Wandrei Faust is inspired by the descendants of those weapons."

"Am I right to assume that you intend to test it against a live target sometime soon?"

"I'm not in the mood to go looking for trouble, but trouble has a habit of finding me nonetheless. All my leads go straight into Hashem territory, so I've got a good feeling that I'll get to give it a test run sooner rather than later..."

In preparation, Krahe loaded six dregshot bullets into two clips; in the first, they alternated with thaumstone-core lead bullets, while in the second, three dregshots came first, followed by three Mescalt solid-cast bullets. Unfortunately, she had found that Mescalt's superior properties didn't function correctly with a core of thaumstone; on impact, the same material reaction that would normally produce a spear of semiliquid metal would crush the thaumstone core and scatter it with the pathetic power of a low-caliber snake shot round. Barely enough to kill small vermin.

She did, indeed, not actively go about antagonizing random Hashem Family members, despite being able to identify them by the quirks of their dress and the tattoos which the more dedicated of them displayed. They weren't nearly so crassly overt as the gang tattoos she was used to, but they were identifiers nonetheless, though subtle enough for deniability.

However, it just so happened that when she went out to investigate at a place known to be under Hashem control, she did so without any disguise whatsoever, wearing the same exact outfit she had when she depopulated the Old Street Butchershop—biosuit, loose green trousers, and Shiva's boots.

CHAPTER 4

A HORNET STEPS INTO A HIVE OF FLIES

In an unremarkable tavern, on an unremarkable street, in an unremarkable corner of Audunpoint, a man sat with his feet up on the table of a bar, grayish-blue smoke pouring from a cigarette in his mouth and gathering into a puddle at his chair's feet. On the table stood a bottle of liquor distilled from a fruit found only on Xaugeth. It was absolutely revolting and cost 500 dregs per bottle. But on the upside, it gained the mild prestige of costing such, and inflicted a clear-headed kind of intoxication that neither left a hangover nor harmed one's health.

From his seat on the upper floor balcony, he surveilled his domain as some two dozen people, a mixture of civilians, contractors, and his subordinates, gambled away. The games were rigged, of course, but in a fair way; the odds were skewed in the house's favor, was all, and anyone who won too much too quickly or even too consistently would be removed. Anything more overt drew too much trouble, and he was content with the profit margins as they were. The gambling was why this place was cheaper than others; the drinks were a loss leader, meant to get asses in seats and stupefy the gamblers' risk assessment. Some of these innovations were his own, but most of what he used to make money hand over fist was based on advice from a friend who owned one of the great gambling houses in the Sultanate.

Cassius Hortator III was his name. He ruled over this one street, as a Hashem Family lieutenant managing this gambling house in addition to three front businesses. There was also the obvious protection racket, book forging, and a small waystation for the family's butchering business. Below him were grunts and made men, though dealing with the latter required a more cautious hand since any made man could replace him if he fucked up. Above him stood the Three Bosses, and above them, Damrus Hashem himself. He was king in this area, and he had both the good wisdom to have eyes on every corner and the raw power to exterminate any invaders. At his rank, he was known for completely disproportionate firepower from a combination of six Lesser Eidolons and the ability to modify Red Reapers into a wide variety of aftermarket subtypes with adjusted properties.

Being part of the Hashem Family wasn't all fleecing gamblers and screwing scaly Saurian whores, of course. Whenever serious shit went down, ripples carried out even to the clever, smaller fish that didn't muddy up the pond, like Cassius. His high-priority tenants—people he had to house and protect, yet whose identities he wasn't allowed to know—were being pissy and sending him requests for extra security. It was all because of that goatfuck at Slaughterhouse 9.

As far as he was aware, some power hungry idiot named Jahangir Panahi had sold out the family to church dogs by arranging for a Banisher Mamon Knight to get broken out of jail. All it got him was slaughtered by that same Mamon Knight and some buttfuck insane Anathemist. Or, so the story went.

Cassius was sure the facts differed, but he didn't care. All that mattered was the shit on his shoulder and the face on his table. A shitty, exaggerated sketch of a razor grinned woman with charred skin and huge, absurdly puffy black hair. The verbal description, at least, was specific enough to get an idea of how she might really look.

He was under orders to report any sightings, to kill her if possible, or to obtain her gun by any means necessary. Of course, he wasn't about to do any of that shit unless she waltzed herself straight into his line of sight.

Which, unfortunately, she did, and Cassius, though not a particularly brave or ambitious man, was a man of principle.

His cowardice and his principles fought inside him for the decision of whether to let her go or foolishly take a shot at her. At first, cowardice won. Alongside most of his subordinates, he watched the woman come in, play cards for half an hour, and leave twenty DDs richer. But he was a man of principle—so, he finished his cigarette, rose from his comfortable seat, and prepared himself alongside a handful of his subordinates to ambush her if she came this way again. That meant side alleys and street corners, the windows of the gambling house, every spot within around twenty meters of where he stood at that exact moment. This way, he could feel good about having done something without actually doing anything.

Meanwhile, Krahe walked straight into an apartment building filled with Vedesian Evoy, because that was the location of her contact, a broker not unlike Garvesh and one of the only individuals who knew something substantial about the Talisman Mistress.

The moment she laid eyes on the structure, with its blacked-out windows, she fully expected to be antagonized or even openly attacked. As she walked through its halls, somewhat to her disappointment, she only got hateful stares from beyond cracked open doors. Before she could reach her informant's basement door, a group of three surprisingly bulky fly-men, each proudly and openly displaying their natural Vedesian markings, emerged. They stopped the moment they saw her, and the largest of the three, over two meters tall and with spiky, armor-like chitin, stepped forward. Until now, she had only received a few random, barked slurs from the locals. This man, who she mentally nicknamed Tsetse after the eponymous giant fly, lambasted her with a tirade of insults pertaining to her species, sex, manner of dress, status as an Anathemist, and finally, the supposed impending extermination and enslavement of all non-Evoy.

It was undoubtedly a withering verbal assault by anyone's standards but having actively participated in communities where such tirades were a part of everyday conversation, it washed off her like water from a turtle's back. The answer which she gave, masterfully controlling her violent impulses, was a venomous smile, marking the moment when she mentally reached her hand into the pool of distilled vitriol in her head, dipping her recently gained knowledge of this world and of Evoy culture in the vile substance.

"I could fry you into the wall right this second if I wanted, but I'm feeling mighty peaceful today, so, my feces-feasting friend..."

This was followed by a tirade of entomological and religious slurs as well as absurdly gruesome threats too graphic and hateful to be recorded in writing. Throughout her tirade, Krahe burned thauma and built up a charge within her left arm, until it cast a light over the whole of the hallway. Meanwhile, as she spoke, she spewed smoke with each word, which she purposely imbued with Isotope to give it the unmistakable rancid quality. The sheer vitriol behind her words was such that, by pure accident, it imbued her thauma with a malicious quality and set her smoke upon the three Evoy, eroding their wards. At the end of her tirade, she said, "Now, if you would, stop wasting my time and go kill yourself some other way."

She was well aware of the fact she had just spent the better part of two minutes doing exactly what she was accusing the speechless, confused Tsetse of doing, but that didn't matter. Before he could realize what was happening, she had already Astro Dived, power-walked through him, and returned to physicality, banging on her contact's door. She was betting that he would choose to remove himself from the situation out of a mixture of confusion and intimidation, and, this time, her bet proved correct when the trio shuffled away, muttering insults and threats to placate themselves.

"Who is it?!" came a buzzy, flighty voice.

"An urgent yellow-banded delivery from Tajik," she answered in code speak.

"I don't 'member orderin' anything from Tajik."

"Open up before I put a reaper through your keyhole. I just want to ask a question."

It was truly a stupidly wide keyhole to go with a stupidly chunky lock.

"What'd you do to Tajik?!" the voice questioned. Light footsteps. A key plugged the keyhole. Rattling of chains and deadbolts followed.

"I got him zonked out of his gourd on Sabbi Root and showed him a yellow talisman paper. He's probably nursing a horrifying hangover by now."

The moment the door cracked open, Krahe pushed her way past, diving to bypass the fly-man altogether. His home was a hoarder's den, and his form, startled and panicking, was the most fly-like she had seen yet. His carapace bore obvious patterns marking him a Vedesian, though they were so slight and faint that it took an active effort to notice them. He ambled about on four spindly legs while ceaselessly, neurotically rubbing his forelimbs together as a proboscis darted in and out of his lamprey-like mouth. A harness was strapped to his body, a backpack power source where his wings may have once been, and a pair of mechanical arms to the sides, gesturing as he spoke.

"Ey, the fuck's that supposed to be, eh?! You can't just break into my home like that! Who the fuck are you, anyway? An... Anathemist? Oh. Oh no. Oh no, no, no. I ain't got no fuckin' Class 3 Painkillers, y'understand?"

"Do I look like I need painkillers? C'mon. I'm looking for the Talisman Mistress," Krahe said, conjuring the yellow talisman paper into the palm of her hand. She waved it back and forth in front of the Evoy's nearly expressionless face. He licked it.

Then, his compound eyes flashed red, and Krahe felt an appraisal attempt smack impotently into her deathsmoke shroud.

"Y'involved with an Outer God by any chance?" he asked with an unsettling calm.

"Don't try to turn shit around on me, Nozar. Tajik sent me to you because he thinks you might know where to find the Talisman Mistress."

"I know. She's moved in recently, just a week after that Archon Flash sent everyone packin' from Jas'raba. Pushed half my clientele out of the market with her product. Half of 'em want her dead, and the other half wanna lick her feet for a peek at her source charts. Question is, which one're you?"

She didn't like this. The fly-man had suddenly become utterly, rapturously calm, as if some realization made him think he had nothing to fear from her, or perhaps a chip to play that would secure his safety.

"The kind with a vendetta against one of her customers."

A tilt of his head. Another cycle of forelimb-rubbing.

"So you're lookin' for her 'cause you want information. Funny thing, she's been lookin' for someone, too. Won't say who, or give any criteria... But hell, maybe bein' able to find her is qualifier enough. I can tell you what I know—for a price."

"Name it."

A finger-wag gesture from his right mech-arm. The insecticidal urge within Krahe grew.

"No. You know how these deals work. You make the offer, or there's no deal."

"How about I spray your brains over that pile of trash? I've got three more leads to get to; one of them has to be less obnoxious than you."

The fly-man rubbed his forelimbs, absently staring at her with his compound eyes.

"Y'willin' to make that bet?"

Krahe conjured a capsule of Class 3 Painkiller and threw it at him. One of his hands caught it.

"Pristine. Original capsule. Unbroken seal. Where'd you get this, I wonder? I won't ask. I know better. The deal's made. Come with me."

Several minutes later, Krahe realized that most of this side of the first floor and the basements below were all Nozar's property. All the piled-up stuff wasn't just trash, but strangely organized piles of records, towers of memslates, scrolls, and books. They arrived at a room with a huge terminal, two rows of three projected screens over an organ-like layered keyboard, and four mechanical arms hanging down from the ceiling. Nozar plugged a pair of black cables with key-like spikes on the ends into his backpack, and the hanging armatures came to life, tapping away.

A portrait appeared on one screen: a vaguely southeast asian woman's face with one eye plastered over by talisman paper and slicked-back black hair. A map came up on another—a central landmass surrounded by countless islands.

"Name: Yao Fu. Likely a pseudonym. Place of origin: the Tiengenzhen Region. Status: Unaffiliated. As I said earlier, she came in and completely fucked the market. Single-use and reusable artifacts, eidolon vessels, charms, weird-ass voidkeys—you name it, she's sold it to someone. They're all variations of paper-charm designs, and they're all way the fuck up there. I'm talkin' the sorta thing you'd expect the Grafters or Wheelers to outfit one a' their saints with. If I was a bettin' man—and I am if I can be sure I'll win—I'd bet a pretty sum that she's some big shot tryin' to lay low as far away from her homeland as possible... and not doin' too hot at it. The woman's turned Audunpoint's underbelly upside down with her supply, and anyone who gets their hands on her product shoots way the hell up on the ladder."

"That doesn't help me find her," Krahe hissed.

"Fuckin' hold on, I'm getting to it. So there's this place..."

* * *

Cassius dared to hope he would get out of this easy. That, come the next day, he would have reported the incident and reaped the rewards without breaking the long streak of no violent incidents within or around his gambling house.

That hope, like a wayward ship, was dashed upon the spiky boulders of reality when *That Woman* swaggered into the building less than two hours after her initial passage. She seated herself, once more gambling in an entirely inconspicuous manner, though the atmosphere of tension within the room was palpable. The keen-eared among the patrons were on edge, aware of what was to come, and, by proxy, so were the others.

Nonetheless, an uneasy illusion of normal goings-on was maintained for the next twenty minutes, during which That Woman played dice at one of the tables while Cassius strained to clandestinely move his men into place for a coup-de-grace. Then one among them, fool that he was, misinterpreted a gesture from Cassius. The man, tall, strong, and not very bright, approached That Woman, looming over her. Cassius knew what was to come; that man, Habib, combined preternatural strength with thaumaturgy to punch with the force of an Atropal. The way he held himself, the tunnel-vision look in his eyes, and the clenching of his fists and calves, all told that he intended to take Her head off right then and there.

"I wouldn't come that close if I were you," That Woman said, not taking her eye off of her opponents' dice, idly swirling her own back and forth.

"There is a high price on your head in these parts," Habib said. His thaumaturgy waxed strong, invisibly at first, then visibly, five golden lines spiraling down his arm. It was subtle, nearly unnoticeable if you didn't know what to look for. The way he stood, even the five lines were hidden from his prey. When they reached his fist, he would kill. That moment never came.

That Woman stopped swirling her dice and raised the cup, revealing they had been stacked into a tower, the topmost one showing a snake-eye.

"I know."

She vanished in a burst of smoke, leaving the cup clattering on the table. Then, Habib lurched forward, and Cassius realized she was somehow behind him. He knew what it was; teleportation, even the extremely short-range kind, was a coveted ability.

Before anyone could act, she had lifted the man off his feet, and a crimson-red light flooded down her arm. His barrier took shape between him and her, but the golden light couldn't remove something that had already bypassed it. Then, came the noise, something between electric snapping and buzzing.

It was only seconds before Habib gruesomely slid down onto the Anathemist's blackened arm, his boiling blood and viscera trickling onto the ground and fountaining from every orifice of his frozen face. The cursed light, redder than blood, burst forth from the man's mouth and eyes, obliterating the latter instantly and projecting his rapidly disintegrating insides over the ceiling. One of the croupiers, a pure-white Inax, had risen up with the intent to take action but froze when the green-eyed demon pulled her gun.

"Don't. I can still leave just one corpse in my wake. Don't give me an excuse to change that to a double-digit number."

She cast Habib to the ground with some effort, her stance wide, a section of his scorched-black spine still in her hand. Letting it fall to the ground, she turned as if to walk out, only to turn into a shape of smoke and burning light as she rushed out the door. Thrown knives and thaumaturgies flew her way, a few of which were on target, yet passed through her unimpeded.

Cassius felt a struggle within himself. Every fiber of his being told him to leave it be, but he couldn't. One of his men lay dead, and the mistake was his. There was no other choice than to pursue, and that was just what he did.

He and five of his best subordinates pursued the woman on motorbikes, catching her before she even got out of his territory. Despite her speedy escape, she obviously couldn't keep up that smoke-form for long, and he knew this area better than the back of his hand, as did his squad of five.

He had her in a back alley, with two behind himself and two at its other end, waiting for his signal to come over the top of the wall.

Cassius drew one of his pistols and fired, unleashing two Pale-Red Reapers that threw him backward with the force of its recoil. These marginally weaker versions of the Red Reaper had the advantage of being much smaller both as bullets and as manifested projectiles, focusing two-thirds the power into one-third the blast radius, while also having a higher maximum velocity and accelerating to that velocity instantly. Plus they operated on Arcane principles, generating the explosion in a manner that would retain effectiveness against barriers. Furthermore, two could be energized with just one Class Three Lesser Eidolon, the same as Yellow Atropals. Being custom-tuned to him alone, his Pale-Reds were still significantly more potent than Yellow Atropals, however. With his double-barreled howdah pistol, even the defenses of his superiors couldn't hold up, allowing him to keep his cushy, comfortable position without politicking.

At this distance, That Woman would have, at best, time to raise a barrier, which would still require exceptionally fast expansion rate and reflexes. Even then, the impact would surely leave her melting down for him to finish off with a third shot from his double-barreled shotgun, into which he had loaded two Crimson Reapers, the opposite of a Pale-Red, being far more forceful but also larger, slower and with a limited range and collateral damage akin to a Bloody Reaper.

But... when the white-red flash passed, and the explosion came, it was not through impact with a human body or a barrier but with the cobblestones and crates right behind her, sending up a spray of dust and debris, ripping into the wall. Confused, he quickly reloaded two more Pale-Reds, and raised his gun, seeing That Woman walking out of the dust with a demented grin on her face, holding up a Pattner-type pistol to her face while running that charred waste of a left arm through her hair. An ember-like glow emerged from the limb, and at that moment, fanged mouths opened down its length, and slick, black tendrils emerged, both from those mouths and from behind her, sprouting from that ridge that ran down the length of her spine.

"Oh man, you have no idea how long I've been waiting for this!" she exclaimed, a melodious laughter ringing out from her as the tendrils continued to expand, enveloping her and even pushing under the edges of that black suit she wore. "How many did you bring? Five? Ten?!"

He wasn't sure if that question was about his ammunition or his reinforcements. He fired again.

Again, his Pale-Reds passed through her like she wasn't even there, but this time, he saw it clearly. Just for a moment, she changed; a devil of smoke and fire, a blazing spine-and-ribcage seething inside her. Green, burning embers in place of eyes, hair billowing as if blasted upward by nonexistent wind. She walked three steps' worth in the span of two, then snapped back into physicality. He instinctively raised his barrier as he loaded two more Pale-Reds, only to find those tar tendrils setting upon him with thunderous impacts, smashing down his barrier before he could set off another shot. He knew better than to risk a meltdown and so allowed himself to be struck on the wards, hoping to be thrown back by the force so he could use the velocity to escape.

It seemed it would work, until he saw the bangle on her wrist flash with light, and felt the ground behind him shudder. When the next strike came, he smacked back-first into a solid stone wall that absolutely wasn't there before. With a snap of his fingers, he fired a whistling, reddish missile straight upward, bursting with a bright flash and loud noise. It was the signal for his squad to go in, and they did—the two of them on the other side.

The Woman's eyes briefly tracked the flare, and, hearing the sound of Cassius' allies, she flicked her gun hand towards him—but didn't shoot. Her finger wasn't even on the trigger. Instead, the bangle on her wrist began to glow, floating and spinning. Protuberances emerged from the wall behind him, seamless as if they'd always been there, followed by thin rods of the same material from the ground and walls. The wall itself grew taller, as if specifically to forestall any aid from that direction. He was stuck; his gun arm was mostly free, as was his left forearm, but they were too far apart to do anything besides fire one more time.

The next moment, it seemed as if something was erupting from inside That Woman's chest, only for her suit to tear open, a black blur flying out. Down the middle of her chest, a fanged maw yawning into a swirling void of eldritch blackness that dragged the eyes. It snapped shut right away, leaving just a tear, which began to close as if even that suit was alive.

The shape landed on her gun's barrel, and Cassius saw clearly what it was: a raven of smoke, with red coals for eyes.

"Barzai. Keep an eye on him," she said to the bird, and it flew off, perching somewhere above Cassius' head while its mistress arrogantly spun around on a bootheel. He held out his hand in an attempt to shoot her in the back but realized that the thrice-damned bird had flicked the break-open switch on his gun. The forward lurch of his arm was enough. The barrel tilted, the extractor pushing his bullets halfway out the chamber—and the thrice-damned bird snatched them in its beak.

* * *

It was somewhat amusing to see three individuals arc overtop the wall as if they were jumping on a trampoline. One was an Evoy with an uncannily humanoid build, wearing a suit. The other was that pure-white Inax from earlier, while the third was a Mamon Knight of the insectile variety with a pair of cleavers as his weapons.

"Barzai. Kill!"

Less like a living thing and more like an autonomous missile, the crow whizzed down into the alleyway and set upon the Evoy, turning him into a maelstrom of whirling ghostly mantis-blades, snapping jaws, and swarming insects. Krahe wasn't sure if he was making a concerted effort to strike down the bird or just panicking.

While the True Eidolon distracted one of her foes, Krahe wasted not a moment more to raise both her hands—her left pointing palm-first at her foe, her right aiming the muzzle of her gun at her bicep. The action, admittedly strange as it was, confused them for just long enough to let her form the necessary construct-shell with her left arm becoming clawed, rocky, and monstrous. Cleavers already moved, and the Croupier already set forth a withering shower of wicked daggers to punch holes into Krahe's wards, but she had time enough; her wards would hold well against kinetic attacks, and no more than half of the Croupier's deluge actually hit head-on to begin with. Of the hits, a third were grazing, causing them to be lacerative and thus ineffectual in more ways than one. Krahe felt sympathy for the inax woman; she, too, had felt the disappointment of a withering barrage leaving its target very much alive.

No matter. Cleavers would tear her to shreds if she let him get close. A pull of the trigger accompanied an incantation in an alien, eldritch tongue.

"Wandrei..."

Click. Boom. No bullet came out; its dregshot form burned up instantly into formless thaumic energy. A stream that empowered the theurgic talisman rolled up inside the shell casing and, in the same moment, carried it out the barrel of the gun. It resembled an exceedingly forceful application of a talisman, its sigils burning with a hateful glow as it adhered to her arm.

"Faust!"

A surge of power—burning and seething—the slithering presence surged through her arm, implicating itself within the construct. The talisman burned up in an instant. With the bursting of a liquid akin to boiling blood, the hollow forearm ripped free and went careening forward. There were two alternate modes in which the Wandrei Faust could be set loose; Chasedown, and Standoff.

Chasedown would try to grab the target and restrain them, requiring a manual detonation command.

In Standoff, the arm would instead try to get within optimal range of its target before firing its payload; the range was around three meters at present.

Despite its speed surpassing that of a Red Reaper, Cleavers deftly side-stepped its approach. He would have successfully struck her, had Krahe not been prepared with a skim to his 4 o'clock blind spot. He quickly spun around and reacquired his target, but a diagonally rising pillar of stone smashed into his groin and threw him backward. He was unharmed but displaced and forced to reorient himself once more.

Meanwhile, as her Wandrei Faust changed targets to the Evoy, Krahe fusion-formed a burster in her hand. Another gunshot carried it, the Six Trees Killer flying right at Croupier's face. She stopped it with her barrier, but the grenade's impact, and the kinetic component of its blast, smashed her off her feet a moment later.

She skimmed in the Croupier's direction and raised a cover wall, already turning to face Cleavers and forming another clawed arm shell. Another shot. Another talisman. Another missile.

Just as it left her arm, she saw the first one passing to her right. It held the Evoy by his torso with its fingers digging through his wards and into his chitin, dragging him against the wall so forcefully that it tore the facing off. Cleavers had righted himself and leapt at her, and despite unfurling his armor's wings, he couldn't dodge. The black-clawed fist struck him and mercilessly dug its fingers into his armor, carrying him away.

At nearly the same moment, both flying forearms smashed their respective victims into the black jade wall by which Cassius was entrapped. With a spark of intent, both arms flashed with reddish-orange light, with streaks of golden-yellow mixed in. It was accompanied by a sound akin to a high-pitched scream, as opposed to the ominous buzz of her own anathemic power ripping the air. The pulse lasted perhaps one-third of a second. From the seams of both the Evoy's and Cleavers' plating, light and boiling fluid burst forth in equal measure, bathing Cassius' horrified face.

GRUDGE-FILLED GRASP
DEATH BORNE UPON CLAWS OF HATE
BLACK HAND OF DESOLATION: WANDREI FAUST

Before she could do anything else, the Croupier dashed past her wall. Krahe had heard her footsteps and prepared a smoke eruption. Before long, she had the Inax in a rear hold, though she had torn an impressive chunk out of her wards, and Krahe was fairly certain she wouldn't have been able to restrain her without using several tar-tendrils and an unconscionable amount of entropy.

"I can still leave only three corpses in my wake. Do you want to continue this?"

She had no reason to take mercy on the Croupier in particular; it was a simple gut feeling. As for killing Cassius, though not something she opposed, it would cause more of a stir than she wanted.

After not receiving a response from the Croupier, she choked her out and instead turned her attention to Cassius.

"Well? Do you want to fire another flare? Call more to their deaths? Or can I just empty your pockets and walk out of here? Either works for me."

"Alright," he sighed, deflating in his stone shackles. "I'll make sure you get to leave my territory without anyone on your tail, but that's all I can do. For all the money on your head, you're fifty times the trouble it's worth."

Krahe sensed no cowardice in the man, yet he wasn't particularly brave either. He lacked the bravado, the ego, that drove others to smash themselves against a wall—the same bravado that had driven *her* to such an end.

"How much is it?"

"A—quarter mil. A-and another quarter mil for the gun, if it turns out to be a legit Pattner."

She felt no particular need to kill Cassius, or bring down his gambling operation. It didn't seem particularly predatory, and she didn't see gambling as a symptom of societal decline or subversion. In her eyes, given what she knew of history, it was a completely natural part of society that couldn't be curtailed any more than recreational sex and intoxication.

Krahe was sure that if she toppled the Hashems, Cassius would go on running his gambling house all the same.

Before she could leave, though, the two others arrived, busting down the iron gate. Krahe was fully prepared to defend herself, but Cassius defused the situation: "Ey, ey, put ya dicks away, alright? We're done. She's leaving. The money ain't worth this."

They didn't need much convincing; the gore of their comrades splattered around was more than enough. While the two new arrivals inspected their boss and slowly waking-up coworker, Krahe got out her souldreg extractor and started pulling Cleavers' dregs.

"Ey. Can't you make this shit go away? It's a construct, no?!" Cassius hissed at her from above while one of his thugs hacked away at one of the bars holding him in place.

"I'm not the one keeping it together. It'll go away after an hour," she said, yanking the syringes out of the dead Mamon Knight, who was a sickly bald man under the rapidly decaying suit. She didn't feel like digging through the gunk and chitin, so she moved onto the Evoy, taking some money and a dregstone from inside his suit. The whole time, she heard Cassius instructing his subordinates that they were not to follow her in-between poor advice on how they ought to best break apart her black jade.

Before they could even think about the option of ganging up on her, Krahe took her spoils and got out of dodge.

It would be another three days before she managed to follow up on Nozar's lead, in part due to pursuing other leads to break up the pattern of her activity to any possible observers. Besides "that one place," her other leads went... straight to the Dead Night Tigers.

This made it an easy choice to pursue Nozar's lead, in no small part because she really didn't feel like marching into the agency's front door and asking for information on one of their members with the only connection being that she had been targeted and that she intended to return the favor to his employer. Oh, Krahe was sure that the Dead Night Tigers were professional enough to handle things reasonably, but that was part of why she went for the alternative. Getting ambushed or a simple investigative stint at a bar was a problem easily solved and potentially a nice bit of practical exercise with profits on the side. An agency filled with actual, professional bounty hunters and contract killers? It would take caution and a light hand, subtle negotiations, adherence to the agency's rules, and very possibly one or more duels against individuals beyond her current level—if what she had read of the DNTs was true.

By comparison, following an annoying cryptographic puzzle to find a secret club for pretentious up-their-own-ass theurgists in a run-down part of town was... preferable.

There were numerous possible qualifiers for entry into the so-called Lost Sun Society; Nozar had referred her to someone who could sponsor her, but, not wanting the loose strings, she decided to go the more direct way: Showcasing an original theurgy as proof of one's skill in the discipline. There was no fortunate coincidence to be found here; it was just one method of entry out of four that Nozar had suggested. Most of them included somehow currying favor with an existing member or proving one's ability in specific disciplines, from theurgy to artifact-crafting and so on.

CHAPTER 5

THE LOST SUN SOCIETY

When she arrived at the door and plainly stated that she intended to join on the grounds of being a theurge, they made a great deal of fuss and played up the ritual of everything to an asinine degree. She was let in and led to a firing range, observed by a procession in ominous robes. The whole thing was officiated by a man in bright yellow robes with a heavy turban over his head, who spoke in pointlessly flowery language. In short, it felt like a crass and shallow attempt to capture the sense of the sublime that the Twin Churches legitimately exuded.

The target was a six-headed chimera whose features Krahe honestly didn't bother discerning. It just looked like a mashup of various predatory beasts on a chunky body with a lizard-like tail and an insect-minotaur lower half, six bug legs and all. The target was its chest, and there, she aimed.

She gave them a standoff shot. With a pull of the trigger, the talisman struck her arm and burned up. Her previously formed forearm carapace was brought to life with the bursting of that weird blood-like fluid upon its detachment, and the missile sprinted across the fifteen-meter gap before stopping. Bright, gold-orange light poured out from its palm, at first a wide cone, only to narrow down and hone in on its target. A burst of light and sound and a bright scream caused four of the chimera's heads to blast flame from their mouths. The arm simply turned to dust and tar, and the spirit animating it returned to her in an instant.

"Fourth-order... fourth-order... It's fourth-order... A Chthonian Eel..." came murmurs from the crowd. It seemed that the Deathsmoke Blessing's obfuscation either didn't extend to her constructs, or there was no relation between Chthonian Eels and Chernobog.

At that moment, all the onlookers flipped up their hoods. Krahe's feeling that this was an initiation into a group of posers desperately LARPing as occultists only grew.

Most of them lacked any edge, exuding the aura of high-level enthusiasts and geeks. The Lost Sun Society decisively leaned on the side of a glorified clubhouse rather than a true occult society; that didn't discredit it as a place for gathering intel, and it certainly made it easier for Krahe. She nonetheless disliked it, simply due to how hokey the occult facade felt in its discordance with what was truly behind the veil.

It felt like walking into a historical orthodox church, only to be met by stage lights and a plastic-faced prosperity preacher behind the pulpit.

"I, Zachariah Ahmadi, who carry the burden of speaker, shall now receive the members' votes and render up my judgment as to whether or not Brunhilde Krahe shall be accepted into our midst."

With one gesture, dozens of yellow talismans flew out from the sleeves of his robe, hovering before each member. Going by the reaction this got, it was new. It also immediately confirmed that the speaker was her contact. Murmurs of the Talisman Mistress abounded while a steady trickle of the papers was sent flying back to Zachariah. One by one, the members touched the papers and sent tiny wisps of thauma into them. They arrayed in a wall in front of him, then, once all were gathered, Zachariah crossed his hands. With a bombastic gesture of throwing his arms wide, he sent them into a swirling, indistinguishable mass, which, after a few moments, separated into two distinct groups. From Krahe's perspective, the left-hand group was three-and-a-half to four times larger than the right-hand one.

"A more contentious vote than I had expected, but I understand why some of our esteemed members may hesitate to admit a late-stage Anathemist into our ranks. For this reason, I would like to make it clear that anathemism alone is not a disqualifying factor. It is the deleterious effects it often has on the practitioner's ability to function within our Society without breaching its other rules."

Another gesture, and the papers all retreated inside his sleeves.

"If anyone wishes to protest the results of this vote, this is your opportunity to do so."

Unsurprisingly, given the vote results, someone did. A lanky Saurian with an appearance on the "humanoid dinosaur" side. It was a woman, going by the voice. By her robes, proximity to Zachariah, and the small wave of murmurs, she seemed to be a respected, higher-ranked member. She managed to pick out the objector's first name as well: Sorayah.

"Regardless of whether or not she is a capable occultist, and regardless of whatever magical means she uses to animate her arm, the advanced stage of Ms. Brunhilde's anathemic poisoning cannot be ignored. It is known that once the carbonization reaches an Anathemist's face, she only has a short and painful few months to live. Many among our number have seen what lengths Anathemists go to in these final months, and though I loath to deny a desperate soul the hope which the Lost Sun Society may seem to offer, I must raise my most severe objection for the good of us all."

While the lizard-woman talked, Krahe raised her hand, rolling her wrist and carrying out various hand exercises while explicitly not channeling an iota of magic, as a way to make it abundantly clear that she wasn't suffering from any such deleterious effects. This garnered her a mix of venomous and envious glares.

"For the record, I do not suffer from any of the effects of acute or chronic anathema poisoning."

"Surely, you cannot expect us to believe such claims at face value," another individual cut in. Male. Pale, soft-voiced, and baby-faced. It was a fair point.

"Surely, in this society of the occult, individuals with abnormal constitutions are both known and present. The fact that the speaker uses the works of Talisman Mistress Yao Fu is proof enough."

Another wave of murmurs came: "Yao Fu?... Is that her name?... How would she know?"

Zachariah's expression changed at that, a brief moment of surprise flashing over his features while Sorayah's face soured.

"I do not see how the Talisman Mistress, whatever her actual name is, plays into this. Are you just trying to distract from your own state?"

"What state? Perfect health?" Krahe laughed. She turned her attention to the Speaker, approaching him, pointedly ignoring Sorayah. "I wish to make it abundantly clear that I neither care for nor intend to participate in whatever clique politics Sorayah is so obviously concerned with. This, in itself, ought to placate her with the knowledge that I am too busy with matters of my own to attempt ousting her from whatever position she holds within this Society. There are only two reasons for me to join your Lost Sun Society: The first is advancement of my occultism, and though I'm sure that those of a higher rank in the Society have easier access to its resources, I would rather contend with the beasts of Jas'raba than power-playing snakes. As for the second... it is the search for a *Tarnished Jade Flower*."

Tarnished Jade Flower was a phrase from one of Nozar's contacts who had done business with Yao. It was, supposedly, the phrase she had given when asked how she might be contacted for further business. The man had used it as payment, and Nozar, in turn, demanded payment for it as well in the form of a second vial of Class 3 Pain Suppressant.

"You have made your point. As I have already mentioned, the practice of anathemism alone is not grounds for rejection, and besides carbodermatism, itself a comorbidity, you do not appear to exhibit any of the acute symptoms of late-stage anathema poisoning."

Zachariah stumbled through a bramble of his own words for another twenty seconds, for whose entire span Sorayah stared daggers into Krahe while Krahe kept her gaze on Zachariah. At last, he said, "Henceforth, Brunhilde Krahe, thou may count thyself among the ranks of the Lost Sun

Society. There yet remain some matters of ritual to deal with in private before you become a true member, and I shall contact you regarding them within the next two hours. For the time being, explore our facilities and library. I trust that you will find its contents second to none besides the greater agencies, the restricted sections of the Twin Churches' Temple of Records, and perhaps some private collections."

With that, he left, exiting by a door behind the chimera, while the others filed out of doors to the sides, doubtlessly to change out of those ridiculous robes. In the meanwhile, Krahe made her way to the common area upstairs.

The Society was legally an agency, but the contract board was minimal and in the corner, and the main public room couldn't be more of a bougie coffeehouse if it tried. The bar, manned by a gynoid automaton with the sigil of the Society on its face, seemed to also serve as the place for taking out and handing in contracts. One-third of the common room's considerable floor space, all the way on the other side from the bar, was dedicated to large tables with elaborate dioramas laid out in the center, as well as shelves and shelves of books and boxes. Idols, statuettes, and miniatures of various sizes completely took up a wall of displays.

Various members started filing in after a few minutes. Despite the tentatively friendly atmosphere, Krahe felt bile rise in her throat every time one of the other members accosted her about her use of anathemism, or, God forbid, Wandrei Faust. Sorayah was nowhere to be found.

Despite all her misgivings, it couldn't be denied that the Society's facilities were very, very nice. It was no surprise why it would be a desirable gathering place. The library, too, held an impressive collection, though she hadn't explored the Temple of Records thoroughly enough to discern how the Society's library compared to the restricted sections. There were certainly some books and scrolls that seemed like they belonged in the higher numbered sections. It was located on an upper floor, up a spiraling, narrow staircase, and the librarian made it abundantly clear that she was not allowed to take most of the books out of the building and some not even out of the library. That was perfectly reasonable.

While she was browsing, a member found her. He looked young, wearing what could be described as a lower-level version of Casus' getup: foppish satin shirt, tight trousers, knee-high boots, a meticulous, oiled short hairstyle. It felt fake. He lacked the confident aura such a getup should dictate. Krahe had met many like him, young idiots who wanted to look like their favorite mercenary-celeb and got themselves killed. He had to be in his twenties at the latest, but the lack of age wasn't the sign; Casus didn't give off this same aura of innocent youth, and even Krahe herself was physically back in her twenties. No, it was the look in his eyes and the way he spoke. He introduced himself as Reuben. Krahe just let him rattle on and on about theurgy, only half-mindedly paying attention to what he said as she idly paged through one book after the next, including his theories of how he thought the Wandrei Faust worked, until he asked a question.

"And how'd you come by a Chthonian Eel? Please don't say a normal spirit-calling ritual. Don't say you were just lucky. Catching Deep Eidolon is something like a one in five thousand chance."

"I can't tell you how I did it," she smiled. "There are methods other than spirit-calling rites."

Disappointed, the young man sighed: "Alright, how about the theurgy at least? I know we're not supposed to ask unless invited, but…"

"Have you read Secrets of the Atropal?"

"That sensationalist dreck?" he asked, furrowing his brow.

Krahe closed the book in her hand and stared straight at him.

"See, that's how I know you haven't even read more than a few pages. The sensationalist dreck ends after the foreword. I'm not trying to fool you; reading Secrets of the Atropal is what helped me get a grip on the fundamentals of theurgy. From there, look into Godbrush. If you can't find it, try Manual of Talisman. The edition I read was from 4599."

"I understand the Talisman Mistress is bringing them back into fashion, but I don't see what would make them better than thaumshot."

Sighing, she summoned a lemon Wandrei Faust talisman into her hand and held it up in his face. A look of taken-aback terror briefly took hold of his face before she could explain.

"Don't worry, this one doesn't work. It's one of my first attempts at Wandrei Faust. It still looks near-perfect, right? But it's a lemon. Now think, what's harder? Just drawing and writing, or carving all these instructions *inside* a little ball of thaumstone? You don't even get the safety net of just tossing a fuckup into an eraser solution so you can try again with the same paper, and one single fifteen-millimeter ball of thaumshot stock costs as much as fifty of these papers. Understand the appeal? The guilds so readily switched to thaumshot not just because of their real advantages, but also because the raised barrier to entry makes it that much less likely that the beginner occultist will be able to make his own instead of just buying them."

That last part wasn't even anything she had read or heard of; Krahe had simply deduced that it had to be the case based on her experience working with talisman paper. She quickly put it away and summoned one of the dregshot Reapers that Garvesh had given her.

"And look here. The outer layer with all the complex patterns isn't dregstone. It's the same thing as just wrapping a dregshot bullet in a talisman."

"I... I see. Thank you for the pointers. And ah... look out for Sorayah. She has a grudge against Anathemists; her brother was one and met a grisly fate due to it."

"Is that so? To what degree? What is the most severe manner in which she came after someone?"

"Well, uh, there was once a new member, not an Anathemist. The story goes he threatened Sorayah's position, and then out of nowhere, he showed up anathema-charred head to toe and threw a huge tantrum right in the common room, then died. Rumor has it…"

"She irradiated and somehow had him kill himself. Interesting. Perhaps the true reason she hates Anathemists is their resistance to such tactics. A late-stage Anathemist can shrug off a dosage that would kill a normal person, after all, so whatever she did to that guy wouldn't work on one."

She noticed Reuben staring at her, aghast, as she thought aloud with her hand to her chin. There was something there; he wasn't aghast because of the far-stretched theory. Did she coincidentally hit close to home? But how would he know? At that moment, Krahe realized. She recognized the rings on his hands and the coin-like earring dangling from his ear. He was one of the people who had stood right next to Sorayah.

"Ah, but it's just a rumor, isn't it," she smiled, trying to diffuse the tension whilst leaning in closer as she continued to speak. "She probably pushed him out through some politicking, and he turned to anathemism thinking it would help him get one over on her, only to fall flat on his face and burn himself out. Either way, as I said earlier, I won't make problems for Sorayah so long as she returns the favor."

The motivation was to "sniff" him, in a manner of speaking. Intimately familiar with Isotope as she was, she found detecting it instinctive… and there it was. Faint, barely even present, but undeniably there, clinging to Reuben and tinging his cologne with an ephemeral acridity that wasn't actually there.

Another member, a red-haired, tan, spunky girl of similar age to Reuben, barreled into the library, calling, "Is Ms. Brunhilde here? Hello?"

A moment later, she heard the librarian hissing at the girl to quiet down, but she had already taken the excuse and called back, "Yes, I'm here."

As for Reuben, he saw the woman turn on her boot heel and walk off, but just as she passed him, she stopped for just a moment and whispered: "If Sorayah's intent was to send a warning through you, let her know that I still don't intend to play at politics. If she comes after me, I'll gladly show her what real anathemism looks like."

A chill ran down his spine as he glimpsed her eyes and bore witness to the cold flame of murder behind them. In an instant, the demon-woman flipped back into her casual demeanor, moving to meet the girl.

Reuben didn't exhale until he heard the two of them leaving, Krahe's voice echoing, "Call me Krahe, please. Brunhilde feels much too formal."

* * *

As Krahe made her way back down, the girl who had come for her only affirmed what she had assumed to begin with. "Speaker Ahmadi wishes to meet with you, to finalize your membership."

"I assumed as much," Krahe said.

Wordlessly, the girl led her to the end of the hallway where the library stairway was located. She gently placed her hand on the door and a pulse of thauma went out from her.

"The Speaker will be with you shortly," she said with a smile, and walked off.

It wasn't even three minutes before the door opened in front of her, with Zachariah waving her into his office: "Come in, come in. Don't mind the door. Take a seat."

Krahe felt her fight-or-flight instinct flaring. It was just like the offices of so many self-proclaimed, all-too-wealthy "collectors." Lacquered wood paneling, a lavish rug covering the whole damn floor, an eclectic variety of artifacts on display... on and on it went. There was a huge, corked, sealed-up bottle standing in the corner; inside it, a lush environment of plants, small lizards, and beetles.

The difference between Zachariah's office and her closest point of reference was that this was fairly normal for someone of Zachariah's position, rather than being a grotesque flex of power through money and connections. This didn't even compare to the grandeur of Twin Churches facilities, yet they didn't offend either, as that imagery hadn't been sullied in her mind. Indeed, an office such as this was only second to a stereotypical corpocrat's office in how hard it yanked on Krahe's death-strings.

"Ms. Krahe?" Zachariah's voice snapped her out of it. She had been staring at that terrarium while her mind wandered.

"Sorry. It just reminded me of something," she said, taking a seat.

"We all wander off, sometimes. It is of no concern!" the Speaker beamed, pushing an ornamental jade box across the table towards her. "The Tarnished Jade Flower lies herein. Do you know what it is? More than a mere code-phrase, it's…"

He slowly opened it for dramatic effect, though his enthusiasm undercut that.

It was an identity token, like from some Chinese period drama. The body was made of dark, polished granite, a braided red cord looped through a hole in the top. In its center was a lotus flower with tattered petals, rendered in mottled jade, mostly white, with gorgeous webs of black and green streaking through. Notably, in the box was also an inkstone and a bright vermilion inkstick, with two symbols that Krahe didn't recognize but looked very much like Old Chinese. Since Cantonese had supplanted it as the dominant form of Chinese with Goujian II's reconguista, she hadn't ever needed to learn it.

"Are you aware of its use, or do you only know the code-phrase?"

"I'm afraid I was not made aware of the specifics, but I might guess as to how the Flower is used given the ink stick. A stamp of some kind, perhaps?"

"Right you are!" he beamed once more. Then, the levity drained from him as he took out the objects in turn, gravely explaining: "Anyone stamped using this flower, this specific ink stick, and this specific inkstone will '*become known*' to the Talisman Mistress. As she described it, a basic snapshot of your capabilities will be taken at the moment of stamping and sent directly to her. Then, for several days or until she removes the mark, your location will be known to her at all times. She made it very clear not to use the Flower unless one has good reason to contact her in the immediate future. Is that your case?"

"It certainly is."

As quick as the snapping of a rubber band, he switched back to his cheerful self: "Excellent! We can get started then. Feel free to get comfortable, this ink takes an eon and a half to grind."

A few minutes passed as Zachariah began the arduous and, indeed, time-consuming prep work. The only sound to fill the silence was the inkstick grinding against the inkstone.

"I'm curious. How does this work? The thing with the Flower. Not on the magical side, the personal one. Why did you take the code-phrase at face value? Did Yao herself order you to do so?"

"You have the right of it, yes. She chose me, and a small handful of others, as middlemen. A first layer of vetting, so to speak."

Slowly, round and round, in steady motions, Zachariah ground away at the ink stick. With each revolution, the water on the flat portion of the inkstone turned to ink, the pigment coalescing into unnatural wisps of perfectly scarlet color, draining away into the reservoir at the other side of the inkstone, leaving only a tiny puddle of water. Time and again, this cycle repeated until no water was left and the reservoir was filled up to a particular line. Zachariah tipped the stone back so the ink would return to its flat portion and took out the Tarnished Jade Flower.

He pressed the hybrid badge/stamp into the stone, which fit together perfectly. Performing a series of signs with his free hand, he poured an impressive torrent of thauma into the stamp—wisps of golden light spiraling around his arm. Just from the aura it gave off, Krahe was certain that it was a greater feat of raw arcane power than she was capable of, and yet, it was contained.

When he raised it, all the ink was gone, and the stamp now shone with a bright red mirrored outline of its symbol.

"Now, Lady Yao did state that this ought to be placed upon as flat an area of skin as possible…"

"Must you apply it?"

"I'm not sure what you mean—"

Krahe unbuckled her pants. The sound of the buckle was clue enough.

"Ah. I see. No, my part is done. You need only hold it strongly to the right spot until the buzzing sensation passes. Shall I…"

"Turn around, yes."

"Right."

With that, Zachariah spun his chair around, awkwardly offering her the stamp behind his back. A few moments later, Krahe had it clamped tightly between her thighs.

"Buzzing sensation" was an understatement; it felt much like having a tattoo done all at once, perhaps due to the fact the stamp's magic was trying very, very hard to pierce anti-scrying defenses that weren't there.

"Er, is… Is everything alright? It has been twice as long as usual."

"And yet it's still going," she remarked dryly.

It was another half-minute before, at last, it gave up, leaving a patch of irritated skin in whose midst Krahe could make out the flower sigil. She popped three tabryxa pills into her mouth. Nonetheless, it was done, and Krahe absolutely did feel an indefinable something exit the stamp when she removed it from her skin and put it back on the table.

"You may turn around now," she said, buckling her trousers.

The Speaker, avoiding mention of the awkward sequence of events, took the stamp, wiped it down, and put it back in its case.

"Now, it is a matter of waiting," he said. "I hope that you find whatever it is you are looking for. And ah… do not mind Sorayah. She and her circle are merely wary of new members."

A lie by way of understatement if Krahe ever heard one, but she didn't feel like confronting the old man after showing her serendipity, so she simply gave him a nod of acknowledgment and left.

CHAPTER 6

THE TARNISHED JADE FLOWER

A woman sat inside an unassuming, yet exceedingly well-warded house on a street just off the city's main arteries. The house, built in millennia past, would have seemed utterly normal, only lightly warded, to all eyes, for even this was part of its warding. Its magical protections, like walls a kilometer tall and wrought of solid steel, had the appearance of mundane stone, neither taller nor thicker than ordinary.

She sat, globs of scarlet ink orbiting her hand like planets around a sun, its ivory fingers and golden joints glistening in the faint light of the light-producing talisman she had affixed to the walls in lieu of using the inbuilt lighting. Like a painter, she mulled over her canvas: a single piece of yellow paper, held fixed in mid-air by the weakest of magics. She cautiously guided the flame in her gut into a roar, ever cautious, feeling like she was fostering a candle flame, yet also feeling that it might burst her open from the inside at any moment. In a few quick gestures and splashes of ink, a new talisman came to be. Meanwhile, her precious brush nestled in the midst of her chest, beneath a curtain of myriad necklaces, from beads to precious stones... unused. So pitifully unused. But it couldn't be helped. In her current, sorry state, she was in no position to use that brush.

Suddenly, a would-be customer made herself known: someone who had either dug in the right places or caught the interest of the right people. Yao Fu pulls on the new metaphorical red string, expecting, truly, just another customer, someone to put in the queue for a simple exchange of goods and services.

But no.

This one demands her attention, her full, unbridled attention.

A woman, named Brunhilde Krahe, also known as "Blackhand," currently located in the Lost Sun Society. The rest of the information was incomplete. No... *tainted.* Obscured by black smoke. Were it a book, its pages would be blackened and glued together by tar. The same tar that now held together Yao's own Soul Furnace, which rightly should have been shattered, irreparable, leaving her forever crippled.

Yet, here she was. Reduced to the lowermost rungs of power, hiding at the other side of the world, sure—but not for long. Either she had just found the soul whose summoning had opened her window to communion with the Black God of the Labyrinth, or the heavens were playing a truly cruel trick indeed.

She would learn which it was soon enough; Brunhilde Krahe instantly shot up to the top of her priority list.

* * *

With not much to do for the moment but wait to be contacted by Mistress Yao, Krahe had taken to occasionally visiting the Society in intervening days. Due to the Tarnished Jade Flower Stamp's tracking properties, she went out of her way to avoid any church safe houses, and the same went for going anywhere that might make it easy to deduce information. She went to the Temple of Records, but not to any restricted section. She avoided Garvesh, and only followed up on leads that led her to mundane places. Despite everything, the Society was well-hidden and secure enough, and the library had some texts she couldn't find in the Temple of Records, and vice-versa. The wargames were also a nice diversion.

On an otherwise unassuming day, she walked through the Society's second-floor corridor and found herself confronted with an equally familiar and unwelcome figure. She had to suppress a smirk; it was an honest surprise that it had taken this long for them to meet again, and she was sure that was no accident.

Sorayah. She was clad in more common attire compared to that stupid robe, but she wore far more jewelry than seemed reasonable, especially rings, several bedecking each of her gangly clawed fingers. Krahe felt magic from some of them, so for all she knew, it might have just been a way to disguise which were magical. Behind her, two others trailed, whom she had not interacted with but remembered as having stood near Sorayah.

She slowed and came to a halt at the sight of Krahe, a seething anger flaring behind her eyes.

"You," she hissed.

Not responding, Krahe merely raised a questioning eyebrow to her.

"Levying false accusations against another member is grounds for expulsion, you know."

"Reuben delivered my message, then? I'm not sure what exactly he said, but I've levied no accusations against you. Neither to other members nor to the Speaker. It was a mere word of caution. You needn't fear any accusations from me. If I must repeat myself; I don't intend to play petty politics with you or anyone else. What was your method, I wonder? A Jas'raban artifact, maybe? Oh, but that power can only be catalyzed by a humanoid soul. I wonder..."

"Tread carefully," Sorayah's right-hand companion growled, arcane-green power winding about him for a brief moment. Krahe figured he was stronger than her, at least in terms of raw statistics. The same went for Sorayah... but they didn't know that. She had felt two appraisal attempts from Sorayah by now, both impotently smothered by Deathsmoke Blessing without sending back any information besides the visceral wrongness of Krahe's appraisal immunity. Casus had made it abundantly clear in the past; the force obscuring Krahe from unwelcome appraisal was something obviously different from any normal anti-appraisal measures. It was this property that made Krahe decide to handle things as she did in this given situation. Merely blocking appraisal was one thing; it could be interpreted as guarding one's weaknesses or lackluster powers. Deathsmoke Blessing made such bluffs infinitely less likely.

"Tread carefully? To avoid being bitten by the snake coiled in the grass?" she asked the right-hand man. Then, staring hard at Sorayah, she added: "If we're speaking of caution, I ought to instead stomp on its head before it can even think to strike at me."

* * *

Elaborate patterns in dark shades of purple flashes across Sorayah's body, clearly displaying her rage as she hissed: "Who do you think I am, to be threatened by some nobody Anathemist? I'm a level thirty-five shaman, I have a fourth-order voidkey, I can—"

Before she could finish, the black-haired woman who had humiliated her in front of the whole Society vanished. In her place, a shape of billowing smoke, with green-burning dots for eyes and an alien rib cage burning in her chest with the color of a hot branding iron. The Green-eyed Demon rushed up to her with inhuman speed, alien whispers and sounds emanating from her form, a raven of the same ethereal countenance upon her shoulder.

Her heretofore loyal companions fled like beaten dogs.

While the mouthless form merely stared at her, tilting her head back and forth, the raven opened its beak, and a garbled, hissing, child-like voice came out. Behind it was a constant, grating sound, weird music from a screeching string instrument, and rapid singing in a language she didn't know. In simple terms, it sounded exactly like a crow talking while alien music played in the background, which itself was then played back from a memslate through a shitty speaker.

"Do nothing. You. Can. Do. Nothing. I don't know what led you to the... Mis-be-got-ten. De-lu-sion. That you could harm me. In a way. That matters. Jas'raba could not. Hashem could not. The Dead. Night. Tigers. Could not. Cease this... or become a stain. Last. Warning."

With those words, she was gone. Sorayah slid down the wall, slowly deflating in a long exhalation.

Meanwhile, just outside, in the gap between this building and the next, Krahe plummeted three stories straight down. She only dared to perform that exit over simply walking away because she knew this back alley was here. Thus, she could safely emerge from her dive mid-air, fall most of the way, and then dive again to break her fall. The velocity reduction from the weakened effect of gravity was nice, but even the sudden deceleration of impact had as little effect as any physical attack; that is to say, none.

She made herself innocuous and turned her mind towards Barzai. The crow was still in the hallway, merely hidden, observing Sorayah. Krahe was perfectly fine with the possibility of the eidolon being detected; it would serve as a nice aftershock for her intimidation tactic.

In fact, once the lizard woman gathered her wits and got back up, Krahe had Barzai follow from a short distance behind. Then, just as she saw Sorayah shifting in a way that suggested she would look back, she willed the spirit to reveal itself, perched on one of the wall lights, staring at her. She stifled a slight laugh when the same woman who had tried to intimidate her ran away. This was Krahe's chosen tactic for the simple reason that Sorayah wasn't lying when she spoke of her own abilities; based on Krahe's cursory investigation, she likely had the superior firepower between the two of them. Deception and terror were tactical powerhouses of human history; they became prime choices when it came to going against a superior force.

The knowledge of how abnormal her astral body appeared had not slipped by her awareness; it didn't match any written description of how it ought to look while in a partial dive, and when she brought it up with Firminus during a checkup, he only confirmed it. With astro diving already being an obscure discipline, it made using her astral form as a tool of psychological warfare all the more appealing. There was the problem that she couldn't speak while diving, but Barzai was under no such restriction, being a native of the Gulf and thus speaking through means other than the physical.

The raven returned at her beck and call, diving into her chest as she began ambling down the alleyway, making her way to a house in the same district of the city, which she had rented specifically to use while she was branded with Yao's sign. Indeed, real estate wasn't exactly hard to come by. Audunpoint was, after all, a young, growing city built atop the bones of an antediluvian megalopolis.

The place she'd rented was barebones to the extreme as a result, with no furniture and only basic amenities, but that wasn't an issue since its sole purpose was the basement, which was large and deep enough to be an indoor firing range. It was in part thanks to the noise of a nearby market and a tram station. Apparently, according to the building's Evoy owner, the whole Audunpoint underground was a vast sprawl of basements and catacombs, such that the tram system had busted through four different ancient crypts during its construction, and one of the stations was located in a repurposed subterranean cathedral. This building was actually the third option, as the previous two only had passive ventilation for the basement, while this one had been hooked right into the tram's tunnel vents.

In the basement, she had set up some steel plates as targets on one end of the room, and on the other end, two fold out tables, a cushion, and a portable burner. Mercifully, the building had its own central water supply, but unlike the church safe houses, there was no central power supply.

As she sat, waiting for her talisman ink to stop bubbling and stabilize into a usable state, Krahe used the other half of the table to chop up vegetables into thin strips: carrot-like roots, peppers, and yellow cabbage. A pan, which she had hammered into the shape of a crude wok, sat atop the burner. Salt alone, rather, a fermented, strongly salty sauce, was more than enough flavoring for her stir-fry.

While the vegetables cooked, she took a mass of cold, leftover rice grain out of storage, leaving it in one chunk for now, followed by the meat component of her dish. It was dark red, almost purple, with veins of fat running between the muscle bundles. The quality was like high-grade beef with a much weaker smell and apparently came from a kind of land tortoise that was a common beast of burden.

She set aside a portion of the meat, mixing half into the vegetables and breaking up the rice into the stir-fry once it was done. Thereafter, having scooped her meal into a bowl, she used the leftover oil to fry individual pieces of meat, partly to enjoy them on their own and because, for some bizarre reason, Barzai incessantly demanded a share. Eidolons had no need for sustenance, and yet not only did Barzai manifest and demand meat, but he demonstrably recovered from exhaustion quicker when she fed him.

Just as he pecked for a piece of meat that she'd plucked out of the oil with a pair of construct-jade chopsticks, she yanked it out of reach, scolding the eidolon: "You won't even do your job, and you have the gall to act like this? Eh?"

She had yet to test the Daemon Core, let alone put it to practical use. Creating the individual constructs that would compose it was well within her ability, that much she had made sure of, but… Barzai wouldn't obey. No matter how many times she tried, though the crow would let her get as far as forming the anathemic core and partly enclosing it, he would refuse to go any further. The moment the core would reach criticality, Barzai always returned to his avian form and vanished, becoming unresponsive for two hours or so.

Barzai hopped up, his head splitting along the line of his beak as he snapped it up.

"You said you wanted to become a Daemon Core. What gives?" she questioned, expecting no answer.

Barzai sat there, tilting his head back and forth. No meat in the oil, no meat to snatch, and for some reason, he didn't so much as spare a glance for the raw stuff or that which had been mixed in with the sauce. He glanced at the oil, then back at Krahe.

"Wah. Awawawawa."

Despite lacking an efficient means of communicating with the spirit, Krahe could still feel his level of exhaustion through the system, and it seemed like he was near-topped up. Resigning to the temperamental not-bird's demands, she fried another slice of meat and gave it to him, leaving her with only one more for herself in addition to her proper meal.

Once more, Barzai opened his beak. This time, a voice came out: a man speaking in a somber, slow manner rather than the typical sound of a crow's mimicry.

"Yea, the Eye of Ruin, in its great and terrible glory, shall not first gaze upon dead stone and steel. It shall scorch the flesh of the wretched, or it shall remain blind."

Raising an eyebrow, she undercut the eidolon's proclamation. "You seemed pretty content to use those eyes of yours on dead wood, and that was the first time I ever made you attack anything."

Going silent, the bird turned his head sideways, staring at Krahe with one eye. As she ate, the passing thought of invoking Chernobog's Mystic Wisdom came to her—the Snare-sign of Blackest Pitch did, after all, carry the Outer God's Touch tag. That thought alone, it seemed, was enough to set it off. A black pinhole appeared amidst the redness of Barzai's eye, and soon encompassed it wholly. Flashes of knowledge flooded in, confirming one out of several theories that she had devised for this conundrum: Barzai couldn't solidify his new form unless it was invoked in the situation for which it had been conceived. She had no choice but to trust that it would work as expected and use it in real combat for the first time.

She finished her meal and took to calligraphy. The ink, now stable, was not yet ready to be used. Beginning with water and an ink stick, she had blended it with the Unguent of Nug-soth, and now it was time to add the final component, a liquid ink that also acted at once as binder and thinner to determine the final viscosity. Finally, after a few minutes of stirring, it was liquid.

Hours passed.

In a meditative state, Krahe repeatedly drew forth her vitriolic hate and wrath, reveling in it, bathing in it, and spitting it onto the talisman paper like a cobra upon its prey.

It was hate not for individuals, not in truth.

Krahe had never been given the easy comfort of names and faces to foist her hate upon.

It was the idea of evil, of subversion, of insidious decay. Wandrei Faust sought its prey based not on simple single-minded malice but on a greater hatred born from outrage towards those who would stand in Krahe's sacred path.

Wandrei Faust was a fist not for slaying random thugs or killing those who merely wronged her. It was wrought for smashing apart those who would forestall her from her ultimate goal.

Within her hand burned an anger altogether greater than that which could be felt by those content in the midst of their own lives. It was anger worthy of the heavens, the sort of anger that would drive one to consider burning a tyrant's city and killing millions as a failure because it didn't annihilate the very ideology for which the tyrant stood.

The hate within her had sprouted silently, and even now, it bubbled, coiling like a serpent, looking out for its rightful prey to strike out. It was the hatred of the righteous, ready and waiting for those who would undermine what is good. Unlike the Saxonian Wars of the early 2200s, there would be no generations-long buildup of vitriol, no century-long reawakening of long forgotten tendencies spurred on by the malice of corporate interest. No, no such thing. Clutching it closely, never once had the flame of righteous hatred within Krahe gone out or sputtered. Never once since that day. She had caught the flare of the bomb, and with plutonium's caustic glow, she had lit a profound hate that not even a lifetime of peace could put out.

Were she to live out her new life searching for an ephemeral, greater evil, never finding it, Krahe would die content, but deep inside, she knew it would not come to pass. A human life could be long, and ever more so if technology's wise hand forestalled the withering march of age. She had a knack for looking in the wrong, or perhaps *right*, places. An inborn skill for noticing patterns that the kinds of people she hated didn't want her to notice. That was, after all, what made her an investigator; a nose that tended to stick itself into the vilest, most wretched cracks in society's facade.

Stroke after stroke, the image of the wrathful, grasping hand was put to paper, time and again.

Barzai, ever curious, watched on.

The raven watched on, enraptured. A maelstrom of dark smoke swirled about the woman, vast quantities of thauma burnt and entropy purged, time and again. Her soul, her astral body, blazed alight, invisible to all but the eyes of the Raven of Ruinous Eyes.

One by one, Krahe prepared talismans.

She stopped not when she ran out of ink but when she was simply too exhausted to continue, when her arm physically gave out, trembling even under the minuscule weight of her brush, when the muscle no longer had even the energy to scream, but instead simply failed.

Hours had passed, and she hadn't even realized it, so engrossed had she been with her task.

A stack of finished talismans sat off to the left side, and off to the right, failures were piled high. A thirty percent success rate.

With a sigh, she used her left arm alone, alongside a few tar-tendrils, to stow everything away and set up the erasing solution to recycle the lemons' paper.

Two more days passed.

Somewhat disappointingly, Sorayah made no attempt to move against her, at least not in the open. Nothing Krahe could use as an excuse to satisfy herself with violent and wildly disproportionate retaliation.

Day by day, she spent her time. Finally, as she sat in her basement shooting range, frying slices of a kind of fish from the River Machine, she felt the Tarnished Jade Flower mark giving her a message. A simple thrum, and the concept of "outside."

Immediately outside the door of the building, beneath the night's pale moonlight, she found herself glancing left and right, looking out for a person or a talisman. She realized that the thrumming of her mark sped up or slowed down depending on her location. Hot and cold. A stupid game of hot and cold. It led her some distance away to a secluded spot in the back alleys, where she was met by a floating talisman just like those Zachariah had used to collect the votes. It simply appeared in mid-air when she reached the spot where the mark's thrumming became continuous.

It ceased, and the talisman appeared with a shimmer entirely too similar to the one produced by the disengagement of active optic camouflage.

Meticulous, yet stilted writing in the Calbian alphabet read:

You may use this talisman as a compass to find me.

Bring Silberblut if you believe him to be trustworthy.

The moment Krahe finished reading, the glow faded and fell into her hand. Curious, she funneled some thauma into it and found that it came alive once more, glowing faintly and sending her a sense of direction—a mental compass, subtler than the floating pointer she had expected. Moreover, from the moment she had found the message talisman, the Tarnished Jade Flower Mark had begun rapidly fading from her thigh. She returned to her rented domicile, and by that point, the feeling of the mark's presence had already vanished. When she checked, she found it to still be there, but it rubbed off with barely any effort.

After finishing her meal, she went right to the safe house and soon met up with Casus.

"Good news, I got in contact with the Talisman Mistress and I have a means of finding her. Mixed news, she wants me to bring you along, meaning that, at bare minimum, she has accurate intel on the Slaughterhouse 9 Incident."

After a few moments of quiet thought, the Banisher said, "Alright. I will finish my coffee, and we can go. A few of my acquaintances have been curious about the Talisman Mistress, anyway."

And just as he said, so it was. They went by foot, using hidden paths and back alleys as always, eventually reaching an out-of-the-way, yet not exceptionally obscure part of the city. Yao's talisman directed them down an alleyway, unsurprisingly, and so, down the alleyway they went.

It was, to no surprise on either of their parts, that the doors and windows of the surrounding buildings swung open, and out came hostile men wielding weapons of various sorts, from swords to guns.

An ambush. But why? Surely, Mistress Yao wouldn't try to use bottom-of-the-barrel goons like this to deal with the two of them.

Casus transformed in a flash and engaged three of the five, rapidly cutting them to bloody shreds.

Krahe blasted one with a short Cinder Strobe. He was dead on the spot, fried into the wall, flesh fused to melting stone. Another, charging right down the middle, met his end by way of Wandrei Faust.

Something felt a bit off. They didn't raise barriers at all, and their wards didn't unravel as much as they collapsed all at once. Not to mention the copious quantities of blood spilling across the ground from just two corpses.

Krahe didn't mind. In fact, she eagerly flooded the alleyway with rancid, isotope-laden smoke. Under its cover she summoned Barzai and began forming the Daemon Core's outer shell. The Wound-like Grin's opening down the length of her chest turned a small tear from earlier into one which spanned most of it, and the raven erupted from the maw. Right away, he nestled himself in the quickly growing hemisphere of black tendrils that floated above her outstretched left hand. Then, he imploded, and as the hemisphere grew closer to fullness, Krahe strode out of the smoke, ready to fry any takers.

Seven more attackers had appeared, with Casus casually keeping four at bay. Yet again, something felt wrong. Krahe tried to set Barzai upon them, but just like the raven had done before, it refused, extricating itself from its nest and returning into her. Casus echoed her realization a moment later after decapitating three of their attackers at once: "Something is off. I can't tell what, but I'm fairly certain these aren't real people."

"An understatement if I've ever heard one," Krahe deadpanned. She couldn't help but smirk at the absurd juxtaposition of Casus' cautious, logical statement compared with the ridiculous scene he was in the middle of. Three corpses, still standing, their necks fountaining absurd amounts of blood, while their comrades just... performed idle animations. That was the only appropriate description. They were idling like goons in some shovelware capeshit tie-in game.

Slow clapping, accompanied by the clack of wooden shoes against stone—perfectly synched, in fact. The illusion fell away; clothing gave way to layers of yellow-red paper with pallid, dead flesh showing through the gaps. These weren't living men, but... puppets? No. Corpses. Corpses mummified in layers of talismans, moved about like puppets and still gushing far more blood than any living human contained. They never had any wards at all, but a layer of protective talismans that was burned away in places where it had felt like their "wards" had collapsed. Nor did they have any real facial features

"I must admit, I'm impressed and disappointed at once!" came a husky, mature woman's voice. The fallen began to move again, dragging themselves to their feet and, in the case of Krahe's victims, peeling themselves off the walls. "I had hoped that it would take you until the fake graft-beast to uncover my little puppet show. Come, we have much to discuss. Don't worry about them; they'll clean up after themselves."

She saw a wood-and-wire scaffold under the melted skin of the men she'd Cinder Strobed. Nothing inside but a great big bladder seeping with blood.

They only got a brief glimpse of the woman, but since neither of them felt hostile intent from her, they followed. They saw no fake graft-beast along the way, probably because it was hidden, and Casus saw fit to detransform. Nonetheless, with disgust at the corpse-puppets, he commented as they walked, "Depending on the methods, this is either borderline heretical, or *highly* fucking heretical."

"Oh, they're not real corpses. Far too much resentful energy, too difficult to work with. I cobbled those puppets together from a grafter's waste solely for this little puppet show."

"Merely objectionable, then," Casus acquiesced.

Before long, she had led them into a two-story house that would've been utterly unremarkable, if not for the fact this place had an ephemeral sense of privacy that Krahe had not felt anywhere other than one of the Church's sanctums or inner chambers.

Finally, for the first time, the woman turned around and faced them.

"I apologize for the crude screening, but I simply had to be sure that you were true killers rather than Zachariah's ilk. That is, powerful, but only in theory. Now… shall we get to business?"

CHAPTER 7

TALISMAN MISTRESS YAO FU

The first things to draw Casus' gaze were her feet, swiftly followed by her hands. The first because his gaze naturally moved upward and stopped when he caught the paper. A substantial portion of the woman's lower left leg was covered in paper talismans, edged in red. He knew of a few Igarian sects that used this format, but there was only one place where these things were common: a place where the presence of the Twin Churches could be charitably described as lightweight and where the Seven Spokes System was not even the fourth most commonly used method by which people harnessed their Soul Furnaces to surpass base humanity.

Her strange sandals only supported Casus' theory: two flat pieces of wood, one perpendicular to the other, created strongly elevated, stilt-like footwear that added an easy twenty centimeters to her height. His gaze then naturally jumped to her hands, and indeed, her entire left arm up to above the elbow was likewise covered in these paper talismans, ragged scars reaching up from beneath them across her bare flesh.

Then, everything clicked when he saw her right hand. Prosthetic, up to and including the wrist. That was not what alarmed him. It was the style. Bone segments. Puppet-like joints. The craftsmanship, the consummate marriage of form and function, it couldn't have been made by any other than the Thousand Puppet Hall of the country of Goujian. The same craftsmen who had wrought Abbot Razem's right arm and legs, these being some of the few foreign-made grafts to be canonized as holy relics in the last two decades.

Calling the woman's attire *extravagant* hardly did it justice. Casus was aware the same could be said of his own fashion choices; as was his intention. But this... Some lesser-learned Seven Spokes adherents might view some parts of her vestment as sacrilege. Indeed, the only substantial article of clothing upon the woman was a pair of loose-legged, bright-red trousers, much like the trousers and long skirts worn by Seven Spokes clergy.

However, these were secured by a red cord laced in a zigzag pattern through numerous loops along the hem, affixed to a belt of red rope that sat on the woman's ample hips. Rather than being solidly affixed around the wearer's waist, they hung in a precarious manner, so low that Casus could readily see the long talisman which, in adhering to her skin, dutifully protected her last, infinitesimal shred of modesty. As if that wasn't enough, there were gaping cutouts in the fabric, exposing her bare legs from the sides and doubtlessly creating windows as she walked.

Her top half was, despite being more exposed, marginally less provocative. Numerous long strings of prayer beads and other spiritual jewelry draped down over her sizable bust, which was nearly bare save for the partial covering afforded by all her jewelry. There were two more horizontal seals, similar to the one down below. Besides prayer beads, she also wore a number of pendants, and a calligraphy brush whose handle was of the same make as her right hand sat wedged in the center of her chest, affixed to her neck by yet more red cord. He couldn't help but stare at it in an attempt to appraise the thing, considering how it seethed with powerful magic, but between the constant shifting of her flesh and jewelry, he couldn't even target it for long enough to hit the undeniable wall of anti-appraisal magic.

"I thought Banishers were going to be immune to my womanly charms. It is good to learn that I was wrong," came the husky voice. Casus forced his gaze up to meet hers, involuntarily passing over one of the two horizontal seals. She was right; he wasn't immune.

"Pilgrims are human. Of course we aren't immune... though, I suspect one of your stature might bewitch even a corpse," he smiled. It wasn't an attempt at flirting but an attempt to guess what sort of unorthodox magic she practiced. Talismans like the ones she displayed were among the more common methods by which corpses could be brought to bear as manpower and certainly among the less grim methods, as they merely puppeteered the body and burned its souldregs as fuel. No worse than a baneworm, and Casus wholly believed that, holding no grudge or prejudice towards baneworms merely for their nature. He still had to suppress his curiosity; when Yao turned, he noticed something, or rather, the absence of it— movement. Either her chest was stiffer than it ought to be, or she had some sort of invisible support both holding up its significant bulk and preventing undue movement. The only reason he'd noticed was that it came across as somewhat uncanny, but he wholly understood the reason for such measures.

Then, out of nowhere and completely brazenly, Krahe squatted down, tilted her head, and peered into the side of Yao's pants.

"Huh. I didn't think anyone wore this kind of stuff here. Nice."

She craned her head to meet the utterly unperturbed woman's gaze.

"So are the talismans just hiding prosthetics, or are they somehow the material?"

That was enough to shift Yao's facial expression into one of faint surprise and amusement—faint, but very much there—a raised eyebrow, slightly upturned corners of the mouth. "Both. The real prosthetic is a spiritual construct. The talismans are suspended within it to make it less obvious, provide structural support, and to give me easy access to a great number of them at a moment's notice. In my state I... cannot reach into my subspace storage with any speed. I did not think they were so obvious; is some of the leg construct shining through?"

"You'll probably get people assuming they're just wrappings. I made an educated guess based on the scars poking past the edge. Looks like the kind of thing gangsters used to do back home to try and destroy the nerves in a stump so you couldn't have new prosthetics fitted."

"I suspect that to have been the intention; the perpetrators of my injuries did much the same spiritually, or at least *made* the attempt. As if I would need working nerves or meridians to replicate something so simple as the function of a limb."

Her otherwise calm tone was tinged half by smug self-satisfaction, half by murderous vitriol towards these perpetrators.

Glancing between the two of them, Casus wasn't sure what he felt. Not himself, but from them. The way they looked at each other—spoke with one another—was like two graft-saints meeting after a century apart. But... Krahe was barely a low mid-ranker, and the Yao woman wasn't a contractor at all. Not a registered one, at least. Even appraising her, Casus saw nothing to suggest that she was a high-ranker, but then... he saw nothing that he had expected, not even the tiny expectations of an insane graft-saint level readout. Yao didn't have a system connection of any kind.

"I ah... As Lady Blackhand stated earlier, I believe it would be best to begin with why you have called us here. And, if you would not mind, why do you believe either of us can help you, given the fact you do not operate under the Seven Spokes System. Our understanding of magic likely does not cross over in the slightest."

"But that is where you would be wrong, pretty boy," Yao said smugly. With a gesture, one of the papers constituting her arm detached. A crimson blob floated out of an ink basin on a nearby table before shaping itself in the palm of her right hand. Half of it splashed onto either side of the paper, forming complex patterns.

"I know that these are not so foreign to you, and neither are the spirits which are often used to empower their consumable versions. Eidolons and Theurgy, you call them. We all work with the same magic; Igaria's System is merely one way of harnessing it. I must admit that I was humbled by the greater world. Despite falling short in all matters of what I know as cultivation, the number of exceptional talents and monstrously powerful individuals matches and, in some places, outstrips my home nonetheless.

Even the weakest among the weak are able to sense and harness Ke, the Breath of Emptiness, if only they reach for it, whereas back home, only perhaps one among a hundred ever has the chance to wield it in its most basic form."

An exasperated laugh took hold of Yao, and she continued: "No wonder, then, that arts which we considered normal are obscure and occult to the people of the outside! Why learn movement techniques and subtle weapon arts when you can throw balls of fire as naturally as breathing?!"

"It is true that natural awakening rates are a fair bit higher than one in a hundred, however..." Casus began, only to be interrupted once more by a laughing Yao.

"Most still need help. But they can get that help! Those things you call voidkeys, which are freely sold in stores on the street, are invaluable relics in Tiengenzhen! The secrets of making them are passed down from master to student and guarded so jealously that they are often lost with the maker's line!"

Yao flicked her wrist, and two voidkeys flew out of a nearby desk drawer. One was a flat, fairly simple key-like design of etched brass, and the other had the form of an eastern serpent-dragon, carved out of solid jade.

"Behold. Identical in performance. One, I exchanged for a few talismans a week ago. The other, I nearly died obtaining and treasured for decades. It is absurd. It is insulting. It is a fact to which those responsible for my state would rather blind and deafen themselves. But enough seething about what I cannot change."

Another gesture, and both keys flew back into the drawer. Yao moved to the conversation pit and sat down, prompting Krahe and Casus to follow suit.

"As for why I believe that you two can help me, and more importantly, why you will *want* to help me... We will get to that point. Let me begin with why I am here. I am certain that my sorry state has already raised some questions; it is one reason. I've been crippled, and coming to this city, halfway across the world, allows me to fulfill two of my goals. The first is hiding myself from those who did this to me. A stronghold of the Twin Churches is as close to a safe place as I can hope for, given that those who would come after me would immediately come to blows with the Churches. The second reason is to rectify my sorry state and rebuild my strength."

"And get revenge?"

"Perhaps. Perhaps not. We will see. For the time being, I am treading the path laid out for me by the same providence that allowed me to put myself back together at all. You see, several weeks ago, a certain event took place in the vicinity of this city. A great rite spurred an even greater machine into motion and pierced a window into the World Wheel's firmament."

Casus's eyes widened as he considered the implications of Yao's account being the correct one. He knew of the World Needle, of its purpose, of the Rite of Amrakas. He had never once considered that the supermassive Archon Flash a few weeks back could be a consequence of that rite, rather than just another of Jas'raba's usual Archon Flashes.

"I had nothing to do with the events leading up to it, of course... But I happened to see that the window was open, so to speak, and I took advantage. The fact I did it is the reason I am here, rather than rotting away a crippled husk. The problem is, I was halfway across the world, and to describe my ritual as "rushed" would be singing its praises. My only leads were, and still are, under here."

She tapped her taped-over eye.

"A gift from the One Beyond the Window. The Master of the Black Labyrinth, Chernobog. To remember him by, to guide me on my path, he said. It led me to this city... And it led me to you two. I'll stop beating around the bush, seeing as your Banisher friend here looks on the verge of an aneurysm, and you look about ready to shoot me. Tell me, Ms. Krahe. Those weeks ago, in the Underground City, was it you who came through the Black Gate? Is the smoke that shrouds you from appraisal merely a way for Chernobog to conceal his touch upon you?"

"Impossible."

It was Casus who interrupted.

"Hm?" Yao raised an eyebrow to him. "Is it so difficult to believe?"

"It was not an expression of disbelief. Lady Blackhand is a graft-apostle. Even a speck of Outer God taint would have been detected before her officiation. If, by some minuscule chance it wasn't, her grafted relic would have violently rejected her. There is no conceivable scenario in which Lady Blackhand could carry the taint of an Outer God."

"Perhaps it isn't taint that I carry, then..." Krahe sighed, deciding to neither lie nor tell the whole truth. "But Yao is right; I did indeed pass into this world during the event which she speaks of, and Chernobog had a direct hand in facilitating that. That is all I know of the event, though."

"How?! Genuinely, how could such a thing be possible?!" he demanded, growing exasperated. His demeanor suggested, more than anything else, that he saw this the same way as someone telling him they could simply choose not to be affected by gravity. It wasn't a question of corruption, never once did he consider that Krahe might secretly be corrupted, having personally witnessed incontrovertible proof to the contrary.

Bubbling with excitement at the possibility, Yao cut in: "Perhaps Ms. Krahe's condition is one which your Grafting Church has not encountered before. Perhaps it is somehow fundamentally different to the methods by which, say, someone like me, benefits from communion with an Outer God. Come, peer into me again. See if you can find the taint."

Casus, though repulsed, did as asked, his eye wandering down to Yao's stomach. At that point, he closed it shut and recoiled, uttering: "Yes, it's... It is there. Like boiling pitch, holding the shards of your Soul Furnace together in an unseemly, yet contiguous single mass."

Krahe cut in, "Regardless of the specifics, it cannot be denied that I carry a relic which would have rightly torn itself free of my flesh if I carried an Outer God's taint, and that neither the divine safeguards of the Grafting Church nor the senses of a High Grafter detected any Outer God's taint within me."

"Nonetheless, I must backtrack for a moment," Casus said, turning to Yao. "You are aware that you have just confessed to high blasphemy in front of two graft-saints, yes?"

"High blasphemy? No such thing. I had no hand in opening the window; my communion rite accelerated its closing, and not only were the local side effects of the rite resolved immediately afterwards, Tiengenzhen is perhaps one of the few places on the face of Zastreon that your Twin Churches consider to be outside their jurisdiction. Please, Silberblut. I am not so foolish as to invite one so known for righteousness as yourself into my temporary home without being certain that I am innocent of any possible crime you could hold against me."

At that rebuttal, Casus froze in place, his brow furrowed in thought. Yao took advantage and returned her attention to Krahe.

"Now, where were we... Ah, right. As things stand at the moment, I am taking a truly perilous risk by bringing you into my home. I've done my best to secure myself, but one can never be too sure."

Krahe responded in kind: "I couldn't agree more. I sought you out in pursuit of my own goals, of course, but I can't help being curious—in what way do you expect that I might be able to help you? If anyone here is knowledgeable enough on the matters of spiritual injury to make that guess, it's you."

Yao observed Krahe for a few seconds in silence before letting out a heavy sigh.

"You would need to permit me to look at you with my left eye before I can make that judgment. I do not expect that it will let me peer through your soul-smoke as if it weren't there, but it will show enough. It... Doesn't see in the true sense. It sees how the world moves and how it might move in the future. A twisted sort of clairvoyance, if you will."

Krahe *really* didn't like how forthcoming Yao was acting. Every cautious voice in her head screamed trouble, and yet... If she was being truthful, it was Yao who was putting it all on the line. Was that why she had invited Casus? To make herself seem trustworthy, knowing the full powers of his Third Eye, including his ability to detect outright lies? After all, the Banisher had kept his eye open for most of the conversation without raising the alarm towards any deceit.

After a moment of consideration, meeting Yao's one-eyed stare, Krahe said, "I need assurances first. What do I get out of this arrangement?"

Yao shrugged, perfectly at ease. "I'll help you to the best of my means. It is that simple. I am sure that, in the process of finding me, you have gained an appreciation for the value of having someone such as I in your debt."

"Casus?" Krahe side-eyed the man.

His Third Eye pulsed with light. He sighed.

"She is not lying, as much as I feel that it should be otherwise."

Yao smiled as if she had just won some battle.

"I'm sure it has become clear why I asked the both of you to come. You've taken care to minimize your footprint, Ms. Krahe, but the one you have left suggests you to be just as cautious as you have been thus far. What better way to assure a new acquaintance than having a Firstborn of the Wheel present?"

Casus once more felt the need to cut in. "Detecting lies is not my strongest point by far, hence why I have been silent. It demands more effort than it is worth, in most cases. Simply using instinct to tell if someone is lying is often easier."

"And yet you fulfilled your role in this exchange perfectly. I apologize for exploiting you in this way; I shall make a talisman for you if you would like. To help smooth over the many bumps of using that belt of yours. We don't have them back home, but we do have something similar. Similar enough, anyway, that I think I can help make yours function better. Your belt inflicts you with a temporary Heart Demon when you transform, isn't that right?"

"Heart... What?"

"It changes your personality in an undesirable way."

"I..." Casus began, hesitating. "I dare not call it an undesirable change, but a change nonetheless."

"Does it not interfere with your ability to use the armor, then?"

"No. I know the reasons for this, but I cannot share them with you. I neither require nor desire your assistance in managing the personality shift."

"Oho? How cold of you. I suppose I shall have to make it up to you some other time, then."

Yao's focus shifted once more to Krahe.

"Well? Shall I take a look at you?"

Krahe wasn't sure of the consequences of the unspoken alternative. Making an enemy of Yao would be a serious problem, she could tell, but she also had no way to know she could actually trust the Talisman Mistress. Nonetheless, she sighed and reluctantly consented. "Very well."

"Good!" Yao smiled, clapping her hands together with an odd sound, being that one hand was hard ivory and the other layers of paper. She rose from her seat, already walking towards the stairwell. "Come, come. I have precautions in place upstairs to ensure nothing undue occurs."

These precautions turned out to be a whole room plastered floor-to-ceiling in talismans, with only a section of the floor left clear. In its center was a ritual circle, including three bronze incense burners on tripods, each designed with a six-legged serpent dragon. The dragons differed in the number of jeweled orbs held in their claws, with the first holding one orb, the second holding two, and the third holding three. Krahe noticed a theme of threes repeating throughout the multilayered circle.

"You may stay, but keep out of the circle," Yao said to Casus as she lit each burner in turn. Turning to Krahe again, she pointed. "Sit."

Krahe well and truly reviled how familiar Yao insisted on acting. Nonetheless, she sat in the circle, and Yao followed suit. The one-eyed woman began a chant, performing a series of hand signs as a steady, rumbling outflow of thauma began to pour out of her. The circle came alive, the incense burners' smoke swirling around them as a handful of talismans detached from Yao's left arm, orbiting quickly around her twice, each time passing her right hand and having one side inked. Then, they took on a golden glow, spiraled out and took posts around the circle's perimeter. Despite no disruption of sight or sound from the outside into the circle, the sense of isolation grew to something not unlike being in a deep-sea diving bell on the sea floor.

"Now, hold still as best you can. This shall only take a few minutes," Yao said. With a simple gesture, she tore the tape off of her eye, and seething anti-light poured out from her seemingly empty left eye socket. Krahe wasn't sure how, but she acclimated to the outpour and managed to glimpse a writhing, tar-like mass embedded in the socket, roots extended into the surrounding flesh and bone. She felt something wrapping around and washing over her, but nothing that tried to penetrate past her shroud of smoke the way appraisal did.

CHAPTER 8

DEIPHAGE

Yao Fu. Devil Woman. Temptress. She had taken that name as a bitter joke, one she knew very few would understand in her place of hiding, if anyone at all. She had truly seen and experienced it all, the highest highs and lowest lows. Risen from nothing to the highest highs one could hope for in Tiengenzhen. It was the dubious honor of being truly unparallelled in one's specialization, to such a degree that the mightiest members of warring sects took the time out of their war just to come after her, knowing and rightly fearing that in all of Tiengenzhen, she was the only person who could single handedly tip the war one way or the other at any moment. So, they had decided to get rid of her.

When she came here, even as she spoke to that green-eyed woman with murder behind her eyes, Yao hadn't expected much. She'd seen the type. She had *been* the type, for a time. Hardened by adversity and human callousness to the point of near-misanthropy, yet still retaining the sense to know that one couldn't isolate oneself completely.

But, as she looked upon Brunhilde Krahe, she saw... Well, not quite her own past, but echoes of it. That was the thing about the Eye of Tar; it was a roundabout, fickle thing, even with this ritual that attempted to focus its gaze. Wars consumed millions of lives for the profit of the wealthy and powerful.

Places whose people were too healthy or prosperous were erased, sabotaged, polluted, or erased with desolation magic altogether, all so they couldn't threaten the power of those who held it. A mighty conqueror, a man born two millennia late through artifice and strange technology, took back a country whose landscapes looked very much like Tiengenzhen from a pathetic, tyrannical regime, though he himself was a tyrant of another sort. Dozens of millions burned in sun-like flame during that conflict.

Then, through the eyes of another, Yao saw Her. She barely recognized Krahe under all that metal and other strange materials. This version of her seemed to be more artifice than flesh, but the murderous spark behind those eyes was unmistakable. Then, their gazes met. A flickering deluge of death in moment long snippets, many directly involving Krahe. So much death. So much killing. The Eye of Tar made her witness and feel what Krahe had felt in the detached manner of memory storage artifacts. Anger beyond rage. Hatred beyond articulation. And against what? Monoliths of power that may as well be sects, controlled by untouchable, elder-like figures who would just start another if the current one was destroyed. No, not the monoliths, nor the elders themselves, but the hidden powerhouses who stood behind them. She had sought to tear out the weed by the root.

In this way, Yao instantaneously knew that she and Krahe were alike.

It was a world so unlike Tiengenzhen, yet so similar in many ways. To Yao, it looked like a twisted, surrealist painting of the worst-case scenario should the great sects' constant vying for power go unchecked for too long.

And then, Krahe died to a simple act of betrayal, driven by one man's fear and greed.

The desolation that followed, wrought by her own contingencies, was a truly marvelous act of revenge, as far as Yao was concerned, but she also saw the futility of it.

Finally, she saw nothing. Not the usual blackness of the Eye when it decided to stop working, but nothingness, the wrong anti-color of the outer cosmos. Kenoma, as it was known in the continental languages. There, among incomprehensible cosmic vastness, shapeless forms stirred, eons passed in an instant, and myriad worlds flickered in the dark like stars in the sky—infinitesimal bright ones among infinite blackness.

Then, Chernobog's unimpeachable vastness enveloped the drifting soul. An embrace of blackest blackness and vastest vastness. A being simultaneously unsurpassed, yet of a capricious nature, with no desire to be a conqueror, but instead to create conquerors, with no ideology of his own but the ideology of giving those mortals with a conqueror's wherewithal the chance to enact their own ideals. Yao knew who it was; she couldn't conceivably not know, for his handiwork was within her—a part of her. In ancient, antediluvian times, before the Wheel, before Igaria, in a time only recorded in legend, Chernobog's apostles were known as the mightiest among the mighty, yet his cult never claimed dominion, for his Paragons warred among one another.

Yao beheld a few tiny flickers of that time from the perspectives of priests and would-be faithfuls, but her vision ended with the firing of the World Needle, and the realization of why the Eye of Tar had led her here and why it had led her to Brunhilde Krahe.

The unlight faded, and Yao quickly sealed her eye once more. She doubled over as she instantly went into a meltdown, shivering as her skin cracked and golden light poured out. Meanwhile, Krahe propped herself up with her hand against her thigh, her meltdown being a comparatively mild coughing fit spitting up ash and soot. The smoke maelstrom dispersed, the burners returning to steady, upward streams of gray.

* * *

Krahe felt like she had sand in her eyes, and the rapid buildup of entropy near the end was certainly unexpected, but she managed. After about half a minute, Yao finally recovered from her meltdown, the cracks in her skin closing as she raised her gaze to meet Krahe with an uncharacteristically manic grin plastered across her face.

The Talisman Mistress soon broke out into a stifled laughing fit. When it waned, she finally said it. "I get it now. It's... It's you. It's all of you."

"Please don't start speaking in riddles."

"I assure you, I am wholly lucid. I saw... Well, I suspect I saw far more than you would like, but most importantly, I now know for certain that it is you who is able to help me mend myself, and I know why there is no apparent corruption to your soul like there is to mine. Chernobog, he... took you. Plucked your True Soul from the void and sheltered it within himself, and in the eon which passed between that point and your rebirth, you took from him. I know not how or why, but perhaps a surpassing will to live and to reach for the power to eradicate those, like the creators of the Sect of White Stones, led to you usurping an infinitesimal piece of the Black God. Then, upon your rebirth, your outer soul, or as you know it, your astral body, formed without the irregularities produced when an Outer God touches and alters a living being's soul. The blessings I gained from communion are still fundamentally part of Chernobog, they will return to him when I die. But you... There was no giving. No communion. The Outer God slumbered, as gods are wont to do, and you, perhaps unknowingly, took from him all you could, and in his vastness, he either didn't notice, didn't care, or found it amusing."

Things clicked into place in Krahe's mind. She tried to query Chernobog's Mystic Knowledge, expecting nothing, only to receive more accurate memory flashes of her own rebirth that all but confirmed Yao's hypothesis. Perhaps most unsettlingly, she felt an unquestionable certainty that Yao was right about one thing: Chernobog had found it terribly amusing when he realized a mortal soul had usurped a piece of him. She also suddenly became aware that she had not been the first and she would not be the last in the Black God's eternal span of existence to do so.

"There was no taint to find," she murmured, still processing the new context. "I came into this world already changed. Chernobog did no more than facilitate my incarnation."

"And upon your death, your next reincarnation will be the same," Yao finished.

Casus chimed in with a skeptical tone, "An unsettling proposition even from the most generous of perspectives. What would that make her, then? Not a saint of Chernobog, certainly not an avatar. Once again, the nature of such empowerment would have been detected and would directly conflict with any Zaveshian relic's implantation."

"A divine parasite, perhaps. Like a tarantula hawk wasp..." Krahe mused. She sighed, deciding that since Yao had already dug up the truth, there was no point avoiding speaking of it. Nonetheless, she wouldn't spill everything. Not that easily.

"As far as I remember, the only time I ever communicated with Chernobog was upon my incarnation," Krahe continued. "Hell, to call it communication is generous. A short time after I woke up, his voice rang in my head commanding me to get out of Jas'raba, and that was that. Afterwards, when I looked inward, I never found anything like Chernobog, no connection to some greater power, nothing that felt truly alien or separate from me. There was always just... this."

She held up her left hand and made it split open into a fanged maw from the palm to the elbow.

"This... nauseating, Wound-like Grin. At first I thought it was a piece Chernobog had left with me on purpose. In retrospect, it was... I don't know. An extra spiritual organ, maybe? It seems my Astral Body is abnormal in the extreme already, wouldn't surprise me if-"

"What did you call it?"

"The Wound-like Grin. That's what it looks like."

"That, in my mind, is proof enough. Never once have I come across any such thing in relation to Chernobog. Always... Always curled horns, labyrinths, giant beasts representing unparalleled power. Your friend is correct, however—the absence of a word for *what* you are gnaws at me."

After a moment of thought, Krahe flatly stated, "Deiphage. God Eater."

"Fitting. As for how exactly you might be able to—"

Krahe exhaled, cutting her off. "I think I already know, at least as far as what I can do right now is concerned. Give me a second."

She turned her focus inward, once more trying to query Chernobog's Mystic Wisdom, this time in regards to how Yao's Soul Furnace might be permanently mended. A vast deluge of information flowed, but trying to take it in felt much like trying to drink a river. Nonetheless, she captured two vital nuggets.

"I can only grasp fragments, but permanently repairing your Soul Furnace will involve Thaumic Fusion, Anathemism, and... something from Xaugeth. I don't know what. I will try again later, but that's all I can get for now."

A spark of hope lit up Yao's eye, and a smile curled her lips.

"Oho, the Land of Beetles and Moths? I shall have to look into that. As for anathemism, that *will* be a difficult one in my state. Perhaps with help..."

"I also happen to have that covered—I can control Thaumic Fusion. Within myself, at the very least. There is no doubt in my mind that I will have to be far stronger if I am to involve myself in such an operation, though, whatever it entails."

"Is that so? Perhaps an effect of your, ah... Deiphagy. I must admit that I am terribly curious as to how your unique constitution compares to the rest of mankind, but I lack the equipment to make such observations safely."

Yao stood slowly as she stretched back and forth, her body popping and cracking with each motion. Krahe took the hint and stood as well.

"Well, I am more than satisfied with the results of my gamble," Yao said. "Ask what you will of me and I will see what I can do."

Stepping out of the ritual circle, Krahe leaned against one of the talisman-plastered walls. "I'm looking for two people. One killed a friend of mine, and another crippled me in an attempt to kill me. Both are assassins. One goes by the pseudonym Crescent Jezail; he is a Dead Night Tiger, though I haven't been able to confirm whether he is a customer of yours. The other is an unknown, but he used a life-saving talisman that formed a partial shell of talismans around his body," Krahe explained, bringing out the talisman Garvesh had given her as evidence.

She only had to reach out, and the paper pulled itself free from Krahe's hand and flew into Yao's waiting grasp.

"Paper Cocoon Talisman, one of my more popular pieces. Come."

Returning to the ground floor, Yao brought out a handful of tools from the desk. A jade bottle, a basin, and ivory tweezers among other things. She shallowly filled the basin and dropped in the paper. Then, she flicked her wrist to extract a tiny, purplish blot of glowing ink that had escaped alongside all the red, and dropped it onto a blank paper strip. As this delicate process took place, she explained, "I do not make an active effort to collect the identities of my customers, but... many of them either take no care to conceal their own magic, or simply identify themselves to me openly, and I happen to have a very good memory. My Paper Cocoon Talismans harness the user's own magic as an ignition source, which results in a trace of it becoming embedded within them, and my Messenger Talismans are wholly powered by the user, causing a similar phenomenon. Thus..."

She raised the paper with the purple blot.

"I can identify who is who even if they never give me their name. Well, as long as I get my hands on it before the trace dissipates. A few more days and this remnant would have been much less useful."

As she funneled some of her golden thauma into the paper and felt out the captured trace's reaction, Yao hummed to herself, her brow furrowed as she fished around her memory. Finally, she turned her singular burning eye towards Krahe.

"Ah, I remember this one. Very pretty handwriting, but a disrespectful little lady. She came off like some spoiled brat who was never smacked as a child. She is an Aspirant-ranked Silversword Agency contractor by the name of Eutropia. I am not wholly familiar with your CQF ranking system, but I believe that places her in the D-One to D-Three range—the low mid ranks."

At that moment, she gestured at the paper and splashed a new pattern onto it, creating an eye-like shape with a dot of purple at its center. It became enveloped by golden light and an image came out, slowly solidifying as Yao sharpened her concentration.

"There. I requested one of my employees to look into her suitability as a customer when she was trying to contact me, and he sent this back as part of his report. I'm afraid I know nothing of interest about her. She is not well known enough for specific information to leak and be circulated."

The image was that of a young woman, and had the unmistakable appearance of a snapshot from a larger photo, enhanced and zoomed in after the fact to pick someone out. She looked... normal. Wealthy and dolled up, but normal from her curled brown hair to her makeup-caked face, notably paler than the rest of her swarthy complexion, to her eyes and lips which were accented by streaks of purple. She looked like any middle-eastern young adult with too much spending money.

"No further information?"

"I'm afraid not," Yao said. Her smile returned, and she added, "Though I am certain that, knowing her identity, you will have no issue finding out more. You got to me, after all, and how long did that take you? A week?"

Before Krahe could respond, Yao moved on, sending the talisman over to Krahe. "You may keep this. Now, Crescent Jezail..."

She took a moment to gather her thoughts, not searching her memory, but considering how much to say.

"He is a customer, that I admit. He signs each of our communication slips, but he is also elusive enough to avoid both my and my employees' efforts to identify him. Moreover, he disfigures his magic such that I cannot trace anything specifically back to him. That is to say, I have traces, but they are no more useful for finding him than traces from any other customer. You already know who he is, so I am sure your next question will pertain as to whether I can help you exact retribution upon him..."

Yao's smiling expression, heretofore nothing more than that, became tinged with a demonic malice. "I assure you that I fully understand the thought process."

Krahe hadn't actually planned on trying to track down and kill Crescent Jezail at the moment; it wasn't a high-priority objective. After all, he was just a hired killer. Odds were, she had been just another job, and killing him would only harm her efforts against Hashem by tipping them off that she was after them. Still, she went along with Yao's not entirely wrong assumption, as it was true that she did want to take precautions against Jezail if she had to fight him in the future.

"Crescent recently sent in an order for a custom offensive talisman, self-powered, with a fairly hefty prepayment for the supplies necessary. It may be intended for you, if his employer realized that you survived."

"How recently?" Krahe asked.

"Four days ago. I had started working on it just before you received the Tarnished Jade Flower stamp."

"That... lines up, I believe. I made myself known to Hashem's people in the process of tracking you down." She wagered that Yao already knew it had to do with Hashem, but she purposely dropped the name to be sure.

"In that case, I will show you." Yao nodded. A gesture brought an unfinished talisman to the surface of her arm, then made it float before her. Just the paper's texture spoke volumes to the higher grade of this talisman, appearing to be an ultra-thin but otherwise unprocessed strip of wood, grain and all. The patterns, too, were mesmerizing and an order of magnitude more complex than Wandrei Faust. It didn't seem so at first, but, like layers of a hologram, different patterns came to the surface and receded depending on the angle of the light.

"Once activated, it will multiply, much like the Paper Cocoon talisman, then surround and envelop the victim before flash-cremating them. Failing that, it will fire off its stored energy as a deluge of individual beams."

Yao took back the talisman once Krahe had gotten a good look, replacing it with a blank paper as she added, "Pour your magic into this. I will add a hidden trigger to the Cremation Cocoon Talisman so that it backfires if used against you. Only a true master of the craft equal to myself could even have a chance to notice it."

"I cannot bring myself to trust your word alone," Krahe admitted. "How about you demonstrate how such a selective disarm trigger would function?"

"Sure." Yao shrugged as if having expected this. She brought out a pair of plain talisman papers and began splashing ink on them. In the time it would take another to cast a normal thaumaturgy, she finished the talismans. The relative simplicity of their designs did nothing to detract from how impressive a feat this was. A single thick-lined, Chinese-adjacent symbol served as the centerpiece.

"These contain the First..." Yao began, then paused, choosing to simplify her explanation. "They create a direct kinetic attack. I only put enough power into them to equal a normal, mundane punch."

With a mere flick of her finger, she sent one of the papers, now strangely rolled in a narrow tube, darting at Krahe. The moment it left her vicinity, a rod mace of golden light took form around it, and it smashed into Krahe with, indeed, the force of a very strong man's punch, albeit concentrated down to the surface area of a fingertip. It punched a small hole into her wards but didn't do much more.

Waiting not a moment more, Yao splashed an extra streak onto the second paper, masterfully camouflaging it among the rest of the pattern. Both Krahe and Casus immediately lost track of it. Once again, Yao set it loose against Krahe. The bar-mace construct formed as normal, but before it could strike, it suddenly exploded into many shards towards Yao, though they dissipated well before they could harm her.

"The backlash will be far more significant in the end result, but as you can see, I am no liar. Should you still not trust me, might I perhaps allow you to watch as I place the contingency upon the finished Cremation Cocoon Talisman?" Yao asked facetiously.

"No, I believe this will suffice. Our business, as it pertains to my investigation, is concluded, but I still have a request—as a customer. To start, you are familiar with the wards and barriers defense paradigm endemic to the Seven Spokes System, yes?"

"Of course," Yao said, waiting for Krahe to continue.

"Would you happen to be familiar with an alternative to barriers which entails becoming semi-intangible through partly submerging oneself into the immaterial?"

"Spirit Walking, yes. I believe it is far more common in Tiengenzhen than the wider world. In fact, there is a nearly even split between those who prefer it over Barriers, though any well-rounded martial expert is expected to be skilled in techniques of both defensive types, and ideally others as well. In this, I find the Seven Spokes System's layout to be a detriment, as it creates such a false dichotomy."

That seemed to grab Casus's attention, snapping him out of his state of silent observation that he had been in for much of the conversation. Nonetheless, he remained quiet, merely paying greater attention. It seemed to amuse Yao a touch.

"Do you think you would be able to procure or produce a voidkey specializing in Spirit Walking, then?"

Yao gave a knowing smile, as if she wanted to say something but decided not to, instead stating, "Procure? No, not in any reasonable amount of time. As for crafting one... As I am now? Perhaps, but I would require materials exceptionally well-suited to it. Parts from a beast naturally able to Spirit Walk, for instance, special resonant metals or stones, and so on. Ideally, an existing key of that type as a core. Whether fully intact or damaged by forcible extraction wouldn't matter. Of course, you would not be asking me this question if you already had such a key, but the limitations of my state are nothing if not suffocating. That is all to say, I cannot fulfill your request right now, but I believe I can help you approach that goal. Before we get into that, however, would you have a more immediate request?"

Krahe stood in silence, thinking. She held eye contact with Yao for a good twenty seconds before she summoned a Wandrei Faust talisman into her hand.

"This talisman harnesses an eidolon. I don't think I need to tell you what it does. Suggest improvements and provide the means to apply them. You *are* the Talisman Mistress, are you not?"

A thread of golden light extended from Yao, enveloping the paper and bringing it to her. She examined it with a mixture of curiosity and amusement until commenting, "How very crude, and yet, profound all the same. The brush strokes, in their roughness, embody a visceral nature which doubtlessly aids in the talisman's combative ability, but it is abundantly clear that the roughness of the brush is a detriment to the delicate components. I presume these centipede-leg-like, or perhaps rib-like patterns around the edges cause the highest number of failures. Am I right? You shall need a clean writing brush for that, no wider than a single hair at the tip. The paper…"

Yao flipped it back and forth, waved it around, and even sniffed it. With a grimace, she admitted, "It's fine. No more, no less. It has no serious flaws but no standout qualities, either. I can sell you some of my stock, so long as you swear not to resell or otherwise redistribute it. The ink, though, is good; I like it very much. There are layers of secrets in its formulation, I can tell. Just one charge of ink for each side, and yet all these colors. Very nice."

She abruptly turned to Casus.

"Silberblut. Do you know of a place where one might be able to hunt soulbeasts?"

Before he even got halfway through his tentative nod, Yao already continued. "Fantastic! We will go there, and you will slay a beast. I will even be so magnanimous as to process it for you, but I must see what you can do for myself in order to be certain, and frankly, I need raw materials to work with."

"For what?" Krahe questioned.

"A better brush, of course. We will find a beast with a nature suited to the kinds of talismans you intend to make and use its body parts and spirit remnants to produce a brush."

"It will be a matter of weeks at the absolute minimum before an appropriate hunting ground can be scouted and perhaps months before we find the right kind of soulbeast. Even being optimistic, I would say up to a month if the only constraint is a destructive, wrathful, or malicious beast with fine fur," Casus remarked.

Yao, smiling, answered, "I don't see how that would be a problem. A truly sublime, custom brush gives twice the results with half the effort, but the minimum effort which it demands is far and above any generalist, mass-produced tool. Not to mention, the process of crafting such an item can be one of months. I, in my unparalleled skill, can do it much faster, of course. I'm sure you understand my intentions, Silberblut. If at all possible, it would be best to hunt both beasts in one hunt, given my limited knowledge of this land's limitations on spirit beast hunting."

Casus nodded in acknowledgment, and Yao continued without pause as she pulled open one of her drawers. She removed a brush with a handle of dark wood and bristles of fine, white hair. A wrist-flick sent both it and the Wandrei Faust talisman flying into Krahe's hand.

"This one ought to be an improvement over what you're using at the moment."

Looking around, Yao's eye landed on a wall-spanning shelf near the writing desk.

The brush was soon joined by an ancient bamboo-slip scroll, pulled out of a partition with at least twelve more identical scrolls. Not just in make and thickness, but the wear patterns, too.

"Ah, and take this as well."

"What's the catch?" Krahe asked suspiciously.

"The scroll is a collection of oft-missed fundamentals and tricks I put together for my disciples, back when I still had any. It is quite outdated now. The brush is one of my many spares; consider it an investment. Have it checked if you so wish; there are no curses or scrying tags. If you wish to pay me, suggest some good texts on this land's counterparts to my art. Advanced or fundamental, it doesn't matter. I will require a full understanding, including the foundations."

Krahe stowed the brush and talisman, her eyes glazing over for a moment as she looked inward. Her inventory now contained a bookshelf's worth of texts from those commonly found to the rare and esoteric, and she named off those which were not too rare but still useful.

"Secrets of the Atropal, The Reaper and its Legacy, Hammer of the North, De Re Theurgia, Thaumshot Modification and You, and… Retracing the Path: A Re-Evaluation of Paper as a Theurgic Medium. Zachariah of the Lost Sun Society should be able to provide copies of them all. The first two may seem like sensationalist slop at first reading, but they contain a wealth of fundamentals."

With a look of pleasant surprise, Yao hesitantly asked, "I shall start with your suggestions, then. I have one last request before you leave. Feel free to reject me, as it is entirely selfish, but…"

Her eye swept over the two of them before landing back on Krahe. A palpable tension built over the few seconds during which she was silent.

"I am well aware of your ability to Spirit Walk, Lady Blackhand. May I see it?"

After a tense pause, Krahe acquiesced, seeing little reason to refuse. At that moment, when flesh gave way to a form of smoke and orange-glowing metal ribs, with only two burning eyes as the sole distinguishable facial feature, what had remained of Yao Fu's doubts was dispelled. Certainly, she had seen incontrovertible evidence of Krahe being who Yao thought her to be, but witnessing the shape of her astral body in person was different to the detached, often fuzzy and disorienting visions granted by the Eye of Tar.

Yao watched them leave and spent some time afterwards re-enabling her lethal defenses. This was one of the reasons she was careful about bringing others directly to her home. In her state, it meant that she had to remove many of her defenses. Neither her many talismans nor her puppets could be disabled remotely; Yao knew better than that. Even failsafe triggers, such as the one she would embed into Crescent Jezail's order, were, in effect, hardwired. Once it was placed, there was no removing or disabling it after the fact. This caution was born from the method by which Yao had destroyed one of the most powerful talisman-specialist sects in Tiengenzhen. Having not just seen remote-control features breached and exploited, but having done it herself, Yao had permanently decided to avoid including such vulnerabilities in her own creations.

One of the downsides of that security was relative unwieldiness when restricted in the way she was at this very moment. It wouldn't be a problem she had to deal with for too long, if things proceeded in the manner she hoped.

CHAPTER 9

RETURN IT TO THE DEPTHS

Far in the south, in the deepest swamps of the Beyond Frontier, a man slept a restless slumber. Growling and chortling, gusts of steam blasting from his nostrils, his scales itching and frills twitching.

The sage, untold hero of the Great Plague, Ibn Ghazi Barzai, twisted and turned as knowledge forbidden to him bubbled up from the depths of his mind. Steered by forces beyond reckoning, he arose from his bed and scraped an angle-web most sublime upon the bamboo floor of his home and sacrificed his own blood in place of the appropriate unguents upon its dark lines. Dozens of lines forming impossible, twisting angles superseded anything he had ever dared to record.

He snapped out of it ere he could begin the rite. The absence of something vital precluded it from taking place; the Liminal Coil. Neither his body nor his soul held the capacity to dive wholly into the Gulf, for he had feared just this.

Deepest dread hung over him as he took his Seven Spokes talisman in hand, gripping it with such fervor its spokes dug through his wards and his scales, drawing blood.

Barzai recited a prayer to Igaria, carrying out occult gestures with his left hand. Some less versed in the true cosmology of the world would call this borderline heresy, but those who knew, knew. The talisman came alive, the world rippling, reality reasserting itself. He was here, far from the Wheel, far from civilization, hidden by this ancient forest's spiritual canopy... and still, they found him—the things from the deep. The things from Beyond the astral gulf.

Ever since that cursed day, he hadn't had a single peaceful night. Once he was certain there were neither rifts nor an impending archon flash, he called out his scimitar, pouring vast arcane power into the artifact. Its metal became wreathed in blue flame, and as he traced arcane sigils in the air with it, it swam through reality just the same as a mundane blade did through water. Its edge, alighted in blue flame, reflected things halfway between the material world and the astral.

For weeks, peaceful sleep had eluded him, but tonight marked the first when things became this dire. Until today, he knew not why it was so, until his blade reflected something familiar. A messenger. A thing from the deep, which had latched itself to his soul decades prior. In his fervent desire to rid himself of the accursed Liminal Coil, he had entrapped The Thing as the guardian of that relic until one arrived who would be able to withstand the Seal of the Great King of Terror.

Even now, as he raised his scimitar, its handle wrought of Mnarian Gray Stone and inscribed with the sign of the Great Fivefold Eye, the Thing From Beyond struggled and writhed to squeeze through the veil. Even now, it whispered to him, speaking truths and knowledge he did not wish to know. To his misfortune, he had underestimated the creature's craftiness, for even the drops of his own blood upon the floor were enough. Its form, obscured from true perception and thus made to look as if slathered in tar, erupted out of the unfinished angle-web in a burst of unlight.

Barzai skewered it to the ground, his scimitar pinning the beast in space and reality alike, its blue flame blazing over its form as the deathless creature thrashed against a restraint it had never known. In its own way, being forced to experience existence in such a mundane manner was as hellish for it as its whispers were for Barzai. He held no hatred for The Thing, only aversion and pity. It wasn't malicious, after all; if anything, the opposite. It just so happened that the favor of a creature such as this was truly ruinous.

For a few minutes, Barzai sat, observing the spirit's struggle, and chanting to himself to drown out its incessant blabbering of knowledge from worlds afar.

The reality of the situation sunk in. The Thing's return could only mean one thing.

The seal which had held it has broken—a seal which even Barzai hadn't been able to withstand. Indeed, in a desperate effort, he had commanded the Thing From Beyond to inhabit a pen and draw a mighty mind-invasion sigil and then sealed it inside, leveraging it against the condition that it would break if someone withstood its effects. The only way he could prevail over the abomination was by betting that the seal would never be broken, by betting against the possible future where it *was* broken. Now that this future had come to pass, he himself held no power over it, and he never would. The only thing keeping him from becoming a mad puppet to an eldritch, inhuman, child-like creature was his beloved scimitar.

Barzai huffed. The Liminal Coil had found its next host.

He knew what must be done to rid himself of the Thing From Beyond. The only method which could dispose of it permanently. The method he had worked so hard to avoid; he had to dive into the Gulf with it skewered upon his blade, and then take it back where it came from, listening to its whispers all along. The odds that he would return at all, let alone with his mind intact, were slim, but he had readied himself for this eventuality.

There was no choice. The preparations were long and grueling, forcing him to venture out into the swamp, where he had buried something he never wished to exhume: His old Gulf Key. The Liminal Coil's sibling. Moreover, he had to carry out several rites to reinforce his spirit. He donned a gruesome contraption of bronze-like metal that clamped onto his spine, ribcage, and skull, reproducing some of the Liminal Coil's benefits in a crude and limited manner. Like a horrific parasite, it held onto him, digging into his skin. The Rite of Dho-Raza and the subsequent astral dive came to him far more easily than he wished they had. Everything was there, irrevocably carved into his brain, alien wisdom with his mind twisted around it like scar tissue around a half-rejected implant.

Barzai barraged The Thing with questions. One after the next. From the mundane to the esoteric. To his regret, he received a vast wealth of knowledge which would have aided him greatly if he had known it sooner. Amidst terrible futures of unprecedented human suffering and horror, invaluable insights were laid. The Thing spoke to him, that much was true, but it was in no language of man. It was in thought and memory. Each unearthly, horrific noise came with a flashing premonition as vivid as if he were truly there to see it.

But, before even the halfway point of the journey, he ran out of questions. He felt The Thing begin to ramble of its own volition, gnawing at his already-scarred sanity. At this rate, he would go mad.

So he asked, "Who broke the Seal?"

For the first time, the Thing was silent. What felt like an eon passed before he received an answer. By then The Thing's home, an inconceivable vastness of pearlescent spires that intersected and stacked atop one another in impossible geometries, had come into view of his soul's sight. The answer was a face, a young woman with green eyes that had murder behind them. She looked at the seal, and the moment The Thing From Beyond moved to empower the seal, the creature felt an absolute terror, as if the power of its prison had been turned inward. It ended when The Thing From Beyond fled its now-broken prison. There, in the Astral Gulf, it glanced back, and beheld a humanoid shape of smoke surrounded by grinning maws filled by shark-like fangs, with tongues or perhaps tendrils of blackest pitch lolling out from some of them. Barzai, unable to fully grasp The Thing's eldritch senses, saw no more than that. It was an astral body abnormal to the extreme, especially given the circumstances. It eliminated the possibility of an Outer God's involvement, but, unlike everything else to do with The Thing From Beyond, it didn't deny conventional logic. If anything it made perfect sense that a freak would be the one to inherit his cursed legacy.

The emotions which The Thing sent to him were a blend of terror and confused familiarity, like seeing something known in a place it absolutely does not belong. Without words, he asked the creature to elaborate on that familiar terror.

His received answer was an image of the Dark Invoker, a divination card representing a boon from a foreign source that carried a corrupting influence or a catch. A loan, a gift given with ulterior motives, a high station given for a bribe, and so on. It was inverted, mirrored, and in photographic negative. Then, as if The Thing was confused, it, for the first time ever, somehow pulled that thought out of Barzai's head. He was struck by a moment of confusion, in which it wriggled off of his blade.

The Thing From Beyond swam about and wrapped itself around his soul, forcing him to understand—pushing knowledge into him. Barzai thought he would split in half and depart for his next life, leaving his astral body as food for The Things From Beyond.

It did not come to pass.

He awoke in his hut, violently hacking up blue-burning sludge, covered in astral gunk... and with knowledge of the Liminal Coil's possessor— Brunhilde Krahe.

It suddenly made sense why That Woman had resisted the Sign of the Great King of Terror, why her Astral Body was so peculiar. Truly, that inverted image of the Dark Invoker had been fitting.

Ibn Ghazi Barzai had long divorced himself from the Liminal Coil, and resolved himself to a hermetic life. As he saw it, the matter was out of his hands. Nonetheless, his fear for the safety of the Liminal Coil's inheritor hadn't been alleviated; it had merely been replaced by a desperate, abiding hope that whatever unshakeable convictions had granted her access to the Liminal Coil wouldn't lead her down a path of ruin... And that she wouldn't think to seek him out.

Sighing, he spent several hours ridding himself of the diving apparatus and replacing his old Gulf Key. Then, he cleaned up his home and removed the angle-web.

When it was done and everything fully sunk in, a bitter laughter reverberated through his hut. Barzai slept well for the first time in weeks and thereafter dredged up flasks of liquor from the swamp—flasks he had put there just for this occasion.

It was, despite everything, a cause to celebrate. The Thing From Beyond the Gulf was gone, back where it belonged, and he no more felt it tugging at his soul. Even the System reflected his severance from that abomination.

By Zavesh and Igaria both, he truly hoped That Woman would not come to seek him out in search of the Coil's counterpart... Or, at least, that by the time she pieced it together, he would be dead.

CHAPTER 10

THE AFTEREFFECTS OF A FEMME FATALE'S INVOLVEMENT

What he had feared was coming to pass. Cassius had chosen to call in a certain incident of his own volition, only to find himself summoned to meet with the incumbent inheritor of the Hashem Family in person. On the surface, it seemed like a friendly meeting at one of the heir's hedonistic parties, which was already in full swing by the time Cassius arrived. Drink, drugs, pretty women from human to Inax and Saurian. A pair of low-level Mamon Knights beating the tar out of each other; one was a purely insectile type with stingers on his arms, the other a locust with a mantis-like blade and a heavy-lift exoframe cladding his upper body.

The tension that took hold the moment of his arrival, however, was palpable. Cassius was stripped of his firearms, ushered to sit with Semzar, and surrounded by his men. Men. Big, burly men, exuding power and violence. That wasn't Semzar's style. Even his own personal guards were eye candy. Sure, they radiated a dangerous aura, but they were, first and foremost, there to look pretty. Semzar himself was only recognizable because of his position, manner of dress, and his face. The body was new, similarly macho to his guards. His face was nothing like his previous body, but it was recognizable in its unnaturally handsome features, which clashed with the body's rugged hands and bearlike build. He emanated a threatening, powerful aura, different from before but far less in control. The bulging, purple tendrils under the skin of his neck, hands, and forehead were subtle by some standards, but they proved he'd gotten sloppy compared to his old self.

Cassius didn't know how many bodies Semzar had gone through, but he could be sure of one thing. He felt cornered, and was desperately trying to get stronger. That was the only possible reason why a baneworm would start burning through one host after the next. Such a method could work, but not for long, and he would pay for it dearly in the future, but knew better than to expect this spoiled brat to look further into the future than the next suck and fuck.

"Wait, so let me get this straight," Semzar started, leaning over the table towards Cassius. It lost some effect since they were still separated by enough distance for Semzar's guards to act before Cassius could do anything. "Blackhand just... waltzed into your bar, and you let her go?"

Semzar spoke as if suppressing a manic laughing fit. His tendrils writhed and made themselves known, deforming his skinsuit's face in absurd ways. One of them snaked out next to his eye, and only when Cassius carefully pointed it out did the mafioso snap out of it. The desire to maintain his self-image was stronger than his anger.

"That is... not how events transpired, no. She entered my casino, and I ordered my people to encircle her right away. Habib, that fool, got ahead of himself and attacked. He lost his life because of it. She... fried him. Just shoved her hand into his back like he didn't have wards at all and boiled him inside out. Then she turned into smoke and ran out the front door. We all shot at her, but it just went right through."

"Turned into smoke?"

"Yeah. Like a person made of it, not a cloud."

Semzar returned to his seat, calming down. It seemed, for a few moments, as though his tension might dissipate, but after drawing from a hookah filled with an unknown blend of herbs, the heir cast a razor-sharp stare Cassius' way.

"Did you get a good look at her face?"

Cassius felt a chill run down his spine. The question was pointed. Purposeful. Despite many being ordered to target the woman, nobody had gotten more than a description, or at best, an artist's rendition that was not even close to the real thing. Her appearance was distinct enough to tell it was her, but it wasn't anywhere close to a real photo. His hesitation to answer tipped the mafioso off.

"Hey, hey, don't worry. I'm not gonna scoop your brain out of your head," Semzar reassured unconvincingly. "I'm just asking. You've seen the pictures, right? Trash. Those self-proclaimed artists don't even know how to draw burnt skin. I just hoped that you might have a good mental snapshot of the target and the ability to draw it, that's all. Get rid of the middleman."

"Ah! Ahahaha... I did get a good look at her, but I'm afraid that I cannot draw."

"It's alright, it's alright. Was that the end of the incident?"

Of course, it wasn't. Semzar knew that. He was just prompting Cassius to continue, and that he did. "No, no. We gave chase. Caught her in a back alley. I know my territory better than anyone. After that, however, it all fell apart. She used that same smoke-like form, as well as short-range teleportation, geomancy, and a sort of... arm-missile. I'm sure it was theurgy. It felt like theurgy. There was certainly anathema in play, but I am not familiar enough with the vile discipline to know."

"You stink of it," Semzar said dryly.

"Is that so? Well, there you have your proof. How else would I get exposed to bane soot?" Cassius latched onto the remark.

"Right you are, right you are, but that does not address my earlier request. I need an accurate image of her face, Cassius. If you can't draw it for me, well... This house happens to contain an relic from my father's collection that may prove useful," Semzar said with a malicious grin. "It's a working Anampictor Automaton. If you make a clear picture come out, I'll let you off the hook."

"Working" and "safe" were two very different things when it came to those machines. They were an ancient and out-of-favor technology, having come into being as one of the only methods of memory *extraction*. A machine that could pull out a particular visual memory and render it. This was opposed to memory *deposition,* entailing special techniques or artifacts that allowed someone to willingly place memories into a vessel. When properly maintained and managed by a trained operator, they were *safe*—but the margin for error was hair-thin, and the process unpleasant at best. An unmaintained anampictor machine could, at worst, just turn the user's brain to mush. They were also notorious for causing "mnemonic burn-in," causing a previously pulled memory to come to the forefront far more easily than others, often in undesirable circumstances. They had been famously manufactured for a little over a year before the makers had their operation shut down and erased by the churches. As it turned out, they achieved what the competitors couldn't through dark magic that violated the soul and left it irreversibly scarred. Cassius knew this. He also knew that Semzar would probably kill him if he refused.

It was tantamount to making him bet his life on double sixes in a game of dice, and the worst part was that Cassius knew it was still his best chance.

"Alright," he agreed with a resigned sigh.

"Very good!" Semzar exclaimed, springing out from his seat with a clap of his hands.

His guards immediately grabbed Cassius and led him to the machine. It was a jumble of essentech that resembled ancient Jas'raban machinery to a degree that couldn't possibly be accidental. Its principal components were a seat, a slot for the subject's arm, an operating panel, and an upper-half automaton in a turban with a glass pen in its hand. The moment they shoved him into the seat, Semzar instructed, "Focus on the subject's memory. Done?"

Semzar didn't wait more than a few seconds before he threw the switch and torment became reality.

Cassius wanted to scream, but the only noise that came out was a strained, wheezing grunt. It felt like an eternity of having his soul pulled out of his body by a claw of red-hot iron, and though it truly only took a few short seconds, it very much looked the way it felt. For a merciful few moments, the torment abated.

"Second subject memory, focus!" came Semzar's voice again. Like a man holding onto the edge of a cliff with broken fingers. Cassius grabbed for that thought, and the torment began with renewed vigor. When it was over, Cassius slumped to the ground, lingering at the edge of consciousness. His mind's eye repeatedly flitted between Blackhand's face, with Habib's mangled corpse hanging on her arm, and her smoke-wrought form, as seen when she walked out of the dust cloud in the back alley. His actual vision was shot; the blood vessels in his eyes had erupted.

An amused whistle came from above.

"Lucky devil. They're both good, even if one of 'em is a touch on the abstract side."

Semzar's leather boot dug into his ribs, and with something between a shove and a kick, he was rolled over onto his back. The mafioso squatted down over him, staring into Cassius' blood-blurred vision. He let out a frustrated sigh.

"His eyes are fucked. Hey, Saeed! We got any spare eyes? Pull some grunt's eye if not."

At that point, Cassius faded out into nothingness.

He woke up strapped into a grafter's chair, unable to move a limb, and utterly blind.

Again, Semzar's voice chimed in, filled with mirthful amusement. "Oh, he's awake! Make a noise if you can hear me. You probably can't talk 'cause of the surgery juice."

Cassius grunted. It was true. His tongue felt like a dead snake in his mouth.

"Good. You're getting some new eyes since you did so well with the anampictor," Semzar said. "I am not pointlessly cruel." That was truly a lie.

His vision returned, but he had no eyelids to blink with, nor could he move his eyes. Moreover, his field of vision was noticeably wider and sharper. Saeed's metal fingers came in from the side and tapped against the glass shield of his vision, followed by the renegade grafter waving his hand in front of his face. Just barely in the corner of this expanded field of vision, he caught the forward-leaning figure of a seated Semzar. Cassius grunted again.

"Alright, you can see me," Saeed said. "Look at that poster over there on the wall. Which one's better? This... or *this*?"

His vision changed very slightly. The second one was better. Cassius grunted twice. This went on for some time, with Saeed dialing in the settings to a point where, as much as he hated to admit it, his natural eyes didn't even come close. At some point, Semzar left, clearly growing bored. Saeed took the opportunity to come in front of Cassius and inject something into his arm. The paralysis abated a bit, but he still couldn't move much at all.

Saeed pulled a cable from his arm, inserting its end into a physical slot on the side of Cassius' head. One which hadn't been there before. With the grafter's cold metal fingers resting against his freshly shaven, sore, stitched-together scalp, he heard the man's abnormally soft voice echo in his head.

"Don't try to move, alright? You're five kinds of fucked up. I had to go digging around in your skull, scoop out, and replace what was left of your visual cortex and some other bits. Lucky you, the astral injuries weren't too severe, and you *might* fully recover, but expect lapses in memory. There are ways to help repair astral injuries, but... I can't help you with that. I have neither the tools nor the know-how. A word of warning: I told Semzar that with this visor you would have to switch between a cripplingly near-sighted or far-sighted visual mode, so keep that in mind. I also gave him a remote control which he believes can forcibly trigger the vismode-switch, but its actual function is to ping his location to you, and to show a heads-up message of the fake vismode-switch. Whenever he uses it, you'll be able to trace his location for a few hours."

Cassius managed to turn his head then tilt it with a questioning grunt.

"I'm a heretic, but Zavyuzz is still my god. It's just not the version of him the Grafting Church believes in."

Another questioning grunt.

"Just think what you want to say. It *might* work."

"Why would an Apocryphal Fundamentalist ever work for a bunch of baneworms?"

"I'm not a fundamentalist, but close enough. My goal is to kill the lot of them, of course. Every last one. They're all abominations against Zavyuzz."

Remaining plugged in, Saeed continued working, tinkering with things. Slowly, elements of a heads-up display flickered into view, and Cassius' vision sharpened even more.

"Is that why you're a renegade?" he asked.

"No," came the answer. "That belief didn't get me in much trouble at all, funnily enough. Baneworms are only still around because they're easier to keep in check than they are to exterminate. You never know how they'll react to a significant change in their surroundings; it's a truly extreme example of polyphenism. The church finds it easier to keep them under control and do what we—sorry, what *they* can to slowly reduce their numbers, like the free body deal. So I figured, if I want to wipe them out, I need to work with them to gather data on how that might be achieved. Hence... well, this situation. As for your question, I left the church of my own volition. A relationship between a man and his god should be personal."

"Why tell me all this?"

"Who would the Hashems believe? A grafter who has been with the family from the very beginning, or a washed-out fuckup? Besides, if you try to fuck me over I'll know, and I'll set off the talisman I wrapped around your brainstem. Don't worry, only I can do that, so if you don't try to fuck me, you don't have to worry about getting your mind blown."

The sound of approaching footsteps could be heard. Saeed quickly pulled the plug out of Cassius' head, and stepped in front of him.

"Try and close your eyes. Look at me—don't blink. That's a different nerve impulse. Close them. And keep them closed. I need to work on something delicate."

To his great relief, Cassius' vision went dark. While he waited in the total blackness, he vaguely sensed Saeed rummaging around and could smell solder.

The door opened. Footsteps approached the chair and Semzar's obnoxious cologne almost instantaneously hit him in the face.

"Well?" he asked Saeed.

"Almost done. Just a moment."

"Does that mean a minute or an hour?" Semzar asked with an impatient tone.

Saeed sighed. "A minute if you sit down. An hour if you keep hovering over my shoulder." There was not the slightest hint of fear or even respect in his voice.

A chair squeaked as it was sat upon.

"Alright, done. Don't open your eyes yet," Saeed advised with annoyance in his voice.

Chair squeak. Footsteps.

"Open."

He saw... not what he had expected.

It wasn't Semzar's insufferable mongrel face.

It was Blackhand.

Rather, a picture of her, a surreal one, like... like a bad memory rendered from a mind on the verge of breaking. It was the second image the anampictor had dragged out of him, derived from his memory of her smoke-like transformation.

Semzar leaned down slightly. Cassius felt his stomach turn, and a violent impulse sparked in the back of his head.

"The other one was much more realistic, but this... I really like this one. I'll frame it, I think," he said in an entirely earnest tone, one which inadvertently came off as mockery.

"Do you have a title in mind? It's your hard work, after all."

"He likely won't be able to speak yet," Saeed warned.

Grinding his teeth, Cassius hissed, "Green-eyed Demon!"

The next day, Crescent Jezail received copies of both images alongside the first half of his quoted payment for the Three Shot Special. That was the absolute maximum he was willing to do for a non-trusted client, to prevent any attempts at draining his resources and leaving him vulnerable. There was also the fourth shot, sure—the full custom from the Talisman Mistress—but it was entirely self-powered, making it a non-issue.

CHAPTER II

CONTRACTORS MAY OR MAY NOT BE LOADED

Relieved to finally be able to return to the safehouse, Krahe set a slow roast before she went out. The oven fortunately had a timer built in, so even if something unforeseen kept her away, it wouldn't burn. At worst, if she were for some reason unable to go back for days, Casus would end up eating it. She surely hoped that would not be the case after the work she had put into that food, however.

Krahe spent the better part of the next day just laying low in the safehouse, attempting to translate Yao's scroll as she familiarized herself with the new brush. It was written in the language of Tiengenzhen, the script close enough to Chinese which was, at once, a blessing and a curse. It was a laborious process, but at least by undertaking it she achieved both her goals and even gleaned a fair few insights from it already. Besides this, she also got in touch with the owner of the building she had been using until now, querying how much he would want for the property.

"Well, eh... Contractors're loaded, right?" the owner prodded.

"High-rankers, maybe," she scoffed. Despite Casus' words, her conception of real-estate prices remained twisted, and so she had decided to manipulate the price downward as much as possible. "I figured I might be able to afford the place given its state and location."

"What state?

"Have you ever lived there? You have to sleep with earplugs in because the basement ventilation is connected to the tramline vents. Not to mention, as I said, the location..."

"Yeah, the location ain't great. Whatever. Fifty thousand, just take the shitheap off my hands."

Krahe almost had a coughing fit, but she just barely managed to suppress it. Thankfully, the owner interpreted it as her balking at such a "high" price, and sighing, said, "Alright, forty-five. I can't go any lower."

"I... Yeah, I guess I can make that work," she said with a heavy, reluctant sigh. She deceived as easily as she breathed.

To the owner, this came across as a completely normal negotiation. The price was a bit on the low side, but considering that basic maintenance on the place had been draining his wallet for years now, he was fine with taking a net loss on the sale.

"Y'want to do it now? Don't matter shit to me. I can draft the contract right now. I'll even sign in thaumine ink and splash some hemolymph on that bitch so you can get it notarized your own self once I've pissed off from this hellhole."

Once inside, the owner drafted the contract atop a rickety foldout table on the ground floor, without much care for his handwriting, resulting in calligraphy that was merely nice rather than utterly meticulous. The atmosphere was a bit tense as Krahe cautiously went over every bit of the three-page document, but that tension evaporated when she admitted, "Looks legit. Just to be clear, I will—"

"Probably kill me if you even think that I'm screwin' you. I know your type. Once this shit's sold I'm gone. I'm moving to... some fuckin' city in Afshan, I dunno. Once your name is on the ownership documents I don't exist anymore as far as you're concerned, and the same goes the other way."

Once they finished signing, the owner was another step closer to being free of this property, and richer by... a moderate sum. It really wasn't much, but then, he was selling an empty shell of a house in an unremarkable part of the city. Really, he figured he should thank her for bringing it up first. He couldn't wait to be out of here. As a silver lining, the anathemist pulled a pair of dregstones, pressing them together for a moment before she showed him one worth the exact amount he was owed.

As he left the house, he murmured under his breath, "Fuckin' Vedesian bullshit. I ain't spendin' another second in a war morph let alone a whole fuckin' molt cycle. Piece o' shit. Can't believe that wise guy expects me to..."

He knew it wasn't smart to mention those kinds of things in front of skinbags, but he didn't *really* give a shit and he had no personal reason to believe that woman could even make sense of what he had said. She could, of course, but he would be in Afshan before it could become his problem.

Krahe branded the owner's words into her brain the moment she heard them, and immediately chased after him. But he was already gone. Somehow, someway, he had vanished from under her nose, and even a meticulous search wasn't enough to find so much as a trail. Frustrated, she took some solace in the fact that the small splash of his hemolymph wasn't yet dry on the paper and the thaumine ink would carry his thaumic signature for some time, as was its purpose. Having no other ideas, she took it to Firminus. She had a good excuse to visit him, since she was three days overdue for a checkup, as he made abundantly and scathingly clear when he realized it was her knocking on his door.

Only once she was in the chair, her suit split down the back and her spine spilling out like some gruesome parasite, did she bring up the owner, what he had said, and her desire to find him again.

"Not so amusing when someone else is able to vanish, is it? I presume you have a lead that you believe I would help you with..." Firminus grumbled, chewing his cigarette as he spoke, poking and prodding at Krahe's back. He pulled and poked at muscle bundles, murmuring about the bonding of her own skin with the graft-muscle and the seemingly total absence of rejection symptoms, theorizing on how the biosuit's presence might be helping the process along.

"He signed the sale contract with imbued thaumine ink and splashed his hemolymph on it. That's all I've got."

"And what do you expect me to do with that?" the grafter balked. "Individual flymen cannot be identified by their hemolymph, and without a sample to compare it against, his thaumic remnants are no more useful. The most I can do is… perhaps cut out the signature and entomb it in a preservation cell. Is that truly worthwhile for the infinitesimal chance of this leading you back to that man? What did he even say to alarm you in such a way? Assuming you are willing to tell me, of course."

Krahe cleared her throat, and recited, "*'Fucking Vedesian bullshit, I'm not spending another second in a war morph, let alone a whole fuckin' molt cycle. Piece of shit, I can't believe that wise guy expects me to…'* And that was it. He also said that he was fleeing to somewhere in Afshan."

"A war morph… There are not many circumstances which can force a mature Evoy to molt into a war morph. However, it could just be a hyperbolic figure of speech; for them, at least for those of them who are not practicing Vedesians, the war morph is a sign of great and terrible upheaval. However, one man's words don't mean much. I would wager he just interpreted recent happenings as signs that upheaval is coming to Audunpoint."

"And if it isn't just a figure of speech?"

"I would prefer not to consider the possibility that he meant it literally, and I am not well-versed in the varied morphs of the Evoy. I specialize in human grafting, after all. Look into it on your own time; you ought to have access to the relevant sections. Texts regarding the Great Plague could be useful, though the involvement of Vedesians in that conflict was tertiary at best. Conflicts going further back into the past would enlighten you more as to how the Evoy became the way they are now, but those records are too dense even for my tastes."

"I presume you cannot simplify them for my own insufficient mental faculties, then."

Firminus stopped his ceaseless testing and sighed, thinking.

"Let us see how much I remember from the schola after all these years. They have… become docile, you could say, but also more clever. Warring with them, rooting them out of our midst, stamping out their influence, it was once among the Twin Churches' most crucial of tasks. It still is, merely not so straightforward. Without a warlord or something greater, many of them strayed from the Vedesian faith and integrated properly into the societies of man, but they're still the envoys of an outer god. The potential remains within each of them to become a weapon for Vedesis, or for someone blessed by her. As I see it, there is only one realistic possibility that can be drawn from the assumption of your man's words being literal. He believes that someone in Audunpoint's Vedesian subpopulation plans to enact a rite of communion at some point in the near future. Why or how, I can't say. Theorizing on the motivations of purely theoretical Vedesians is not my specialty… It's making sure you don't stroke out in the street because you forgot your rejection suppressants."

"I've not missed a single dose. Do relic grafts not have a near-zero rejection index?" she complained, though she was well aware it was a matter of accounting for edge-cases and making sure everything was going well, even if it wasn't truly necessary.

"Near-zero. Not zero," Firminus rebutted. "Even then, it is not a flaw in the graft, but merely accounts for non-ideal compatibility, issues with the implantation, or the aftercare. Some individuals are simply not cut out for grafting. It is the same as any other natural predisposition. We can do much to lessen the impact, but you are still changing your worldly shell far faster than any training could achieve. Also, I made it abundantly clear that spines are some of the most complication-prone grafts possible. Even without rejection, you can suffer severe issues due to small hitches in connectivity. That's what I am trying to prevent."

She spent another half-hour there, going through various tests and exercises meant to expose any flaws in the integration of both spinal and rib cage grafts. Once all was done, Firminus applied an oil of some kind to the exposed musculature on her back and commented, "As expected, there was some marginal desiccation due to the rushed procedure. You likely would not have noticed any issues, but this will help smooth out the bumps and accelerate the melding of individual muscle bundles. The graft muscle should fully merge within the next two months, keep it covered as much as possible until then; not that I expect you would do anything to the contrary even if I did not tell you. That looks about done—you may go now."

Krahe rolled her shoulders and stretched after getting up off the chair, and Firminus rolled off across the room to grab another cigarette. He'd smoked the whole thing, unbothered and unburnt by it somehow. As she closed up the back of her suit, Krahe remarked, "You're much less ill-humored of a doctor than I had anticipated."

He responded with a somewhat sour chuckle. "And you're much less of a headache to work on than I had anticipated," he said, lighting the new cigarette. Wisps of blue smoke, alongside ash, rose up from it. "I have some experience working with anathemists. Torment, hair-pulling torment to work on. Every single one is a different tangle of comorbidities and horrific internal damage. Like a puzzle box made of rusty razors. As far as I have seen, it appears that you indeed possess the faculties for metabolizing anathema and its remnants."

"A puzzle-box made of rusty razors, huh. Reminds me of something. Would you happen to know of methods to harness anathema without exposing oneself to it?"

"There are some. Why?"

"It's not for me. I'm looking into someone at the Lost Sun Society whom I believe may be involved in something of that sort. I insinuated the suspicion on a hunch, and got a reaction that suggested I hit close to the truth."

"I will disappoint you; the most help I can render on this matter is pointing you to a particular restricted section in the Temple of Records and submitting the access request in your stead. Section Fifty-three. If they approve it, I will send you the access permit through Casus, or failing that, give it to you when you next come for a checkup."

* * *

The day before, Casus had brought her a message. It was a request from Garvesh to come visit within a few days, so she had it set aside in her mental calendar.

"Since you're here already, could you put in a requisition request at the church for me?" Krahe asked Casus.

"I have grown to dislike being treated as an errand-boy, but I understand that your situation necessitates it. Perhaps consider training Barzai to deliver messages. Until such time, though, what is the request?"

"Physical training equipment. It would be easier if I could just train in private rather than showing my face at church gymnasiums. Weights, bars, some roll-up mats. I don't need any expensive machines."

"Alright. Do you have space for them, or do you intend to rearrange the furniture here?"

"I bought a place."

"Where?"

"Where do you think?"

"A below-average part of town? Out of sight and out of mind?"

"Bingo."

"I could have it delivered to a nearby storehouse in a warded crate."

"Works for me." She shrugged, raising her legs and flipping forwards off the sofa onto her feet. "The house is number ninety-four on Gashward Road. Want some stir-fry?"

"Gashward?" the Banisher questioned, setting down his book and following in her stead. "You truly did find a hole. I don't actually know where that is. And yes, I would like stir-fry. Same as last time?"

"Spicier, but more or less the same. Found these mushrooms that have a texture and flavor sort of like pork, but also contain hot pepper oils," she said, half-mindedly setting the burner to full blast. White flame erupted from the ring, and a small bubble gurgled up through the stove's fuel tank with shimmering white liquid swirling behind a translucent gauge.

"Are overly spiced foods another one of those foldover things for you? A matter of nostalgia?"

"You could say that," she said with a slightly somber tone. "Everything was either spiced all to hell with synthetic filth or full of sweet corn syrup. Or both…"

A few moments and mouthfuls of the colorful dish passed.

"But stir-fry just doesn't taste right if it's not spicy, at least to me. Is it too much? I expected you to have a high tolerance for heat."

Casus curiously scooped rice and individual pieces of vegetables, roots, and meat-mushrooms as he replied, "I do, but I cannot help but notice the glaring discrepancy between foods I eat in restaurants or at the temple, versus your cooking. I also cannot help but find it strange that you cook at all. I expected you to take full advantage of the city's street vendors."

"Who says I don't?"

"Touché."

* * *

More investigation. Another direction. Another lead. It was an awkward hour, early in the morning, when the place was all but deserted save for a small group of diehards in the lobby, trudging onward through a more than twelve-hour session of wargames. Krahe wagered that her arrha paled in comparison to the stuff they were hopped up on; she'd seen them drinking and smoking various things, as well as chewing roots of some kind.

A pile of ash and cigarette butts began to occupy some of her Kenoma Pocket as she searched through the Lost Sun Society's library. Despite its comparatively small size, it took her far longer to go through any single row of books due to their greater substance. In a public library, she skimmed all but one out of seven or eight books, and only read into one out of fifteen, but here, every third and sometimes every other book had some thread of promise begging for Krahe to pull and unravel.

Inevitably, however, she found what she was searching for. The library's contents were all clustered together by topic if applicable, except for one—Anathemism. These books and scrolls were conveniently scattered in weird places with most of their neighbors covered in dust and cobwebs. The anathemism books themselves seemed to be purposely covered in fake coats of these things. She referenced everything she found against the index of the library's volumes to find that none were missing, but a few volumes had pages that were... wrong. They were there, very much so, but they weren't the original pages.

She checked the index again.

The downright demonic-looking book in her hand, Anathemia Oscura, had been repaired recently. Pages had been found missing. The dust cover also concealed a slip with the information those pages would have contained, as well as a bounty offer from the librarian for whoever found the culprit. It wasn't much.

This, alone, was just a grain atop a pile of golden sand that Krahe would melt down to later use for joining the shards of this case together. Her study of Anathemia Oscura yielded little headway in the case; the removed pages pertained to various obscure methods by which someone could protect themselves against anathema, as well as how one could prepare and mitigate the deleterious effects of using anathemism.

Krahe felt the mounting weight of exhaustion crawling up her back as she rolled open another scroll, and found that it was a fragment. What little of it was intact detailed the gruesome fate of some anathemists, and the similarly gruesome things that had been done to harness their unrotting corpses. It only barely began to describe the anatomical effects of bone-deep anathema burns before it cut off. She recorded everything she could from the partial scroll, put everything back where it had been, and left like a ghost. She exited into the side alley rather than out the front door.

She was sure she would find what she needed in the Temple of Records, and upon visiting that place, that hunch turned out true. Speaking with the librarian went as such:

"I came upon a partial scroll pertaining to the ultimate fates of certain extreme anathemists, titled Burning Torment Wrought in Black. Does the Temple of Records carry a complete copy?"

"That is the case, yes. However, it is in a restricted section that appears to be beyond your clearance."

"Figures. Someone should have already put in an elevated access request on my behalf. What is the status of that?"

"Still processing. I expect that it will be no more than two or three days, so I will have the text prepared and held in reserve. If the request is approved, you may bring the proof and pick up your scroll the same day."

Two to three days was a fair bit sooner than her next checkup with Firminus, but she supposed it was acceptable. She banished bureaucracy from her mind for now. Garvesh was waiting.

And he was, indeed, waiting, not just in the figurative sense.

"You're an hour fuckin' late!" he chided her when she arrived. It was a lie. She was only half an hour late, and it was only because she had to shake someone she was sure had begun following her. "Egh, fuckin' whatever. Come into the back. This isn't something for the front end."

He led her into the storeroom, where two heavy-duty cases sat atop a similarly heavy-duty metal crate—one small and the other large. Alongside them, there were several pieces of chunky equipment, with black cables all around. More than anything, it felt like corporate prototype hardware. Her hunch turned out to be correct when she asked, "What is it?"

"A Mamon Coupler. For when you have a go at Hashem."

"You know I've never used one, right? I'm open to the *idea* of using one, but I won't bet my life on something I can't use properly."

"Yeah, I know, I know. I'm not stupid. I have a good reason. Let me get to it."

After fiddling with the cases' holeless locks, he flipped them open. Their interiors were lined in velvet, molded to fit only their contents. Furthermore, they were so densely warded it was tangible. It was not by way of paper talismans, but through protective glyphs embroidered directly into the lining, and that was just the visible layer.

Besides the audible hiss of air rushing in, Krahe also felt a more esoteric form of the same phenomenon, like the stuff inside had just come into existence the moment the seal was broken. Within the larger one was a set of partial body armor. Front and back plates for the upper chest, bracers and shin-guards with quarter-spheroid extensions to partly protect the middle joints, and sizable flat plates that she guessed had to be shoulder guards. It looked like extra plating that would be issued to some corpo death squad to wear over their standard armor. All of it was a dark, matte metal.

As for the smaller case, it contained a belt in the same starkly utilitarian design. Some of its curves, tubes, and exposed mechanics gave off the impression of an overgrown dregsteamer belt. It had two distinct slots; one contained a metal cell of some kind with a readout marked 'full,' while the other, on the belt's left-hand side, was a clearly marked slot for a voidkey. Well, to call it a slot was generous. It was a circular recess about ten centimeters across and no more than two centimeters deep. Its interior was filled by twisting, etched patterns, while its perimeter was outlined by the word VOIDKEY repeating over and over, stamped straight into the metal. On the inside of the smaller case, she noticed a thin, unassuming dossier. The only text on its exterior was smack dab in the middle. Three words.

PROJECT BLACK SUN

The combination of roughshod construction and razor-sharp design had already set off alarm bells in her head. The ominously classified dossier only made her certain that she was right.

"It's..." Garvesh began.

"A prototype?" Krahe interrupted.

"Yeah. A real, bleedin' edge prototype. Not like that Silver Slip Key I've got on display. Straight from Kristoffen Heavy Ironworks. Y'know, the folks that make the dregsteamers. The Black Sun Project is their answer to the lucrative mid-ranker market. Idea is you start off with a dregsteamer and then buy one of these when you '*make it.*' They want their special catalyst to adapt to the user at first coupling, and then have it re-adapt to any new souldregs the user decides to introduce. Ambitious if nothing else."

"And the armor?"

"Part of the coupler system. It's a support framework for the suit to form around, supposed to make the end result more resilient. They also haven't been able to make the coupler work with a full-construct framework. It was either compatibility grafts for the user, or this framework. You're supposed to be able to customize the supports in the final version. Y'know, get your own custom armor fitted to it and shit. 'Leasteast that's how they plan to advertise it so they can upsell the users on overpriced premium supports."

"Not my problem," Krahe shrugged. "What is my problem, though, is that using a dregsteamer is bad enough. I've seen the state Casus ended up in. What's the catch with this one? Is it the same side effects as a dregsteamer, but even worse? I can cope, but I'd rather know that the crash is coming."

"High cognitive strain factor and Throughput requirements for the performance. The catalyst doesn't even respond to some 80% of testers, and the prototypes have a habit of just burning out within a handful of uses, or even sooner if you push them too hard. This one, uh... Let's say it had some *quality control issues* and got sent off for inspection. If it responds to you, I'll make the call and my friend will have an '*accident*' that destroys the unit. Hold on, I'll plug it into the diagnostic unit."

The unit was a chunky box twice the belt's size with a projection eye and black cables coming out of it, one of which was connected to a similarly cubular unit with a small thaumine fuel cell. The others, Garvesh cautiously plugged into an out-of-place port on the prototype coupler's belt, connected to the main unit with a thin cable.

As he did so, he continued speaking in a surprisingly enthusiastic manner. "I figured it would work for you, since you've got that funky new spine. You'll still be fine if it doesn't. It's not like—Uch, this one really doesn't want to go in. There we go. As I was saying, it's not like the Silberblut Coupler. At worst you'll get a splitting headache and detransform. They worked out the aneurysm problem three iterations ago. Put on the framework armor for now while I set this up."

Krahe did as was asked of her, finding that besides belts, the armor also had quite complex internal frames that automatically shifted to fit her. She couldn't help but smile. This—*all this*—from Garvesh's spiel to the bleeding-edge prototype, was bringing back a slew of memories. She couldn't help but notice the asymmetry in the bracers and the shoulder plates. The right bracer had lighter plating in exchange for a socket of some kind, while the left bracer and shoulder plate were both substantially chunkier, with the left bracer almost forming a small shield.

"Alright... Just a few more..." Garvesh rumbled under his breath. The lizard finally managed to get the diagnostic unit to flicker from a continuous downpour of readouts to a single floating message.

AWAITING TEST USER

"Now pull your key and slot it into the belt. You haven't had it in for long so it shouldn't be difficult to extract."

Garvesh was right in that it wasn't difficult, but it was an order of magnitude harder than Krahe had expected. It was a sickly, ticklish sensation that sent waves of shivers down her back with every centimeter.

Once it was out, she felt a yawning emptiness that slowly closed up like biorepair gel rushing in to fill a wound. The Black Sun Coupler took in the key without issue, and the stamped readout around the slot shifted to form a dial with a handful of increments with the head of her voidkey becoming the selector. Donning the belt, it was somewhat loose until she buckled it in the back, at which point it shrunk to fit.

After pulling the dossier out of its box, Garvesh flipped through it, muttering, "Insert fuel cell... Release the safety switch... Connect contactor... Ah, here it is. Rotate the dial forward until it clicks once—from the first position into the second position."

Krahe gave him an incredulous look at the wannabe-idiotproof instructions. She still did as he said. There was some initial resistance, but once it was overcome the dial spun freely until it snapped into the second position. The belt awakened, several connections clicking into place as it emitted a rising tone. It reminded her of a fusion bomb being armed.

"Now turn the dial forward until it circles back around to the first position. This should initiate the transformation since the prototype doesn't have a cognitive trigger safety. Fair word of warning, it comes with an arm-mounted hardpoint catalyst. Like a gun that spits out a basic offensive thaumaturgy at a rapid rate of fire."

"So that's what it was. Should've said so sooner," she sighed as she started undoing the straps of her bracers so she could swap them around. Once both bracers and shoulder guards had been switched, she finally completed the sequence. The gaped-open serpent maw that was her voidkey's head spun around and came to a halt.

For all her effort, she found herself briefly losing awareness of her surroundings. A typical symptom of momentary nervous overload caused by abrupt integration of new hardware—a type of benign seizure. It was all too much like getting into fancy power armor and quick-booting the unit. Her spine felt like it was buzzing for a few seconds after the fact, but it soon settled down.

When she returned to awareness, she saw two things. First, a gobsmacked Garvesh. Second, the diagnostic unit spewing lines of data, yet with a distinct absence of errors. A homely HUD partly filled her sight. It even had an ultra-retro searcher reticle! Looking herself over, Krahe raised her hand to see that her bracers had not only grown, but bulked up significantly and changed in shape, including armored gloves and upper-arm guards. The undersuit, visible on the palms and in the elbows, was innocuous dark-gray, almost matte-black, looking like a dense ballistic weave. Reaching up, she raised her hand into her field of vision, and couldn't help but notice the short barreled machine gun bolted to her forearm. It had something resembling an action but devoid of the mechanics of such a thing, with a cable shaped like an ammo conveyor snaking up her arm and under the shield-like shoulder plate. The HUD pointed out where the "gun" was aiming with a separate crosshair.

"Mirror?" she asked.

"Uh..." was the reply.

Garvesh looked around, and after manhandling some very heavy looking boxes, he hauled out an antique full body mirror in a frame of precious metals, or at least one made to look the part.

Krahe almost laughed when she saw herself in full. On her head was a helmet whose shape was only a half step from the infamous stahlhelm, and her face was concealed by a plague doctor-esque beaked gas mask with green glowing eye ports. Not even an iota of humanity shone through that ominous guise. The pattern of stark, aggressive shape language rendered in dark metal continued with the rest of the armor, though nothing quite matched the helmet's ominous impact. The upper half of her torso had a full chest plate, while the midsection was covered by segmented, interlocked plates to preserve mobility. Her right arm's forearm and shoulder plates were big and thick enough to act as effective shields.

A skirt of plates hung over her upper legs. Her normal pants were still there, seemingly unaltered, though with some focus she could *feel* the undersuit beneath them. Much like her pants, the Black Sun armor had incorporated her boots into itself. The armor's boots were half her own, and half the Black Sun shin guards, merged and amplified into the platonic ideal of death squad doorkickers.

"I look like some activist's rendition of a tyrannical regime's enforcer," she said, barely suppressing an amused chuckle.

Garvesh, caught up in checking and rechecking the diagnostic readouts, ignored the remark and said, "Do some squats."

When she fulfilled his request, he continued. "Alright, now hop in place."

This banal game of "simon says" continued for a few minutes before he finally, mercifully, brought out an unreasonably handsome bust of some guy and set it on a crate.

"Last test. Shoot. No need to worry about the noise, I've got this place warded."

The sound of bassy thumping ripped through the storeroom, and a deluge of abnormally large Tracers flowed through the air. Flashes of orange-red colored everything. The burst lasted a number of seconds that could be counted on one hand, but half of the bust was gone by the time she was done.

The lizard looked at Krahe, then at the bust, then back at Krahe. With a somewhat accusatory tone, he said, "You know I've tried to smash that thing with hammers before."

"So we can call the test a success, then."

"The system's throwing alerts about anathema contamination, but otherwise, yeah. I'll turn off the safeguards for when you take it out for a ride for real. Don't expect it to survive. Right now it's the diagnostic unit powering it, but that cell will melt down once it's out of juice and it'll be a coin toss if it takes the whole belt with it. On the optimistic side, you might get five minutes out of the thing if you pace yourself."

"Five minutes of this kind of performance are all I'll need. Just need a Mamon Knight name, now."

"Seriously? For five minutes."

"You never know. I might get myself one of these once all the kinks get ironed out. I'm thinking *'Viridaimon.'*"

"Please do not explain the wordplay behind it."

"Casus told you, huh."

"Of course he told me."

"How much do you want for it?"

"Just take the damn thing. I couldn't source a gulf key no matter what strings I pulled in any reasonable amount of time, so consider this the replacement. I still have people looking for one, they're just a bitch to find. So long as the belt's wick gets burnt in the process of getting revenge for my cousin, I'll consider us even."

"How specific is that criteria? Should Viridaimon grind the assassin into paste, or is it alright if I just off her without the suit and then use it to come after her employers?"

"Ah, I don't care," the lizard huffed. "Keep it and try to reverse engineer it for all I care, so long as the assassin—Wait, her? Was that a slip of the tongue or do you already know who did it?"

"I have my sources."

"Better than mine, it seems. Y'mind sharing? Could look into her some more. Promise I won't do anything stupid. I'm not some hot-blooded whelp... I'd want to do it myself anyhow, and I'm not much stronger than Imraal in my state."

A melancholic resignation came over him as he said that. Krahe weighed the risks, and deemed them minimal: "She's with the Silversword Agency. A young human by the name of Eutropia."

"I will attempt to look into her, though I expect that I will not find more than you already know."

"Do so discreetly. It would not do for her to be on guard when I come to collect."

"Come now. You think too little of me." Garvesh chuckled wryly. "Take the diagnostic kit as well. If possible, run the full battery of checks before using the coupler."

Detransforming left her feeling strange and her head thrumming with a dull ache, but grinding a couple Tabryxas between her teeth helped set her back in line. After doffing the extra support armor and packing everything up, she tried to waste no time in leaving Garvesh in peace. Her departure was delayed by an offer she couldn't refuse. "Y'want some Machine Crab Juice? I was making some just as you arrived."

Casus waited for her back at the safehouse. His expectant, excited reaction to the Black Sun Coupler proved that he had known about it in advance. Despite the distrustful voices niggling in the back of her head when he took to fiddling with the diagnostic equipment, she didn't say anything.

It wasn't long before this short time of peace came to an end.

At the end of each investigative thread, more often than not, violence awaited.

Getting access to the necessary restricted section in the Temple of Records only confirmed what she had already assumed, and built upon her suspicions beyond what she had dared to theorize.

The texts she found were more a collection of notes and letters than actual books, leading her to believe these were the originals which the Lost Sun Society's books were based on, or at least copies of the originals. The text was recorded as "The Human Charcoal Letters." They were dated in the time window of 4127AB to 4183AB. Over a millennium ago.

They spoke of a fate supposedly worse than death. An exceedingly rare condition wherein, over the course of an extended period, an anathemist could somehow self-mummify into a state akin to a living ember, not quite truly alive, but not quite truly dead; so-called Adustocorpus. The bodies of such anathemists could, supposedly, be split up and harnessed as power sources or for the creation of anathemic relics. The rarity of this occurring naturally was such that information was scarce prior to 4127, but cases had spiked to the extreme during the writing of the Human Charcoal Letters, and so had knowledge on the condition.

In particular, the Human Charcoal Letters spoke at length on several occult practices that all boiled down to variations of the same thing: Methods of manipulation and occult rituals designed to aid in driving someone to the point of Adustocorpus, so that they may be harvested for the practitioner's own use. Uncensored, surviving excerpts from retrieved ritual books described the subject as "human charcoal," hence the name of these documents. These practices were described simply as "charring," which was obviously for the purpose of dehumanizing the victims to soothe the practitioner's conscience.

The same chamber also contained extensive documentation on the Twin Churches' joint effort in stamping out the individuals and occult groups which had created and used these methods. Krahe only skimmed through these records, finding not much more of use for the Lost Sun Killer Myth case. Regardless, she had gotten what she was looking for.

Upon next visiting the Lost Sun Society, she found that, curiously enough, the texts she had touched were now no longer missing any pages, and had been replaced into their proper places. Krahe asked the librarian about it in a roundabout way, who claimed to be unaware of any recent repairs to any of the texts.

On her way out, she ever so briefly glimpsed a lithe lizard. She assumed it to be Sorayah, since all the other Saurians in the Society were on the heavy, crocodilian side. One of them, a man revered as a god-like miniature painter, resembled a humanoid komodo dragon, and smelled the part too, despite his efforts.

Krahe didn't think much of it as she randomly chose a direction away from the Society, remaining no more and no less on guard than she normally was. Of course, by any normal person's standards her baseline was a schizophrenic level of constant vigilance. She wouldn't have survived Crescent Jezail otherwise.

So it was to her surprise, and, admittedly, excitement, when she realized she was not only being tailed by several people but surrounded by them at that. They... weren't great. They were good, yes, but not great. About the best one could expect from amateurs. Their outfits were too homogenous, and at least two of them wore openly visible Lost Sun jewelry. Krahe had to give them credit; they didn't know that she could see through Barzai, or that Barzai was even there. Truly, a flying, camouflaged pair of extra eyes and ears was an immensely powerful tool.

CHAPTER 12

LOST SUN KILLER MYTH: THE HAND IS SHOWN

They eventually "got her" in the loading/unloading area of a small warehouse, insofar as she led them to this place because the layout was advantageous to her and the warehouse, being out of use, would be an easy way to split them up or lose them if things went badly. It was an apparent dead end, but she had been around this area before and knew that the "dead end" wall was just a thin divider separating this unloading area from one of the main roads.

Krahe waited for a short time with her back turned, making it look like she was looking into the warehouse as she lit up a cigarette. Meanwhile, Barzai perched on a nearby railing, covering her blind spot.

"I figured I was being tailed," she said aloud when the group of five entered after her. No other entrance, no way for them to surround her.

No response. From what Barzai saw, they looked... marginally professional, with masked faces and some armor. Two Mamon Knights with dregsteamers, three thaumaturges, none exuding a particularly impressive aura. The apparent leader was a large, bird-like Saurian with a hooked beak for a mouth; thus, she dubbed him *Beak*. To his right, an unsettlingly humanlike Saurian with a long beard of feathers and a second, weasley looking one. She named them Beardo and Weasel, with Weasel having a dregsteamer belt. To his left, a second Saurian with a lighter, raptor-like build, and a blonde woman who had the second dregsteamer— Raptor and Blondie. Now that she looked at him, she was sure Raptor was the one she saw earlier. They clearly weren't true pros, but hired muscle that knew the basic opsec practice of "shut the fuck up."

Turning on her boot heel, hand already on her gun, Krahe asked, "Let me guess. Sorayah?"

"The identity of our employer is not yours to guess at," Raptor hissed, but the speed and manner of his reaction betrayed that she was right.

C'mon, oldest trick in the book. She gave the weaseley looking man an amused look. His compatriots stared daggers through him. He squinted, glaring at her, as if he recognized her.

Not one to give up the first mover's advantage, Krahe dragged down the rest of her cigarette. Simultaneously, she fusion formed a high-pressure burster that would be weak, but loud and messy, erupting into a short-lived burst of smoke and ash. A prototype Concussion Burster by any other name.

With a spark of intent, she willed Barzai to reveal himself and set upon the five. In the split-second where he pulled their attention, she fired the concussion burster into their midst by way of Six Trees Killer. The bullet itself struck one of the Mamon Knights, throwing him off and delaying his transformation by two seconds compared to his counterpart.

The strobe-bursts of Barzai's eyes briefly preceded bursts of small explosions, springing out of nowhere right on the bodies of Blondie and Raptor. They weren't enough to break or even seriously damage their wards, but that wasn't their purpose. Krahe exhaled, shrouding her surroundings in a Smoke Eruption. The rancid taste of Isotope burned her mouth. Despite this onslaught, three of them regained their bearings, firing into the smoke. Krahe felt a mixture of wildly varied projectiles zip by her as she raised a wall from the ground.

Rapid footsteps combined with a dregsteamer's synthesized voice betrayed one of the Mamon Knights trying to close in. "WARNING: High velocity. Explosive pressure. Stand free."

Beginning to form the Faust Construct, Krahe met the freshly transformed Mamon Knight in battle. Not a fair, straightforward fight, of course. She skimmed twice in a row around him and dived to further improve her own mobility, emerging only once the construct's formation had finished and Weasel was facing away from her, around six meters away. A single shot was all it took to send it his way, but true to his armor, he reacted to the gunshot with blistering speed and whipped around to come at her. At this rate, she had maybe a second and a half before he punched her lights out. In this moment of adrenaline, she realized the suppressive fire from before had stopped; the only reason Weasel's allies stopped shooting, she wagered, had to be that they didn't want to hit him.

Krahe took the risk and ran ahead to intercept him, unable to dive for a few more seconds. With her rather limited control over the missile, she willed Wandrei Faust to slow down. Another transformation announcement, this time for Omniphage, sounded, and Blondie's armored feet approached as well.

In the absence of better options, Krahe changed plans from a pincer attack on Weasel to splitting up her resources. She smashed into Weasel with a tendril extended straight punch, pushing dangerously close to meltdown to keep him at bay long enough to regain a skimming charge. Afterwards, she skimmed straight through him, using the opportunity to turn herself around.

With every bit of what little entropy she had, she swung again and sent him flying into her Wandrei Faust. At the moment that punch connected, her tendrils rotted away. At that same moment, right as she punched Weasel with her left hand, she gestured up with her right to impel the Forming Toroid into raising another wall.

Her smoke was dispersing by now due to the battle going on inside it, so despite her best judgment she took a moment to refresh her Smoke Eruption. Barzai, upon Krahe's command, dive-bombed into Blondie, momentarily keeping her at bay. The attack was enough to exhaust his astral form, and so she bid him to return as she exhaled the next blast of smoke. Her mouth and throat were burning and raw from the Isotope.

Meanwhile, outside the smoke, Beardo fled. He simply turned tail and ran, much to Beak's and Beardo's vocal chagrin. The two men gathered their wits, unused to such unreasonable combat conditions. The smoke clearly wasn't normal; both their eyes were sharp enough to pierce most obscuring thaumaturgies.

That smoke had to be some anathemist trick, but what fool would resort to the risks of anathemism to enhance a mere obscuring thaumaturgy? Then again, it clearly worked wonders, and those summoned walls were far too durable to be simple constructs. That had to be an artifact of some kind. That was what Beak told himself, hoping and praying they weren't up against some insanely strong mid-ranker with a bottomless entropy tolerance. His cousin certainly hadn't made it sound like that when she called in a favor to have her dealt with.

Both of them being practitioners of the same thaumaturgic style, Beak and Raptor joined forces in trying to salvage their original plan of attack: The Basilisk Dive, a combination thaumaturgy drawing on their thinned-out Drasaurian genes. While Beak showed some of the signs, Raptor's only proof of his Drasaurian lineage was his shitty blowtorch breath and his ability to invoke draconic powers via thaumaturgy.

Out from the smoke, a monstrous, flying forearm appeared, dragging Weasel and Blondie over the stone. Weasel screamed while Blondie grunted and struggled to free herself. She slipped out thanks to the fact she had merely been caught in its trajectory and wasn't actually in the construct's grasp, but Weasel wasn't so fortunate; the black arm made an unsteady 180 degree turn, smashing him into the left-hand wall and dragging him back into the smoke. A bright yellow flash followed, accompanied by a horrific sound that neither of the Saurians could describe—the sound of a man in Mamon Armor exploding from the pressure of his own boiling blood.

By now, Blondie had circled around from the right, and the smoke had dissipated enough to see at least silhouettes. What Beak and Raptor beheld were alien shapes erupting from the anathemist's body, striking at Blondie without regard for the Omniphage armor's caustic properties. Their sightline was broken by a pair of ominous, blackened jade obelisks, and further disrupted by the fact Weasel had been turned into nothing more than a shadow on the wall and a red puddle spreading over the cobbles below.

* * *

Krahe knew better than to fight a fresh Mamon Knight in a melee while her entropy was pushing eighty percent, doubly so when her two other foes were using this time to build a ghostly dragon head.

So, she dived, sprinting to the back wall with the intent to skim through it. As she ran, mere steps away, she felt a wave of searing heat surround her, and blinding light filled her vision. She passed unto the other side, emerging and instantly beginning a purge, but as she spun around as to not have her back turned towards the trio, she saw that the thin wall was melting. Unsure of whether those lizards could pull this trick again, she raised her third jade wall today just in case.

By the sound of their shouting, the three weren't dumb enough to assume she was gone altogether. That was fine. She just needed time to purge. Enveloped in an aura of gray-black smoke, she watched and prepared, cycling her gun to eject the current thaumshot-core cartridge and chamber the next Wandrei Faust. Then, a plan took form in her mind.

A second attack came just moments before her purge finished, and this time she witnessed some of its execution. The ghostly dragon head flew upward and came diving down, spewing some kind of boiling, burning liquid. It was most easily described as acid napalm. The original wall was broken down by now, and the burning acid was eating away at her jade slab. She was certain Goldie was helping it along with the Omniphage armor's abilities, but she hadn't heard a Coupler Charge callout, so her caustic output had to be limited.

Meanwhile, Krahe formed a Wandrei Faust, forming a Tar-tendril from her upper arm and wrapping it around the construct. She steadied her feet, aimed her arm upwards, visualized Beak in her mind's eye... and shot herself. She felt the construct detaching to fly after its target, and willed the tendril to extend, giving her around a meter and a half of standoff from the missile. Once it seemed long enough, she launched herself in the same direction using a diagonally rising pillar of jade. Soaring over the wall, Krahe Fusion-Formed and fired a weak Smoke Eruption grenade into the Saurian brothers' midst, herself letting go of the Wandrei Faust as she came barreling downward.

She stifled a grin when she saw Blondie moving to eagerly play into her hand by attempting to swat her out of the air. For once, she made use of her barrier, wanting to preserve her access to diving as a safety net. Her downward approach was punctuated by the ominous cracking of the Cinder Strobe, smashing down on Blondie like a cruel sun, visibly deforming her armor. Just before she came into Blondie's melee range, Krahe executed her premeditated plan: She used one of the secondary features of Astro Skimming to reorient herself, ensuring that Blondie got closely acquainted with the stone underfoot for the second time today.

As Krahe slid that short distance, she wasted no time in giving Blondie a full-tilt Cinder Flash at near-point-blank. The woman, previously struggling, boiled inside her suit before it could even fall apart, blood and fluids gushing out of the joint seams, the undersuit cracking and peeling apart. A visibly charred outline formed around her on the ground, but it was washed away by the continuous leakage from her corpse. As Krahe turned to finish dealing with the Saurian pair, Blondie's armor emitted a kettle-like whistle for a few moments before it utterly crumbled. The residual omniphage would leave no corpse behind.

Despite the smoke, Krahe saw the two still valiantly maintaining the ghostly dragon.

"Well, since you're pulling out the big guns..." she thought, holding out her left arm that still glowed an ominous anathemic red. Without an explicit prompt, Barzai erupted from her chest and perched atop her palm, imploding into a seething ball of crimson as Krahe already began forming his tendrilous casement.

Raptor and Beak's ghostly, somewhat bird-like dragon head turned to glare at her, alarm gripping the two of them at the sight of her.

Krahe pushed and pushed, closing up the shell until, at last, it wouldn't enclose any further. She briefly thought Barzai was refusing again for some petulant reason, but the next moment, alien words pushed into her mind's eye. Indistinct and formless, exuding not a linguistic meaning but an altogether more primordial sort of truth. In that instant, she knew that they were the incantation necessary to make the Daemon Core function, just as the talisman was necessary for Wandrei Faust. Despite Barzai serving as the power source, it had to be her who triggered the theurgy.

But no matter how she tried, she couldn't speak them. They just hung in her mind, three burning keys awaiting a hand to grasp them. The Saurian duo's dragon head reared back, its form becoming more concrete, and Krahe knew she had only moments before it would drown her in burning acid. She wagered, at best, a fifty-fifty chance that she would manage to get out of the zone of death, given her rapidly rising entropy level and the initial burst of hard entropy she suffered whenever diving. Such was the cost of this theurgy; a high price in entropy to give the shell the necessary properties.

The only option she could think of, besides pushing harder, was to attempt, somehow, someway, using the Wound-like Grin. After all, it manifested itself readily upon her left arm when she wished to access her Kenoma Pocket or to conjure a Tar-tendril. She mentally envisioned a black tendril wrapping around the first word, channeling it into her arm.

A fanged maw yawned open, and Krahe spoke from it. Despite speaking it, she couldn't hear it. As far as she could tell, no sound came out at all. Beak and Raptor stumbled, clutching their heads. Nonetheless, they persevered in their effort.

The second word came out all the same as the first, opening a second mouth on her forearm. At this point, it felt as if time came to a standstill. Nonetheless, with the mouth in the palm of her hand, she spoke the third, and time resumed.

THREE KEYS TO SWING WIDE THE GATES OF BLACKEST BLACKNESS
THREE WORDS SO MIGHTY NO MORTAL MIND CAN HOLD THEM
THREE BREATHLESS MOUTHS WITH WHICH TO SPEAK THEM

In the palm of her hand, a gordian knot of blackest pitch now hovered. An ominous, rising hum emitted from it, and every once in a while, arcs of black lightning jumped off of it, almost as if the flares of a black sun.

With only a thought and a gesture, she impelled it forwards. This, too, was an advantage of using a True Eidolon; it solved the delivery issue.

Panicking now, Beak and Raptor exchanged glances and began feverishly gesturing, taking more direct control of their dragon head construct to try and shoot down the projectile. The Daemon Core simply dodged past the ghost dragon's snapping jaws, coming to a halt in mid-air right above the two Saurians.

Krahe engaged a dive and pulled the mental trigger. The Daemon Core's exterior shifted.

The last thing Beak or Raptor ever saw was that ominous spheroid and a green-eyed demon of billowing smoke.

With a flash of impossibly vivid scarlet and thunderous burst of buzzing noise, they were erased. Neither flesh, nor bones, nor any of their possessions remained; only shadows scorched into the red-hot stones. Only a seething ember was left behind, and it, too, popped out of existence a moment later.

AN EYE OF CRIMSON IMPRISONED IN BLACKNESS
ITS GAZE ERUPTS FORTH TO SCOUR AWAY THE UNWORTHY
BLACK HAND OF DESOLATION: DAEMON CORE

She felt sick.

Not due to her surroundings or what she'd just done, but some strange, non-physical exhaustion. It felt, for lack of a better description, as if the muscle involved in theurgy had been strained to the point of exhaustion. Just thinking about using Wandrei Faust again made feelings of exhaustion and sickliness bubble up… and the words were gone. She decided to try asking Barzai later. For now, she pulled the souldregs out of Blondie's corpse, taking her dregsteamer belt and moving on to try and find what was left of Weasel. She managed to find his mangled head, which was good enough for the souldreg extractor. His Dregsteamer had also outlived him; it would just need a replacement belt.

Knowing that she wouldn't have a great deal of time before someone came to investigate the commotion, Krahe dragged Blondie to the wall and rifled through her pockets, managing to find a wallet with some ring-cash, a DD gem, and a contractor ID card.

An hour, a shower, and a cursory investigation at a church branch later, Krahe had learned that Weasel had a bounty on his head for several crimes, though it was slashed for bringing in only his souldregs. Blondie turned out to have been a completely unassuming independent contractor with no particular negative or positive marks on her record.

When she had the time to herself, she queried Chernobog's Mystic Wisdom regarding those words. No knowledge came. So, back to theurgic texts she turned, and found nothing. Not a word in any of the books she owned. Barzai, however, gave the answer she sought, once he woke up. He simply pulled up her memory of the first time she drew the Wandrei Faust medallion, specifically the final strokes, and sent her the sentiment that speaking those words was somewhat equivalent to that. He also, as if to placate her, made her aware that she would not need to repeat the feat each time she wished to invoke the Daemon Core.

Meanwhile, Zachariah was in a huff, as were several of his acquaintances, as they had all felt it—the creation of a new High Theurgy. It wasn't necessarily a once-in-a-lifetime event, but the fact it was so detectable meant that the feat had been performed by someone who either didn't know or didn't care enough to take concealing precautions.

CHAPTER 13

LOST SUN KILLER MYTH: TRACKING DOWN THE SUSPECT'S RESIDENCE

For the next few days, Krahe dedicated a portion of her time to stalking Sorayah. Barzai made it a trivial matter, as she could be quite far removed from her target for limited periods of time. Additionally, Sorayah became somewhat careless when Krahe stopped coming to the Society after the attack.

It didn't take long to track down where she lived, and somewhat to Krahe's disappointment in her quarry, there seemed to be no third or fourth location. On the third day, at a time when she knew Sorayah was out, she tried skimming into the basement through the locked outside door, but found herself ejected.

Frustrated at her own carelessness, Krahe let out a heavy sigh.

She probably conducts human charcoal experiments in there. Of course it's warded. Just hope my skimming attempt didn't leave a mark.

Rather than try again, she hit the door with a simple appraisal attempt. The Prospector's Eyes detected magic from the door, but, being what they were, they didn't give her much info beyond that. Upon examination, there were the remnants of an inbuilt lock and turning handle core, but it was now held shut by an external padlock with a familiar maker's mark—the same maker's mark as a Dregsteamer belt. She squatted down, looking into the keyhole, and though it was sealed on the other side, she still managed to shove her pinkie into it. A grin took hold on her face when she felt it;

Isotope. The tiniest bit, like a draft going into a door hidden behind a bookcase, but undeniably there.

Before she left, Krahe took another moment to get a close look at the lock. Thick, heavy, sturdy, but seemingly mundane, with a wide keyway. The Prospector's Eyes detected no magic coming off of it. There was a good chance something on the other side would prevent her from opening the door, but there was no harm in picking the lock and trying to get in this way either.

This plan to pick the lock went out the window when she returned to the safehouse and found Casus sleeping there. She brought it up to him once he woke. A curious, respirator-like mask sat on the coffee table alongside an empty coffee cup and some pill bottles. Krahe only recognized the Purge Pills. The Banisher's pallid countenance betrayed the fact he had made heavy use of the Silberblut Coupler recently.

"Sounds like a Kristoffen lock. Their locks are notorious for being some of the best you can find for a reasonable price. If you need to get into a building with one, perhaps consider skimming inside instead. Assuming it's not warded against such intrusion, of course."

"That's my problem; it *is* warded. I don't know to what degree, but I couldn't just skim inside. Not through that door, at least."

"Hrm... Why exactly do you require entry into this building? Assuming, that is, you are willing to share that information."

Given the fact this was a secondary investigation and the fact the church would inevitably be involved when she resolved it, she saw no reason to keep it from Casus: "I'm fairly sure someone at the Lost Sun Society is practicing the arts detailed in the Human Charcoal Letters; manipulating people into undergoing Adustocorpus, then using their bodies as fuel for artifacts that allow them to use anathema without risk to themselves. Not certain of the motive. Could be power, eliminating competition, simple curiosity."

"The Human Charcoal Letters?" the Banisher asked with a serious tone. "I see, they are why you required elevated access. Is this matter related to Hashem and his Benefactors?"

"No. I just happened to come across a lead while I was trying to get in contact with Yao," Krahe said, summoning a cigarette and placing it into the corner of her mouth. She lit it with just a touch of her thumb.

"I could—" Casus started.

"Don't even think about it," Krahe interrupted. Exhaling a long puff of smoke, she gave him a chiding look over the top of her glasses. "Yesterday was the third day in a row I found you slumped down by the door with your coupler still on. I ought to report you to Firminus for doing the exact shit he told you to stop. Bet you haven't even been properly oiling your arm. Besides, you would be overkill. I need to break into an apartment building, not demolish it."

Casus shrank back somewhat, furrowing his eyebrows in a look of befuddled surprise.

With an amused grin, Krahe took another puff of her cigarette and asked, "What? Did you think I wouldn't take graft maintenance seriously? Forget that I used to be more graft than original flesh? I bet you haven't even realized why your arm is getting slower. The A-Three Tricep Bundle is fucked."

At that, Casus raised his arm, twisting it well beyond a normal range of motion.

"How did you…"

"Come on, I'm not an all-knowing genius. Firminus guessed that would be the issue when I last visited him. When I went for my final post-graft checkup, he wouldn't stop bitching about how you ran out on him before he could even start with the maintenance."

"I could not help it. An urgent alert came in from the Central Temple. I will take care to visit him tomorrow."

"An urgent alert, huh? What was it?"

Casus smiled, leaning forwards. "I know where Semzar Hashem will be not too long from now. The alert was a trustworthy source from his inner circle asking for a secure evacuation into Seven Spokes custody. Thanks to my request for priority on any matters pertaining to the Hashem heir, I was alerted first. The man wanted protection until Hashem was dealt with, erasure of his bounty record, permission to legally operate his gambling business, and to have his grafts looked at by a sanctioned grafter. This, in exchange for giving his testimony and leading us to Semzar. He even offered to have us bring in an Inquisitor to prove he was telling the truth."

"How does our man know where to find the brat?"

"I will get to that part soon..." he said, standing up and stretching to the sound of popping joints. "Once my throat is not dry as a desert."

A few minutes later, two cups of coffee steaming on the table, Casus began recounting the incident.

Casus had never ventured into this area of Audunpoint before. Considering the unusually high number of gangsters, he couldn't help but notice that building. The one with blocked-out windows and Evoy lingering about the entrance. It screamed trouble.

He knew he was all but begging for trouble by coming here. That was, after all, why he had gone so far as to don a disguise that concealed his nature as a Banisher. However, a man in subtle full-body armor and a long coat drew attention all the same. At least he'd had the good judgment to avoid using anything identifiable as Church equipment. That was a mistake he had only made once, and it had nearly cost him his life. As he was, he looked like someone who absolutely didn't want to be seen in this part of town, but also wanted the ability to protect himself, which meant he had a bare minimum level of plausible deniability; the local gangsters couldn't reasonably walk up and start trouble right from the start.

He was currently equipped with The Black Magnum Coupler. A unique urban stealth model designed to make the wearer forgettable, emitting a weak sensory deterrence enchantment. Adding onto its stealth design, it emitted a minimal magical aura mimicking a normal person, and no two Black Magnum suits looked the same. Its combat capabilities were slightly superior to a Dregsteam Coupler with the high velocity cartridge, but its cost was over twenty times that unit. It also had the unique feature of a self-contained, ultra-low-interference design, meaning he was able to wear the Silberblut Coupler under the Black Magnum suit without issues.

Rather than a belt, the coupler was a lower face mask that expanded out to form the helmet and then the rest of the suit, and it was a monolithic black box unit, without a typical catalyst or voidkey-adjacent power source. It was not a well known or widely produced model, certainly not enough to be known to some random gangsters; it was just one out of Casus' collection of couplers, which he had begun during the time he was not yet able to handle Silberblut. It also hadn't been produced in over a century since the introduction of the Black Magnum G, the improved model, but Casus personally far preferred the original's aesthetics.

At the moment, his greatest concern was that Evoy building, particularly one of the Evoy out front—a huge, spiky specimen with thick chitin. Casus nearly did a double take when he saw him, briefly thinking it was a war-morph. Simultaneously to his relief and concern, the giant Evoy lacked most of the signs of a war-morph. It was just a freakishly large and powerful individual... But considering his demeanor when interacting with his two lackeys, he would likely pick a fight for any reason—or even no reason at all—if Casus grabbed his attention. He felt the giant Evoy's gaze pass over him, linger for a moment, then move on a moment later. One of the Black Magnum's chief advantages was the sensory suite, featuring strong visual amplification, B-piercing appraisal capabilities, and even an audio telescope.

As he made his way to the building that had been stated as the meeting place, Casus kept an eye on the giant Evoy to ensure he didn't stand up or do anything else to suggest he intended to attack him. It even had built-in triggers to reduce sound and darken the field of vision to counter bright flashes and deafening noises. Moreover, it had its own small voicebox, which he would use to speak instead of his own voice, so that his identity would not be revealed.

On the approach, Casus's attention was immediately captured by a row of wanted posters with surprisingly accurate portraits of Lady Blackhand, at least in terms of appearance. The portrayal of her was still exaggerated, just like it was on the previous, even less accurate posters. She was depicted with a malicious grin on her face, her left arm glowing orange with fanged maws opened along its surface, running its fingers through her hair. Her gun was raised to the side of her face, drawn to the exact specifications of a true Pattner rather than the reproduction it likely was. Rather than bearing the designs or watermarks of any agency, they bore a serpentine design, openly claiming:

WANTED: Dead or Alive
"BLACKHAND"
500,000 DD

There was no delivery address, but then, they probably assumed anyone who did the job would already know where to take her, or would be able to find out. Right below the row of posters for Lady Blackhand, similar ones for himself were found:

WANTED: Dead or Alive
Casus Aristedes
"Mamon Knight Silberblut"
500,000 DD

He didn't give much thought to the bounty payment; it was clearly just an amount that Hashem thought would suffice to get the target killed through sheer volume of attempts. That is, whichever Hashem of the father-son duo was responsible for these posters. No doubt they would figure out some way to shave the cost down if someone actually delivered. When he entered the building, Casus immediately knew it was a gambling house. Many pairs of eyes lingered on him as he slowly walked across the floor, approaching the bartender. "I am here in regards to the owner's inquiry into a refurbished Samstani slot machine for sale."

A thumb pointed to a recessed door in the back of the room. Hammer-forged black iron. Tougher than anything in this building. These doors were one of the Heavy Ironworks' best products, as they came with a door frame and were thus highly breach-resistant relative to their price. Such was the Ironworks' business model: Advanced manufacturing applied to achieve above average quality/price ratio. He didn't think he could break the door down in a reasonable time unless he transformed into Silberblut.

The peephole slid shut, and the door opened for him. The guard, an Inax woman in a pinstripe suit, slipped out and shut the door behind him when he entered. External sounds fell silent, and Casus made his way through the short hallway to a well lit, but windowless room. There was a table with quite a few chairs.

The whole room gave off a markedly more refined feeling than the rest of the gambling house, from the dark wood floor to the walls and furniture. It was... still nothing much compared to a church safehouse.

There was only one man at the table, whom Casus presumed to be his contact. He appraised him, and it stuck without an iota of resistance. The man was a Lv. 17 Occultist. His attribute scores were nothing special, and he didn't bother trying to dig further. What grabbed his attention were not the man's system readouts, but his appearance; more specifically, it was his head. A heavy-duty optical apparatus was affixed to it, a type that had been neither made nor sold in this region in at least twenty years. Its design was emblematic of certain Samstani manufacturers aligned with strongly synthetic-leaning grafters. Even more eye catching was the swelling and scabbing, both proof of recent installation and subpar-at-best aftercare.

"Ah, Mister..." the man began.

"Ahmed," Casus answered.

"Mister Ahmed, thank you for coming on such short notice regarding my inquiry into that Samstani one-armed bandit you offered for sale. I am Cassius; as of recently also known as Seer, for a reason I am sure is, heh... plain to see. I am the proprietor of this humble establishment. As you can surely understand from seeing the front of the house, the machine's self-adjusting mechanism would do wonders for my business."

The visored man went on and on with an undeniably sleazy smoothness of speech. As his words shifted over to the contract of sale, he brought out a paper, but curiously went out of his way to not look at it. It was typed, and had quite a number of mistakes. Considering its contents, Casus assumed the man had typed it quickly and without looking at neither the paper nor the keyboard:

DO NTO SHOW THIS TEXT TO ME. MY OCULAR GRAFT MAY BE COPMROMISED.

I can find Semzar Hashem for you. I'll make this same claim befoer an Inquisitro if I have to.

The terms of my coopreatoin:

Firstly: Protection until Sezmar is gone.

Secondly: A total wipe of my bounty record.

Thirdyl: Full legal permit to operate my estabilshment as-is. It's alreafy nine-tenths of the way above-boar, I jsut need the papers.

LAST: I demnad that an orthrodonx grafter examins this thing onmy head and removes any and all malicious modificatnios, icnluding trakcers, kill switches, etc.

answer as if you are answernig to my offer for the slto mahcine

After looking over the paper and folding it away inside his coat, Casus answered, "Yes, I do believe we could work out something along your suggested terms of purchase. The matter comes down to the manner, time, and method of delivery, as well as any potential issues you believe may arise. I am not familiar with this region, you see. How much danger, do you think, such a delivery would face? Additional insurance is, as always, available. I would hate to see the machine meet an untimely end; far too often we have seen them stolen before they could reach their destination and dismantled for parts when the thieves realized the machine wouldn't open for anyone not designated by the rightful owner..."

"It er... would be best to see it delivered as soon and as securely as possible. Such is life in the Free Cities, the cost of true freedom is caution, as they say..." he trailed off, clearing his throat. With a joking tone that would've convinced any normal person, he added, "Why, if you had it right here, I would take it on the spot!"

They sat in tense silence for a few seconds.

"Are you certain?" Casus asked.

"Of course. My employees already know to look out for a courier and not cause them any trouble. You know how security personnel can be, and they have been even more on edge these past months, first with the Evoy moving in and then that Blackhand woman coming around…"

"Alright. Regarding the first stipulation of the contract—the additional security equipment—would you prefer to have the delivery made here, or pick it up in person?"

"In-person pickup would be preferable."

Seer went on talking in circles for a short time, and Casus played along until he managed to steer things in the right direction in a way that wouldn't sound suspicious to any possible listeners-in. He wasn't worried about Seer's graft—it was a purely ocular piece, and he hadn't noticed any signs of auditory grafts. It was a matter of possible unwelcome ears in the immediate vicinity; it was a common misconception that a room having outside-in sound insulation also meant the opposite.

The two men made their way out of the back room, and exited through the front to keep up the facade of a friendly business relationship, talking about a whole lot of nothing as they went. Doing it so openly lessened the appearance of suspicious activity. Unfortunately, someone took suspicion all the same. Casus realized this quite quickly, as, being a Banisher, he did have an eye on his back, and could thus easily see the large Evoy following them.

Casus recalled Krahe mentioning her encounter with a large Evoy and naming him "Tsetse" after a kind of giant stinging fly from her world. The name took root in Casus' mind, because he hadn't had a particular name for that man until now.

Tsetse's gaze, despite being ever pointed in their direction, never focused on them, and he turned into a different street too abruptly. At this point, Casus wasn't too worried about the Evoy, he was merely paying attention to his surroundings. However, before they could get anywhere close to the nearest branch temple, Tsetse just so happened to be there right past a bend, waiting for them. He was leaning on a wall, his giant form making even this otherwise casual stance seem aggressive.

Viewed from this close, it was obvious there was something off about his body. He couldn't quite place it, but an alarm went off in his mind that even an Evoy this built shouldn't look like this. Only war-morphs were ever this bulky, but they were bulky in ways different to Tsetse.

"Unlucky," he said, craning his armored neck towards the duo. His empty, composite eyes shifted, focusing on Seer. "Someone wanted an eye on you, skinbag. Didn't want you doing something stupid. And you—"

"Unlucky. Too close. Nice suit. Look-away field. Looks expensive."

His manner of speech was different, that much Krahe made clear when Casus recounted this part, but it wasn't just that. Everything about his demeanor had changed. There was no more uncontrolled, bubbling anger. He didn't spout slurs and diatribes willy-nilly. The posturing of a big bully had been replaced by cold professionalism.

"Feel free to remind me when trying to buy a new slot machine for my gambling house became something stupid to do," Seer retorted, masterfully hiding the fear in his voice with irritation, leveling the flyman with the unflinching, stone-faced glare of his visor.

Tsetse shrugged. "It never did. I will come along. See for myself. Maybe I was wrong. I doubt it."

"Fine, go on." Seer gestured uncaringly for Tsetse to proceed.

With a tinge of smugness, Tsetse refused. "No, I walk behind."

"Very well," Casus said, walking ahead. He tapped Seer on the back to signal him to move, and as they approached, Tsetse tensed in place, obviously expecting an attack. Casus, however, just walked on by. Once they had passed, he leaned over to Seer and spoke just loudly enough to be overheard. "I do not expect that even seeing the slot machine in person will suffice to satisfy our insectile friend."

The true purpose was to get his hand on his helmet and twist the dial on its side once. A quasi-liquid, shadow-like substance began spilling out of his respirator; so dark that it appeared like a hole in the world. A waterfall of the same followed from under his coat, racing across the pavement. Despite Tsetse's blindingly fast reactions given his size, the moment he came into the substance's vicinity he was enveloped in a whirlpool of cosmic blackness. It quickly coalesced into sticky threads and restrained the Evoy, covering his eyes and mouth as well as binding his arms to his body. As this took place, Casus quickly made his escape while dragging Seer along. The reason he used the low-output coupler charge was that the full-power version was designed for the wearer's escape; it would tremendously enhance his mobility and stealth, but Seer would be left behind.

Tsetse unfortunately turned out to possess far greater capabilities than previously expected. He not only broke free of the Black Magnum's restraints quite quickly, but also caught up with the duo only one street over. His arrival was heralded by deep, thunderously loud buzzing as he flew overtop the apartment buildings with a strange grace that belied his non-aerodynamic build. Casus didn't recall seeing anything on Tsetse's back to suggest that he had wings; he thus concluded they had to be constructs. This was supported further by the fact his wings were covered in hemolymph and began rotting away the moment he landed, sending up a spray of dust and pebbles as his armored feet broke several cobblestones.

While the slight tremor threw Seer off his feet, Casus regained his bearings and faced Tsetse properly this time. Taking into account Tsetse's intense killing intent, his previously observed speed, his build, and the fact he had freed himself so quickly, Casus arrived at the conclusion that trying to win this using the Black Magnum would pointlessly endanger both himself and Seer.

* * *

"That strong? He didn't feel that way when I met him," Krahe remarked.

"You fought him?"

"No, but I can feel it if someone is a real threat."

"A killer recognizes a killer, I suppose. Perhaps you didn't sense any killing intent when you met him because he had none towards you."

"Guess so. The moment he saw me, he went on a tirade about how all non-Evoy were animals and how the Vedesian Swarm would inevitably rule the world."

"Fairly typical Vedesian talking points. I must admit I am curious how you avoided escalating into a fight."

Krahe went on to briefly summarize her encounter with Tsetse and his two lackeys, including a few choice highlights from the deluge of insults, slurs and threats she had leveled against him. It left Casus with a ghastly expression, and, after a sip of coffee to recenter himself, the Banisher said, "Well, I suppose I have no right to be surprised by your continued use of shock and intimidation tactics. Right, where was I..."

* * *

"Unlucky," rumbled the insectile giant of a man. Chunks of chitin, flesh, and wing membrane sloughed off his back. A pair of pale-red bolts shot past Casus before he could react. One struck Tsetse dead-on, while the other missed, both detonating in a burst of light and dust. They felt like Red Reapers, only much faster and somewhat weaker. Casus, not one to waste an opportunity given to him, hopped back and pulled the Black Magnum Coupler off of his face, throwing it to Seer.

"Don't even think of stealing it," he warned, smacking his fist against the Silberblut Coupler's eye.

His body was enveloped in a burst of silver-gold flame, the undersuit forming just as both Seer and Tsetse recognized him. Simultaneously, they said, "Silberblut?!"

Tsetse knew better than to attack him mid-transformation; many modern low-mid grade couplers lacked the iconic Transformation Burst feature, but Tsetse, it seemed, either knew what it was or just had the good judgment to stay away from a man enveloped in golden fire. As his armor's numerous plates clicked into place and his arm-blade emerged, the Silberblut Coupler's stern voice echoed through the street. **"BLIND JUSTICE, THE LAWMAKER!"**

Silberblut took stock of the situation; Seer was backing away and feverishly trying to reload his howdah pistol, while Tsetse calmly approached. A shallow crater had been melted into the flyman's exoskeleton by Seer's attack, with rivulets of yellow hemolymph seeping out, but he seemed relatively unharmed. More than that, the wound was healing right then and there, the chitin melding back together and buckling outward. The scar was plain to see, and it would be a weak point until it healed properly, but such resilience was still astonishing. It was also extremely suspicious. Evoy could form barriers and wards just the same as anyone else, so why was he so poorly protected? A consideration passed Silberblut's mind, but he dismissed it. This couldn't be an Evoy version of Mamon Armor. Surely not.

Dashing in, Tsetse unleashed a barrage of side kicks against Silberblut, using the length of his legs to control the spacing. Despite using his arm-blade to defend himself, it couldn't get a good cut on the chitin of Tsetse's calves. It bulged outward strangely in the lower half, and its surface was extremely slick. It felt like trying to cut glass, and Tsetse's technique didn't make it any easier either. It was clear he was highly skilled in whatever bizarre martial art this was. Then, the punches came in. Without dropping his focus on kicks, Tsetse flexed his arms, causing the segments of his forearms to rise, exposing a fleshy membrane with three glassy orbs on each arm. With short punches, the orbs emitted a high-pitched noise and Silberblut felt as if he had been struck. The force was comparable to a Yellow Atropal. A sound-based concussive blaster of some kind. Minimal charge-up, great power output, so the flaw had to be range... And those membranes sure looked fragile.

This exchange continued for some time, high-pitched whirrs and thunderous impacts reverberating through the street. At one point, Silberblut got his fingers into an exoskeletal crease on Tsetse's upper foreleg, taking this opportunity to put his other arm to work by grabbing his foot. Tsetse blasted him in the chest twice in a row in an attempt to stop this, but by then Silberblut had already moved him enough that only one of the sonic blasts struck, and even this was a glancing blow. With a mighty heave, he swung Tsetse overhead and smashed him into the pavement. The man bounced; his chitin buckled and cracked in a few places with yellow bursting out, but its flexible nature absorbed much of the impact.

Grunting with anger and exertion, Tsetse punched the ground and blasted himself into a quasi-upright position. Silberblut let go as to not get dragged along, and Tsetse now spun on his free foot while using the one Silberblut had grabbed to now try to deliver a spinning kick. Silberblut let his knees fall out from under himself, bending backwards just in time. The strange bulge on Tsetse's lower leg had slid down and over the top of his foot, revealing a single large sonic lens. As the kick followed through, Silberblut heard a high-pitched whirr. A deep gash was torn across the facade of the building to his left.

He followed through on the momentum, delivering a downward spinning left hook. Silberblut had seen through it, and opened the Second Eye. In a bright flash, the force of Tsetse's blow was absorbed, and Silberblut was able to handspring backwards, onto his feet and into a safer range. Seer, at this point, fired two more Pale-Reds in quick succession, which Tsetse dodged, followed by a slow, deep-red missile. It was obviously positioned to try and catch Tsetse after dodging, but the flyman rushed towards it, closing within only a few steps of Seer... And punched the Reaper back the way it came. Rather than detonate, it imploded and fizzled out.

"Unlucky," Tsetse repeated yet again, turning his attention back towards Silberblut, even as he continued talking. "You put a safety primer on them. They don't detonate if it would hit you too. Heard you mention it once. Don't try to remember. I had a different face."

In the meanwhile, Silberblut had been looking for an opening, circling around, but even as he spoke, Tsetse meticulously kept up his guarded stance, adjusting to counter Silberblut's own changes in posture. Not wasting another moment, Tsetse closed the distance with a barrage of side kicks, but this time, every once in a while, he would fire one of the sonic emitters on his legs.

There was no way to predict when it would come besides trying to find a pattern, which Silberblut did find several of. Firstly, Tsetse favored his forward leg, maximizing range, while also using his opposite arm to attack. Secondly, he couldn't fire two of his sonic emitters at once, and there was a clear cooldown period for each of them. Thirdly, there wasn't a particular pattern to when he used the emitters, but there was a tell. The membrane shuddered a split-second before the equally split-second audible charge-up, giving him one third, perhaps four-tenths of a second to react to the tell. Silberblut hit the center of his belt to prime a coupler charge, feeling anathema pressure build within the device, waiting to be directed. A subtle aura of silver-gold flame built up around him.

Just after dodging a sonic blast punch, he slipped under Tsetse's leg and delivered an overhand casting punch, lodging his arm-blade right between two of the sonic lenses. Silberblut then raised his left arm to intercept Tsetse's right, positioning it perpendicularly to invalidate the sonic emitter, then released his coupler charge and the power he had captured with the Second Eye—a mere three of Tsetse's sonic punches, but it added up, especially with Tsetse. Something about him drove the Silberblut Coupler into a frenzy. It wasn't mere guilt; the belt reacted to anything and everything from someone's inner evil nature to the wretchedness of an existence, like the Tindalos graft-beast.

An outpouring of Anathema rushed into his arm. Silver flame came pouring out around his blade, and a jet of it erupted out of his elbow, pushing it further in. Tsetse's flesh came apart like wet paper with the flame tearing and shredding more than it burned.

Silberblut got halfway up his arm before the giant Evoy twisted free and used its blast to propel himself backwards, wings exploding out of his back at the same time. Despite the catastrophic damage to his limb, Tsetse appeared mostly unharmed. That didn't add up. Evoy didn't have compartmentalized bodies like that, and it seemed there was a cavity in the center of the upper arm.

For a few moments, they stood some ten meters across from one another in a standoff. Tsetse retracted his sonic emitters, only for several plates on his chest to slide out of the way and expose a dinner plate sized emitter lens. A rising whirr began to issue out of it as the surrounding membranes shuddered. The blood vessels within them bulged out, and then it died down as the covers slid back into place.

"No point. You're prepared. You would just turn it against me," he said, his apathetic tone now tinged by resignation and mild disappointment. His wings began beating, gradually speeding up as he turned his head to Seer. "Lucky."

Though he attempted to close the distance before Tsetse could flee, driven by the righteous will to exact the full extent of his deserved punishment upon Tsetse, Silberblut found himself thwarted. The flyman simply caught his blade by skewering his good hand upon it and leapt away into full flight a moment later, leaving the entirety of his forelimb seamlessly detached at the elbow.

Silberblut exerted a herculean force of will to draw back the flame of his arm-blade, instantly dropping out of his transformation and stumbling to the ground. He hadn't quite realized just how mighty all of Tsetse's blows had actually been; the immediate surroundings had been demolished by their fight, with several civilians worriedly peeking out through broken windows. It was, in part, due to the Silberblut Coupler's eponymous Silver Blood, which invasively reinforced his body from the inside; were his compatibility with the coupler sub-ideal, he would risk massive rejection each time he transformed. Even without taking a single hit, transforming left him sore all over for several hours—a painful side effect he fully prepared to bear. A few bloody coughs came up, their violent contractions making him distinctly aware he had some cracked ribs.

"Nothing broken, that's good..." he uttered as he got back up to his feet. He glanced around, and saw that Seer was gone. After reassuring the local civilians that the Seven Spokes would foot the repair bill and then some, he questioned them to see if someone had seen where Seer had gone. The three testimonies he got all lined up to suggest he had run off towards their original destination, which was the nearest branch temple. Casus ended up finding him just there, hunched over before the statue of Igaria muttering a generic prayer for protection that betrayed his lack of familiarity with real scripture.

"I hope you kept an eye on my mask."

Saying that made Seer jump up like a Reaper had just whizzed past his head. Once he realized it was Casus, however, he deflated with relief and gestured to one of the pews. After this, Seer was moved via a daisy chain of underground passages to a secure holding place beneath another Seven Spokes branch temple. Casus left him there for the time being while he went to visit an ordained grafter in one of the city's shrine clinics. Based on questioning the man, he brought Tsetse's forearm to a church-affiliated independent grafter known for his research into insectoid biology. His clinic happened to be halfway across the city, deep in the bowels of the unfinished tram line. Afterwards, he returned to the safehouse, arriving only two hours before Krahe.

* * *

It had become abundantly clear that Krahe had something to say about the incident the moment Casus mentioned the combination of a gambling house and the Evoy apartment building. She nonetheless waited until he was done before bringing it up, all the while bearing an unsettling smirk on her face.

"Well, well, well. Half a million each? How convenient. If 'Seer' can point the finger for us, we ought to go collect the bounty in person. Just hope he's reliable."

"What exactly would you have in mind for 'collecting the bounty in person?'"

"An anonymous individual makes contact with Semzar, offering to have us both brought before him at a given date. Semzar prepares the money and, quite likely, some sort of spectacle for Audunpoint's underworld, if he is as much of an idiot as I think he is. We show up and make Slaughterhouse Nine look like a fucking joke, possibly with church support depending on projected enemy forces. His father may even be involved in an attempt to redeem himself for getting me involved in the first place. He just talked about your capture in the open in a smokery. Can you believe that?"

"We shall know for sure in a few days once Seer has been properly interrogated and any leads he provides have been checked. I doubt that his case is anywhere near high-profile enough to grab the attention of the inquisition, but..."

"Hold, hold, stop. You mentioned inquisitors earlier. Explain."

"They are an arm of the Inner Wheel specializing in investigation and severe edge cases. For instance, if you had not gotten involved with my kidnapping, and if one of the Hashems took my body for himself, an inquisitor could have investigated the case and carried out judgment. I've only met inquisitors a handful of times. Severe people. Scarily competent. Not well known besides the fact their powers of truth extraction are nearly unmatched."

"Secret church police. Outstanding!"

"Comparing inquisitors to night watchmen is a severe insult. An Inquisitor's work is not so far from yours, they are nothing less than specialist investigators for the Inner Wheel."

"I'll be sure to be more respectful if I ever meet an inquisitor. Wouldn't want to be accused of heresy and burned at the stake."

Seeing the confused look which she received for that statement, Krahe exhaled and said, "The inquisition had extremely negative connotations in my world. Let's move onto Tsetse, give me more specific details. I've got an uneasy feeling that one of us will run into him again. Start with those sonic emitters."

Krahe questioned Casus on Tsetse's combat characteristics for some time afterward, going so far as to draw out a surprisingly accurate diagram. Her rendering of Tsetse's forearm got astonishingly close after a few rounds of edits.

"Still, the absence of either wards or barriers is worrying. Combined with everything else, I almost want to guess he might have been some evoy version of Mamon Armor. If not that, maybe he was grafted to be as close to a war-morph as he could get. Despite the absence of orthodox wards, his armor did hold up against Silberblut, and he did keep up with you in that form..."

CHAPTER 14

LOST SUN KILLER MYTH: TYING UP LOOSE ENDS

Days passed. Krahe couldn't find an easy route of ingress into Sorayah's home, until she tested the route that was often forgotten—entering from above. Climbing a nearby building, Krahe got onto the roof of Sorayah's home and skimmed down. Hot, stale air assaulted her and the darkness of a disused attic choked her senses. After getting some light by pouring thauma into her arm she saw that the attic was completely empty, and had clearly not been used in a long while. She took a moment to bring a small DD-fuelled light out of storage, using a small tendril to affix it to her shoulder. Krahe didn't even try skimming down again, assuming the presence of wards; she simply looked around and found the door. It was old, dusty, and didn't even have a lock, but it didn't open, suggesting a latch at the other side. Its hinges were on this side, however.

Krahe left, deciding to prepare before committing. She sourced a tubular lock pick from Garvesh, and learned that, apparently, artifacts and talismans capable of breaking local wards were fairly difficult to come by. And so, Krahe gave up on subtlety. If she had the time, she would've tried to source such an item or even develop a Theurgy capable of it, but as she saw it, she didn't have that much time. Sorayah's case was a loose end that needed tying up. It didn't need to be a perfect, cleanly executed ghost operation.

She returned the next day around two hours before Sorayah usually came home, once more skimming into the attic. Ten minutes and a few usages of the Forming Toroid later, Krahe had succeeded in knocking the hinge pins out and propped the door against the wall. A narrow stairway led directly to a hallway on the floor below. The house was quite small, with one bedroom, a reading room, kitchen, and basement. Rugs, wood, bronze, and semiprecious stones made up the decorations, with simple glowing stones set into the walls as lights. It was, just like much of Audunpoint, an ancient building that had been renovated.

The bedroom was locked and warded, as was the basement, but the same couldn't be said for the kitchen or the reading room. She picked the locks on both, taking only a few minutes for each, given the fact the locks weren't particularly strong and didn't have any particular anti-picking measures. There was nothing suspicious in the kitchen, unsurprisingly. Going through the reading room, Krahe found a variety of books, including several interesting books on the interactions between theurgy and anathemism, none of which were to be found in the Society's library. There was also a complete copy of Burning Torment Wrought in Black, and fragmentary copies of several Human Charcoal Letters. Besides occult texts, a surprising volume of Sorayah's personal collection was made up of human-saurian interspecies smut.

Unfortunately, Krahe didn't find any spare keys inside a book, even after searching the writing desk and finding three different hidden drawers. One of these contained a smut manuscript involving a painfully obvious self-insert being taken advantage of by men whose appearances lined up a bit too closely with members of the Society. It also got human sexual anatomy comically wrong, ascribing them with what Krahe assumed to be Saurian traits.

What she did find, however, was a book that lit up as an anathema hazard on the Prospector's Eyes, far out of reach on a high shelf. After getting it down with a tar tendril, Krahe found it to be locked with a padlock that had no keyhole. Trying to get into Sorayah's mindset under the assumption this was one of her locks and not just something she had found, the first thing she thought to try was to simply pour some anathema into it. At first, it didn't work. The lock lit up with runes, only for a snap to sound from inside. Gradually, after a number of attempts, Krahe got it open by pouring in as little anathema as she could. It was a tiny amount, the smallest she had ever produced at one time, and it felt horrid. Barely starting the fusion reaction only to snuff it out felt *wrong*.

While Krahe shuddered in place at the unpleasant feeling, lines of eldritch runes pulsed over the lock's surface and it popped open. The book was indeed hollow, containing a poorly shielded box within which there sat a piece of coal shaped like a human hand. IIt couldn't be described as charcoal, as its surface had a gleaming luster, with an orange glow only coming out of a few thin cracks and the cross-section of the wrist. It was much closer to anthracite in appearance. It constantly radiated anathema, twitching in a claw-like rigor as if it was still attached, and as if its owner was in the throes of terrible pain.

"Ohoho, there's exhibit A..." she uttered as she smiled to herself. Truthfully, Krahe wasn't even slightly opposed to making use of anything she found for herself. If human charcoal could be used to somehow boost her own capabilities, she would use it. However, given its documented uses, she didn't expect this to be the case. Every application seemed to be some variation of allowing the user to control Thaumic Fusion and/or to shield herself from exposure.

Krahe closed the hollow book, set it down on the writing desk, and sat down with the chair turned to the door, gun in hand. While she waited, she read through Sorayah's manuscript. She couldn't take it seriously in any sense of the word, and ended up turning her attention to the other texts, such as a book on theurgy titled "Dreaming of Hyperion Shore."

Around two-thirds of the way through the first chapter, the front door opened. Krahe continued waiting, listening to Sorayah walk around for a few minutes, watching her through Barzai's eyes. Then, abruptly, her footsteps stopped in the hallway outside the writing room. She had realized that something was amiss—the door was ajar.

Barzai saw her conjure a brass apparatus, presumably from her own Kenoma Pocket, resembling a bullseye lantern. Soon enough, Krahe was staring her in the face. She conjured a cigarette, raising it to her lips as Sorayah stared at her with a mixture of bewilderment and pure, seething hate. An angry-red spotlight spilled out of her lantern, containing a continuous stream of faint anathema. The way it scattered strangely looked like two beams converged into one.

"*You...*" she hissed.

"What? *Me*?" Krahe laughed. "Did you assume I was dead just because I stopped showing up at the Society? Did you really think the *amateurs* you sent actually succeeded? I admit I didn't leave much in the way of survivors that could report back, or even identifiable corpses, but c'mon. You didn't hear back from them, and it didn't seem suspicious? Even a little bit?"

"I assumed they *taught you a lesson* that you took *to heart*."

"My, so intimidating. Let me guess; that lantern has human charcoal in it and you intend to blast me with anathema. Is that right?"

Sorayah didn't answer, but her grip on the lantern tightened, and her eyes narrowed.

"Well? Hit me. Better turn me into a shadow fried into your carpet all at once. *Better make sure it kills me in one hit.* Y'know what? Let's make it easier for you to pull the trigger. Let's go to your basement, shall we? That's where you carry out the final step to turn your victims into human charcoal, isn't it? I'm sure you won't be so hesitant when your interspecies porno isn't at risk of getting incinerated alongside me. Y'know, I've seen my share, and I'm fairly certain human penises don't actually have bones in them, and they certainly don't have *knots*."

A noise somewhere between an angry snake's hiss and an angry crocodile's rumble began to issue from Sorayah, her throat visibly reverberating. Her teeth ground together, and she gripped the lantern ever tighter. Even the beam grew in intensity as something mechanical inside the device moved, now starting to lightly burn away at Krahe's wards. Nonetheless, Sorayah backed out of the door, slowly, keeping both her eyes and the lantern pointed at Krahe. To her surprise, that offhanded suggestion had worked. She had fully expected to be breaking into a dead woman's basement ten minutes from now, but it seemed Sorayah's sensibility—or perhaps love for her book collection—won out.

Krahe, not yet trying to stand up, casually picked up the hollow book.

"Leave it!" Sorayah snapped. "Get up. If you want to see the basement before you die, I can give you that much." Her attempt at control sounded feeble, her voice far too angry and not nearly confident enough. Krahe couldn't help but derive great amusement from this classical scenario; Sorayah's demeanor reeked of a serial killer caught metaphorically with her pants down, thrown far off-kilter, struggling to convince herself she was still in control.

Her original intention was to split her forearm open lengthwise while placing the item into her Kenoma Pocket, but she decided against it. Considering that course of action triggered a revulsion akin to the thought of consuming something far beyond one's ability. So, she did leave it. A puzzled expression came over Sorayah when she saw that the lock was undone, but she maintained her focus on Krahe while backing out into the hallway. Krahe followed, openly raising her barrier as she went. It had changed quite noticeably. The swirling umbrella of grayish ash and smoke had grown darker, and glistening, obsidian-like chips were now included within it.

Sorayah stopped some distance down the hallway. Her features tensed, and she raised the lantern. Something inside it moved, and the beam narrowed down to a diameter even smaller than Krahe's barrier, shifting in hue towards purple. Then, in a near instant, a deluge of strange sigils burst out, crackling with an eldritch energy that was neither lightning, nor fire, nor any single definable force. The charge-up was far faster than she had expected, and since she hadn't seen the minimal telegraphing before, she had no way to predict when the artifact would fire.

Despite Astro Diving on reflex right when the beam hit, even the quarter-second of blocking it had built up an intimidating amount of hard entropy. The beam had to be anywhere from two and a half to five times stronger than Krahe's strongest Cinder Flash, based on whether it was Energetic or Arcane in nature. If it was Energetic, it would completely obliterate her wards and fry the living hell out of her if she got hit straight on. If it was Arcane, she wagered she might be able to weather one hit and be fine. Two hits would definitely be very fucking bad, but maybe survivable if it hit a particularly resilient area like her left arm or anywhere armored by her Biosuit. These were all worst-case scenarios, of course. Krahe wouldn't take the risk of eating another hit head-on.

Seeing Sorayah's eyes go wide and her stance falter at the sight of her astral form, Krahe surfaced once again.

"The flame of a candle," she lied.

But Sorayah didn't know that. She was too busy reeling from the backlash of Krahe's barrier. Angry serpents made of smoke and ash manifested in her vicinity and spewed outbursts of burning cinders at the lizard woman with unerring accuracy, their flame reddened by Isotope and their constituent smoke a rich, sooty black from the abundance of hard entropy. It was burning filth in the purest sense.

Five seconds passed. Sorayah, wild-eyed, raised the lantern again. The charge-up was even shorter this time, but Krahe reacted based on the tensing of Sorayah's arm and avoided the vast majority of the blast with another dive. Nonetheless, the attack did graze her, and what little she had to block still filled up over two-thirds of her entropy tolerance. Even then, it felt like being sprayed with acid in the way the Isotope-filled blast corroded her wards and wormed into her. One more blast like that would fill her arm's ability to contain, and it wouldn't take much more after that to make her get sick.

"I don't know what you expected. I can just keep doing that, y'know. While I admit that there is some effort to *doing it*, your attacks can't affect me once I've transformed... And I'd wager you can't fire that thing faster than I can disperse what little entropy nullifying its effects costs me," Krahe lied again, omitting the five-second dive recovery time. She took a step forward, prompting Sorayah to take a step back, grasping the lantern with her other arm much like someone whose giant penis-metaphor revolver just bounced off of a cyborg's subdermal armor. She started manipulating something in the lantern's rear for the third time, and the beam began narrowing for the third time, but Krahe interrupted her—

"I wouldn't. I gave you two chances, and there won't be a third. Next time I'll dislocate your arms instead of just standing here. Now be smart and take me to your basement."

"You can't expect me to believe that you can break my wards that quickly. Mine are especially resilient."

Krahe stepped forward as if preparing to sprint, skimmed towards Sorayah, and mid-skim adjusted her exit position and facing so she would come out into a ground slide, or as close as she could with her current Control attribute. It was rough at best—she slammed onto the ground in a somewhat awkward slide-kick position, but her momentum carried her through and the smooth rug provided some assistance. She was able to get behind Sorayah in the commotion. The Saurian exerted a level of strength and grapple resistance well beyond what her size suggested, but Krahe had three things that allowed her to come on top:

Firstly, knowledge of real grappling arts. This included bits from various martial arts learned throughout her life, followed by the mnemonic imprints for the *Whitestone and Bergmann Security Grappling Manual V.3* burned into her memory, all culminating with Sector 7 Style's brutal joint-locks designed to counter an opponent's superior strength and exploit the common weak points of most cyborgs.

Secondly, the Left Arm of Chernobog. Specifically, it was the unique property that had allowed her to lift a man weighing more than a hundred kilos back in Cassius's—or rather, Seer's—gambling house. The Left Arm's physical attributes grew not just based on her own pure strength, but also her arcane attributes. At this point, it was far stronger than her right arm.

Thirdly, *tar*; she could throw the full weight of her magic into a grapple through Tar-tendrils.

By exploiting all three of these factors to the fullest, Krahe managed to get Sorayah into an arm-lock. In the process, the Saurian had fired two more blasts from her artifact, imprinting reams of purple, smoldering eldritch script into the walls and carpet.

"I won't *need* to break them, unless you've got some truly special wards that protect against grappling," she hissed into Sorayah's ear. "Now drop the artifact or I'll make you drop it."

"I cannot. It's volatile. Who knows what will happen if I let go."

With a smirk, Krahe extended the tendril she had winding down Sorayah's arm and wrapped it around the lantern.

"No excuses. Let go."

Sorayah didn't, so Krahe wrenched her arm—not enough to dislocate the shoulder, but enough to make it abundantly clear that she was able and willing to do so. It was not out of mercy, but because Krahe didn't want to risk the possibility of the basement's wards requiring both hands to open. Once she had the lantern grasped in a Tar-tendril, Krahe skimmed backwards, raising her arms into the firing configuration of Wandrei Faust.

"Basement. Now."

A few uneasy minutes later, Sorayah unlocked the door and proceeded to move her hands over its surface. Her palms, held in stiff gestures, snapped through a sequence of three specific positions while Sorayah uttered a sequence of three inaudible keywords.

When it finally swung open, Krahe ensured that the two of them stepped in at the same time so that Sorayah couldn't try slamming the door in her face. Beyond was a short stairway into the earth, leading into the basement proper. It was fairly spacious, a single large rectangular room, mostly plain, smoothed stone. It resembled a laboratory of a sort, with bookshelves and a large L-shaped table that included a sink in its design. A mixture of glassware and occult implements made from a mixture of brass and strange dark stone were strewn across its surface. Shards of coal-like material pulsing with red light were suspended in clamps, contained in flasks, and so on. A few of them could be recognized as human parts—mostly fingers, toes, and other such small pieces. None of them moved like the hand in the book; in fact, none of them quite looked like it either, truly resembling charcoal. Krahe realized what the hand reminded her of: high-grade rock coal, anthracite.

On the left side of the room, Krahe saw the door she had tried to break through earlier, barely visible behind a large device that was shaped like a vending machine, clearly placed there as a barricade. It was a power supply unit, based on the tank with Thaumine sloshing about inside, and the black cable hanging from it and snaking to the various devices through the room.

"Are these your best results?" Krahe asked, glancing towards the table. She decided to pretend she knew more than she truly did, making the assumption that Sorayah hadn't gotten far in her research.

"Yes. My materials have been sub-par. Perhaps we could work together—"

"Very compelling offer, I'll consider it," Krahe interrupted facetiously. "Move, open the next door."

As Sorayah carried out the same unlocking and ward opening procedure as before, Krahe added, "If you've only gotten so far with the resources available to you, it means I caught you early."

She was just blowing smoke, of course, speaking from extremely fragmentary evidence and wild assumptions. But it had its effect nonetheless, and Sorayah, with shaking hands, opened the door. Forcing her through the door and sticking close, Krahe was struck by a grim sight.

The walls, floor, and ceiling were all reinforced by metal sheets, crudely riveted into the walls and glimmering with enchanted runes, with the exception of a 2m wide circle in the middle of the room. In it knelt a man with his arms chained to the ceiling, or rather, what had once been a man. He had turned completely into glowing charcoal, radiating heat and anathema, the burnt scraps of high-quality clothing still hanging off of him. His posture was arched and tense, knees wide, face contorted in a voiceless, agonized grimace. Not screaming, but rather with gritted teeth. Around him, filling the circle, was a layered, extraordinarily complex glyph carved into the stone. Dried blood filled its grooves. Krahe tried to discern whether the man had been cut, but with the number of straight, narrow cracks covering him, she couldn't tell whether any of them were simple cuts.

Walking around, dragging Sorayah along, she noticed a hammer and chisel on the ground just outside the circle. The man's right leg had been chipped off halfway up the calf. She'd seen worse, much worse, but Krahe was nonetheless disgusted at the scene. Even if it wouldn't haunt her, even if it couldn't unsettle her to the point of tremors, that grimace of torment still sparked a visceral blend of disgust and anger somewhere deep inside. It would've died out, buried under decades of growing numbness, but she stoked it, gladly taking the ember of righteous fury into her mind's hand.

"In the corner. Now," Krahe said, pointing at the far end of the room with one hand and shoving Sorayah with the other.

"Really? It gets to you *that much*? I've seen the posters. You must've done far worse than I if the Hashems want you dead so badly." Sorayah scoffed, but she nonetheless did as she was told.

"To feel disgust and anger at the sight of evil is no sin, and to tolerate it is no virtue."

"There is no such thing in the scriptures of the Twin Churches."

"I didn't say it was. I also didn't say I was an apostle," Krahe said, approaching within the Forming Toroid's range. Raising her hand, she pointed her gun at Sorayah.

"Don't move, I won't shoot you..." she trailed off. The Forming Toroid began to glow and Krahe flicked her wrist, using the gun as a pointer. In moments, Sorayah was restrained by a series of smoky jade rods.

"Wgh—What is that? Archon-forged?" Sorayah questioned, audibly struggling to keep herself together. The panic was starting to overtake her voice. Krahe didn't care much. Oh, she was sure that Sorayah was sorry; sorry that she got caught; sorry she encountered a fish too big for her.

"Correct. I get it, you're clever. It won't save you."

Krahe conjured and lit a cigarette, taking a drag as she observed the man-turned-coal.

"That phrase about evil—a philosopher in a faraway land said it, once, thousands of years ago. You know what happens now, don't you? I promised to show you *real anathemism. D*id I not? Barzai, come."

She outstretched her left hand. The eidolon simply stopped hiding and flew into her palm.

"Why?" Sorayah questioned.

"You came after me. I warned you. You persevered. Actions, consequences," Krahe deadpanned. Slowly, tendrils began to grow out of her arm, forming a hemispherical nest in which Barzai stood.

"No. Not me! Why?!" Sorayah demanded, growing audibly frustrated. "The Society, the Talisman Mistress, everything. You're a saint; don't pretend otherwise. Only the Temple of Records holds texts listed as the Human Charcoal Letters, and only a saint would have such high-level access. I know. I tried, through an apostle who owed me. What I don't understand is why you would come after me. I am of no consequence. The Grafting Church doesn't send saints after small-fries like me. They're too busy dealing with things like rogue grafters and body theft. Am I just... a diversion? A convenient notch to pad your record with?! *That's* all my hard work to unearth these ancient arts will amount to?!"

By the end, Sorayah was nearly screaming.

Krahe turned to look at her.

"You put yourself in my sights at a time when I was looking for a target to test *this* on." She glanced at her left hand. "Just bad luck. Is that what you want to hear? It's *half* of the truth. The other half is that, in truth, I would have come for you sooner or later. Surely, you can't have deluded yourself into thinking what you are doing is permissible."

"You still haven't answered me. Why?!" Sorayah demanded, wild-eyed and ignoring what was happening in Krahe's left hand in favor of locking her gaze on her To facilitate their conversation, Krahe kept Barzai as he was, simply building the shell around him, fully aware that she could will him to transform into the core at any moment.

After staring into those wild eyes for a few moments, Krahe explained herself: "This is what I do. This is what I am. I *don't know how* to do anything else. After you, it will be Semzar Hashem. After him, his father. After him, whomever is pulling his strings. I mean to follow the roots of infestation spreading through this land all the way to the source, because evil has a name. A face. Perhaps a mansion and a family. Many of society's ills do not spring up from nothing. There are oft-powerful men who proliferate them, perhaps for their own gain or because they are driven by an ideology. And just as evil has a face, so does the hand that will strangle the puppet master with his own strings; you're looking at it. *That* is what I am."

"You're mad," said a wide-eyed Sorayah in a hushed tone. "So what? You mean to just keep killing until the world is 'rid of evil?!'"

"Come now," she sneered. "The world is much too large for one woman to personally fry every shitbag businessman into his office chair. A gardener never runs out of weeds to pluck. I only need to make sure I never get the wrong man! Easy enough."

At this point, Krahe was just messing with Sorayah, purposely using extreme rhetoric while remaining quasi-accurate to her true beliefs. Alas, nuance didn't make for a good monologue.

"What of the churches, then?! You don't mean to claim—"

"What makes you think I *won't* come after a corrupt priest? By rights, I ought to root out corruption within the church with absolute prejudice. It would be a disservice to the divine not to do so. It's almost time now—there won't be much left of you after this; just a shadow on the wall. I'm sure the higher-ups would prefer it if I just pulled out your voidkey and had you taken in for questioning, but I *did* promise to show you *real anathemism...*"

"No, wait! Wait, wait, wait! Please! I don't need to see it, and my key, it's—"

Sorayah desperately thrashed against her restraints. Krahe genuinely didn't understand why she hadn't tried to fight back or free herself; surely, she wasn't so reliant on that lantern device as to be incapable of normal thaumaturgy. Or perhaps she was smart, and rightly thought that fighting back would only serve to worsen her situation.

"-it's here. Take it, just don't kill me," she said, twisting her head. A sigil on her neck began to glow - it was a triangle with small circles at its corners, each circle containing an eldritch sigil. They were some of the same sigils as those which filled the ritual circle. Sorayah gritted her teeth, hissing, and a hexagonal rod bearing that triangular mark slowly emerged from her scales. It was an extraordinarily simple design in physical shape, this simplicity offset by the fact its body was covered with countless more angular patterns with sigils in circles at the angles. Krahe's mind immediately jumped to circuitry.

It looked to be a stony, reddish material at first, only to seamlessly transition to the anthracite-like, glowing material one-third of the way down its length.

"The church will reward you more for bringing me in alive. You should know that!"

Krahe manifested a tar tendril, using it to reach over and begin pulling on the key. Though it took quite a bit of effort, it came out without incident. It was around 20cm in length, with its lower 2/3 made from the same anthracite-like matter as the hand. She didn't bother to appraise it yet, slipping it into her pocket, because her attention was solely on Sorayah. The saurian looked disappointed and frustrated; despite trying to hide it, Krahe noticed the shift in her demeanor and the rumbling in her throat. For this reason, Krahe kept her hand in her pocket, fusion-forming a smoke burster packed with as much isotope as she could fit. Out of sight and beyond her notice, concealed by clothing, reams of eldritch symbology pulsed across Sorayah's back, eidolons swimming beneath her skin like predatory fish waiting to leap out of the water.

"Disappointed that I didn't come close enough for you to set off a contingency or something of the sort? Come on." Krahe scoffed. "What kind of fool did you take me for? Every member of the Society is a theurge, and you were a high-ranking one. Of course you would have contingencies."

Raising her left hand just above her head, she willed Barzai to collapse into the Daemon Core. Despite the lack of need for an incantation, Krahe nonetheless recited one, to see if Sorayah would try to interrupt it.

"Lei-Amul, Thelder, Wandrei, great sages of the Astral Gulf, hold fast the Three Keys and uncoil the chains that bind—"

As expected, Sorayah's pupils became hair-thin lines and she emitted a shrill, ear-splitting screech. Her entire body was enveloped in pulsating strings of runes, and, on reflex, Krahe decided to dive while she finished casting. She had seen these runes displayed earlier during their confrontation at the Society, but this time, they were far denser and brighter, and they leapt off of Sorayah's skin, lashing her surroundings.

The Saurian freed herself and carved deep gashes into everything around her in an instant; the human charcoal fell apart, scattering into pieces. Krahe honestly wasn't sure why she hadn't done this sooner, but the reason revealed itself when she got a look at Sorayah and saw that she hadn't been entirely spared, either. There were deep gashes covering her whole body, all the way into the meat. Moreover, she seemed to have become feral, based on her hunched stance, bestially heavy breathing, and glazed-over eyes.

"Where..." Sorayah growled, looking around. Her eyes locked onto Krahe, and she lunged across the room. With that leap, yet more reams of script exploded out of her, shredding the ceiling and floor, but passing through Krahe unimpeded. Being able to see it up close and while partly submerged in the Gulf, Krahe got a front row seat to serpent-like creatures covered in those runes tearing their way out of their master's body before transforming fully into their theurgic forms.

It was done.

Krahe emerged from her dive, raising her hand.

Sorayah leapt right at her without a moment wasted, but by the time she or her absurdly lethal, self-destructive theurgy could reach Krahe, she had already burned both her skim charges to get out of the way.

Desperation—and with it, sapience—flashed over Sorayah's contorted features. With a swing of her arm, arabesque runes flashed down its length. A deep gash along the same spiral appeared on the limb as the runes tore themselves free, lashing towards the Daemon Core rather than Krahe herself. A last-ditch effort to try and shoot down the theurgic vessel before it could carry out its function.

It was too late.

The spear of eldritch script did pierce the shell, but it only hastened Sorayah's demise.

A narrow beam of red light shot out, accompanied by a thunderous buzzing sound. It obliterated both Sorayah's theurgy and her arm, and before she could even scream in pain, it expanded to consume her entirely.

Then, just as quickly as it had begun, the deluge was over, and a disjointed shadow had been burned into the reinforced metal that covered the ritual chamber's interior.

CHAPTER 15

AND YET, LOOSE ENDS REMAIN

A flaw of the Daemon Core had already become apparent due to its overwhelming firepower; Krahe didn't know how to get souldregs out of a nuclear shadow. Being a problem that she could only try to avoid moving forward, she left the scene as it was. Undisturbed. Her chest briefly split open down the middle as Barzai, now a formless mass of smoldering smoke, returned into the confines of her soul.

She returned to the lab, and there read through Sorayah's notes. Much of the material pertained to translations of the code used in her source texts, as well as attempts at improving the ritual. Clinical descriptions, one after another, described the macabre failures of her efforts. After four subjects that died after only partial transmutation, Sorayah had given up and returned to the original method.

Mentions of a particular item stood out—the locked book. That was how it was referred to, as it had no external identifying markings besides the fact it was locked. Sorayah seemed to be completely stumped by what it was or how to open it, describing several unlocking experiments that had led her to believe somehow exposing it to anathema could be the key, but that was as far as she had gotten. From these notes, Krahe also learned that the book had been found in the same place as the hexagonal voidkey, but the specific place was referred to only as "the dig site."

Krahe took care to minimize how much she disturbed Sorayah's workspace, as she had not yet decided whether to keep the case of the Lost Sun Killer Myth to herself, report it to the church, or to do something between these two extremes. One of the considerations in her mind, despite the wretchedness of it, was the potential usefulness of human charcoal. Sorayah's stock of the substance was already made, and even the church's disposal method involved burning it down to ash after a fashion—so if it turned out to be useful to her, simply handing it over would be wasteful and pointless.

In the course of going through Sorayah's home more thoroughly, things turned out to be inconveniently nuanced.

Everything that Krahe was able to find, from texts in the lab to those in the library, pertained to the process of turning someone into human charcoal and to artifacts that directly burned human charcoal as fuel. The problem came in with the mention of a substance described as "Black-flesh Jewel" in the older, more mystical texts. Meanwhile, newer fragments in Sorayah's possession referred to the same substance in more grounded terms: "anthrocite" or "astral rock coal."

Over the course of a few hours, Krahe arrived at two undeniable conclusions. Whomever invented and developed these occult arts had clearly gone much further than just human charcoal, and the Human Charcoal Letters didn't reveal the full scope and severity of the goings-on during the century they spoke of. To say she was surprised would have been a bald-faced lie.

Krahe honestly wasn't sure what course of action to take, but she had the small comfort of knowing that Sorayah wasn't likely to have visitors any time soon, at least speaking on the time scale of weeks. With that in mind, Krahe took the keyring Sorayah had left inside the ritual chamber's doors, as well as the one with the house keys. After placing Sorayah's lantern, the locked book, and several samples of human charcoal into her Kenoma Sack, he left the place behind for now. The key, after closer inspection, was not entirely homogeneous in shape. The side of it which would be inserted had a narrow hexagonal hole about a centimeter across and of an indeterminate depth.

After spending the rest of the day looking into the Human Charcoal Letters at the Temple of Records, she reconvened with Casus at the safehouse and, since she needed his assistance in this matter, let him know of what had transpired.

"As Mamon Knight Silberblut, I would say she met a fate rightly deserved... Though I would likely put it less politely. Out of the armor, however, I cannot help but feel she would have been more useful if she had been interrogated in an official setting," Casus remarked, drinking his coffee and reading a book as was typical of him. This time, he had borrowed Krahe's copy of *De Re Theurgia*.

He turned his gaze up from the book in his hands, nodding towards the hexagonal voidkey standing upright on the coffee table. "You mentioned that you managed to coax her into giving over her voidkey and needed help identifying it. Is that right?"

"I wouldn't say there was much convincing on my part, she tried to use it as bait to get me within range of her last-ditch theurgy attack... But yes, I do need it identified."

Unsurprisingly, Sorayah's voidkey had robust anti-appraisal enchantments. Casus managed to break them after trying for a few minutes. He described them as "fortress walls built to hide an ancient mausoleum."

"They're new. I would guess they were made by Sorayah herself or by someone on her behalf," he clarified afterwards. "Rather than being incorporated into the key's construction, they were merely layered around it. Moreover, there are traces of anathema—er, isotope suppression glyphs, never activated. Whatever radiation the key gives off, it is merely *very close* to anathema. Give me a moment..."

Casus got up, returning with an Oculon-branded device and a handful of bronze memslates. Its design language was the same as the eyebox Krahe had taken from the dead prospector, but it was thrice as large and far more complex. It very slightly resembled a 20th-century tape recorder in shape.

It had sockets for four memslates, a more expansive keyboard, and a row of cable sockets on one side. A vial of thaumine sloshed around on the other side.

Casus popped in a pair of memslates and plugged a black cable into the device. Nerve-like endings surged to life from the cable to complete the connection when brought near one of the sockets. With a hiss and the turn of a locking ring, the cable was connected. At its other end was a flat, key-like plug, and much like a voidkey, Casus inserted it into his temple.

After a few seconds of focus and unsettling undulations going down the cable, he disconnected himself and popped the memslates out, handing one over. "The appraisal readings. I would strongly suggest that you report the case to the Grafting Church. Besides being properly rewarded for resolving it, you would be able to easily levy support, such as access to restricted information relevant to the case."

"Yeah, I know, I know…" Krahe snapped offhandedly as she popped the memslate into her eyebox. Logically, she knew she would likely only benefit from reporting the case, but she didn't *want to*. The same part of her that fundamentally distrusted large organizations also made her overthink the consequences of involving the church. Would the church ride her ass for killing Sorayah? What would they confiscate besides just the human charcoal? Krahe figured she could keep the house untouched for some time under the guise of investigating the scene, but that wouldn't last forever. Her eyebox took a moment to project the appraisal readout. It was garbled and barely legible, an issue fixed by replacing the DD battery.

While she looked over the record, she got started on placing the Hexkey into storage, not wanting to have it sitting out and about where it could be seen or Zavesh-forbid scried for. As far as she was concerned, it was safer inside her Kenoma Sack, shrouded by the Deathsmoke Blessing.

The characteristics of Sorayah's voidkey explained why she didn't wield thaumaturgy in self defense; It wasn't intended for thaumaturgy. The "Flame's Collapse Hexkey" was a cursed relic that, upon implantation, would grant the user the *"Collapsing Flame"* Boon. This boon would make it easier for the user to carry out Thaumic Fusion while severely worsening their ability to burn thauma normally. The curse part came into play in two ways:

Firstly, the boon wouldn't go away even if the key was removed, but it *would* degenerate into Collapsed Flame; a version without the positive effect, until the key was reimplanted.

Secondly, it contained a unique theurgic pattern. By applying this pattern, the user could brand others with a cursed mark that would confer a version of the Collapsing Flame boon, tying it back to the curse-layer, so at any point the user could pull out the key to cripple everyone they had cursed in exchange for also crippling themselves. The *Hexbrand Curse* made the victim constantly aware of these facts, but it also concealed that it artificially induced the beginning stages of adustocorpus, starting from the spot where the curse mark was branded onto the victim. The key specified that the curse mark would vanish and remain invisible unless in the near vicinity of the curse-layer, and that removing the flesh it was on would just cause it to move.

Moreover, it granted a second boon, "Pyremaster," which was exclusive to the user. This boon would enable the user to easily carry out the rites that would initiate and accelerate a victim's adustocorpus, as well as the rites to finish the full transmutation into human charcoal.

It had the usual features as a normal voidkey, sure, but despite being classed as fourth-order it was barely better than Shiva's Warding Chain in attribute reinforcement. As a ward and barrier catalyst, it was basic, with only low-level hardening. Its best feature was how it affected the user's powers as a theurge, granting three additional Lesser Eidolon Vaults and strengthening all theurgies. This was obviously intended to make its features usable even for someone without their own natural eidolon vaults.

Despite everything, despite the Hexkey's foreboding nature and the implications of its creation, the most alarming was the last line in the "Details" section.

"This voidkey's characteristics will evolve when Anthrocite Transmutation reaches 100%."

The Anthrocite Transmutation gauge was right below, sitting at 63.71%.

"An evolving voidkey, huh?"

"I have never heard of such a thing, but I can see how it would explain its classification—it must be in relation to its potential. I would guess that key's fulfilled potential would likely be at least fourth-order, else I cannot see how it would be worthwhile. The question is—"

Krahe interrupted him. "How does the transmutation progress? My first guess would be feeding it human charcoal, perhaps through a ritual or a specialized tool. I did not find any such thing in Sorayah's home, but she may have had it in personal storage... Speaking of, what happens to the contents—"

This time, Casus interrupted. "Of someone's Kenoma storage after death? It drifts away, just like their True Soul. Sometimes the items return naturally, and sometimes the Wheel catches them, outfitting its Banishers with them or using them as rewards. They might get caught by an Archon Flash and return as archon-forged versions of themselves. Your bracelet was likely one of those. There are rites for detecting and summoning a Kenoma Storage stash, but it must be very soon after someone's death. The church—"

For the third and final time, Krahe interrupted. "Can help me with it. I get it, you want me to report the case. Fine. I needed to look something up in the Temple of Records anyway."

With that, she took the Hexkey and left. Why did she feel so irritated? She genuinely couldn't tell.

She had also not told him the whole truth; before heading to the Temple of Records, she went to her second home on Gashward Road 94. At this point, she had managed to outfit it with some ultra-basic furniture on top of the exercise equipment, but it wasn't much. Frankly, if it was an option, she would be willing to take Sorayah's home for herself. That was assuming someone else didn't lay a claim to the property, but even then, Krahe was sure she could take most of the furniture as "evidence" to furnish Gashward Road 94.

After secreting herself away in the basement gym, she brought out the locked book to inspect it in detail. Immediately, something caught her eye. The twitching hand clasped an additional piece of anthracite-like stone, worked into the shape of a narrow rectangle.

When she took it out, Krahe still felt it giving off a faint, barely noticeable aura of anathema. Its surface was inscribed with two lines of writing, the stone's glow illuminating it. It was a bit tricky to read due to the text's tiny size and differences from what she had grown used to reading. It wasn't clear print-type, but rather stylized calligraphy. Krahe assumed it was due to the age of these two items, but after getting a good look at the anthrocite slip, she managed to decipher it.

"For ye, who hath mastered the high magic: Burn this hand of mine to fuel thine ambitions."

"It should suffice to complete my key, if you have not done so already."

She was still suspicious of it, of course, and so she closed the book and locked it up again. The lock now obeyed as easily as her glasses. It would be a convenient little trinket in the future, especially once she put it on a more resilient box or at least had the book reinforced. For all its craftsmanship, the shielding inside the book was *leaky*. But then, perhaps it was by design if whoever had put it where Sorayah found it *wanted* it to be found. For now, she tucked it away behind a rack of weight plates.

She spent a short time experimenting with Sorayah's Lantern, and learned that it rejected her; she could neither control nor appraise it. Thus, she placed it into her Kenoma Sack. The human charcoal still loaded in it made this a laborious process.

While she had the sack open, she retrieved a change of clothes; a darker, closer-fit pair of trousers, as well as the ice-user's jacket and a pair of gloves to conceal her arm. To finish, she swept her hair forward over her left shoulder such that it would hide the charred section of her face. It wasn't much, but it would be enough in a crowd.

With that, Krahe made her way to the Zaveshian Central Temple. She wasn't entirely certain which church's jurisdiction the Lost Sun Killer fell under, since it was not only a severe form of body theft and desecration, but it also pertained to heretical magic, which was generally the purview of the Seven Spokes. In the end, however, the Twin Churches were called that for a reason. Their operations, faiths, and jurisdictions bled into one another in many places; they were effectively joined at the hip. Her decision was influenced, more than anything, by her status as a graft-apostle and the lower average number of people at Zaveshian temples. In reality, Zaveshian temples got more visitors than Igarian ones—many of the faithful were just out of sight, either being treated, having grafts done, or exercising as a form of worship.

Despite her hopes, the number of people milling about surpassed her expectations.

There was a line of seven at the main counter, now manned by a different banisher than before. However, the same banisher receptionist whom Krahe had met upon her first arrival was at the counter to the right, with a warning sign that it was for urgent matters only and that one should not come there unless they had a bounty to turn in. While Krahe waited, she indulged in people-watching, though she didn't bring out Barzai lest someone *somehow* spot him.

Near the contract board, a group of five had gathered around that muscular contractor. She was even more muscular than before, apparently having had grafting work done which was made clear by the swelled lines going down her arms and the noticeable increase in their size. Her blade was replaced by an even bigger one—a huge saber with two cutouts on the back, wrapped to serve as extra grips. Its handle was excessively bulky and contained a small engine. The guard was two-layered, with a solid piece guarding a motorbike throttle, while the handle itself had a brake-like lever. Two dark gray, barely purplish lines of crystal ran down the blade on each side where the fuller grooves would normally go. Krahe didn't even need to try to listen in to learn about the weapon as the contractor was currently in the process of loudly boasting about how she had paid some famous craftsman half a million to have it put together, despite providing all the parts herself. She claimed she could now cut through a building when transformed. Krahe didn't even doubt the veracity of that assertion. If anything, she was thankful to the loudmouth for drawing all the attention.

Krahe committed the loudmouth and her weapon to memory, knowing full well that Casus would be terribly interested, and she felt bad for snapping at him earlier. Her reaction wasn't even extreme, but it was akin to scolding a cat for killing mice. This was also one of the reasons Krahe hated dealing with genuinely good people. It was much easier to justify her own prickly personality when everyone else was just as bad or worse.

The original receptionist recognized Krahe when she turned to glance that way, and called her over.

"Ah, I was wondering when I would see you again, Lady Blackhand," the receptionist said in a low, yet bubbly tone. "You might be disappointed to learn that we do not have another kidnapped Pilgrim for you to rescue."

"He talked," Krahe deadpanned. She suddenly felt less bad for snapping at him.

"Of course he did!" the receptionist beamed. "But he didn't need to. The Slaughterhouse Nine Incident left both witnesses and survivors... And people were more than eager to talk and ask questions about the commotion. I heard that one of the graft-beasts was even intact enough to pull a visual recording. Ah, apologies. What can I do for you today?"

Taking a deep breath to calm herself, Krahe moved on from the matter of her failure to keep a low profile. She had decided that it would be fine to get a reputation after all! But not every part of her had realized that yet. The paranoid schizo part that saw a camera on every corner and behind every civvie's eyes still wanted to be invisible.

"I have a case to report," she said. "There was no contract set beforehand as I uncovered it myself. It pertains to restricted material in the Temple of Records. Section fifty-three."

The receptionist sat still for a moment, thinking. Her cheerful demeanor fell away in an instant, and she regarded Krahe with a hard gaze, her eyes running up her arm before they met her own. Her third eye opened, its cruciform pupil burning in a pool of radiant green-blue.

"Are you absolutely certain?"

Krahe just nodded.

"Very well…" she trailed off, taking a piece of off-white, watermarked paper and writing on it by hand in immaculate calligraphy. "It so happens that an ex-inquisitor who worked on the case is present in the city. I will refer you to him. Go to the Seven Spokes Central Temple and ask for Razem."

The letter was then folded and sealed with a large, rectangular stamp that burned a complex sigil onto the paper, holding it shut without wax or any other physical glue. She silently nodded, took the letter, and went on her way.

It almost seemed like Razem was waiting for her. In fact, the front end of the Igarian temple was conspicuously deserted; not entirely, but the number of people was significantly lower than she would have expected.

He stood at the precipice between the chapel and the temple's halls, and simply met her gaze with a nod.

"I did not expect to see you so soon. Certainly not in these circumstances. You look well," he said, gesturing for her to follow as he turned to walk down the hall. He led her deeper and deeper, eventually into a subterranean area of the temple, but only perhaps two floors underground. As they walked, he explained, "The letter you hold in your hand—it's little more than an identifying token. I already know what it says."

He brought out a second letter, identical to the first, but not sealed. When the two letters touched, they merged together and burned up into nothing. The room he was leading her to was a reliquary, but the security was not nearly as stringent. There were the giant doors with the complex opening sequence, sure, but that was it. Within was a large room with walls of reflective black stone. Razem snapped his fingers. A pulse of thauma radiated out of him, blanketing the whole room, and several sections of the wall became transparent, revealing artifacts previously concealed within. All of them shared various design elements with Sorayah's lantern, and some of them Krahe recognized from having read their descriptions.

"Hoh? I thought you would be more impressed," the ex-inquisitor remarked. "New church contractors always like the polarized quartz trick."

Seeing her apprehensive glance at those words, Razem acquiesced. "You said you had a matter related to these relics to report, yes?"

With those words, he held his hand out to another section of the wall, causing it to recede and slide to the side with a rumble, revealing a far less impressive, but far more practical room. A small archive of texts and scrolls, with a few tables against the walls, but otherwise blank. He led her into that other room and seamlessly conjured several items onto the table. This conjuring manifested as reams of paper unwinding from inside the sleeve of his robe to wrap around a nonexistent item. Once finished, the layer of paper burned away to reveal the item inside, now very real and present. In the span of a few seconds, he summoned a typewriter, a memslate record player deck that looked far too much like his hands to not be custom, and, weirdly, a full pitcher of amethyst-colored liquid, plus two tall glasses.

Krahe had no reason to be taken aback. It was a perfectly sensible application of Kenoma storage. And yet, she was—just a little.

"This may take a short while, but I am sure you already knew that. Please, give your full and unabridged account of your findings."

And so, Krahe did. Mostly, anyway. The fairly large amount of information she withheld didn't factor into Sorayah's case specifically, and she simply didn't drink any of the amethyst liquid on the off-chance it was a truth serum of some kind.

Razem, however, didn't express doubt as to her words. He did ask her to restate a few things while holding a band of seals that he conjured, and Krahe did feel like she physically couldn't lie while holding it. Deception, however, didn't necessitate lies, and her purposes didn't require a great deal of deception to begin with.

Eventually, she brought out the lantern, and Razem, openly displaying his interest in the thing, took several similar artifacts from their displays to compare. He told her some things she already knew, and others she didn't.

"We did a great deal in the effort to wipe these out, but, as you can see, the knowledge of their creation yet persists. The problem with these devices, besides the manner of their creation, is the occult corruption their use inflicts on the user and the fact they demand 'human charcoal' to operate. Some versions of the device even demand that the fuel comes from someone who trusted the user. It will be a challenge to discern how many based on the residue inside the mechanism, but if I were to guess... Seventeen, or perhaps eighteen people must have been turned into charcoal to power this thing over the years. How many of them can be blamed on Sorayah, I cannot guess."

He looked up from the lantern, adding, "That's a small number, to be clear. You caught her early. Most of the specimens in our collection have burned through volumes of human charcoal equivalent to several hundred people. At their heights, the Human Charcoal Cults were powerful enough to make an entire town disappear overnight..."

They spoke on the matter of the Human Charcoal Cults and their occult practices for about another hour, and Krahe came to the conclusion that Razem held some similarities to Casus. He was a genuinely, truly good person. But he wasn't. Not entirely. The difference hit her quite quickly: Effort. Casus didn't try to be what he was. He just was. Razem was trying terribly, terribly hard, at all times. He didn't come across like he was faking it, but Krahe sensed that he had to try to be like this.

So, she took a risk.

"You don't have to put on appearances in front of me, you know. I can tell."

He didn't suddenly transform or completely change his demeanor, but he *did* let out a breath and sink into his chair. It wasn't his personality that fell away. It was the faintly regal, detached aura that he had been giving off until now. Suddenly, that vanished. He was just an old man with a fire in his eyes and an aura that felt like the surface of a vast ocean; tranquil yet prepared to churn into a storm at a moment's notice. A former killer who had become a man of the law, and then a priest. A walking, talking narrative stereotype.

"Ah, you've detected my dark secret! Razem, High Priest of the Seven Spokes Audunpoint Branch Central Temple, is just an unenlightened old coot," he said with a mischievous smirk. He reached out and a band of paper whipped towards one of the glasses. He downed half of it in one swig. "It's not truth serum, if that's what you were thinking. The glassware doesn't have anti-appraisal enchantments either."

He knew. Not exactly, but he guessed basically what she had been thinking. She hesitantly took the other glass and sipped from it. It *smelled* great, a soft herbal scent. It *tasted* atrocious. Bitter and sour. And yet, once it went down, it felt like she'd just shot up a cocktail of nootropics; her thoughts ran a hundred miles an hour and her mind felt clearer than ever.

"The taste, however, is an acquired one," the priest added after the fact, sipping from his glass with a malicious grin.

Krahe appraised the drink.

[Decoction of Mind's Dawn]
Status
Exceptional (High Quality, Low Concentration)
Details
Perfect Recall A1
Memory Formation Amp C2
Mental Energy Amp C2
Mental Clarity Amp C1
Sleep Replacement D3

She was, much to Razem's amusement, taken aback by the litany of effects.

"It's my personal blend. What do you think? Sorun used to pester me for the recipe whenever he came by to get a refill. Wonder why he hasn't come by lately. I hope his overgrafting hasn't finally caught up with him..." he trailed off, swirling his partially full glass. He grew somber, before taking another sip and perking up again. "Anyhow. Let us get back on track."

"Right, right. It's not really surprising that there are remnants floating around. The church is too big and ponderous to effectively exterminate such an elusive enemy, and the inquisition, despite being the Inner Wheel's dedicated scalpel, suffers to some degree from the same issues. It doesn't help that they're eternally stretched hair-thin. One inquisitor is really good. Two? Great. Outstanding. Three? Nearly guaranteed that it will get solved, and solved quickly."

Razem took a sip. His expression soured, as if the flavor had suddenly caught up to him. With a sigh, he placed the glass back on the table and continued speaking."But that never happens. One is usually good enough, and they're spread thin as it is. They put me on the case because they hoped I was the right man for the job, being the only anathemist inquisitor in a while. I was, but not for the reasons they thought. Turns out someone who dives into anathemism for his own reasons is much worse as material for the human charcoal process than a normal person. The curse struggles to take hold due to built up tolerance, and the resulting charcoal is laden with Bane Soot. Knowing how widespread and how slippery those bastards were back in their heyday, I'm not surprised that people are still finding remnants. Did you find anything as significant as the lantern? Another relic or tool?"

"I haven't combed through all of the perpetrator's home yet. I was thinking of trying to summon the contents of her personal Kenoma storage, if she had one."

"Well, I can give you a one-use kit for that, but don't expect much. You're placing yourself at the mercy of the Gulf's tides, and given the circumstances of her death, her storage will have likely dispersed even more rapidly than normal. Oh, and uh... Don't open the kit until you're ready to use it."

"One of the rooms is also ward-locked."

"I... Cannot *give you* ward-breaking equipment, as it's fairly delicate work with oft-lethal consequences for failure, but I *can* assign someone to your case with the skills and qualifications to break the local warding. Come, let us handle the rest of the paperwork so that you may be rid of this old man."

With that, Razem got up and packed up his things, and suddenly, the aura of regal detachment returned to him. He led Krahe back to the surface and into an office decorated similarly to the one in which he had examined and treated her. The report had already been written; Razem now updated Krahe's contractor ID. Then, he asked her, "How would you prefer to be paid? Solid-state? Coinage? Thaumine?"

"Rings."

Utterly unsurprised, the old man smiled and gave a nod. "Very well, but I'll have to account for the market exchange rate. I'm sure you understand. It will take a few days to turn the cogs of bureaucracy given the magnitude of this case. Do you have an address where you would prefer to have the reward delivered, or would you rather pick it up at the temple?"

She honestly wanted to say Gashward Road 94, but she didn't spend enough time there to not worry about the package being stolen.

"Can you send it to the Seven Spokes shrine on Gashward Road?" she asked. There was only one on that street, well away from 94.

"Of course. I shall have the ward-breaker contact you using that address as well. Ah, not to forget. Wait here for a moment."

Razem left, returning with an elongated box of dark wood, taped shut lengthwise with fabric covered in holy symbols."

"I must reiterate. Do not open it until you intend to use it and do not place it in Kenoma storage *under any circumstances.*"

* * *

Inside the box was a clump of flesh with a face. No skin, no hair, just purplish meat with a face.

It was tiny, just a bit larger than her fist, and contained in a sealed jar. Various equipment filled the remaining space, including instructions for what looked suspiciously close to Barzai's angle-web, the reagents to draw it, and a sheet of vellum with an intensely herbal, nose-stinging scent. She was to draw the sigil on the vellum, place it as close to the site of death as possible, then set the "gulfcaller" in the middle and supply thauma.

The purpose of the weird homunculus revealed itself when Krahe did as instructed, and the gulfcaller began reciting a complex incantation whilst throat singing in a second voice. It grew arms and legs, immediately doubled over and began dry heaving. It stopped half a minute later and, looking up at Krahe, turned side to side as if it was shaking its head. The weird little creature then climbed back into the jar, fell limp, and shriveled up to barely half of its original size. Disappointed, she left everything as it was, locked the place up, and left. Her end goal was to simply return to the safehouse before she went out to look into Eutropia in the evening.

Krahe meandered through the city for longer than she needed, eventually visiting a craftsman's workshop whose repertoire included both eyeglasses and low-level artifacts. The place was deserted and run by a shriveled little man with an equally bushy mustache and eyebrows. She queried him on how much it would cost to have her glasses upgraded and how long it would take.

This was, in fact, the sixth craftsman who did this kind of work that she had visited. As such, she confidently requested a specific upgrade. "I'll need at-will Appraise Object of C-Three or B-One grade, Extended Highlight Magic Object Plus C-One, Detect Baneworm D-Three, and Detect Life D-Three."

"These... Quite right. These seem like something one would take to Jas'raba. Typical construction, notably the frame is much better than the lenses. Since the lens shape is standard round stock, I can pencil your order in for... Next month on the twentieth. Is that acceptable?"

She nodded. "Sure."

"Good, good. The down payment will be fifty percent; if you don't show up, I won't be able to easily sell the lenses to someone else. Pick them up within another month of the agreed upon date."

"With my hard requirements out of the way, I would also like Anti-Appraisal Penetration of C-One or better. Can you do that?"

The craftsman stopped at that request, regarding her with a dubious gaze. It was a bit more than usual, but within norms. She couldn't ask a random craftsman to give her glasses that could see through anything efficiently, but she wanted at least something that could reliably defeat low-mid level shielding.

"I understand that such things are desirable for many people, but you must understand that I cannot risk the guilt of equipping a thief or perhaps a scoundrel…"

They looked at each other for a few seconds. He was waiting for a response.

"Well? Do I seem like a *thief or perhaps a scoundrel?*"

Then, the old man laughed.

"I'm kidding. I don't give a shit what you do with my work. It's not as if I'm selling anything *truly* valuable like high-grade voidkeys."

From the way he awkwardly transitioned from one sentence to the next, it felt like she had failed to provide a keyword. Then, Krahe noticed the spark of recognition in his eye, and the way he glanced at her arm, which was fully covered by both her jacket and a glove. She didn't bring it up, but she did give him a lowball counteroffer when he quoted her his price. He didn't fight her on it.

* * *

First thing upon returning to the safehouse, Krahe questioned Casus on the matter of Seer.

"I had expected you to ask sooner. We had him checked over, as promised. The grafter found widespread modifications to the ocular module, as well as extraordinarily precise repairs carried out to mitigate damage to his brain and material soul. According to Seer, all of his grafting work was carried out by an apostate grafter in the Hashems' employ. An extremist who, by his own admittance, lives and works with baneworms to better devise ways to exterminate them without triggering a polyphemic reaction. He also claims that he can track Semzar thanks to the modifications made by this grafter. Supposedly he had done this as a way of subverting his employer out of spite."

As he spoke, a mirthful tone bled into Casus' words, and a faint smirk formed on his lips.

"And?" Krahe asked.

"We have to wait." He shrugged. "His description lined up with certain restricted records of apostate grafters, so they're calling in an inquisitor who happens to be operating in this region to confirm his testimony."

Rather than dwell on the matter, Krahe raised her legs and hopped out of her seat, walking to the kitchen. She decided to finish off a leftover tortoise steak. No complicated cookery, just salt and "Powder No. 7," a spice mix that she had learned was preferred over ground peppercorn for meat. Its flavor and complexity put white and black pepper to shame. She seared the marbled slab of meat on both sides using an iron pan with clarified butter, and then sautéd a chopped up vegetable as a side. It was an alien root, but its culinary role was adjacent to broccoli.

With her sole proper meal for the day, she returned to the living room and decided to regale Casus with a description of the musclewoman's Mamon Coupler saber.

This topic naturally led into the matter of Tsetse's torn-off arm and Casus' excitement grew serious.

"My acquaintance says he thought it was a construct at first, due to how rapidly it decayed, but placing it into a preservation tank halted that process. Regenerative agents also functioned normally. However, it is not *true* flesh."

At Krahe's raised eyebrows, he continued. "It appears to exist within the same gray area as Mamon Armor. Not quite a full construct, but not quite permanent matter. The difference is that Tsetse's arm is much closer to permanence than anything generated by a Mamon Armor, *except* for the sonic blaster array, which is within normal Mamon Armor parameters..."

He trailed off, waiting for her to guess the reason. It was obvious, but she had a mouth full of turtle meat, and she absolutely wouldn't choke down this ambrosia of the gods unchewed. It was at once incredibly rich and filling, yet light enough that she could eat a 12oz, or 340g tortoise steak without it feeling like a heavy meal. Beef didn't even compete.

Weathering the Banisher's patient gaze, Krahe savored chewing the meat properly and flushing it down with a sip of ekarone juice.

Then, she stated her hypothesis. "So Tsetse's body is some sort of imitation war-morph, or perhaps an Evoy innovation on the principles behind Mamon Armor."

"Exactly!" Casus exclaimed with a snap of his fingers. It was as loud as a firecracker.

"Show me your hand for a moment," she asked, and Casus eagerly obliged. It was as she had suspected. The shade of his muscles was much lighter, and the layout had been altered. The blackveins didn't protrude anymore, and he now had alarite studs that seemed to be embedded in his knuckles and fingertips.

"L-Sixes for the full arm *and* alarite joint reinforcement, huh?" she muttered with a half-full mouth.

"A full alarite secondary endoskeleton, in fact. I was intended to receive it to begin with, but it has special anchors that only interface correctly with the L-Six cultured fibers. They double as blackvein connections, meaning that my arm is now truly monolithic. Anything powerful enough to render it inoperable will also kill me in one hit."

"So it was an all or nothing high-spec package," Krahe mused, marveling over the arm.

"Precisely," Casus agreed. Letting his vanity take over, he more than happily displayed the graft-limb from every possible angle, even doffing his shirt just to show how it was joined to the rest of him. It truly was a work of art. Neither of them thought any more of this, despite how it may have looked to a purely theoretical third-party observer.

Compared to everything surrounding Sorayah, dealing with Eutropia was a fresh change of pace.

To begin with, Krahe had managed to dig up some more information on the woman by paying Nozar another visit. She was conspicuously left alone this go round, with the Evoy building's inhabitants peeking out curiously only to slam their doors shut at the sight of her. Nozar didn't have much on her, but he did have *some* interesting info, such as the fact she was a disfavored eighth daughter of some Afshani merchant clan. She was an E1-rank contractor, but Nozar noted that there was something fishy about her CQF record.

"Gut feeling. I'd say she's more of an F3," the flyman guessed. This info wasn't nearly as expensive as what he had on Yao, but it was still pricey. At least she was able to pay him in cash this go 'round.

Despite the fact Eutropia had wronged her personally by killing a street vendor she liked, killing her wasn't a primary goal; even at Garvesh's request. It was the same reason she didn't go after Jezail, and that was that Eutropia was just the hand that held the knife. If she wanted to get proper revenge, she would have to extract the identity of Eutropia's employer and come after *them*. Her anger was, in the same way, directed in Eutropia's direction because she happened to be a stepping stone between Krahe and whomever had paid to have Imraal killed. She had her own guesses, of course—it was more likely than not Semzar—but she wanted to be sure.

Krahe didn't know what made hired killers less guilty in her eyes than normal murderers, and she frankly didn't dwell on it, because she knew that, like many other avenues of introspection, it would only lead her to the conclusion that Megacity Gamma had left her sense of morality irrevocably distorted.

Eutropia was a minor celebrity, a performer in one of the city's lesser known, yet still reputable establishments. Despite the marginally sleazy name "Hot Legs," everything else about the venue gave the impression of an upstanding establishment.

Eutropia, alongside the establishment's in-house band, wore costumes styled after the Mamon Armors worn by an all-female group of independent contractors from the Samstani capital. Though, Eutropia's stage getup was far from a real Mamon Armor, of course. It was an all-too-tight black body glove with sections of blue-painted armor fitted around it, with a chestplate that only covered the top half of her torso and was shaped to exaggerate her curves. The rest of the suit was much the same, with "metal bikini type" bottoms and chunky, high-heeled knee-high boots, with gauntlets that matched their rounded shape. Sizable pauldrons that swung about freely during the performance rounded out the whole thing.

As for the performance, it was fun. It brought back memories of attending underground concerts, both for fun and to discuss things that were best covered up by the eardrum-rupturing noise. Krahe also learned that this world had equivalents to some modern instruments, including distorted guitars and synthesizers. Unsurprisingly, all powered by souldregs. Musically, the songs were familiar, being similar to the New Wave of Synth-Rock which had swept through Megacity Gamma's Sectors 7, 8 and 9 in her lifetime. As for lyrical subjects, they covered the usual topics. Love, sorrow, living in the big city, tearing down the road as fast as your machine would go—etcetera, etcetera. Timeless subjects, really. A song including the words "tonight, there's a hurricane" in the refrain stood out among the others, being the opener and also being repeated once more after the audience demanded an encore.

The question was whether Eutropia moonlighted as a Silversword Agency Contractor, or the other way around; the bar's advertising used her contractor status as a selling point.

Tracking her back to her home wasn't difficult. In fact, Krahe wasn't the only one to do it that night. A pair of drunk fans, out of an audience of about a hundred, had followed their idol back to a building in one of the city's more affluent residential areas. Given her reaction—shooing them off and throwing spare pieces of her costume—this seemed to be a regular occurrence. Like feral raccoons who had been given leftovers, the two obsessives scurried off with their prize.

Krahe was well out of sight, but with Barzai as her eyes, she got a good look at the building and at Eutropia herself.

CHAPTER 16

VS. CRESCENT JEZAIL

Eutropia regarded Krahe with a questioning look that seemed to say, *"Another fan?"*

But as she approached, emerging into the pallid glow of a streetlamp, curiosity turned to recognition, and recognition turned to wide-eyed terror.

"Blackhand…" the girl muttered. She didn't seem to even consider fleeing, merely backing up against the front door of her home.

"W-why're you here? I… I'm not with Hashem anymore, I swear! I paid off my debt! I'm clean!"

.Oh, I've missed these reactions. Best thank Semzar for doing my PR.

Somewhat confused, Krahe asked, "Why do you *think* I'm here?"

"They say you used to run with the Hands of Purgation," Eutropia said. She hastily shoved her keys into the door without ever turning around. She unlocked it, opened it, and slowly backed into her home. The whole time, she kept talking. "They say you've come back to take vengeance on the whole Hashem Family. But I—I swear, I'm not with them! I just… I just owed them and I did some work to repay it."

She… wasn't lying. At least, not as far as Krahe could tell. Though increasingly puzzled, she decided to play along, and followed her inside. This wasn't a conversation to be had out in the open street if it could be helped, and Eutropia clearly understood that.

Krahe shut the door behind herself, leaning against it, leaving Barzai just outside to cover her blind spot—especially the rooftops.

"Did that *work* happen to include the killing of a Saurian street vendor? The one that blasted you with a reaper and set off Mistress Yao's protection talisman?"

"How do you—"

"Answer the question."

Krahe didn't need to try to put an edge in her voice. Just interrupting Eutropia was enough to make her crumple. Well, she supposed it wasn't too big a surprise. She was a hired killer, sure, but she had killed a *civilian*. Frankly, Krahe wasn't sure why Yao had taken an interest in her or sold her that protective talisman.

"That..." Eutropia tensed up. "It was the last thing I did for him. I swear on my family name!"

"I don't recall finding anything about a family name when I looked into you," Krahe said plainly. Eutropia's terror became tinged by shame.

"I... Well, I'm the eighth daughter of the Kartier Family's Ulthar branch," she admitted with a sad smile, averting her gaze. She didn't seem to feel the need to elaborate, probably because there was none. The Kartiers were an ancient and absurdly wealthy family, with the core branch controlling all the businesses while the secondary branches specialized in a wide variety of research and development. It was such surface information that even a book on the general history of Afshan included it. They were, in every sense, old money.

Raising her eyes to look at Krahe again, she added, "I would swear that my family will reward you if you spare my life, but I would be lying to both of us. So, if you spare me, my family will not be able to use my death as an excuse if your interests ever conflict with theirs."

"Point me to the one who hired you, and I'll let you get away."

"It was—"

"Shut up. I wasn't finished. I'll let you *get away*. Not let you go. You will vanish from Audunpoint and take only what you can carry. Make it look like someone made you disappear. Run off to Afshan or something, change your name, start another tribute band—Zavesh knows there's a hundred of them just in this city. Someone wants you dead for that street merchant. So, Eutropia Kartier is dead starting today. Understand?"

Krahe had just guessed that part about tribute bands. She was sure Hot Legs would have no trouble finding another singer for their in-house band. Eutropia nodded along, both intimidated and relieved.

"I'm sure you can guess," Eutropia said with a wry smile. "I can't say who contacted me personally, but I'm deathly certain the man who gave the order was Semzar Hashem. The message was worded in an exceedingly *him* manner. Egotistical shit brat with less of a brain than the corpse he's riding on any given month."

As if on cue, Krahe saw a strange shape shimmering on a nearby rooftop through Barzai's eyes—just the next street over and less than a hundred meters away. It was a human figure, one obscured somehow, and difficult to focus on. She noticed it due to the disturbance of the air around it; like overly aggressive active camo, standing out against a comparatively tranquil backdrop. There was a good chance she would've missed it if she hadn't been actively scanning the rooftops, windows, and other such vantage points in Barzai's field of view.

She would have warned Eutropia, if there had been time. The figure appeared on the roof one moment and the next, the cloak broke as the person underneath opened it to raise a long weapon into a crouched firing position. Through Barzai's superior vision, Krahe was able to catch the shape of Crescent Jezail's eponymous weapon.

There were all of four, perhaps five seconds between when Krahe initially spotted a weird shimmering shape on a rooftop and when a ray of arcane death tore the air apart on its warpath towards her back. Of these seconds, three were filled by what would come to be Eutropia's final words.

Krahe skimmed straight upwards twice in rapid succession, placing herself on the balcony, and turned herself to see better. Her reason to abandon cover was the assumption that Jezail could see her through walls somehow, considering he had been able to target and shoot through a heavily warded safehouse window, let alone a stone brick wall.

* * *

A gulf skimmer.

That was a problem, but she couldn't have more than three charges, and Jezail could compensate by predicting the likely direction she might skim next. That stunt had to have cost her one charge at least, and Jezail was willing to bet it had cost two, given the structure's dimensions and typical skimmer ranges. It could be a longer-ranged technique, but then it would have a lengthier recharge time and likely only two charges. The third option was that she just had the brute attribute ratings to force a standard skimmer's range that far, but he couldn't very well do anything about that if it were the case, so he didn't worry about it. Jezail was, of course, wrong. It was none of these. The characteristics of Krahe's skimming ability were, in fact, objectively subpar. Its range was above average, but not *long*.

Four shots; Semzar had paid Jezail for four shots and impact confirmation. Or rather, three of his standard catalog, the Three Shot Special, plus the Full Custom. A shot tailored specifically to the target, and what a shot it was. Jezail honestly hoped she would dodge the next two just so he would get to use it.

The collateral damage was Semzar's problem. Eutropia was a loose end whose death was included in the contract as a secondary objective, which he had now fulfilled, but his current ammo was rather destructive by nature. All of the buildings behind his target were at risk of unintended destruction, and given the area, some of those buildings were the homes of people Semzar couldn't afford to anger.

That wasn't Jezail's problem.

You wanted me to use the Oblivion Flow, you get the Oblivion Flow...

In the same breath, he briefly considered waiving the fee for Eutropia and only charging for the shot that killed her, since information on her was, in the end, what allowed him to catch Blackhand like this. He banished the thought. For a better customer, maybe. For Damrus, even, perhaps. Not for Semzar.

Blackhand raised a wall of strange, black-green stone, as if it would shield her. It probably would against most attacks, but not against his.

He fired the second shot. It didn't burst out of his staff, but rather poured out. It thereafter flowed through the air, an unearthly river of power in a color darker than black, creating a trail not through the violence of its passage, but mere incident. Bits of dust, errant feathers, even the air itself were all erased by the flow, sweeping up a light breeze and leaving shreds of impossible blackness in its wake.

It was nearly instantaneous. It traveled no slower than lightning itself with a fraction of the commotion and far more focused power than such a brutish bolt. Jezail had no particular talent, no particular elemental affinity, but he felt no need for it. The reassuring absoluteness of Arcane magic's outcomes was one of the reasons *he* was Crescent Jezail, instead of some idiot with a cooked brain and too much love for literal beams of fire. The Oblivion Flow brought an altogether more elegant and literal kind of obliteration. Eutropia wasn't torn apart, and neither were the walls caught in the Flow's path; they were simply erased, directly destroyed by magic.

Given the lack of overpenetration, that wall had put up a significant amount of resistance, but not enough to stop the Flow from passing through.

Two shots. Half a million DDs without hit confirmation accounted for. The first shot had gotten hit confirmation on Eutropia, bringing it to 600,000. The second, too, had passed through a living target, raising his *base* payout to 700,000. Jezail didn't relax, however. His method of hit confirmation wasn't foolproof, as he had warned Semzar earlier, despite Semzar's refusal to acknowledge that fact during the negotiations for this very job. Two shots left, and Semzar had in the end caved and paid for direct kill confirmation. Thus, Jezail would circle the target to get a line of sight and make damn sure she was dead.

He reloaded, securing a new talisman around his staff. An adjustment of his fingers on the haft, translating to subtle adjustments to the next shot's properties. The air still crackled with remnant energy as Jezail regained sight and recalculated trajectories. Jezail's mind ran far faster than any normal person's, apropos of his heavy cerebral grafts and a cocktail of elixirs he had taken beforehand. He got up and stalked over the rooftops, eventually jumping across the street to the next roof over.

There he was met by a grinning face, sitting slumped against the stone slab. He raised his staff again, but she skimmed into the building before he could fire.

The game of cat and mouse which followed went on for three hours.

Jezail eventually managed to set up a decoy trap using his camouflage cloak, which seemed to be what she had used to detect him. At this moment, he was buried in a pile of trash on the flat-top roof of a three-story apartment building. He was waiting for Blackhand to cross a sightline from beyond a street corner where she would be out of his decoy's sightline. She did, and he took the shot...

...Only for her to still be standing once the remnants cleared, grinning at him straight through his camouflage. How? Yes, he was blind for a few brief moments after firing, but her posture wasn't changing at all, let alone enough to suggest any kind of evasive maneuver! The feedback he was receiving could only mean his attack wasn't being blocked, as the arcane reverb of a barrier and the various feelings of ward impact were distinct from a true, direct hit on target. By every reasonable metric, Blackhand should be dead.

Something clicked in his head.

She must have taken and implanted Eutropia's special voidkey at some point before he took the first shot. He wasn't familiar with it or its strange mechanics, but he knew enough to lay the blame on it. That was the only reasonable explanation for this havoc that was being played with his magic, and it also explained why Eutropia died properly—she didn't have the same defenses that had protected her from that street vendor's Reaper. Jezail came to these conclusions in moments of real-time and decided to take a risk.

Barriers took time to raise. Skimming, too, had a recovery time. It stood to reason this esoteric means of attack avoidance had to also have limitations. So, he brought out Mistress Yao's talisman, wrapped it around his staff, and took the shot.

* * *

Krahe had been screwing with Jezail all night, and she had to admit she enjoyed it. For all its lethality, there was no network layer to deal with, no hacking and counter-hacking, making the game an enjoyable balance of real danger versus relative safety. She'd guessed that he couldn't see shit after firing right away. That black beam just left too much mess behind; it obscured him but also obscured his vision. It was possible he could see through it, as she could through her smokescreen, but her vision was still impaired somewhat. At this distance, even that slight level of cover was a big fucking problem.

Once she saw that dead-still decoy and that sightline straight out of a sniper's wet dream, she knew she had the right bait for him.

He swallowed it hook, line, and sinker.

A golden-yellow light flashed from the talisman, filling the many spiraling grooves that covered the staff's surface. A burst of that same light erupted from the rod, sending the talisman itself flying at a velocity that rightly should have obliterated it. As it flew, it rapidly multiplied into dozens, at first flying as a swarm and eventually reaching such a density they *flowed* at their target.

Yet, something was wrong. Jezail had felt a sense of foreboding when he took aim, as if something was warning him not to take the shot, but he had encountered similar dissuasion magic before.

For this same reason, seeing his target turn into a green-eyed smoke demon didn't intimidate him.

Jezail started reconsidering his odds only once he saw the swarm of talismans surround their target and begin orbiting. By now, they should have mummified and vaporized her.

* * *

Krahe didn't trust Yao enough to just eat that talisman face-first unguarded, and there was no guarantee that this talisman was the one Yao had agreed to rig with a rebound trigger. For all she knew, Jezail might have acquired more offensive talismans from the mistress for general use.

Her distrust was once again proved wrong when, a split-second after being surrounded by that swarm, it suddenly went zipping back to sender, spewing beams of golden light at Jezail from all directions. It didn't even look like he was supposed to get hit, but rather as though the swarm was corralling him, trying to chase him away. It worked, as the sniper-wizard fired off a scattered version of his earlier attack and vanished in the aftermath.

The last Krahe saw of Jezail for that night was his blurred silhouette as he leapt atop his staff and went blasting over the rooftops, using it as a hoverbike of some sort. It certainly didn't look like real flight.

Despite his best efforts, however, Yao's talismans chased after him. He had, after all, tied himself to them as the caster, and Yao had purposely altered their homing mechanism so it could go both ways. The tie between Jezail and Krahe was much like that of a curse, if shorter-lived. If anything, the rebound was even more powerful than the original attack; rather than homing in on an arbitrary target, it was following the chain of retribution to a perpetrator. At least, such was Krahe's limited understanding of sympathetic magic.

Krahe wasted no time returning to Eutropia's home, taking a moment to change her clothes in a back alley on the way there. Her caution was rewarded when she found a handful of curious eyes peering from the windows of nearby buildings. She extracted Eutropia's souldregs and her voidkey, knowing that Garvesh would appreciate seeing hard proof of her death. The key snapped, with a sizable chunk of it just bursting apart and disintegrating, but she got most of it anyway. It felt familiar, somehow. Before anyone in the neighborhood could muster up the courage to investigate, and before the night-watchmen could reach the place, Krahe was gone.

* * *

That night, there was a brief light show in the sky just above the city. A swarm of glowing papers chasing after a deep-blue comet, each letting off a shining beam of light before disintegrating.

It ended with a dozen rays of light scattering into the sky all at once and the body of their target—a willowy, unassuming man—plummeting onto a rooftop. He rolled off the side, smashing into a balcony railing on his way down, leaving it bent. Nothing else broke his fall save for the hard stone, but that was fine. He wasn't as fragile as most.

Emitting an entirely inhuman groan of pain and effort, Jezail dragged himself off the ground and propped himself up against a nearby wall. He let out a wheezing, strained laugh. Despite the discomfort of a punctured lung and numerous small wounds that riddled his whole body, that laugh was the only appropriate reaction to his predicament.

"Hazard pay... here I come," he cackled to himself as he conjured an injector out of his quick-access storage. Relief flooded him when he pressed it against his neck; a Class 3 painkiller, able to take the bite out of any pain without impairing other senses while also providing a minor regenerative factor for several hours.

Once he was able to move again, Jezail simply returned to one of his hideouts in the city. He had done his job to the extent of the contract.

For the next hour, he sat there injecting himself, smoking, and slathering graft-paste on his wounds. Tens, hundreds of thousands of DDs in restoratives, spent without a second thought. After all, it was in his contract that his employer had to cover any expenses for injuries sustained on the job. Semzar wouldn't willingly shell out for that policy; he knew that. But he also knew that Damrus *would* pay. The Hashems were already in dire straits. The patriarch was smart enough to not risk souring his relationship with Jezail, or Zavesh forbid, risk having the assassin come after him personally.

Jezail still wasn't quite sure what had happened, and he was quite close to giving up on trying to figure it out. There had been no sign of the talisman being corrupt, and he had no way to discern how exactly Blackhand had turned it against him. A part of him wondered if she used some alternative to traditional barriers, and since he himself used a "Distortion Impulse Barrier," that was where his mind wandered. While demanding a higher level of skill and active attention even for basic usage, a DI barrier conversely had a far higher performance ceiling. As per the words of his master, it was "the parry to an archetypal barrier's simple block."

He knocked the burnt waste out of his pipe and absent mindedly stuffed it with various mind-clearing herbs. He was so used to it the taste didn't even register anymore. The initial kick was a flood of menthol, heat, and sour astringency, forcibly opening his airways and ensuring maximum absorption of the active ingredient, a specially cultivated Cassia strain of Jezail's own creation.

However, now that he thought about it with a clearer mind, Blackhand using a DI barrier was unlikely. As a user of this unique defensive technique himself, Jezail was certain he would have been able to detect it. It was also exceedingly unlikely outside the DI barrier's region of origin, which was on another continent. Looking back, he hadn't even sensed the normal thaumic upsurge caused by raising a standard barrier. There had been an undeniable disturbance, but not one that felt like any kind of barrier. Moreover, his attacks weren't deflected but seemed to merely pass through her space as if she was dodging them. But to where? She hadn't moved. He saw it; she had stood in the same spot yet was unharmed.

"How? Is that smoke form simply invulnerable?" he questioned aloud. "No, that's not how thaumaturgy works. It's not omnipotent. If it was truly a self-transmutation into smoke, the Oblivion Flow would have erased it all the same. Then how?"

Crescent Jezail decided it was high time to broaden his horizons, starting with obscure defensive techniques. For all his fame, he was far from a true veteran. He saw this incident as a stark reminder to not get complacent just because he was in the top 10%. That still left a whole 9% that could put him in the ground. Just a few years of being *the* Crescent Jezail had nearly made him stop polishing his edge.

"Next time, Blackhand..." He chuckled to himself. "Hopefully there won't be a next time. Best to prepare regardless."

CHAPTER 17

SOMETHING WRONG

Something was wrong. Casus felt it in his gut.

Cornelius, the man to whom he had entrusted Tsetse's arm, was supposed to have contacted him by now. They had no official agreement of a particular time or method, but Cornelius was an exceedingly scrupulous and consistent man, despite his veneer of a quasi-rogue grafter. For this reason, Casus had developed a strong sense for when Cornelius would contact him. Even if his tests on the arm hadn't progressed by a millimeter, Cornelius would still have sent a message to update Casus on his efforts.

Therefore, Casus decided to check up on him. He hoped that Cornelius had made a breakthrough and had been too engrossed in his work to report back, or that he had worked himself into an exhaustion coma. The alternative was just too unpleasant to consider.

An unsettling sense of urgency began to grow in his chest as he went. Eventually, he ended up riding a motorbike as fast as it would go through the city and even down into the underground, abusing its generous suspension by forcing it to go down stairways. He simply left it at the furthest possible spot it could take him.

Something was wrong. He could feel it in his gut. Cornelius wasn't the type to not check in just because of a breakthrough or simply because he was tired. He wasn't that irresponsible. Something *had* to be wrong.

He smelled it long before he reached the lab. The sweet smell of rotting meat, but not quite like the real thing, tinged with musky pungency and the sting of pheromones not intended for his nostrils. The stench only led him to rush even more, driving him to transform into Silberblut preemptively.

His fears were only further affirmed by the sounds of commotion as he sprinted through subterranean corridors lit only by old, flickering lamps. Three layers of black-iron doors had separated the lab from the corridor, but now, there was just a tunnel of torn-up stone. The doors were embedded into a wall inside the lab, one atop the other, having been blasted from their hinges and smashed into a monolith of abused metal by immense concussive force.

The unmistakable voice of Tsetse echoed from within, "Possess something that was stolen from me. Return it, and I will let you live. Lucky you."

"I—I don't know what you mean! Truly!" Cornelius insisted unconvincingly. His eyes jumped to Casus when he passed through the door. Scanning the situation before him, the first thing that hit him was the state of the lab; surprisingly, it was not wrecked. There was damage, yes, and quite a few pieces of equipment had been destroyed, but it looked plausibly collateral. As for Tsetse, he had cornered the swarthy grafter, who was keeping the flyman at bay thanks to a quarter-circle of blood drawn on the floor. Using it as a catalyst, Cornelius generated an immensely potent barrier. Its weakness against Tsetse's Kinetic attacks was offset by the fact it lashed back at him, as evidenced by the still-smoking Seven Spokes insignias that had been mercilessly branded onto Tsetse's body.

Indeed, Cornelius was exceptional when it came to purely defensive thaumaturgy, and not just in terms of barriers. His wards, too, were downright excessively thick, interlayered, and compound—unreasonably complex for his distinct lack of combative tendency. That was, after all, why he was so defensive; he utterly lacked the nerve to even fight back. He was the one worm who would sooner grow a spiked shell on the spot rather than turn and strike back. No matter his talent, however, Cornelius couldn't hold that barrier up for long. He knew this, Tsetse knew this, and Casus knew that Tsetse knew.

For that reason, a flash of hope lit up in the grafter's eyes when he saw Casus, and he immediately called out to him: "Ah, thank Zavesh you're here! A-as you can see there has been a bit of a misunderstanding. Please explain to my friend here that I don't know anything about his arm!"

Not only did he lack the nerve to fight, he also couldn't lie to save his skin.

Tsetse turned to meet his gaze, and despite the flyman's stoic visage, the noise he emitted was very much that of a chuckle.

"Ah. Lucky me. Silberblut," he said, sounding genuinely glad to see Casus. "I must thank you. The data from our fight led to quite a few improvements to my morph, as you can see, and as you will soon feel for yourself. Worry not; I can feel your confusion. If you survive a head-on strike from me, I will freely divulge the nature of my existence."

While he spoke, Casus used these precious moments to inspect Tsetse's altered form. The sonic emitter bulges over his ankles had been joined by another pair just above the knees, both of which were now more elegantly melded into the curvature of his plating, with eye-like slits in the chitin. His arms were completely different from before. The right still missed its lower half, with a crude-looking machine prosthetic in its place, cables winding up the limb to a compact power unit embedded in his back. As for his left arm, it had bulked up as if to compensate, individual plates now spread apart by bulging muscle. Any trace of sonic emitters was gone from the limb.

"I presume you know where it is. Please, disappoint me by disclosing its location without a fight."

Casus knew, of course. The arm was beneath them, its container one among dozens within a mechanized storage system. The access panel was, in fact, right behind Cornelius.

Rather than respond verbally, he simply dropped into his fighting stance. Having been transformed for a short time already, he felt assured that he could pull out a coupler charge right on the spot. It wasn't a good idea as he risked backlash, and even if successful, it would severely cut into his stamina. However, given the state of those doors and Tsetse's confidence, Casus wagered it was his best bet.

Tsetse raised his left arm to waist height, hand clenched into a downright weird fist. The exposed muscles of his torso flexed, and plates snapped out of place to reveal an array of three large and nine small sonic emitter lenses. Their placement was awkward, spaced out widely near the sides to make space for Tsetse's powerful core musculature. That explained the thick plates on his sides—their purpose was to protect the emitters.

Tsetse followed with a short punch, the kind one might use in tight quarters to hit an opponent's stomach. Casus, reading it as the trigger gesture for the greater emitter cluster, opened the Second Eye. Just as a wall of force came bearing down on him, he devoured it, skidding back just a bit. However, another blast of force came just as the Second Eye's window of effectiveness petered out. Viciously focused, it wasn't just enough to throw him against the wall, it embedded him into the brickwork and continued on *through* him, carving a hole into the stone.

The Silberblut armor's internal structure was a relic of the highest order, and the only thing that prevented it from turning his insides into mush. Nothing could severely harm him until the armor's durability was depleted, no matter how focused the attack was. Unfortunately, after weathering *that*, there really wasn't much durability left. He wagered he could take maybe one more of those hits, and perhaps one or two regular strikes after that before he was forced out of his transformation.

As he ripped himself free, he caught a glimpse of the source of that second attack. Just a flash, but it was unmistakable. A damascened membrane in the palm of Tsetse's hand. That was the reason for the weird fist; to cover it up. His thoughts ran rampant. Had Tsetse devised that *specifically* to counter the Second Eye?

Tsetse, however, seemed amused, remarking: "Impressive. Very well. I am certain the question has been gnawing at you: Am I a war morph? An overgrafter? A simple freak of nature?"

He stepped towards Casus, lunging at him with an absurdly long kick. It looked like a straight side kick, then like a hook kick, only to become a question-mark kick instead, all in the span of moments. The sonic blast sent stones and dust flying as it tore into the wall; Casus ducked and rushed in, the obvious answer to all three of the possible kicks. He also anticipated a mixup afterwards, but Tsetse engaged him in an exchange of punches and kicks. Each of them checked or blocked the other while throwing in a few truly lethal surprises; Casus with his blade, and Tsetse with his sonic emitters. He wasn't using the one on his left arm at all, but the limb itself was monstrously strong. It didn't match up to the Right Arm of Silberblut in its current state, but it didn't need to. At this moment, Casus was painfully aware of the fact Tsetse was simply stronger than him. His only chance to tip the scales was to push himself as far as he could, to use and abuse the Second Eye, and to steal Tsetse's own strength to use it against him. Tsetse also knew this, given how he took care not to use his sonic blasts when Casus was likely to devour them.

It was obvious he was just playing, just using this fight as the stage for his continued monologue. "The answer is neither of those three above, yet also all of them. I am something new. This form... it *is* my body, yet I can shed it and survive. In this manner and beyond, we are alike."

Out of nowhere, with no apparent inhale, Tsetse exhaled—and contined to breath out far past a natural breath. In one immense exhalation, he flooded the whole room with mist. At first Casus thought it to be a poorly conceived smoke screen, but then he felt it gnawing at him. It wasn't mist; it was omniphage, the same ruinous substance that made the Omniphage Dregsteam cartridge so potent. This single breath contained as much omniphage as two or perhaps three cartridges, and it was of a higher order than the breed used in those. Rather than clumping together like living mercury, it seemed to be the opposite.

Casus stood strong, continuing to fight and weathering the onslaught as the silver of his armor tarnished and soon turned black. He wasn't under threat here—Cornelius was. His barrier would hold, but everything around it wouldn't. Even if Cornelius had the nerve to banish and reform his barrier anew without the hemomantic catalyst, his barrier didn't have full-dome coverage. He *had to* get him out of the room.

So, he burned what power he had stocked up on empowering a coupler charge. Not an attack, but a movement. The Silberblut armor wasn't suited to it, but desperate times called for desperate measures. He timed it to the moment he noticed Cornelius' barrier faltering due to the destruction of its catalyst.

At first, it seemed to work. With flame erupting from his back and propelling him, Casus dropped to the ground, sliding between Tsetse's legs. There was a burst of high-pitched noise, pain, and the realization that Cornelius had a chunk missing from his side all of a sudden. It wasn't much, just surface tissue, but it meant his wards had been breached. The grafter, perhaps thanks to shock, immediately drew a circle around the wound using his suddenly abundant blood and formed a temporary plug of metal over it, then layered a barrier over that.

At first, Casus didn't even realize that the force of the blast had embedded his outstretched limbs into the walls and floor. His attention was wholly fixed on Cornelius. He had to get him out of the omniphage mist. There was no time. Casus shook off the pain and swiftly freed himself, spinning on his heel to face down the flyman. Unsteady, bleeding internally, and a hair's breadth from detransforming, his resolve was no less ironclad than at the beginning of this fight.

"The arm, Silberblut. Give me the arm and you may go," Tsetse said, already approaching. Casus, without a moment's hesitation, grabbed a brick and pulled it out of place. Behind it was a handle, a pull on which opened the masterfully disguised panel. Behind that panel was a yawning recess and a keyboard. He punched in the code and waited as the mechanism stirred into motion.

"Why? Why the mercy, I mean," came a hushed, strained voice from below.

"Not mercy," Tsetse scoffed, approaching yet closer, looming over them with amused apathy. "I want my arm back. I do *not* want a fight with whomever your deaths would alert."

His eyes shifted to Casus, and he added, "Not yet. I can't beat a *real* Mamon Knight yet."

At that moment, the container popped up in the recess, and Tsetse grabbed it immediately. Not only did he not try to stop them, he simply walked away with the container in hand. It seemed at first as though he would leave them in peace, but he met them outside. Casus had to drag an inconsolable Cornelius out of his own laboratory as the most delicate of his equipment was rendered into scrap. There, well outside the lab, he found Tsetse. The flyman was just sitting there, legs crossed, pulling the cables out of his right arm. Casus stopped short of passing him because he was simply exhausted. At some point between the lab and here, he had fallen out of his transformation without even noticing it.

As the flyman performed a simple grafting operation on himself out in the open, he said, "I almost pity you. You must think highly of Silberblut. It must be difficult to know you will never live up to what he was. To know you tarnish his legacy with this deluded impersonation. Perhaps I was wrong to fear you after all—if such a pale imitation is all you can manage."

His apathetic tone was tinged by a smug sense of superiority, but also true, genuine pity.

"You like the sound of your own voice far too much for that man-of-a-few-words affectation," Cornelius seethed.

"I am no such thing, and this is no affectation. This is just how I speak. I understand why you accuse me, however, if such poor pretenders as *Casus*

Aristedes are the norm within the church," Tsetse retorted, pulling out the last of several pins around the base of his mechanical forearm. They had been previously hidden under a ring-shaped protective shroud that also served as an adapter for the power cables. It was a crude design, but effective, and also entirely defiant of common design principles. The prosthetic was either a one-off or the work of someone unknown. Alongside itself, it pulled out a bone of some description, leaving a hollow cavity inside the upper arm, which now dangled uselessly.

The moment Tsetse pressed his original forearm to the stump, however, tendrils of flesh whipped forth to join the two together. There was the sound of flowing fluid, accompanied by the hissing of air being forced out of the limb's internal cavity. With a final shift that weirdly resembled someone shoving his arm into a sleeve from the inside of a zipped-up jacket, Tsetse's arm sprung back into motion as if it had never been detached.

Wrapping the cables of his detached replacement around his wrist, the flyman took his machine forearm, got up, and walked away. Casus vividly felt both his own and the Silberblut coupler's desire to come after him, but he was aware of his inability to do so just as vividly. Over the next twenty minutes, Cornelius fashioned a temporary plug for his wound, being a grafter after all, and the two men painstakingly made their way to the nearest safe place that could properly treat their injuries. It was a small shrine clinic. One of the resident grafters, a red-haired woman, gave them both an earful about how the clinic wasn't equipped to treat serious injuries. Nonetheless, their injuries were treated to an admirable standard. It turned out that out of the clinic's four resident grafters, three were sisters who looked just different enough to be distinguished but still unsettlingly similar.

Afterwards, the two men retreated to the shrine's inner sanctum for some rest and privacy.

"How did he find you?" Casus asked eventually.

Cornelius looked up at Casus with tired eyes, giving a weary smile.

"How did you find your belt?" He shrugged, as if the answer was as obvious as the color of the sky. "Direct sympathetic resonance. The arm reacted when he focused on it, so I had *some* forewarning... but not enough. Not nearly enough. Shame. I was halfway to unraveling the Abara Morph."

Casus hated that habit of his; dropping jargon and waiting for him to ask what it meant. So he just sat, and stared, and Cornelius broke. His desire to share the fruits of his research was stronger than his desire to be asked questions about it.

"You're joyless sometimes, you know that? You sure the coupler isn't giving you a permanent personality shift?" Cornelius complained. "Alright, fine. You saw how he looks, right? Sort of like a war morph, but not quite. And the insides of his arms. Those aren't *just* hemolymph cavities."

Shifting in place, Cornelius began listing off on his hands: "Additional internal reinforcement, improved muscular design, body segment detachment musculature, latticed chitin structure for extra hardness without loss of flexibility. Casus, the arm contained *dedicated, physicalized Thauma channels.* A new subtype of them at that, with a superior delivery rate and pressurization to the closest equivalent I am aware of. If I can replicate *just* these 'Tsetse-type' channels, adapted for a Mamon Armor design, I could create a full-organic unit that would—urhk!"

Cornelius grew more and more excited until his gesturing became too violent, and the irritation of his wound made him crumple up into himself in pain, clutching his side. After a minute or so of silence, he continued. "You know what all these things have in common, and you know that I know how a War Morph is built. They are the extremification of Evoy biology for the purposes of warfare, but Tsetse defies baseline Evoy biology without clear evidence of grafting. Whatever your Tsetse is, he isn't a War Morph."

"He is an Abara Morph; you've made that much clear. Now, explain what the term means. I am sure you feel terribly proud of inventing it."

Cornelius gave Casus the kind of stare that only fell half a step from openly asking if he really hadn't figured it out yet, or if he was just trying to make him say it out loud. It took Casus *some* effort to prevent a smirk from pushing its way onto his face.

"He's an Evoy-specific version, or rather a counterpart, for the Mamon Knight. You know, funny thing is, I don't think I could've learned much more from that arm than I did. The last thing I did was a simple saturation test. Positive. The ratio was all wrong, but there was a distinct host and catalyst signature. Can't expect our tests to work perfectly on their technology, I suppose."

"You know what this means."

"Of course. Whether we like it or not, this *must* be reported to the church."

CHAPTER 18

CASE THREE CLOSED

Krahe wasted no time in taking the proof of Eutropia's death back to Garvesh. Right next to the door in that back alley, near the cobbles that were stained with Evoy hemolymph, she found a pile of scrap. After taking a closer look, she recognized a few parts. A rack, a mangled burner, a burst-open thaumine tank. Her stomach wrenched when she realized it was none other than Imraal's food cart, mangled by what was likely an explosion.

Despite her deep and profound sorrow, she mustered the will to enter the building. She knocked on the old lizard's door and called out, "Open up, it's me!" He readily opened up upon hearing her voice.

The lock turned, and the door swung open, but Garvesh was nowhere near it.

"Close and lock the door. I'm in the bathroom. Come in, it's fine."

"Something happened," Krahe deadpanned as she did as he asked.

"You saw Imraal's cart out front. I took it out on the street. Didn't want to disappoint his customers, y'know. Some overly ambitious assclown just came up and blasted me point-blank with a Red Reaper. Can you believe that?"

There was effort in his voice, strain even, but the way he spoke about being shot with a Red Reaper carried a tone of disbelief and ridicule more than anything. Krahe was somewhat confused, but it wasn't because of that. It was the aura. Like some giant monster, unable to act in any way befitting its size yet inconceivable in its immensity.

Garvesh was, indeed, in the bathroom. The old lizard turned his eyes up to meet Krahe's as she walked in. He was sprawled out in the small pool he called a bathtub, leaning on one hand while his other was twisted into a stiff gesture—thumb, index, and ring fingers forming an eye, while the middle and pinkie were held straight. He hovered his hand over his stomach, a thin stream of blue-glowing magic pouring out through the eye to join a large, metallic scale of a blue shade so dark it was nearly black. Slowly, tiny bit by tiny bit, the scale grew. Others around it were also visible, transitioning from solid metallic to ghostly and to nothing. Krahe immediately knew what was happening. Wards. He was repairing his wards.

Across the room, chained up to the radiator, was a gagged man who may have been handsome at some point before the front of his body had been shredded and burned. A baneworm's bulging tendrils could be seen beneath his skin, and some even dangled out of the cavity of his torn stomach, tangled amongst his intestines.

"I'm not moving until this one is finished, so you may as well speak now," he remarked, refocusing his eyes on his own stomach. They momentarily flicked upwards at Krahe as he added, "Please tell me you came to tell me Imraal's killer is dead. I need some good news after this shitshow."

Krahe gave a slow nod, still processing the scene.

"Yeah. I have her souldregs if you want them."

"You said she's dead, so she's dead. You can show me the dregs later." He shrugged. A short time passed in heavy silence as Krahe remained captivated by the complex internal pattern of Garvesh's wards.

"I thought wards were at least partly tied to your attributes."

"They are. I wouldn't be able to form one of these from scratch in my state, and I've got a couple thin spots in places I won't tell you. But as long as one of these scales doesn't break, I can fix it. It's a bitch and a half, tell you what. The damage this wormy fuck did will be at least a week's work to repair. Just maintaining my wards is hard enough."

An aura of pure anger and hatred spilled out of Garvesh as he spoke, doubtlessly fuelled by awareness of the meticulous and strenuous work he had ahead of him. Krahe knew it all too well; for several years, she used a type of armor that, despite its high defensive performance, was no longer being manufactured. Manufacturing replacement graph-fullerene without the original machinery was perhaps among her least favorite memories. The inside of Garvesh's ward-scales didn't quite look as complex as a graphene mesh with fullerene balls instead of single carbon atoms, but it probably felt just as complex given that he was rebuilding it by hand. Krahe continued to watch for some time, drawing closer as Garvesh allowed her to observe.

"Feel free to try an' copy me, so long as you let me know when you fail so I can laugh at you. You wouldn't believe how many times I've seen someone try."

"I'm sure I'll figure something out. I've been using the same ward design far too long," she admitted. They had worked well enough when she needed them, and with the Liminal Coil, simply not getting hit had become her go-to defensive tactic.

"Think Semzar's going crazy and trying to have anyone who dealt with me killed?" she asked, assuming the worst.

"No, he's stupid, but not insane." Garvesh shook his head. "I know why dumbfuck here shot at me; he spilled his guts the moment I spilled *his* guts. One of the side effects of my crippled state is that so long as I do not burn Thauma, I come off exactly as weak as I feel. This fool, turns out, was the one who hired the assassin on Semzar's behalf. He saw me, saw Imraal's cart, and, puttin' two and two together, got five. He thought Imraal had somehow survived and faked his death, so he panicked and shot me."

Garvesh emitted a rumbling, engine-like chuckle.

"He saw a Drasaurian and thought a single juiced up Red Reaper would kill me. Even without wards that wouldn't be enough, not for me. Ey, you hear me?! Y'forget why yer filthy kind love to steal our bodies so much?!"

The noise didn't wake the baneworm, but what Garvesh did right after his outburst served that purpose. He gathered spit in his mouth, and spat out a piece of the same bluish metal as his ward-scales, enveloped in a thick layer of mucus. It landed right in the would-be assassin's eviscerated intestines, and quickly became enveloped in spitting, angry, blue flame. It looked like white phosphorus, just prettier and without the poisonous smoke.

The baneworm's host awoke. His eyes flashed with panic and tendrils bulged under his skin as he began screaming into his gag.

"Shut up, or the next one is going in your mouth," Garvesh threatened, gesturing at the burning mass currently eating its way into the prisoner's guts, somehow going deeper rather than following gravity.

Outright screaming tuned down to sounds of pain, until the worm's tendrils retracted from that area of his stolen body, and he fell silent. His gaze almost immediately became an analyzing one, darting back and forth, shamelessly looking for an opportunity to escape.

"What do you plan to do with him?" she gestured to the prisoner.

"I'll turn the body into the church. It should get back to any relatives he might have. The wormy fuck didn't even bother to change the face, and kept the original contractor ID. As for the worm... I'll debeak and swallow him whole. You've got an acid bath to look forward to, my friend."

The fear gripping the baneworm's host seemed to get to be too much, as his tendrils began writhing wildly. The body's eyes rolled into the back of its head, with tendrils bursting out of their sockets. The worm exploded out of the host's mouth, trying to jump for Krahe. Before it could reach her, Barzai erupted out of her chest, catching the worm in his beak as he darted across the room. The eidolon proceeded to tear into the worm, seemingly killing it instantly, and continued eating it from there on, piece by piece.

"Sorry. Looks like my pet eldritch monstrosity stole your dinner," Krahe said, genuinely unsure whether Garvesh would be angry. The old Saurian finally finished repairing the one ward-scale and erupted with guttural laughter.

"You didn't really think I'd eat that nasty fuck, did you?" He cackled, slapping his thigh. It sounded nearly like a gunshot.

"I've eaten worse." She shrugged. "Was that a total lie, or some niche delicacy?"

"It's a niche delicacy even among Saurians," Garvesh confirmed. "Baneworm meat's nasty and stringy, and you must carefully remove the venom glands without rupturing them. We used to do it as a ritual execution for any baneworms we caught."

The hatred dripping from each of his words made it abundantly clear how much he reviled baneworms as a whole, not just this particular individual. He shook his head as if to clear his thoughts, sighed, and glanced down at his chest, running his hand over it. The ward-scales revealed themselves beneath his fingers in a truly draconic suit of armor, though many of its scales were chipped or even broken.

"Fuckin'... They're getting more brittle by the year. Unless you've got more to tell me, you should go. I'll be here for a while."

Krahe glanced at Barzai, then replied, "I figure I'll be stuck here for at least fifteen minutes. Got any crab juice?"

Garvesh's face lit up, and nodding, he gestured vaguely towards his kitchen.

"Yeah, in the fridge. Pour yourself a glass. And bring me the whole jar after that."

Despite Garvesh's incident and the resulting tragic death of Imraal's food cart, things were going quite well. While she was still there, she presented him both Eutropia's souldregs and her broken voidkey, hoping he might be able to appraise it where her glasses failed. She had attempted to do so herself, but the reading in question was garbled and illegible.

Unfortunately, appraising a broken key's original effects turned out to be far more complex than appraising a functioning one. Audibly pleased with himself, Garvesh explained, "Think about it. Think a rando on the street could look at the pile of scrap out front and tell that it used to be a food cart, let alone the specific kind of burners it had or what kinda food it used to make? It's... Alright, it's not actually like that with broken artifacts, but the analogy still works. Takes specialized knowledge or equipment to make sense of it. If you want."

"No, you don't need to find someone who can appraise it for me. I'll let you know if I run out of my own options. You just... fix yourself. You'll be useless to me if you get whittled down and killed."

She spoke as if her motivations were entirely selfish, but in truth, she had grown at least enough of an attachment to Garvesh to not want him to die. Krahe, of course, was not self-aware of this fact, nor would she be willing to admit it to herself, let alone to someone else.

Returning to the safehouse, she found it empty. In the absence of anything urgent to do, she spent further time studying Yao's scroll. Having jumped ahead a few times, she found that the later sections were exceptionally dense and frequently referred back to earlier parts of the text, so she stuck to going through it from the start for now. The parts she had managed to digest so far mostly covered small tips and optimizations for the basic act of drawing a talisman. Rather than cosmic secrets, the scroll's early parts contained the wisdom of countless hours spent doing a precise, repetitive task. Krahe couldn't draw a Wandrei Faust with the new brush yet, but she found it to be far more pleasant and better balanced in the hand. It would only take time and practice to get used to it.

The reason she went straight to Yao's scroll was simply the fact that Yao was on her mind as she left Garvesh to his work. The Talisman Mistress was, after all, the first person who came to mind when it came to appraising the broken key.

Once she had built up a pile of wastepaper, her grip on the brush was noticeably unsteady, and she saw occult symbols when she closed her eyes; Krahe decided it was enough for now. She spent the rest of the day resting and casually reading, occasionally making basically futile attempts to pierce deeper into the dense mass of Yao's scroll.

The next day, she visited the shrine on Gashward Road as a stop along her way to her house on that street. A young, nervous woman manned the shrine. She couldn't be more than sixteen, yet Krahe felt a tangible degree of strength from her, both physical and magical. Despite being visibly intimidated by the sight of Krahe, apparently knowing who she was, the shrine maiden moved with trained grace. Her arms had well-defined muscles from what was visible of them.

"Would you happen to be Lady Blackhand?" the girl asked.

"That would be me, yes. I suspect I'll be visiting your shrine in the future."

"Ah, my name is Eliana. There are packages here for you, if you could come with me."

One of these aforementioned packages was heavy and the size of a small suitcase, while the other was about the size of a letter and half a centimeter thick. Both were wrapped in narrow reams of paper and stamped with a sigil with lines of smaller sigils spreading out across the package in a chain-like pattern.

"A pulse of your thauma, please," Eliana prompted, and Krahe complied. The central seals pulsed with golden light, and the sigil-chains gradually disappeared as if it was burning them away. With all the sigils gone, the packages looked a bit strange, but not particularly churchy, so she just carried them to house No. 94 the normal way.

Opening a box full of cash never got old. The paper wraps disintegrated the moment she tore them off, revealing a dark, wooden surface. Despite being wood, it was just as cold, firm and reflective as solid granite.

A brass insignia of the Seven Spokes stared back at her from the lid, which she lifted. Not the faintest sound issued forth when the lid swung back and knocked against itself. Rows of rings nestled into a tray awaited within. They were set with gems and engraved with glowing runes. For a shining moment, Krahe felt a child-like joy, grinning ear-to-ear. She could swear the rings glowed with purplish light, and a tangible wave of power washed over her. It was stony, impassive, utterly homogenous, and unlike the aura of a person, but the quantity of arcane currency contained within this suitcase was such that it could match the intensity of Casus' presence when he became Silberblut.

Lifting the tray, she found two more beneath it, decreasing in denomination, with the bottom-most one holding densely packed cylinders of plain bronze bands. Krahe appreciated that she wouldn't have to bother exchanging the rings. Beneath the bottom-most tray, she found a second, much simpler box, which she took out but left alone for now.

Moving onto the letter, it contained two papers. One was a talisman, and the other was the actual letter. It detailed her payout, specifying a hefty deduction for the suitcase with the options of keeping or returning it. It also mentioned that this payout was for Sorayah and that any further progress in the investigation would merit further compensation, specifically any information pertaining to potential Human Charcoal Cult cells and the recovery of relevant items such as further relics and human charcoal itself. A substantial portion of the payout was, in fact, for Sorayah's lantern and the human charcoal Krahe brought along.

A second, smaller sum came directly from Razem himself, the reason unexplained beyond the word 'Bonus.' The total money in the box fell shy of even half the posted bounty on her head, but it was still in the six digits. If she was being optimistic, even if Sorayah's case didn't lead to a greater cult, just the occult material in her home could furnish her with quite a bit of money. How much of that stuff she would turn in depended on whether she found a use for it. The post-script clarified that the talisman was for the ward-breaker; once activated, it would resonate with its twin in the ward-breaker's possession and call him to its location as pre-arranged by Razem. He would supposedly arrive within an hour if it was anywhere in the city.

As for the smaller box, it contained several paper bags and had another note from Razem on the inside. It was the herbal mixture for the Decoction of Mind's Dawn, with the note containing directions for brewing and drinking it. Most notable were dosage instructions and for how long it would be good after brewing.

"*You will surely find it to be of use.*"

To start with, she wanted to visit Yao again to see if the woman could answer some questions for her. There was the Hexkey, Eutropia's broken voidkey, as well as human charcoal in general. As for the anthrocite hand, she wanted to keep its existence to herself until she knew its potential value, so she decided to bring up anthrocite if Yao turned out to know about the base substance. She had not mentioned it to Razem out of caution.

There was the matter of her gunmanship, which was *acceptable*. She didn't consider the ability to hit a still target at a given distance to be the peak priority, especially since it was so contingent on the gun, the ammo, and the environmental factors. Target tracking and acquisition could be improved beyond just training and real combat, but those improvements would likely be grafts or combat drugs. As she saw it right now, her most pressing shortfalls were to do with getting the right ammo in the chamber at the right time. Alternating-load clips were a start, but awkward, and since the Pattner wasn't tube-fed, she couldn't do something like add a second tube magazine and a selector for which one was feeding. Without modifying the gun, the two options that came to mind were manually placing a bullet onto the bolt face while it was cycled forward or pushing the round into the top of the clip, assuming the clip was one bullet short. The second option was a bit problematic due to the fact the clips were held inside the gun only by friction and the same spring that pushed cartridges up through the clip.

There was no choice left but to see for herself. Simply pushing a bullet into a partially empty clip turned out to be the easiest solution. Sliding a bullet into the chamber directly also worked, counter to reason. The clip itself shifted downward slightly when a bullet was chambered, as if the follower spring was pulling it down in response. Krahe brought out the manual and went into the section with the blueprints. The magazine retainer—which was also the clip release lever—was the culprit. It was a single part that gripped a lip on the back of the clip, stopping the follower spring from sending the whole clip out the top of the breech. By disengaging it with one's thumb, it also allowed a non-empty clip to be ejected. The blueprint noted that it was enchanted to shorten subtly when a bullet was in the chamber *specifically* for the purpose of letting the user manually load a bullet.

Now that she gave it deeper thought, she remembered reading the manual only so far as it was relevant to maintenance of the weapon and loading the ammo. That left a good one-fifth of the book, which turned out to hold the answers to her questions, including the reason for the gun's specific design. This late section was absent from the table of contents, and its nonstandard nature was evidenced by the fact it was handwritten and not truly ordered. It stood to reason Pattner had made this one-off edition of the manual for Audun Sorun specifically, or possibly for early adopters in general.

"The revolving cylinder design, albeit convenient, is limited in capacity. My design can be modified to accommodate alternate and/or expanded magazine designs at any time; I have included example blueprints for two types on the next page. Any craftsman of mediocre skill can manufacture the modification. The same cannot be said for a revolving cylinder design. I shall not speak of contemporary revolvers' countless issues with structural integrity, sealing, reloading, etc."

The first modification was an unusual apparatus that would turn the Pattner into a belt-fed pistol, with designs for a disintegrating sheet-metal belt included.

The second one was, effectively, a Mauser C96-style self-contained integral magazine, including a design for a stripper clip. Its design even accounted for the possibility of the user wanting to convert the gun back to en-bloc clips.

These options might be useful in the future but were useless in the now. Krahe went through the rest of the manual just in case, finding a great deal of interesting technical details and various modifications or features that just didn't make it into the production version for one reason or another. Better sights, a rounded barrel, different grip, different trigger, a wooden stock that doubled as a holster, a rimless cartridge and a bolt to match it. So on and so forth. She spent enough time committing it to memory that she was confident it would float to the surface if it was ever directly relevant.

After dealing with the delivery and stashing most of her money away in the vent duct, she made her way to back Sorayah's place. The main reason for coming here—breaching her bedroom—turned out to be a bust. The ward-breaker, a Pilgrim Banisher with his horizontal eyes still closed, did his job and left right away like the meat-robot he was for the time being. Sorayah's bedroom was perfectly normal. Yes, there were occult materials scattered about, but Krahe found nothing that stood out—certainly nothing like the Hexkey or the anthrocite hand.

Disappointed, Krahe continued digging around the house. While reading the various occult texts, she spent time polishing her chamber-loading technique. The fact she needed two hands to do it gnawed at her, because an errant thought had come to her and stuck; a memory of what she had dismissed as a stupid gimmick when she saw it in her past life. A tiny appendage that would pop out of her forearm and shove a round into the chamber or a whole new clip into the mag well. The reason was obvious—she needed her left hand free to cast Wandrei Faust, and to carry out thaumaturgy in general. Eventually, after several hours and several infuriatingly similar manuscripts, it clicked. Why settle for a graft when she could achieve the same effect with thaumaturgy? She could simply conjure a bullet or a whole clip just like she did cigarettes. While any large tendrils were beyond her as far as manifestation from uncharred skin went, something this small was not an issue. Still, it added an Entropy cost to reloading, so simple manual dexterity would remain king. Another option in the arsenal.

Krahe gradually gathered Sorayah's texts in the writing room, keeping several open in the hopes of coming upon something, anything. Occasionally she would come to the ritual room in the basement to clear her head and look around the scene in the vain hope she would magically find something new.

Mistress Yao came to mind again. How would she even contact the woman?

"It's not as if she gave me a…"

She conjured the talisman that Yao gave to her. It held a captured trace of Eutropia's thauma, but it was still one of Yao's communication talismans, in theory.

"Well, might as well try."

CHAPTER 19

SPIRITUAL GUIDANCE

Yao had expected many possibilities. That the self-styled hero of justice would come to her of his own volition, alone, and unannounced, was not among them. She had assumed Blackhand would either figure out that the eye talisman she had given to her had a communication theurgy on the back, or that she would find the one hidden inside the scroll's spindle. She sent out a flesh-puppet to greet and ask him to wait before disarming her defences to let him in.

"I've come to claim what you owe," he said to her.

"Sounds to me like you're sick with a heart devil, after all," the woman smirked.

Casus wanted to argue, but she silenced him with a mere glance as she turned and gestured for him to follow. She brought him upstairs and examined him, carrying out various strange rites, some of which tangentially reminded him of Zaveshian and Igarian practices. Others, though, were completely unorthodox. It all involved a great number of talismans and needles that he barely felt. Moreover, with each round of tests Yao's confidence in her prognosis waned and her confusion grew.

"As it appears, it truly is not a heart devil. There's no corruption, no psychosis, no astral instability... How strange. The only alternative is the opposite, then. You've gleaned a piece of enlightenment recently but haven't fully processed it. Perhaps it runs counter to your pre-existing beliefs, and you have yet to reconcile the dissonance. How troublesome. I have many ways of dealing with heart devils, but nothing for this. I am afraid that I cannot help you with such a thing. However, I am not so callous as to pretend this cursory examination makes us even."

Nearly every part of Casus wanted to reject that, but he knew it was true. He had just hoped for the infinitesimal possibility that the issue was something easier to fix, such as internal bodily damage.

In the end, Casus left the woman and found himself wandering the city without any particular aim. He fell into a strange stupor and only came to his senses when he found himself in a particularly nasty part of town, tangling with random nameless scum from the gutter. Trash on legs, making a bid for Hashem's bounty. Two baneworms in Saurian bodies and four humans. There were six of them, and three brought out belts—two Dregsteamers and some homemade piece of shit with a motorbike throttle and a cracked, cloudy Locust Stone catalyst. This was a point where he would usually transform, but he simply couldn't. It wasn't that the Silberblut Coupler wouldn't respond; he couldn't even flip the mental switch that would initiate the transformation.

So, he fought as Casus Aristedes. He came out at the other end with several new bruises both to his body and his ego. A fight like this ought to have been trivial, but had it not been for his arm, he wasn't sure he would have walked out of that back alley. Even the bounty money for the baneworms had a bitter taste somehow.

For lack of direction, he turned to faith. Not directly asking Zavesh or Igaria for an answer—that just wasn't how things worked. No, he went to a man who had guided him on his path to taming the Silberblut Coupler to begin with. A man who spent much of his time within the city's central temple, volunteering as one of the gymnasium trainers between his excursions, all in pursuit of cultivating a perfect body and mind. His hair was white, and the centuries showed on his face the way a few decades past 20 showed on any other man, but his gaze burned like fire, and he held in one finger more strength than Casus held in his entire right arm.

Ambrosius, the Saint Ungrafted.

The saint lived in a small house about half an hour's walk from the central temple. It was downright ascetic compared to a church safehouse; the only luxury to be found was in the exercise equipment, books, and war games that filled much of the dwelling. Ambrosius was, as always, busy training when Casus found him, and as always, he found time to speak without uttering a word of complaint.

Ambrosius simply led Casus into the basement, where a miniature urban landscape of astonishing detail stretched across a table. In the span of a few minutes, he brought out boxes of miniatures and re-set the battle state as it was nearly a year ago when they had last spoken like this. The saint didn't say a word, simply playing his turn. Two of his thaumaturge units got a lucky strike in and cut down Casus' graft-beast.

So it went for around three hours, finishing that battle and beginning another before Casus managed to order his thoughts enough to put some of them into words. "I have lived my life with the unwavering belief that I was to be the next Silberblut. If that is not my role, then why... What..."

Three turns, about half an hour, passed before Ambrosius answered.

"Tell me, young one. Is a man no more than a flesh-automaton? Is a son no more than the sum of his parents? Is a Fullgraft no more than the sum of the saints from whose parts their body was crafted?"

"No," Casus answered without hesitation.

"And what, pray tell, is the reason? What differentiates you from your unthinking brethren, who tirelessly maintain the Wheel?"

"The indomitable spirit of divinity which burns within all mankind."

"Straight from the scriptures," said the saint, smiling.

They continued to play in silence for some time, and spoke for far longer than that, into the night and unto dawn. Eventually, Casus reached a conclusion. "I believe I shall be able to move past this, but I will require time in the Chamber of Reflection."

"Are you certain? You know the risks," Ambrosius cautioned, but didn't try to dissuade him.

"I know them better than most. I believe a day will be enough."

"Very well. Besides Favonia, Firminus, and Fidelia, is there anyone who should be informed regarding your status should complications occur?"

"Yeah." Casus nodded.

Several hours later, he was floating in a tank of fluid deep beneath the central temple, in a chamber whose walls held two dozen such tanks. It was not a dreamless, peaceful slumber, but a journey into his own psyche induced through elixirs and absolute sensory deprivation. He'd done this before, once. It wasn't fun then. It wasn't fun now. The risks were many; mental damage, delusions, and even permanent catatonia. The fluid was, in fact, a vast colony of engineered omniphage that at once drew out bodily waste and supplied the body with nutrients. To call this particular strain 'omniphage' was a stretch, but it was the correct term.

Nonetheless, he found at least part of the answer he had been searching for.

* * *

Krahe, as much as she disliked it, understood why Casus decided to send that message back to the safehouse. If she was not mistaken, he was taking a significant risk, comparable to her own choice to dive into the Astral Gulf not long ago.

He returned seemingly no better or worse off, but there was something different about him.

When he started asking about how she saw the matters of legacy and inheritance, she knew he'd chanced upon *something* in that glorified sensory deprivation tank. She gave it some thought, and, at first, she decided to just parrot the words of someone who had given this matter far more thought than she.

"A great philosopher from my world's ancient past once said that tradition is the preservation of fire, not the worship of ashes. But that's not what you need to hear. What you need to hear is that you will never be the Silberblut of legend. The only thing you'll achieve by mirroring your predecessor is to become a distorted echo of him in our era."

"Then how would you see it if someone did for you as I have been doing for Silberblut?"

"Honestly?"

"Lady Blackhand, my convictions are not so fragile as to break this easily," said the Banisher, not entirely certain of his own words. "I have come to learn that you are more honest than most when it comes to giving your unfiltered thoughts. Of course I want your honesty."

"If I learned of someone trying to embody the idea of me five centuries after my death, let alone five millennia, I would be confused at best. Most likely, I would be a bit disturbed. It would be an imitator, not a successor. But if someone were to, let's say, discover some of my old grafts, use them to unearth a conspiracy and bring down the masterminds in their own time, I might consider such a person a worthwhile successor. I don't know what Silberblut was like when he still lived, but if I were him, I would prefer for a would-be successor to use my coupler for his own ideals, not for slavish imitation of mine."

Krahe took a long swig of ekarone juice as she watched Casus absorb her words.

She then added, "That being said, I think I prefer your idealism to Silberblut's cold judgment. I mean, 'guilt repaid with cold blood, each and every guilty man?' A bit harsh. Even I wouldn't chop off a petty thief's hands."

"I admit that some of my predecessor's recorded judgments gave me pause as well. It is why I worked so hard to ensure I had full control of myself before using the belt..." Casus trailed off, his gaze shifting across the table to the Silberblut Coupler's vacant eye. His features hardened, and newfound determination crept into the banisher's voice. "I suppose now it is time to take full control of the belt itself. Tell me another, Lady Blackhand, before I go."

"Another what?"

"Another quote from one of your world's saints."

"Hmm, I never did study ancient history much. I usually read these whenever one extremist or another used them on a poster." Krahe shrugged, but nonetheless furrowed her brow as she went rooting around in her memory. "I think I recall that Saint Augustine once said... What was it he said? Barzai, help me here. The one about anger and courage."

She held out her arm, splitting it open lengthwise to let the eidolon manifest itself. Barzai popped out and took up a perch on her open palm, tilting his head back and forth before locking his gaze on Krahe.

"Beef," the raven demanded in a large black man's voice.

"I'll give you some if you give me that quote."

"Beef, twelve ounces," he reiterated.

"We have tortoise. You liked it better than beef."

The whole time, Casus observed, his stoic visage admirably masking his mild bewilderment at the scene. That thing really wasn't a normal eidolon; not only did it eat, it even made *demands* of its master.

Nonetheless, the offer of tortoise steak convinced the crow. It opened and closed its beak a few times, snippets of various sounds and voices coming out as if it was scrolling through radio stations. After a solid two minutes, Barzai opened his beak one final time. A scratchy voice came out, like that of a man who yelled a lot, made even grainier by the hiss of a low-quality speaker.

"Hope has two equally glorious and terrible daughters, for they drive men to action like none other; their names are Anger and

Courage. Anger at the world's wrongs, and Courage to see that these wrongs might be righted. Or something like that, I'm kinda stupid…"

At that point, Krahe recalled the raven.

"Alright, that's enough. You'll get your meat in a bit."

She couldn't help but notice that Casus had a profound look on his face as he left, but she didn't give it much thought. After all, it felt like the Banisher had a profound expression more often than not.

* * *

Underground, in the privacy of a Zaveshian indoor gymnasium, Casus Aristedes engaged in an ill-conceived exercise in self-abuse. His hair was draped in front of his face as he stood, leaning on a wall, the Silberblut Coupler clasped about his waist. He was emitting sounds of struggle utterly unbefitting of his image—be it as Silberblut, or as Casus Aristedes.

The belt's eye, vacant of its four-pronged star, whipped back and forth like the eye of a panicked animal. Bursts of golden flame issued from the coupler as it tried to transform its user into Silberblut, only to find itself rejected with an unimpeachable will demanding its subjugation to ideals that clashed with what it was accustomed to. The half-sentient artifact didn't understand. It had, up until this point, been fooled into thinking its user had never changed at all.

Casus, meanwhile, struggled to stand, even with support. He hadn't experienced struggle like this since his first attempts to use the Silberblut coupler. The sole, singular saving grace of this torturous power struggle was the fact he didn't need to worry about Isotope poisoning. Each exposure was so brief and minimal that even dozens of attempts didn't match to the full suit operating at combat output levels.

That didn't make this any less unpleasant. His head and soul threatened to split open as he tried to assert himself over the belt's tendencies rather than letting the transformation go through. Casus was well aware that what he was trying to do was the labor of months and years, but he had never been the patient, slow-going type. Becoming a suitable user for the Silberblut Coupler was the work of decades, they had told him, and he had achieved it in less than two years.

[SHINING KNIGHT OF SILVER]
Tags
Self-Adaptation
Mamon Coupler Compatibility
Details
This boon forcibly maximizes the holder's compatibility with any Mamon Coupler. The nature and severity of side effects is variable. Severity of side effects can be mitigated in various ways depending on their nature.

That Boon—the pride and great achievement of Casus' hard work—was now a shackle. He now understood that it was fundamentally flawed.

He continued his struggle with the belt until he lost consciousness from exhaustion. After the attendants from the shrine above helped him recover, he continued on without delay, prompting reactions of mixed respect and concern. They were familiar.

He's doing it again. What could possibly drive one to such horrific training? the shrine maidens thought. Nonetheless, he was a Banisher, and so they didn't question his choices.

Their fear for him wasn't unfounded. The more he pushed, the more a fear grew inside him—a fear he would cripple or kill himself.

In the end, he began to feel the coupler's confused panic. Through the pain and the constant immolation with sacred flame of transformation, the sacred relic eventually reached out to him, and he readily grasped its metaphorical hand.

It didn't communicate in words, or even clear thoughts, but vague sentiments. From what little Casus understood, it had finally realized that he wasn't Silberblut, but rather a successor... and now it wanted to know why he was doing this. In effect, it was asking him the same question he himself had sought an answer to. *"Why refuse the transformation? Why would you want to be anything other than a shadow of Him?"*

Casus, however, had a pure, burning determination in his chest, a flame born from his own ruminations, from the guidance of the Saint Ungrafted, and from his conversation with Lady Blackhand. She, in particular, had been the one to pour the accelerant onto the pile and set it alight, with her straightforwardness of expression.

The sentiment which he poured into the Silberblut Coupler in response was as pure and brilliant as the pain that scorched his being. *"I am not Magnus Aristedes. I will never be Magnus Aristedes. To pretend is a dishonor upon his name. I am the next in line, the successor. Walk with me out of his shadow or join me in the void."*

At that moment, something broke. Casus wasn't sure if he had finally burst his Soul Furnace or inflicted some other crippling astral injury in his bullheaded efforts, or if it was the belt's stubbornness that broke. But something undeniably did break.

The pain that came after would have sent any human into the bliss of shock-induced unconsciousness, but, grinding his teeth, Casus persevered. At that moment, as the man of faith he was, Casus prayed with a fervor worthy of any saint, crumbling to his knees as he thoughtlessly repeated an advanced, seventy-seven lines long prayer to Zavesh.

There, in the depths of struggle and pain, he found an abiding and invincible will to move forward. For the briefest moment, he could swear someone was pulling him back to his feet and speaking encouragement in his ear. He couldn't make out most of the words, only an immense sense of pride and agreement with the idea that he had no choice but to move forward as something new.

For a few moments, he was able to claw back true clarity of mind. As he leaned against the wall, drawing in sharp, ragged breaths, he felt and saw something truly strange—the Right Arm of Silberblut, moving of its own accord. It took him a moment to realize it was using one-handed sign language to spell out individual letters.

YOUR
TURN

He felt his mind being pulled inward, into his system, towards the Shining Knight of Silver. The Boon changed right before his mind's eye, the letters themselves torturously shifting in a manner unlike anything Casus had seen from the system. His boons had changed in the past, but it was never like this. It almost looked as though the Boon was being melted and forced into a new shape.

[CRUSADER OF BLACK AND GOLD]
Tags

Imposition of One's Will

Mamon Coupler Compatibility

Details

This boon forcibly maximizes any Mamon Coupler's and/or Catalyst's compatibility with the holder through "Heroic Subjugation."

Carrying out Heroic Subjugation incurs backlash, the nature and severity of which are highly variable. The severity of backlash can be mitigated in various ways depending on its nature. The holder may suffer astral injury due to subjugation backlash.

The effects of Heroic Subjugation are permanent for Couplers and Catalysts with which the holder has a strong bond of possession. In other cases, the effects last until the item is used by someone other than the holder.

Without thinking, Casus transformed. None beheld the form he took, and even he was in no state to maintain or remember it. He could do it, and that was enough for his utterly drained self, so he detransformed and collapsed on the spot.

When he returned to his senses, the pain was gone. Or rather, he was still wracked with an ache as if he'd been fed through a rock crusher, but he no longer felt as though his Soul Furnace might burst at any moment. Glancing down, he saw that the Silberblut Coupler's outer frame was, for the lack of a better term, shedding. It was now covered in dark, brittle slag. Casus unbuckled the belt, and as he took it off, the mere motion was enough to shake the slag off.

Underneath was alarite. Pure alarite, flickering as if reflecting a dancing flame. As for the belt's eye, it now bore a new pattern; in the stead of Silberblut's four-pointed star, a cross mimicking the pattern of Casus' own eyes shone over the blue abyss in the eye's depths. It also seemed unsettlingly alive. Whereas it had been stony and motionless before this endeavor, frozen in a forward stare, it now shone with a not-quite-human awareness. It was as if the Silberblut Coupler had been asleep until now, carrying out its duties by simple instinct, and only now had it been roused and made to acknowledge its new master.

The Banisher, completely drained, spent the better part of the next day resting.

Meanwhile, Krahe burned away the daytime hours in seclusion, occupying herself with a mixture of reading, physical training, and calligraphy practice. The Decoction of Mind's Dawn felt miraculous at first, too good to be true, even, allowing her to compile several different Human Charcoal Cult scriptures, using them to fill in one another's gaps. It grew increasingly obvious that the individual texts were purposely left with gaping holes—a fairly typical infosec tactic. In several cases, strange phrases or even oddly written words served as indexing marks for where a section of text should be replaced with another, changing the meaning of a passage. Disappointingly, the information that came together entailed superior, more complete versions of the rites and manipulation methods detailed within each scripture, with an implied anthrocite yield of around 3-4% of the victim's body mass.

Krahe didn't doubt that informing the church of these hidden rites would mean a good payday, but she wanted to know more about the uses of anthrocite and the Hexkey. The Decoction's side effects showed themselves sometime after she set aside the cultist texts and began making headway into Yao's scroll. The flavor suddenly became violently acidic and astringent, her body rejecting the liquid altogether, and a thumping pressure made itself known inside her head, threatening to turn into a splitting headache if she took another sip. Fortunately, that she had followed Razem's guidelines, and had made only one day's dose of the liquid. The preparation guide also warned that it was volatile, losing potency in mere hours.

Despite that limitation, the Decoction of Mind's Dawn nonetheless pushed her past the edge of comprehension. As the sun dipped past the horizon, she grasped Yao's brush in hand with a new understanding of its previously awkward weight distribution. The Chimerahair Brush, as her glasses identified it, demanded a grip that felt like it would fall from her grasp at any moment, but it didn't. Once she got it moving, she finished the back side of a Wandrei Faust talisman in less than half her previous fastest time, and the same went for the front. The limitation was no longer the brush, but her own skill, manual dexterity, and ability to mentally parse the patterns she was imbuing in the paper.

She found that with this new brush, the patterns felt even more angry than before; the theurgic pattern felt almost alive. The claw almost seemed to twitch on the paper, waiting for a neck to grab. Krahe took the time to load three fresh cartridges with these improved papers, marking each with a painted ring midway down the length of the case. She stored these, along with three of their earlier counterparts, in her Kenoma Pocket. Thereafter, she loaded a clip full of six mescalt bullets into the Pattner, and a seventh straight into the chamber before sealing the gun.

The only thing left to do was to write a message and send Yao's communication talisman back to its owner. It was a relatively simple process, though laborious due to the talisman's ravenous appetite for thauma. The message was brief, informing the talisman mistress of Krahe's intent to visit and requesting confirmation that she could do so without taking as much of a risk as Casus had. Half an hour later, when she walked out back to check, she found a camouflaged talisman hovering in the exact same spot as the time before.

Not too long after, she made her way to Yao's home. It was without incident, insofar as her own journey went. However, about a third of the way there, the ground shuddered. A huge impact, akin to a thunderclap, sounded in the distance, past the horizon—likely several kilometers outside the city. Then came another, and a third for good measure. A few seconds later she saw a burning yellow comet screaming into the heavens. Two more followed it; one blue and one purple. The blue one resembled an actual comet, violently tearing through the air with a rocket-like tail, whereas the purple one was smooth, its flight seeming nearly effortless save for the huge arcs of lightning it gave off.

A swarm of smaller lights separated from the yellow comet, surrounding the others, turning a swath of the sky into a field of explosions, only for blue and purple to emerge seemingly unscathed. The sky was lit up by a dance of lights as these three chased one another, unleashing arcane death upon each other. Distant sonic booms and explosions filled the night, and the conflict of nameless demigods illuminated the city like a wild thunderstorm.

Krahe almost felt at home for the span of her walk across the city. It drew out a great number of curious civilians, with a surprising number of people climbing out onto the roofs of their homes and apartment buildings. Despite the number of eyes, Krahe felt even safer from notice.

Attention was being directed in the exact opposite direction of where she was, after all. The three comets were still fighting by the time she reached Yao's place.

The two of them walked through Yao's death-gauntlet of trapped alleyways and corridors. Not a word was exchanged until they entered her home.

"First him, now you. I am flattered by such trust," the mistress remarked with a decidedly hag-like, facetious smugness. She spun on a heel, conjured a slender pipe from between the talismans on her left arm, lit it, and took a long drag, all in a single motion lasting no more than three seconds.

"In exchange, I *trust* that you are not here for help with a crisis of ideology," she added.

"Of course not. I have two things that I believe will interest you," Krahe replied, sitting down as she began the process of opening her Kenoma Sack. She found it increasingly easier to do if she gave it a bodily medium rather than just using the black tablet directly. So, with a yawning maw splitting her forearm down the middle, she brought out two items of interest: Eutropia's broken key came first.

"I need to have this appraised. It... well it sings, for lack of a better term. My gut tells me it has something to do with Astro Diving- Spirit Walking, as you call it."

With a long exhalation of smoke, the talisman mistress near-enough stalked over to the table. The interest couldn't be more evident in her eyes as she sat down, crossed her legs, and leaned forward to get a better look at the broken voidkey's pieces.

"Yes, I recall a scripture which described it as a certain inaudible song that, once heard, one cannot help but keep noticing..." Yao trailed off, curiously picking up the key's pieces with either hand, the pipe sticking to the corner of her mouth in a gravity-defying manner. "It is a typical post-mortem extraction strain fracture. The voidkey is still mostly intact - you could implant it, and it *might* function as-is, albeit to a fraction of its original specifications. That unfortunately means the bloodline lock is also mostly intact. The lock doesn't appear to be particularly profound. I will be able to subvert it, perhaps even maintain the functionality and merely alter it to recognize you as the rightful host. The craftsmanship speaks of a highly skilled craftsman purposely working to a lower standard than he is used to. Nonetheless, it is still better than anything you can readily find on the open market."

Yao put the key's pieces back down, leaning back in her seat.

"I will contact you with any relevant information once I have had the time to carry out the necessary rites. While the key *is* relevant, I suspect it is the less important of the two, seeing as you left the other matter for second," Yao said, glancing down at Krahe's split-open forearm.

Giving a nod of affirmation, Krahe continued her effort to extract the human charcoal piece from storage. Slowly, painstakingly, a black tendril lifted it out of her forearm-maw and placed it right next to her arm. The moment it was out, Krahe snapped the maw shut and began purging, letting out a deep sigh of relief. For reasons that escaped her, this time the purge remnants manifested as a scentless smoke, spilling out of her mouth and nose without ceasing for the whole duration of the purge. Human charcoal was truly infernally impractical to store in Kenoma storage, taking up many times more space than its actual physical mass. The same phenomenon applied to other magical items, but human charcoal was the most extreme example she had encountered by far.

Yao remained silent as she tilted her head back and forth, inspecting the human charcoal. It was as if she was trying to judge whether it would be safe to even touch it, or perhaps waiting for Krahe to explain what it was.

"It's an anathema radiation source, but not actively hazardous. I won't say any more until you inspect it for yourself," said Krahe.

Reaching out with her left hand, several papers split off from Yao's arm and wrapped around the chunk, bringing it closer to her. She silently inspected it for a few moments, subjecting it to four separate talisman-based tests. Twice, the paper's patterns changed color, and twice more, it burned on contact with the stone. The first time was instant, like flash paper, and the second slowly blackened the paper as if the charcoal piece was just a hot ember. After contemplating for a further minute, Yao simply asked, "Are you yourself aware of what this is?"

"Yes," Krahe confirmed. "I'll make this simpler for the both of us. I will not reveal how much I know—and from what perspective that information comes—until you do the same. I believe we can both benefit from an exchange of knowledge."

After a few more moments of contemplation, Yao took the chunk in hand and began speaking.

"This is... Well, there is no direct equivalent word that comes to mind."

"Charcoal?" Krahe suggested. It *looked like* charcoal, so she wasn't giving up much by suggesting that word.

With a nod, Yao continued: "It is charcoal made from a human, body and soul both. In Tiengenzhen, this is the *waste*, or perhaps more accurately, the *side product* of the Onyx-black Puppet Hall's human refinement arts. Even this *waste* is considered immensely valuable to all artifact cultivators, as it is the cheapest fuel for certain artifacts and tools. Its value is such that inferior versions of the Onyx-black Puppet Hall's rites that are only capable of producing this have spread throughout the land. The strongest battle puppets devour a hundred convicts' worth of this in a day of operation, but they are still used by the mortal kingdoms because the number of lives they save far surpasses the price. Even so, it is—"

Turning the chunk in her hand, Yao's expression shifted from one of consideration to disgust, and she placed it back on the table.

"Wretched. Human refinement is, by its very nature. The victim's suffering is part of the process. It simply does not work without it. I believe the Onyx-black Puppet Hall's method is called the Five Torments Blast Furnace Refinement. It involves a specially constructed furnace chamber that deprives the victim of all senses, keeps them alive, and allows for the introduction of hallucinogenic poisons throughout the process. Only reincarnation ends the victim's suffering, despite the rumors of the uneducated that claim the victim's soul is imprisoned in the coal. That is my understanding of this substance, its origins, and its uses. Now, I believe, it would be your turn."

Digesting the information, Krahe started with an easy one. "This Onyx-black Puppet Hall. Are they related to the Thousand Puppets Hall?"

"I am surprised that you are aware of them. Yes, they are related. The Onyx-black Puppet Hall was formed by a group of demonic artifact cultivators who left the Thousand Puppet Hall rather than let themselves be judged for their crimes. I must ask, if you do not mind, how do you know of the Thousand Puppets Hall?"

"I have met a man with strange-looking arms, looked into the matter, and learned that one of them was of Tiengenzhen origin. Not much else, unfortunately. Now, regarding what I know of this stone..."

Krahe went on to recount some of her knowledge regarding human charcoal and the Human Charcoal Cults, taking care not to stray or to go too deep, so that the knowledge she shared would not surpass what Yao had shared, or otherwise reveal what she wanted to keep concealed. The talisman mistress gradually became more visibly interested, particularly at the mention of the Human Charcoal Cults.

"You would not happen to know when these cults were active, would you?" Yao asked.

"At least a century, starting in the late 4120s. Presumably earlier, but I don't know enough to make any guesses."

A smirk took hold on Yao's face.

"What a curious coincidence. An acquaintance of mine made off with copies of the Onyx-black Puppet Hall's ritual scrolls only thirteen years prior to that time, and vanished from Tiengenzhen in... Oh, I think it was 4112. But he would've left inheritances. That bastard was not the sort to put all his eggs in one basket. Perhaps the church was just very thorough."

"And perhaps they still take such great care specifically to curtail cases like Sorayah. Even what she found was enough to sow the seeds of a serious issue for the city, given how well they paid me for rooting her out," Krahe said.

Knowledge of Sorayah and the fact Krahe had dealt with her was a minor detail. It was convenient to use as a framing device for how she had obtained human charcoal and knowledge of it, and she hadn't spoken so much as a word regarding the Hexkey or the Anthrocite Hand.

Nonetheless, this game was still frustrating. After some further circular conversation, Krahe decided to just ask the question outright: "Considering everything, do you think human charcoal would be of any use to either of us?"

"No," Yao said without hesitation, shaking her head. "It's too volatile for ink or any other artifact crafting. Its only use is as fuel for artifacts and certain demonic rituals, of which I know a few, but none would be useful. There is a good reason it is considered a borderline waste product. The energy output by its burning is far too unstable to use in the manner I desire, and besides sheer burst output, your own natural abilities are superior to the burning of human charcoal. Its greater counterpart, however, is another matter."

"What if I happen to come upon it?" Krahe asked, allowing her tone of voice and expression to make it clear she had anthrocite or knew where to find it. "You wouldn't happen to know and be willing to share methods of distinguishing it from the chaff and making use of it?"

"That depends on the quantity, quality, and use case. I do not own any written texts, but I am certain I could aid in preparing and performing any channeling rituals."

Krahe weighed her options. There was the chance that the Hexkey's evolution would turn out not so useful, and either way, Yao was still one of a vanishingly small minority with reason to not screw her over and the skills to craft a higher-order voidkey. If she kept this course, she would eventually have to disclose the Hexkey's existence to Yao regardless.

"Alright, fine, enough games," Krahe huffed, deciding to just spill everything about the Hexkey. As it was, both it and the anthrocite hand were completely useless to her. "To start with, I know the superior counterpart to human charcoal under the name 'anthrocite.' Secondly, I found what I believe to be an inheritance from the Human Charcoal Cults. The first part is a cursed voidkey that promises it will evolve at some ill-defined point, claiming that it will 'evolve once Anthrocite Transmutation reaches 100%.' It currently sits at around 66%. The second part is a full hand made of anthrocite, found in a purposely poorly sealed box disguised as a book. It was locked with a holeless lock that demanded painstakingly precise anathema manipulation to open. The box also contained a message that directly stated the hand should somehow be sufficient to 'finish' the cursed voidkey."

"I see why you would be cautious about disclosing this to anyone you do not fully trust," Yao acknowledged. "Do you know the nature of the curse, or is the voidkey warded against appraisal?"

Krahe had no qualms about explaining the nature of the Flame's Collapse Hexkey, since there was no reason to withhold this information after what she had already disclosed. The mistress listened with interest, concluding, "It's clearly intended to hook a prospective disciple and *encourage* commitment. I would not be surprised if there was at least one more link in the chain that could somehow override the Hexkey. Did you bring either the key or the anthrocite hand? While I cannot be certain until I've examined both relics, I believe I may be able to aid you in completing the Hexkey."

She turned, glancing out the window. Despite the ground-level windows not facing the open street, the battle in the sky still reached them in the form of occasional flashes of light and moving shadows on the surrounding buildings.

"And if we are to carry out such a rite, it would be best to do it tonight, if at all possible. We are not likely to receive such a convenient cover for some time," Yao added.

"You expect the process to create a large energy signature, and you think that the battle will be a sufficient distraction," Krahe stated.

Turning back to face her again, Yao nodded. "In more ways than one. The protections I already have in place, combined with the protections I will create for the rite, will do most of the work, but I am not an anathema specialist."

She got up and walked to the window, leaning on its edge. Outside was a narrow alleyway, with the walls and roof of the next building over being plastered in talismans, included as part of Yao's defensive perimeter. A shimmering wall of scrolling symbols rose from the wall of the building across the alley, becoming visible when Yao came into its vicinity. Staring up at the sky, face lit by intermittent flashes from above, she continued to speak.

"At best, assuming you contribute your expertise, I would estimate that at least one-tenth of the ritual's waste energy will leak into the environment. The arcane winds stirred up by tonight's heavenly battle will suffice to sweep it away, and the battle itself will provide us with plausible deniability. I do not expect individuals of that level to disclose their trump cards to dispel accusations of anathema usage, given the fact that anathema seems to be regarded as a force that can only be safely wielded by high-level practitioners. Perhaps one of the participants made use of an anathemic technique in desperation. It would make perfect sense for one of them to use it, perhaps the red one..."

Yao became drawn into her own words, a sense of melancholy, nostalgia even, creeping into her speech.

"I must admit that I am curious. How does that display compare to your own experiences?" Krahe asked. It was, indeed, somewhat familiar to her. She had seen power-armored superhumans soaring through the sky on jets of plasma, firing off rays of death and hypersonic slugs, forming wings made of nanomachines for protection. Krahe had seen it, but despite a degree of familiarity, it was still different and new in some ways.

"Feels the same as looking at the stars here. Familiar, but different," the talisman mistress croaked, taking another drag from her pipe. It was a perfect description for how Krahe felt about it, too. She watched in silence. Krahe walked up to the window and hopped up on the ledge, sitting down with her legs hanging out. It was wide enough to still leave about a meter of empty space between the two of them. Without a thought, Krahe conjured an arrha cigarette and joined Yao in smoking. The smoke mixed together into a medicinal, incense-like compound, and a cloud formed around them as it dissipated slower than new smoke was added.

The talisman mistress spoke up again some ten minutes later. "They want *someone* in the city to see them fight, yet they also fear the consequences of causing collateral damage. I was observing them before you arrived; even with my impaired senses, I noticed six instances where an opening was not taken advantage of out of fear it might strike a building. At my peak, I would have mocked them for not having the person above the city lord in their pockets, or for not being able to quickly set up precautions so that an all-out battle would not ever threaten the city, even as close to its perimeter as this."

They watched for a few more minutes before Krahe eventually brought out the Hexkey and set it down on the windowsill between them. After sparing a brief glance, Yao took it in hand and stepped back from the window, turning away from it. Resting her pipe in the corner of her mouth, she brought the key to her left eye and pulled back the talisman plastered over its socket. An ominous, invasive sensation filled the room as a floodlight of eldritch darkness emanated from her eye, with shimmering wisps of indescribable color whirling in the blackness.

As quickly as it had begun, it ceased. With a sound somewhere between a wheezing inhalation, the scraping of glass, and the creak of a bone being slowly bent to breaking, the unlight was drawn back into Yao's left eye socket, once more sealed away.

"It certainly matches your description, for better or worse. I cannot predict what form it will take upon its evolution, but I shall gain a deeper understanding given some time to examine it more thoroughly," Yao said. She turned to Krahe, who had by now hopped down from the window. "Have you brought the hand as well?"

Krahe shook her head. "It would have left a trail."

"And you did not wish to bring both items, just in case," Yao added the quiet part, walking over to the table. She set the Hexkey upon it and brought out six talisman papers. "How large is the container?"

She conjured the book closest in size, stating, "Same height, slightly wider, two and a half times as thick. The internal volume suffices to fit a man's severed hand in a loosely curled-up position without much free space."

Manipulating the papers in mid-air, Yao added several more, going well beyond what was needed to cover the whole thing. Then, she arranged them in mid-air and got to work. Grinding a red ink stick into a small puddle of scarlet liquid with a few meticulous motions, Yao pulled droplets into the air and, using mere gestures, manipulated them into forming complex symbols upon the paper. She turned the talismans into indistinguishable copies of one another, with complex patterns that exuded a powerful, pure meaning. Krahe's instincts warned her to avoid getting them on herself; they would likely cripple her ability to dissipate Isotope and expel Anathema in any form, even if temporarily.

With a wave of her hand, Yao collected the papers into a bundle and set them on the side of the table where Krahe had sat.

"I would ask that you bring the hand," she said. "I would like to keep the Hexkey in the meanwhile so that I may examine it, but I shall not stop you if you wish to take it with you for safety."

Krahe suppressed the part of her which intensely distrusted the unsettlingly familiar stranger that Yao was and simply took the papers while leaving the Hexkey where it stood.

She left Yao's home without a word, with the talisman mistress turning her attention to examining the relic in greater depth. Yao wasn't at all offended or put off by her guest's behavior; they had interacted a grand total of *once* before now, and even then, Yao had offered up admittance of her position in relation to Krahe as a token to buy some trust. Despite it being the purest truth, Yao had assessed Krahe's character, and she was not surprised that it had curried her only a tentative level of trust. It would take substantive shows of trustworthiness from both sides before they truly had confidence in one another. Building rapport was, in fact, Yao's main reason to suggest hunting a soulbeast for materials. Such an outing would be the most expedient way to increase trust and bond with her new, fate-ordained allies.

Even still, in the here and now, Krahe showed more trust than Yao had expected. She nearly did a double take when the anathemist took off and she realized the Hexkey was still there, on the table. Yao made her way upstairs, where she took to carrying out a deeper, more conventional examination of this voidkey, forgoing the use of her Left Eye in favor of the skills she had developed over centuries prior.

CHAPTER 20

CHARCOAL GAMES

As Krahe made her way through the city back to Gashward 94, she quickly came to understand what exactly Yao had meant when she spoke of the battle whipping up arcane winds that would scour away any signs of their anthrocite transmutation ritual.

The air was *thick* with an almost oppressive, dense feeling pervading every breath. Her heretofore unnamed sense for magic was completely dulled, much like how an overpowering stench can smother a more subtle scent. She even felt the waxing and waning of the "winds"—a nonphysical pressure that, with its stronger gusts, sanded away bits of her wards.

Yao's sealing papers demanded some finesse to use properly, and Krahe spent a few minutes meticulously activating each one before plastering it onto the fake book-box. Despite expecting *something* to go wrong, nothing did; Krahe reached Yao's residence without incident, though she took a roundabout path. Several streets away from Yao's place, Krahe noticed one of Yao's talismans stuck to a wall amidst old posters and charms. As she approached, carefully observing just how far and wide Yao's talismans were spread out, Krahe came to the conclusion that Yao likely had an area larger than Slaughterhouse 9 secured as her personal fortress without most, if any, of her neighbors being aware of this fact.

Upon her return, Krahe found that Yao had left her main defenses inactive. Instead, there was a fake wall. It looked convincing from a distance, and it nudged one's gaze away from itself, but perhaps due to being a welcome guest, Krahe had no issue discerning that it was an illusion. She walked through, feeling a brief bout of confusion as she entered the next section, somewhat like walking into a room and forgetting the reason. This also passed quickly.

Yao called her upstairs when she entered, and Krahe heard the monstrous defender puppets stirring back to life as the door closed behind her.

"I expected the confusion array to slow you down more," the talisman mistress stated plainly, glancing up to meet Krahe's eyes before looking down at the box in her hand. Krahe placed the box on the table, and with a snap of her fingers, Yao ignited the talisman papers in golden flames. Krahe then unlocked and opened the box, leaving Yao to examine the hand while her own attention was drawn to the Hexkey. It was suspended in mid-air in the center of the room, revolving clockwise while six rings of faintly glowing talismans revolved around it, themselves also spinning at various rates, much like an armillary sphere. The whole array was contained inside a pillar of floating talismans, emitting a deep, yet noticeably muted hum. The light, much in the same way, was also muted such that one could look straight at it without discomfort. It reminded Krahe of an innovative 3D printer design that was bought out and subsequently permanently shelved by the dominant 3D printer manufacturer, Vishvakarma Manufacturing.

Krahe's brief bout of reminiscence was broken by Yao's voice.

"This is... not anthrocite," the talisman mistress said without looking away from the hand for so much as a second. The tone of her voice and the expression on her face spoke of a mixture of surprise, mild confusion, concern, and slight excitement. In short, she knew what the hand really was made of, and it was probably above anthrocite in value.

"Any clue what it *is*?" Krahe prodded.

Yao gave a slow nod, her focus remaining on the hand.

"I cannot be entirely certain, as it does not exactly match the usual signs, but I can make a guess," the older woman said. Finally, she tore her gaze away from the relic, shutting the book-box.

"Where to start... I suppose the beginning would be easiest. The myth of human charcoal containing the ritual subject's soul as part of its material is not entirely without basis. It came about from suicide rituals, carried out by the elders of the Onyx-black Puppet Hall to pass down some of their cultivation to their students before they departed for the wheel of reincarnation. The practice died out early in the Onyx-black Hall's history, as the ritual is, for lack of a better term, a spiritual suicide by a thousand cuts. The master would gradually break down his astral body, while compressing it into as small a region as possible, creating something much like this. It's... well, I suppose the continental term would be something like astrocite."

"And you believe your *acquaintance* carried out that ritual with the intention of creating an inheritance?"

"Not quite the same, but something similar. He must have been crippled and near death at the time, but I can sense it. He condensed his remaining cultivation into *this*. It would be useless to me even if I stole it from you—your anathema signature is imprinted upon the astrocite. It likely took place when you opened the keyless lock," Yao said.

A wry smile appeared on her face as she added, "Shang was ever the cautious one."

"How much longer?" Krahe nodded towards the Hexkey.

"Twenty minutes, assuming no further disruptions," Yao replied, rising from her seat. She approached the ritual circle, performing various gestures that caused the talisman rings to accelerate in their rotation.

And so, Krahe waited.

Two cigarettes and twenty minutes later, it was finished. The talisman rings came to a halt, returning to the mass of Yao's left arm the moment she plucked the Hexkey from their midst. In the same manner, the papers making up the sound and light suppression barrier rejoined her right leg when she stepped outside the barrier.

Clack. Clack. Clack. The sound of her sandals echoed through the room, the commotion outside having quieted for the moment.

"That scoundrel," she muttered as she took a seat at the table, turning the Hexkey back and forth in her hand. "He buried a trap array in the key's structure. It's not active at the moment, but there is a switch keyed specifically to Shang's cultivation. Using his hand to complete the key would activate the array. I cannot guess the specifics, but I recognize the pattern. A curse, guidelines to remove it partially, which would likely include steps to make you a suitable vessel, then a guiding impulse to lead you somewhere for the 'full cure,' most likely a tomb with Shang's True Soul and facilities for its transplantation into your body. An insidious body-theft scheme, but I cannot say I am surprised."

By the sound of it, the trap array would bypass her direct immunity to mental manipulation through indirect coercion. Even if it wasn't direct mind control, Krahe didn't want to take the unnecessary risk.

"Can you remove the array?" she asked. "If not, would it be a better idea to simply use human charcoal in bulk? I have access to... I would guess at best two adult humans worth."

Yao shook her head. "Not good enough. Anthrocite is the bare minimum, and it would require at least six more humans who've undergone the Five Torments Blast Furnace Refinement. Sorayah likely used an inferior version of the ritual as well, reducing the anthrocite ratio, thus raising the likely minimum to eight or nine rather than six."

"Her offensive artifact likely went through seventeen people's worth of fuel in its lifespan, and she had a nearly intact victim in her ritual chamber. The numbers line up, but I doubt she was responsible for all eighteen," Krahe mused.

Yao followed her line of thought. "It is entirely possible she found the artifact and the box together with an already partially complete Hexkey, subsequently continuing the work of one or more individuals who attempted its completion before her. Regardless, deactivating the array is not possible, Shang was the superior array master between the two of us by far."

There was a "however" hidden in those words, and with a self-satisfied tone, Yao spoke it soon enough, looking up from her work.

"He was, however, not my equal in artifact crafting. I can remove the array altogether. I have determined that the voidkey's fundamental functions will not be harmed by this, but it will lose all defensive qualities, as Shang purposely embedded the array within as precarious a section as possible—I suspect to prevent exactly what I am about to do."

"And his True Soul will be left to rot in some tomb, probably for a thousand years until the vessel fails," Krahe guessed.

"A thousand years of dreamless slumber means little compared to the chance at a fresh start without the downsides of starting from nothing."

"How long will it take to remove the trap array?"

The noise outside picked up again. Wasting no time with a verbal answer, Yao waved her hand over the voidkey and towards the ritual circle in the room's center. A swarm of talismans from her arm carried it there, forming an armillary-like structure yet again, now enveloped in a spherical barrier of seething golden symbols.

Yao proceeded to carry out a feverish series of hand-signs and gestures that incorporated her whole body, taking a few methodical steps, each ringing out with a loud CLACK. With each sign, the talisman rings spun faster, each at a different rate, as did the intensity of their glow. Soon, the room was bathed in blinding light and a loud thrumming sound. It lasted, by Krahe's reckoning, for nine seconds, at which point it flickered out and died in an instant. When her sight returned to her, the Hexkey floated over Yao's left hand. Between two fingers of her right hand, she grasped a hair-thin, cylindrical piece of the Hexkey, about a centimeter wide and twice as long. A complex cluster of glyphs shone both on and beneath its surface, the faint reddish glow fading with each passing moment.

"Done," Yao breathed. Her good eye twitched, sweat trickled down her forehead, and her chest heaved with labored breaths. She held out the cylinder of removed material. "Here. You might be able to find Shang's tomb one day. He is bound to have left treasures for himself."

Krahe took it, knowing all too well that Yao would be involved in such an endeavor more likely than not. This was a simple show of trust.

"Now..." Yao began again, taking a moment to catch her breath. "We can move on to the simpler, yet more laborious part. I shall begin preparing the ritual circle whilst describing its properties, feel free to interrupt at any point. It is not a delicate operation, so modifications can be as crude as necessary."

They spent the next half-hour or so preparing the ritual while the battle in the sky raged on. Krahe learned more about ritual circles and ritualism in general in that half-hour than she had from most of her reading combined, but she also spent most of that time kneeling on the ground, building. An icosahedral framework, entwined through and through by tendrils of Tar impregnated with anathema-reflective particulate to form a sphere; it was a larger, sturdier version of the Daemon Core's reflector shell. The most obvious issue was maintaining the construct-matter, but Yao wasted no time in lightening this burden; in moments, she created six new talismans and bound them to the sample chunk of human charcoal with spectral threads of golden light. Thereafter, she suspended the coal chunk above the dome and placed the talismans on the inside of its perimeter. With each one placed, Krahe felt the burden lift and saw the coal chunk flaring more brightly with crimson flame. It shrank moment by moment. By the end, only a small hole was left in the shell, large enough to insert the hand and Hexkey.

"It will hold for a few minutes. Long enough," Yao said, regarding the shell with a critical, yet satisfied eye before glancing Krahe's way. "Once it begins, the ritual's own energies will feed my stabilization talismans. I could have achieved the same effect with lesser ink, but better to waste it than to have the shell burst open. I shall take hold of the shell for a moment, but it must be you who inserts the material."

And so, Krahe did. After placing the Hexkey into the Astrocite Hand's grasp, she wrapped its wrist with a tendril and carefully inserted both into the shell's center, wherein it became weightlessly suspended. Thereafter, she sealed the shell, and they both examined the whole assembly with a final pass.

"Is there anything we're waiting for?" Krahe asked.

"No, I do not suppose there is. We do require an incantation, however. I have my own, but you are the primary ritemaster in the end. I am only here to ensure everything proceeds correctly. The incantation can be nearly anything; grasping for it should be no more difficult than grasping for a theurgic sigil. It must have an initiating and a finishing component; I can signal for the latter when the time comes, but I do not expect you to need it."

An incantation to set off a ritual such as this; the complete transmutation of a voidkey via what was effectively a crude reactor. Krahe chuckled to herself as a memory surfaced. In her time, she had seen many things she was not supposed to. Technologies that were said to be vaporware for decades after their invention, because someone powerful didn't want them in the open. For this reason, she had just the speech to parrot as an incantation. She took a few moments to mentally shift gears, recalling the words and muttering a Japanese tongue-twister to get her mouth used to speaking that language again.

Krahe mentally returned to a time and place far removed from here and now. Her eyes saw what was before her and her body remained fully present and aware of her surroundings, but the majority of her attention turned inward. Megacity Gamma. Sector 8. The observation deck of a hidden, highly illegal research facility. She had infiltrated the place as part of an investigation, and though it ended up being a dead end, it at least gave her this precious memory.

Once she felt confident that she wouldn't stumble over her own words, she held out her hand to the ritual circle, with Yao doing the same in response. Krahe began reciting, "Neptunius Heavy Industries experimental atomic transmutation reactor 'Solomon' v7.9.108 Test No. 66, ready to proceed. Reaction mass in place. Estimated transmutation ratio: 87%. Preliminary computations loaded. Biocomputer array reads as operational. Hyper composite capacitor arrays operational."

Blending with her intent, a thread of Thauma flowed out to connect with the ritual circle. It was the simplest thing; she just had to build up enough pressure to set off the reaction, keeping in mind the general intended course of the ritual. No more and no less than the consumption of the Astrocite Hand for the transmutation of the Hexkey into its final form. The reflector shell floated about a meter off the ground as it began rotating clockwise. A quartet of talismans from Yao followed after it, followed by another, and a third, each forming another ring that, in turn, revolved at different speeds and in different directions, once more like an armillary sphere.

Krahe continued reciting. "Capacitor charge at 80% projected capacity. 90%. 100%. 110%. 120%. Capacitor charge stable at 124% of projected capacity. Preparing laser pump array for connection. Connection successful. Initiating ignition. Capacitor discharge… successful."

The revolutions intensified, as did the reaction. Anathema began leaking out, coalescing around the shell's exterior, granting it the appearance of a blood-red star. The room was bathed in red light. It even occasionally erupted with flare-like tongues, these soon being pacified when the talisman mistress adjusted her containment array.

"Capacitors 87 through 143 sending alerts, replacement in progress. Fusion reaction initiating. Activating TK Containment Field Emitters. TK Field operators injecting Psi-Amp fluid. Plasma field contained successfully. Fusion proceeding. Exotic particle emission within projected boundaries. Transmutation in progress."

As Krahe recited the NHI reactor operator's test report, the containment array's revolutions grew to a fever pitch, as did the tangible tension within the room. It felt as if the entire structure might fly apart at any moment. It went on for a span of time that Krahe could not discern; it felt simultaneously like mere seconds and hours, so wholly focused was she on the process itself. She couldn't see it, but she felt it. The building pressure within the shell, the Hexkey's gradual transmutation, the spindown of the reaction before the final surge. Yao gave a signal to say the final lines, but Krahe didn't see it as her mind was wholly consumed by the star-like patterns of crimson light.

"Finalizing. Maximizing TK Field output. Venting remnant plasma. Test No. 66 complete. Estimated final transmutation ratio: 98.7348%. TK Field operators, inject Psi-Suppressant. Dispatching drones to extract reaction material. Rapid spectrometry has just confirmed: We have elemental platinum. King Solomon lives."

The array abruptly halted, as if frozen in time. A momentous and undeniable sense of change washed over them as the shell began cracking. Blinding light shone through the cracks, piercing the layer of red. Yao's eyes went wide and it seemed as if she wanted to call out in alarm, but she didn't get the opportunity. With a thunderous, roaring sound, the reflector shell flew apart in a hundred pieces, and a deluge of anathema poured out, only to be quickly drawn back in. Though abrupt and forceful, the blast was delayed and sapped from most of its force by Yao's precautions, rendering it little more than a messy and noisy firework.

There, between the two of them, floated the Hexkey with the Astrocite Hand still grasping it. In the next moment, the hand crumbled to dust. The key's shape had not changed, but all else was different. Its composition was neither stone nor coal nor anthrocite, but a perfectly homogenous mass of red, opaque crystal. A constant outpour of anathema flowed from the artifact, possessed of an equal purity and furious brilliance, a beacon of power.

Yao instinctively threw up her barrier, taking the shape of nine talismans with a golden lattice of symbols between them. Krahe, meanwhile, bathed in the baleful brilliance, for as long as it lasted. It only took the talisman mistress moments to isolate the artifact. With the voidkey enveloped in a spherical barrier, Yao sent it over to Krahe, barrier and all. It stopped in front of her, facing her with one of the papers which was positioned out of step with the pattern. The specific paper's symbols slowly filled in, absorbing the voidkey's emanations, and once complete, it projected an appraisal readout. Krahe couldn't help but notice that it was as detailed as her system readouts, unlike the shallower appraisals given by her glasses.

[ATOMICA REFULGENT, FRACTURED SOLOMONIC KEY]

Tags

Fourth-order

Voidkey

Incomplete

Unstable (Temporary)

Imprinted (Brunhilde "Blackhand" Krahe)

Details

Thaumic Throughput +C1

Entropy Tolerance +D3

Entropy Dissipation +D3

Thaumic Fusion Efficiency +15%

Isotope Tolerance +D1

Isotope Dissipation +D2

First-time implantation of this voidkey will reshape the holder's Soul Furnace, permanently conferring the following Boon: "Astral Implosion Furnace"

This voidkey may be safely implanted only by the Imprinted individual. Implantation by any other individual will result in catastrophic Soul Furnace rupture (as with simultaneous implantation of two voidkeys).

[ASTRAL IMPLOSION FURNACE]
Tags
External Source (Voidkey)
Details
The holder's natural Thauma-burning will take on some of the properties of Thaumic Fusion: Increased efficiency and heightened intensity of output energy. Lesser Thauma-burning methods will remain possible.
The holder's natural ability to initiate and carry out Thaumic Fusion will grow in efficiency. This efficiency increase will compound with the improvement of the voidkey's direct fusion efficiency.
The holder's natural arcane attributes will be improved to a variable degree, with possible secondary physical effects.

"It's as you said. No defenses whatsoever," Krahe remarked, looking to Yao. "Do you think you would be able to complete it? If you were to have a suitable voidkey, could you simply graft its defensive capabilities onto the Atomica?"

"Were higher-order voidkey crafting so straightforward." Yao grimaced, turning away and stepping to the writing desk. She sent a talisman paper downstairs, and moments later it flew back up, carrying a partly filled inkstone. She began drawing another series of talisman papers as she continued to speak. "The voidkey is in a state of flux, highly unstable. If you implanted it right now, it could very well tear you apart, or worse, injure you such that it can never be removed. It must be left to sit for some time, then quenched via first implantation. You will know when it is stable enough; it is not a subtle change. Such a quenching implantation tends to be... energetic at the best of times. I suggest implanting it at a time and in a place where collateral damage will not be an issue. After that, I will require a suitable donor key *and* a suitable binder, such as material from a soulbeast, possibly other materials as needed. Depending on the voidkey's stabilized form, it may even be better to avoid using another voidkey altogether. For now, we can only speculate. Here."

With a gesture, the papers containing the voidkey flew back to Yao, replaced by a swarm of no less than twelve others that plastered themselves all over the item, creating two or possibly even three layers. Their symbols quickly began to exude the same glow as Atomica itself, but much weaker. The voidkey's presence diminished until it felt only slightly more significant than the Twin Serpent key.

Yao walked downstairs, with Krahe following.

"This seal will have the secondary benefit of further compressing the voidkey's energies," Yao said on the way down. She proceeded to collapse onto a sofa, and, in a manner strangely similar to Razem, any sense of transcendence vanished from her. It even felt as if she had aged by decades in an instant. "It may slow the stabilization process, however. Now, please go. I am exhausted, and if you and the voidkey were to remain here, the energy signature would linger."

Krahe complied without hesitation, placing Atomica into the book-box, giving a simple nod as goodbye, and walking out. The Talisman Mistress' fortifications fell into place right behind her, one after the next. This was the first time she got a close look at them. Graftbeasts, walls of talismans, traps, dozens of layers. Despite the appearance of normal alleyways and the open sky, this whole section of Audunpoint was a fortress meant to withstand direct assault from a small army, if not perhaps individuals such as the three comets still waging fierce battle in the sky.

After Lady Blackhand's departure, the domicile of Talisman Mistress Yao Fu was filled by an exhilarated, yet also exasperated laughter. The crippled old monster had predicted a potent result, but what had emerged was beyond her expectation. Perhaps Shang had carried out the suicide ritual in a far better state than she had assumed, or perhaps Lady Blackhand held some profound insight that altered the transmutation rite's course. It had to be both to some degree.

The voidkey's new name was beyond Yao's understanding, but she perfectly grasped the magnitude of difference between what it had become, its past incarnation, and what it had been intended to become. There was one thing for certain; Shang had not intended the transmutation to yield this result. The voidkey's fundamental nature was altered by the concepts carried in Lady Blackhand's prolonged incantation. Atomica Refulgent was not even remotely suitable for the Onyx-black Hall's practices; if anything, it was ideal for the type of person that would go against them, a natural anathemist. In other words, it was ideal for Blackhand.

Yes, Yao laughed, pulling out an ensorcelled bottle-gourd that she had brought all the way from Tiengenzhen. She took a long swig from it in celebration; it was filled with a small lake's worth of quality baijiu. If things proceeded at this rate, she might be fully mended before the decade was out. That was the uttermost extremity of everything going as well as the transmutation rite, but even a few decades or a century were an outstanding time frame for undoing the mutilation that had been perpetrated upon her Soul Furnace.

In the end, she had done less than half of the work she had been ready to do. In the time Lady Blackhand took to retrieve the Hexkey, Yao had made preparations, she had taken things out of storage, readied herself to deal with the consequences of carrying out a strenuous ritual that she didn't fully understand. While she was exhausted, it was an exhaustion that would be gone before the end of this new day, rather than demanding several days of active rest. In short, Yao was pleasantly surprised by how this whole thing had gone.

CHAPTER 21

SIX-EYED DREAM SERPENT

Krahe, too, was pleasantly surprised by how the transmutation ritual had gone. Compared to her deep-dive excursion into the Astral Gulf, it had been simplicity itself. Nonetheless, she felt utterly drained—not physically, but mentally. She had felt this before, especially after Slaughterhouse 9, but it had been masked by a far more vivid feeling of tiredness back then. She cut a jagged path through the city, stopping at a small bar. Rather than being seedy, like she was used to, this establishment gave off the feeling of a decent place purposely located out of the way to filter out those who didn't do their research, such as tourists and the like. There was a substantial entry fee, enough to pay for a week's food. It was nearly deserted, with most of the patrons entranced by the light show overhead, meaning that Krahe got all the privacy she could want.

She spent the next half-hour simply drinking and smoking, permitting herself to truly relax for once, without trying to find something to do, without thinking about what she should be doing, without constantly thinking over the possibilities of who was working for whom or what groups could possibly get involved. Keeping local political webs in mind was enough of a pain when one had lived in an area for years, but Krahe was simultaneously learning Audunpoint and causing changes in the process.

It was nice to retreat to a tiny world populated by four people total, including the bartender. Some of the drinks were familiar—the typical grain alcohols and fruit mash distillates—but others were more in-line with crab juice. Shots of mild hallucinogens and psychedelics that took effect and wore off equally fast were exceedingly common on the menu. It was obvious why; most of them tasted tolerable at worst, and they universally provided an enjoyable experience. One could zone out for a few minutes without such consequences as a hangover or withdrawals.

Various mixed cocktails included not only the blending of flavors and fragrances, but also the alchemical blending of different psychoactives for altered effects. A cluster of beverages warned away anyone with oral sores or stomach ulcers and listed comparatively high prices for antidotes. Yes, even the venoms of various creatures were drunk for fun. Krahe tested out a few, noting with some amusement that the bartender insisted that one particular venom was from a "properly fed" specimen of some kind of giant spider, stating that it had no aphrodisiac qualities whatsoever.

One offer in particular advertised the fact it came from a live snake and supposedly could bring about an epiphany if one consumed it. Krahe saw it as literal snake oil, but she decided to bite the hook anyway, out of curiosity.

The snake, after all, was right inside the terrarium behind the bar, hiding in its artificial environment. It slithered into view when Krahe expressed her interest in its venom. Its head shape was similar to a horned desert viper, but it had six blue-glowing eyes with hairpin pupils, including three pairs of horns—one for each eye. Its scales were varying shades of creamy and sandy off-white, glistening with an eldritch pearlescence that reminded her of the Astral Gulf.

"I'm curious, is the snake actually called a Six-eyed Dream Serpent, or is that just the menu name?" Krahe prodded.

"That is the most common name for them. It is... arguably a soulbeast, arguably not," the bartender said with a practiced cadence that betrayed the fact he was both used to and fond of talking about his pet. "There is a tribe of snake mystics out west who think these creatures form when a lost soul accidentally incarnates into a snake egg."

"Interesting. Does the venom have any truly mystical properties, then? Or is it just a particularly potent drug? In other words, will I see things based purely on my own psyche, or do its effects veer into the realm of true clairvoyance?"

He shrugged. "It depends on the snake; I can guarantee nothing. But I do not believe you will be disappointed. Nobody ever is, at least when it glows like that."

The bartender put on a truly amusing show of handling the snake, which, itself, pretended to be furious, lashing out and snapping mere millimeters from his face before he grasped it by the base of the head and pressed his thumb between its eyes as he held it over a *tiny* shot glass such that its fangs hooked just over the edge. A spray of opaque, glowing, blue-colored venom filled the glass three-quarters of the way, before the snake's eyes glistened as if it was taking her measure, and another spurt filled the shot glass the rest of the way. In a flurry of motion, the bartender placed the serpent back in its terrarium whilst also dumping the shot into the half-filled glass. The venom spread out through the liquor, bubbling in a violent reaction as the bartender poured in a salt of some kind while stirring the mixture. After several seconds, the reaction ended, letting it all coalesce into a slightly thick, glowing blue liquid with streaks of light pulsing within it as if lit by an unseen, fluttering candle.

"I suggest you try to get it down all at once," the bartender recommended.

Krahe had consumed far worse before, so it was no issue; the shot was fine, taste-wise, sour-sweet with a slight burning heat. Its aftertaste was one of buzzing numbness. The effects that followed were akin to a DMT-induced vision of a dream-like alternate reality, but rather than seeing angels or devils, Krahe found herself momentarily spirited away to a particularly filthy alley in Megacity Gamma's Sector 5. In this back alley, a local gang dumped the bodies of their victims, because the local cleanup drones were faulty and just mulched the corpses alongside the trash. A man with no arms crawled out of the trash container, muttering. It was... something about Chernobog and Jas'raba. And it was in the continental tongue of Ashametan. His eyes met Krahe's, and in the next moment, she was elsewhere, at another time.

She found herself on the coast of a dark lake, with an ancient city at her back, the alien stars of Zastreon overhead and the Banishment Wheel in the far distance. There came a deep, sonorous sound; Krahe heard and felt it in equal measure. It rumbled up from underfoot, reverberating through her ribcage and her spine—resonating with the Liminal Coil. There was a question in that frequency, a question and a sense of advice, but she could not comprehend it.

Sector 7. That old bastard's... Sauer's hut. He was out in front, going through a form Krahe had never seen and using a cybernetic arm he had never worn before. Its outer shell closely mirrored naturalistic muscle curves in shining chrome, following old-style aesthetics. It bristled with plasma nozzles from palm to shoulder, and with each of Sauer's movements, greenish flame erupted from them, amplifying the motions. The old man was a whirling dervish one moment, then stone-still the next, his face hard and coldly angry in a way Krahe had never seen while she studied with him. Krahe watched for what had to be several minutes, but from this distance, with these eyes, she could only follow the general gist of it at best; even then, it was because she recognized parts. As the mutant art that Sector 7 Style was, even this advanced form of it incorporated elements from other parts. The occasional thunderclaps and accompanying shockwaves from Sauer's more forceful movements, however, made it no easier to comprehend. Her next impulse was to look closer, but the old man froze and stared *through* her. Then, she was once more spirited away.

In a staccato of flashes, Krahe beheld the same scene playing out in wildly different settings. The founding of a small town on the frontier of civilization, the type that were frequently founded in an effort to reclaim or unearth ancient ruins. Growth, both of the town and its church. Then, corruption. Even the declaration of a splinter faith. The people suffer. Conveniently, as if by divine providence, a Saint arrives and tears out the corruption by the roots. Again. And again. And again. Thousands of iterations with wild and great variation, yet the same overall arc.

The vision lingered on a particularly egregious case, wherein the church's presence in an isolated town degenerated into corruption to the point of being little more than a bandit band extorting the townsfolk. A skull-faced saint, covered head to toe in exposed, root-like musculature, arrived, annihilated them, and took over, restoring the town only to disappear once things settled for the better. The vision lingered on that skull-masked face, with lilac flame burning in his skull's hollow sockets and the sigil of the Seven Spokes emblazoned on his forehead.

Another staccato of thought-flashes followed, far more rapid, showing similar scenes of growth, but without corruption this time. Saints arrived all the same but passed through without incident after solving small problems. It was obvious what it meant; a juxtaposition of some kind, perhaps even a vision sent from on high, seeing as she was an apostle after all. Krahe didn't understand what exactly it all meant, lacking the mental bandwidth to process it so quickly, but the visions all burned themselves into her memory with unnatural clarity.

When she next blinked, she was back at that bar, in the exact moment after she had swallowed the shot, and the aftertaste was just beginning to set in. She found her gaze slowly drifting over to the snake as she regained full awareness, not unlike waking up from a dream.

The bartender and his snake both gave her an amused look, with the former remarking, "I would advise you to not get addicted. You'll have a near-immunity to the positive effects for... Oh, I would say a few years at least given the dose. It would require a blood sample to be sure."

"What, did you have to get an apothecary license to sell snake venom as a drink?" Krahe slurred, still not quite mentally back together. Some echoes of psychedelia still lingered, and her mind was busy parsing the visions. Before the bartender could respond, the ground shuddered. Noticing the difficulty of keeping her balance, Krahe decided that it was high time to head back to the safe house. She left, having paid for each drink individually so she could keep track of her tab. It totaled an irresponsible sum, but she somehow didn't regret it. More than half her total was the Six-eyed Dream Serpent Venom. The safe house was empty when she got there, but a note on the coffee table clued her into the state of things. The Inquisitor had finally gotten around to dealing with Seer, and Casus was, at this very moment, one of the participants in the interrogation. The note nearly begged her to wait and not take action on her own.

Krahe smoked a cigarette of Adefron Incense, only to wake up to the sun high well above the horizon.

Five hours, she thought. From what she knew of Adefron, this meant she would have likely slept around twenty hours had she not used it. In the absence of any particular goal besides waiting—which she hated—she took Atomica back to Gashward Road. Two days passed without any notable events, which was absolutely agonizing. Krahe tried to find that bar again, but it was nowhere to be found. The location was burned into her mind, but it was as if the place had just up and disappeared. There was a bar there, yes, and it was even in the same building, but it wasn't *that bar.* The floor plan was the same, but everything from the floorboards to the counter, the furniture, and the staff—nearly *everything* was different. So as not to seem suspicious or otherwise stand out, she spent a few minutes there and bought a shot of cheap, nasty, funky rum before leaving.

After this excursion, she busied herself by attempting to recall and reconstruct the kata she had seen Sauer performing in her vision. When that turned out to be a dead end, she turned to Yao's scroll, and after that, to improving the design of her wards.

In the end, she hit a dead end with all three of these endeavors.

She was already struggling to digest her thoughts, trying to comprehend Yao's ultra-dense writing style only made it worse. Sure, it was clear and largely devoid of pointless obfuscation, but it was still written in a quasi-Cantonese equivalent to Renaissance-era scholarly writing.

Improving her wards was theoretically plausible, but she simply lacked whatever made it practical, and she didn't even understand wards well enough to know what she didn't know. No matter what she did, her wards always settled into a homogenous ablative layer of compacted ash. At best she could add some resilience by incorporating obsidian, which *did* help, but it was just applying the benefits of the Forming Toroid rather than improving the fundamental design or technique.

The trial-and-error process was only made worse by the limitations of her voidkey, which gnawed ever more keenly when it came to something so thauma-intensive as reconstructing her wards over and over again. Moreover, it was a reminder that the Twin Serpent Voidkey was merely at the borderline between second-order and third-order.

It took every bit of strength she had, but Krahe went to Garvesh and, without a bit of pretense, simply asked for help.

"Can't help with your Wards, not the same as mine. And as I said already, the Twin Serpent Key really *was* my best. But... I *have* been looking for one ever since you first asked, and a guy who owes me a couple favors just recently got one for me. Only reason I haven't picked it up yet or sent you a message is, well..."

The old lizard looked around. He was still in the tub, in the exact same pose.

"Been otherwise preoccupied, let's say. So, here's how you get to his place—"

It wasn't a particular building, but an even more obscure shop than Garvesh's, one that shifted locations periodically and required an invitation to enter even if you found it. For this reason, he went on for a few minutes and had to repeat himself so that Krahe could write it down. Well outside the city, it was a particular ship ferrying people and goods across the river.

"You'll have to dial the number, it's 5-8-3-7-9-1. Remember that. You got it? Good. The code word... I don't remember. Just tell him Garvesh sent you, and that this is about that favor I called in recently. If he doubts you, just say I hope he hasn't forgotten what I did for him at the Spire of Glass."

"What did you do?" Krahe asked, not expecting an answer.

"I'm not telling you," Garvesh grinned. "Just mention it. He will know. As for payment... we can work that out later. Call it a favor for now."

And so, Krahe set off for that place; the ship was not nestled quietly in the corner but was, in fact, the largest one. Garvesh's debtor plied his trade from deep within its bowels, and given the fact that none of the crew stopped her as she walked into areas obviously not meant for normal passengers, she wagered that they had been paid off. She arrived at a modified bulkhead with a small vault door embedded in it at roughly chest height, and an intercom to the side. Well, not quite an intercom. It was an antique-looking telephone handset bolted to the wall just above the keyboard from a Dregstrider, requiring her to dial the six-digit number Garvesh had given her to even speak to the proprietor.

"Who..." a hissing, snake-like voice came from past the bulkhead.

"Garvesh sent me regarding his recently called-in favor."

"I don't know who..." came the voice again, uncertain.

"I wasn't finished," Krahe interrupted. "He wants you to know that he hopes you haven't forgotten what he did at the Spire of Glass."

An agitated hiss burst from the earpiece, and the sound cut out as the other side hung up. Before she could grow uneasy, the vault door slowly opened inward, revealing the scarred face of a serpent-man staring at her from the other side. He was no mythical gorgon, but a lanky humanoid with a neck that transitioned into a diamond-shaped head, his neck curved in a question-mark shape to allow him a forward head orientation. An eyepatch-like prosthetic supplanted his left eye, and numerous scars marred his poisonous-looking, red-yellow scale pattern. He set a small sandstone box on the counter, slid it over to her side, and shut the window forcefully enough to blow a gust of wind in her face. It smelled astonishingly similar to Firminus' office, only more herbal. As for the box, it had no hinges, only a rectangular lid which bore cuneiform symbols on its surface. Krahe wasted no time in bringing it back, as awkward as transporting it was.

CHAPTER 22

MINIATURE SARCOPHAGUS

"Aristedes! Wake up!" came a stern woman's voice. Casus slowly returned to consciousness, having fallen asleep in his seat a few hours prior. A set of ominous, purple-glowing eyes stared down at him from a pale, narrow face framed by black hair at the sides, blunt bangs tracing the woman's browline in a dull V-shape, intensifying her already owl-like countenance. The glossy blackness of her hair was broken up by eye-like sigils in white, defiantly remaining congruent even as her hair shifted about, creating an unsettling appearance. Casus was accustomed to the idea of having eyes in the back, and he was slowly growing used to Lady Blackhand's detached second set of eyes, but this woman felt more all-seeing than the two of them combined, exuding an aura of constant, unwavering vigilance.

The Witch Inquisitor, Yazata Heptaxia.

She wore a partially unbuttoned satin shirt and tight black pants with cutouts on the outer sides of the thighs. It was a mode of dress similar to Casus' own, but the similarities ended there. Of the countless differences between the two of them, the most obvious were the "Black Bindings" visibly crisscrossing Yazata's skin, visible upon her thighs, over the very top of her chest, and going all the way up her neck, even peeking out of the bottoms of her sleeves. Eldritch symbols shone upon them in hues of purple the same as the glow of the inquisitor's eyes. A rapier-hilted bar mace hung from her belt, held by steel rings rather than a scabbard. It was a weapon of countless diamond-shaped, razor-sharp facets.

She walked away from him the moment she saw he was awake, turning to the one-way observation window. A minimalistic control console rose from the ground in front of the window, with a handful of black cables leading down from it to beneath the floor. Yazata's footsteps were punctuated by sharp click-clacking sounds, not because she wore heels, but because her feet were metal, as were her legs all the way up to the knees. Her trousers were bound down to her prosthetics with those Black Bindings of hers, leaving them exposed halfway up the calves. The craftsmanship was of a standard equaled by few—they were Inner Relics, after all, made by the church for Yazata specifically. Rather than mimicking human anatomy to the fullest extent, her prosthetics traded biomimicry for improved functionality and resilience with a simpler, more heavy-duty foot and ankle design.

There was no need for her to speak of the situation; Seer was doing all the talking that was necessary.

"I've got him! The little shit's fuckin' pinging me! Can you hear me, inquisitor?! I know where Semzar Hashem is RIGHT NOW!" Seer yelled in desperation, doubtlessly because he worried there was not much time.

Yazata reached for the console, and with the flick of a switch, the observation window shifted to go both ways. Pressing an adjacent button, she took a mouthpiece in hand and spoke. "You may now give your testimony, we are recording."

Seer continued without the need for any further prompting. "He's been intermittently pinging me for the last hour or so. I didn't speak up until I was sure he was in one place and not just passing through. It's the mansion on Mirzaii Two."

"Old Ishmail Two-snakes' mansion... isn't it owned by a Silversword administrator?" Casus mused aloud. He didn't know who exactly owned Mirzaii Two, but he knew her position due to the controversy surrounding her acquisition of the property. Ishmail had been a once-famous ex-contractor who pioneered the Twin Serpent Voidkey design as standard equipment for his agency's full-member contractors. The so-called Iron Adder Agency competed fiercely with the Silversword Agency for dominance in Audunpoint's early years but collapsed after Ishmail's disappearance under dubious circumstances.

"I wouldn't know about that. I just know that Semzar likes to host his degenerate parties there. It's where *this* happened to me, so I won't weep if you send a saint to level the place," Seer replied, gesturing to his visor with hatred seeping from every word.

"Just a moment," Yazata said into the mouthpiece before hanging it up and once more turning the window back to a one-way mirror.

"Was that enough information for you to decide on a plan of attack, Aristedes?" she asked, an undercurrent of annoyance in her voice. He couldn't blame her. He was withholding information from an Inquisitor. That was to be expected from civilians and even witnesses, but not from coworkers, even less so from apostles, and *absolutely not* from Pilgrim Banisher apostles. Casus fully understood where she was coming from, because he hated it too, but he couldn't reconcile his own sense of right with betraying Lady Blackhand's trust.

Casus got up, and walked to the table that occupied a third of the room's floor space. It was a "Strategic Planning Unit SPR-4735-C." It was an enormous and highly advanced piece of machinery, combining a massive memory bank called a *Memory Obelisk*, countless memslate slots, a cognition engine the size of a small building, all feeding into a combination of projector lenses and a geomantic mapping module. The module was a mass of thaumetically treated "clay" that could work as an erasable writing surface, form a 3D map, and perform several other fancy functions that rarely if ever got used. Unsurprisingly, these things were rare due to their impracticality compared to simpler and more modular solutions.

He exerted quite a bit of force pressing one of the large buttons on the side. A loud CLACK betrayed the fact it set a great clockwork mechanism into motion. The SPU whirred to life, the scribe-automata underfoot coming alive and reading off of the Memory Obelisk as the boot sequence.

"I need to ask a few more questions. Patch him through and keep it open; just let him see," he said. Yazata did as asked, and stepped away as she began walking around the room's perimeter to reach Casus' side without breaking his sightline with Seer.

"I'll ask simply. Do you know of any means of entry into the mansion that wouldn't be on official maps or blueprints?" Casus questioned. "Secret entrances or passages through the mansion, illegal tunnels for trafficking contraband..."

"Or people," Seer finished, his reluctant tone betraying the fact he did know. He sighed, leaning forward in his chair, grasping his head. He ran his hands over his visor, then emitted a noise of annoyance as his vision was overtaken by smudges. While cleaning the outer shell with his shirt, he began talking again.

"When Semzar 'invited' me to that mansion, I was led through one of *those* tunnels. The ones that nobody but its builders and their victims know about. It was connected to the mansion's underground supply line. I can point out where it was on a map; it was this underpass somewhere near... I think it was somewhere near Jafarnejad Gardens, with the big tree."

"That's nearly ten kilometers by air from the mansion..." Casus thought aloud, operating the SPU. The lenses set around its outer edge came alive, projecting a map of that section of the city. With the adjustment of a slider, he turned it so that Seer could see it from a bird's eye view. Immediately, he pointed out the spot.

"There. Some stones on the left side look out of place. Not sure how it opens; I couldn't see. Probably a combination of illusion and deterrence field."

"You let us deal with *that*. How much did you see inside the tunnel?"

"I already told you. The tunnel goes on for a while, twisting left and right, loads of sealed off side passages from the looks of the walls. Some of 'em are just locked doors, and some of 'em are just bars, like the rusty barred ones off of old elevators. Saw some nasty shit behind those, but it all looked to have been abandoned for a while. As for the subterrain, it looked like a private tram line or something. It's way too nice to *not* be on maps."

Casus shifted the map. Both the projection and the clay model shifted, showing a sprawling, vein-like tangle of tunnels and vents.

"Looks like it connects the mansion to several other buildings; they even come under the same deed as the mansion. A butcher shop, a grocer, library, anything you would need without having to interact with the *common rabble*," Casus mused as he inspected the map.

"One more thing about the tramline—it was flooded. Wasn't much. About two, three finger-widths of old rainwater. Won't stop you, but they'll hear you coming."

Casus nodded. "Very well. You've been helpful."

He glanced at Yazata, and without him needing to say a word, she once more separated them from Seer. With that, Casus got to work, operating the giant machine with gusto. It wasn't the most practical device; it didn't conform to more common standards of design and learning it had been a nightmare, but Casus couldn't help but love the SPU. It was as much a holy relic of the Inner Wheel as it was a machine, possessing a sense of the sublime not found in its mass-production counterparts. In a few minutes, he had a plan of attack worked out—not because he could think that quickly, but because he had considered this possibility before. Audunpoint's subterrain layer wasn't quite as vast as those of capital cities, but there were so many ancient and forgotten passages from the city's time as a Jas'raban metropolis that there was no chance in hell to keep track of them all.

The SPU rendered the subterrain on the clay layer, while the surface level was projected above.

"You want me to lead a contingent of 'Red Hood' semi-autonomous graft-beasts, encircle the mansion, and mount a direct assault? Truly?" Yazata questioned for the third time.

Nodding, Casus reaffirmed his intent. "I will join up with Lady Blackhand to infiltrate through the subterrain while the security force is distracted. After we eliminate Semzar and his officers, we will be able to mop up the rest from within and without. Should we falter, other tactics will remain viable."

Sighing, the witch-inquisitor agreed. "Very well."

"I expected you to outright object to the plan. I even prepared two alternatives," Casus admitted.

"I *am* an Inquisitor, even if my direct combat capabilities are on the lower end. If I could not stand against odds like these, I would not qualify for my title. I must admit that I am curious. What were these alternatives of yours?"

"The first one... I shan't say. It is neither relevant nor interesting. As for the second, I intended to enlist the aid of a particular independent contractor by leveraging personal connections as well as dipping into mine and my sister's money."

"Who?"

"An... unpleasant individual. One I would rather not deal with if I can help it. He recently purged a Hazard Zone and lost the entire payout on collateral damage, including any claims on Archon-forged items. His combat capabilities are some of the best out of anyone within my reach, but the strings are wrought of razor wire dipped in corrosive venom..." Casus trailed off for a moment as the mental image of that madman floated up from memory. He banished it, and refocused on Yazata. "Fortunately, you didn't veto my plan. Thus, there is no need to involve him."

The part he didn't mention was that he was *afraid* of that man. Trying to rope in the man known as "The Cleaner Krait" was about as extreme as trying to get official help from the public-facing church, while posing far greater personal danger for Casus. The one upside was that doing so would allow him to bypass the church bureaucracy. In short, it was an absolute last resort.

"Speaking of combat capabilities…" Yazata looked sidelong at Casus while zooming in the clay model. "Are you certain this 'Lady Blackhand' is qualified? I admit that her track record, assuming it is accurate, would be impressive for a low-ranker, but this is not a matter that can be resolved by a handful of low-rankers, even if you yourself are borderline. Semzar Hashem alone is known to possess a near-cap archetype and a high third-order voidkey, and we do not know who will be with him. His father's presence would all but guarantee the failure of this endeavor."

"Semzar is a fool who lacks the skill to properly make use of the power he has stolen from his hosts. He is no different from some grafted-to-the-gills Kartier brat," Casus responded, also shifting the clay model. "Moreover, he fears his father as much as he hates him, doubly so given the current circumstances. You yourself confirmed the truthfulness of Seer's testimony regarding the Hashem Family's internal political state. Between us and Semzar, Semzar has the greatest personal investment in staying apart from Damrus."

After a shallow nod of acknowledgement, Yazata interrupted. "But he is likely to be accompanied by individuals who could be a real threat. A threat to you or even I, let alone a relatively unknown low-ranker. Make no mistake; I trust your judgment, Aristedes, but I would prefer more than a single man's testimony."

Casus didn't like deception. It went against his nature. But nonetheless, he opened his mouth and said, "With all due respect, Inquisitor, I would not bet against Blackhand even if she were stripped of all wards and surrounded by gunmen."

And Yazata didn't sense a lie because there wasn't one. The feat of deception which took place was not one of spoken words, but of the mind; Casus wrenched his own consciousness away from everything Yazata didn't know that she had a right to know. He forced himself to not think about Blackhand's status as an unlettered apostle, nor the fact he had leveraged his status to secure the option of access to a voidkey beyond her qualifications should she require it. Casus did not have the power or the guile to keep such a requisition quiet should it go through, so he kept it to a possibility rooted in the truth of his recent training. His plan, at this moment, was to bring it up with Blackhand and let her decide, hoping she would make the wise choice. Some part of him genuinely believed that she would manage to secure a third-order voidkey before then; if only to avoid having to put her trust in the church.

They separated after going over the details, with Casus loading the map and the plan of approach onto a memslate before leaving to join up with Blackhand. Yazata would, in the meanwhile, continue interrogating Seer until the time came to rendezvous at the staging point, which was a randomly selected safe house that was close enough to be practical but not the single closest, on the off-chance it was being watched.

Meanwhile, elsewhere in the city...

* * *

The first thing Krahe did, once she was a safe distance from the ferry, was to verify that there was, in fact, a voidkey in the box, and to ping it with an appraisal attempt. The key was in there, but her appraisal washed off it in a manner that suggested her glasses couldn't appraise it properly for reasons other than anti-appraisal measures. That most likely meant it was third-order.

Rather than heading straight back to Gashward 94 or any other place she normally frequented, Krahe stopped by a small Zaveshian shrine which she had scoped out beforehand without visiting. It was more of a church-owned gymnasium with a small shrine at the front end. After paying for an hour of use and receiving a disposable timer-talisman, she ducked into one of the showers, taking the time to store the voidkey-sarcophagus in her Kenoma Sack. The container seemed to be designed for such storage, as it came alive when she brought it into the storage rift's vicinity with the intent to put it in. Some of the symbols lit up with purple light, and the lid shifted slightly, becoming firmly fixed. It even took up far less capacity than it rightly should have, just based on knowing the key was third-order.

With that out of the way, Krahe decided to make use of the gymnasium, showering once she was done. Only then did she make her way to Garvesh's, taking a detour to a food cart that she liked on the way there. She wanted to let him know that all had gone well, and to confirm that the voidkey was of a standard he had expected from his contact.

The malformed corpse of Imraal's cart was still out front, now joined by a trail of dried blood leading inside the building. Krahe half-jokingly muttered a prayer to the deceased machine, then went inside, following the blood trail up the stairs to Garvesh's apartment. From the direction, it was clear a corpse had been dragged out—obviously the baneworm. This guess was confirmed when Krahe entered the bathroom, finding Garvesh still in his pool-sized tub, with the corpse gone.

"Couldn't they clean the blood after they took the corpse away?" she asked.

"Hrrm?" Garvesh grumbled, the sound more akin to the deep rumble of a cyber-gator than the vocalization of a person. He looked up at her, a predatory glow in his eyes, pupils constricted. Then, it suddenly melted away, and he returned to his normal self. "Oh, it's you. Thought it was the cleaner. You just came in after he left to dispose of the meat. He *will* clean the blood too, if he knows what's good for him. Well? How'd it go?"

"The snake guy I met with didn't sound too happy when I brought up the Spire of Glass. Gave me this box that looks like a miniature sarcophagus," she said, holding out her arm as she began the process of opening the Kenoma Sack.

Garvesh simply watched in silence while continuing to repair another of his ward-scales, this one two rows down and three to the right of the previous. A glint of recognition lit up his eyes at the sight of the box alone, but in the next moment, his gaze became distant. The Thousand-yard Stare—it was unmistakable. Coming closer and kneeling in a spot free of blood next to the tub, she set it on the edge and finally opened it. Immediately, a strong, dense aura spilled out, like a wall of smell hitting her in the face, only it didn't smell like anything.

For the first time, she took the voidkey out of its container. It was a comet-like shape formed by a three-pronged bronze spiral, suspending in its center a shard of jagged black metal that thrummed with a mysterious and ominous aura. Cuneiform symbols were etched down the length of each of the voidkey's prongs, as well as on one facet of the shard. Though, in the shard's case, they were fragmented.

Something further inside the box grabbed her eye. It was a rectangular piece of the bottom, as wide as a memory slate and twice as long, with a cutout for a finger on one side so it could be easily pried out.

"Oh, it's one of *these...*" the lizard muttered at the sight of the key. Krahe pinged the rectangular stone, and received confirmation that it was, indeed, a memslate, and even that it contained the voidkey's specifications. Setting the key down, she brought out her eyebox and finagled it to get the too-long memslate into its slot. It only went in halfway, leaving the spring loaded cover open, but the eyebox read it just fine. She wondered if this was an old, outdated design, or perhaps just an alternate style of memslate that was still in use.

[SHARDKEY OF HESHMAD ABBASI, No. 7624]

Tags

Third-order

Voidkey

Ancient

Series 7/8

Details

Thaumic Throughput +D1

Entropy Tolerance +D1

Entropy Dissipation +D1
Barrier Catalyst (Hardened, Form-fitting, Shatter-type Anti-Meltdown Safety)
Barrier Hardening +D2
Barrier Formation Rate +E1
Barrier Upkeep Reduction +D1
Ward Catalyst (Hardened, Interlaced, Trinity Composite)
Ward Hardening +C1
This voidkey was wrought of the 7624th fragment of the armor of Heshmad Abbasi. May each among the 8888 Immortals of his great army forever bear a piece of his unfaltering strength.

"A shardkey. Bastard thinks he's funny throwing it back in my face," Garvesh muttered, his words laced with anger. He shook his head, asking with a calmer tone, "What number is it?"

"Seven-thousand six-hundred twenty-four, Series 7/8. Whoever made it seemed to be under the delusion that it was for some truly elite army."

"The 8888 Immortals *were* one of the most elite armies of their time. You just got the second weakest kind of shardkey, the kind used by those of them who didn't see combat or were not important enough to worry about assassins," he quickly corrected, seeming as insulted as if she had described a high-caliber revolver as "primitive" to the average droid-wrangler. He held out his free hand to grab the key. Krahe, seeing the dissociation in his eyes, handed it over. As he examined it, he continued speaking. His accent thinned out, as if he were forgetting to use it. "Each series of 1111 delineates a jump in the voidkey's power based on the size and quality of the armor shards they're built around. I'd even say that one of these is the epitome of a low mid-ranker voidkey; solid allrounder with exceptional defensive characteristics. They're even designed to be compatible with upgrades *and* are highly collectible, so either way if you keep it or sell it later on you can't go wrong."

"How much would it have cost me in DDs?" Krahe asked in the same tone she used when haggling. That pulled him back.

"Who's to say?" the old lizard grinned, his accent returning in full force.

"I'm sure you'll call in that favor I owe you for a tenfold profit." She grinned back, taking the shardkey out of his hand.

"We'll see when that time comes. Now go, I—"

Garvesh plainly struggled to finish repairing the scale, his eyes constricting as steam erupted from his nostrils, followed by a trickle of blood. With superhuman effort he completed the task, and stumbled to his feet, staring ahead like a warrior on the precipice of death. A rumbling noise could be heard from his stomach, and he turned to look at Krahe.

"I really hope this is yesterday's dinner instead of the alternative."

He coughed, and another trickle of blood ran from the corner of his mouth. Again he glanced her way, nodding for her to leave, and so she did, trying to ignore the gruesome sounds coming from the bathroom as she left. By the rancid stench that reached her just before she exited the apartment, it seemed the lizard had gotten his preferred outcome.

As Krahe made her way from Garvesh's place and turned the corner, she heard footsteps nearby, entering the same alleyway but from the other end. Rapid, but decisive or agitated. They were accompanied by a whistled melody. Though she never once glimpsed that stranger, a sense of unease washed over her. She walked aimlessly for a short time, looking out for signs of someone following her or laying in ambush, but found no evidence of such a thing, and so continued on her way back to Gashward 94. Her intention was to replace her voidkey and reuse the miniature sarcophagus for Atomica. However, she still had quite a bit of built-up Isotope stored in her arm, so she decided to dissipate most of it first before she carried out a voidkey change. She had, after all, plenty of time to burn.

In the blink of an eye, several hours passed.

If only that were the case. In truth, Krahe could feel the blood pounding in her head and her eyes glazing over as she read the same strip of Yao's scroll over and over. It was one of the few outright mystical sections, and was presented as such, with the scroll openly stating it was a riddle, a way of preparing the reader for other texts that were likely to be this obtuse in their entirety. She pulled the last dregs of Isotope into herself, lit a cigarette, and decided to just wait it out, laying back on the sofa as she turned the shardkey over in her hand. She could have taken more purge pills to speed up the process, but besides being unpleasant at best, they were also caustic enough to threaten stomach lining damage with repeat dosage. This was not a problem when they were used as intended—to help purge minor curses.

As she felt the last of her Isotope scatter and fade, Krahe sat up, mentally glancing at her arm's Isotope capacity—20% full. Enough to do something with but not enough to be a problem. She conjured a talisman into her hand. One among the insights she had managed to glean from Yao's scroll was a truly rudimentary talisman for easing the extraction of a "set" voidkey. It required no external power, only good ink and a steady hand to draw its symbol, a winding "spiral" of straight lines and right angles.

Extracting the Twin Serpent Key felt just as sickly ticklish and unpleasant as it had been when she did it for the Black Sun Coupler's test run. If she had to assume the talisman had done anything, she would guess it might have reduced the stress on the voidkey itself, or it might have sped up the fading of that sickly, wound-like sensation of absence. The Shardkey went in easily, but the moment it was seated, Krahe felt a faint wrongness. After mentally feeling around in the dark, a subtle mental pull clued her in on the culprit: her wards were wrong. Or rather, they didn't match the key's embedded ward design.

After she dispersed and began reconstructing her wards, Krahe found that the shardkey was guiding her. At first, she couldn't help but feel as if her wards were forming far too quickly, twice or thrice faster than normal, but it turned out to be only the first layer. Bit by bit, Krahe built up the multi-layered structure, and the reason for the term "Trinity Composite" became clear. A "padding" underlayer of homogenous, compressed pyroclast. A "flexible armor" layer of interlocking segments, serving as a smooth transition into the outermost, "articulated plates" layer, resembling obsidian in color and reflectiveness. The Trinity Composite design was somewhere between antique full-plate and modern hardsuit armor. Krahe still couldn't quite tell why this worked, unlike most of her previous attempts. She well and truly hoped it was up to her own lacking understanding of how wards functioned, rather than some glaring flaw in her thinking that she couldn't perceive. After all, she had no clue how they didn't get in the way, why they only showed themselves to protect their user, or how they determined what was an attack. If she could grasp the fundamental nature of wards, the ability to reshape her own as she saw fit would follow.

Frustrated, she finished reworking her wards, before placing Atomica in the stone box and storing it away. She immediately left for the Temple of Records, leveraging her access to restricted texts on wards. She left with a total of three books, two being publicly available foundational texts while the third contained records of nontraditional ward compositions, as well as various methods for embedding and extracting the ward composition of a voidkey. Their titles and authors read as such:

Armor of the Spirit
by Hashmail Ibn-Abbasi

The Wizard's Aegis:
A comprehensive history of personal wards.
by Audun Sorun

**Record of Transcending Human Resilience: Chapter of Wards
translation by Hashmail Ibn-Abbasi
original by Unknown**

The *Record of Transcending Human Resilience* was the restricted text. While the others were typical leather-bound tomes, this text was a scroll, with the translator explaining that he disliked scrolls and only used this form factor because the record didn't work within a book format.

Krahe got as far as learning the most prevalent theory of ward invention. This theory was based on countless historical accounts corroborating it, and it stated itself that they were most likely invented as a defense against melee attackers, originally intended to buy a magic user enough time to create distance. At that point, as she was getting into the historical usage of personal wards, Casus came into the safe house.

A simple phrase followed with his entrance. "Ah. You are here. Good. We know where Semzar is and how to get to him."

Those words were all it took for Krahe to stick a blank talisman paper into her book and jump to her feet. Just like that, a switch flipped in her head, and she took the Black Sun Coupler from its spot in a hidden compartment under the kitchen stove. She strapped it to her waist, donned the supporting armor, and covered it all with a long coat she used to disguise herself. They spoke briefly as she did this, exchanging basic operational info and the plan of attack. It was a straightforward plan, but it made sense.

"Do we get Red Hood support, or are they all needed for the frontal assault?" she asked as she locked the gun-like catalyst to her left arm's bracer.

"Unfortunately, we shall be on our own in the subterrain," Casus said.

And so, they were off, riding through the city until they reached a nearby nook to stash the motorbike in. As they approached their goal, Krahe sent Barzai further and further ahead. Even if it was secret, given its nature, it was not unlikely for Semzar or one of his subordinates to station guards or at least lookouts nearby.

There were no guards stationed outside the secret entrance, and it was walled up just as Seer had described, but Barzai did see *something*. A woman, walking down the street with a boy in tow. He couldn't be more than seven or eight, dressed in brand new, generic clothes. The woman's manner of dress was the same, generic to the point of being suspicious, and imperfect at points. Her fingers bore numerous rings, some of which were Calbian currency, and tattoos peeked out from the insides of her sleeves. Something about the two of them, about that boy's demeanor and the way he seemed to be dragged along, set Krahe off.

She had seen human trafficking countless times; in fact, she had personally depopulated entire sub-sectors that had been used for that revolting practice. Seeing that woman all but dragging the child along was dubious enough, but the fact that she shared no resemblance with the boy was another nail in her coffin. In fact, she didn't look much like a real person at all. It wasn't obvious at a glance, not something a normal person would easily notice; no baneworm tendrils visible under her skin, no evidence of heavy cosmetic grafting, or any other surface-level give-aways. It was her entire being, particularly her face and the manner in which she moved. Krahe had seen it countless times in gangsters, merchants of death, loan sharks, corporate ladder-climbers, and politicians.

If Krahe's measure of her was right, the fundamental thread of humanity inside that woman was too severely corroded for her to mask it at all times, and as far as she knew, there was nobody looking right now.

"There's someone approaching the entrance. Stay out of sight if you can," she said to Casus. She rushed forward, sending Barzai to the underpass, where she left him hovering in a manner impossible for a living bird. Hidden from sight, the eidolon hung there, flapping his wings without disturbing the air. Closer and closer. Krahe timed her approach so she would entrap the woman, while Casus hung back, ducking into an alleyway.

From this close, she could be sure. She just needed the woman to face her. Eventually, she did. At first she turned slightly to face the hidden entrance, glimpsing Krahe in the periphery, after which she whipped around and reached for something on her hip.

"It's... it's you... The one from the posters!" came an alarmed utterance. The woman raised her barrier, forming a translucent shield of greenish-blue hexagons. It was about a meter tall, a bit less wide, and flat rather than domed. Meanwhile, she raised one hand, forming octahedral spikes in front of each finger. With her other hand, she held onto the boy. There was a feral kind of fear in her eyes.

"Oh? You know me? Then this'll be easier. Just answer me one question. Just one. Easy, right? Where are you taking the kid? Tell the truth for once in your wretched life, and I won't kill or maim you."

Krahe genuinely meant that. If the woman spoke truthfully, she would choke her out, tie her up, and have Casus drag her off to be detained by the church. She also knew that was astronomically unlikely to come to pass.

"H-huh? Him? I—He's my cousin's little brother! I'm taking him home! Yeah! Taking him home!"

Even without the kid's eyes screaming that it was a lie, it would've been obvious. Slowly approaching, raising her own barrier just in case, Krahe reiterated, "That's a lie. One more chance, c'mon. I won't pretend to be an Inquisitor, but I have my own means of getting the truth when I want it. If you lie, or even try to avoid the question, may the spirit of a raven peck out your eyes. Well?"

Obviously, a human trafficker wouldn't openly admit to being one.

She opened her mouth to speak, and the moment the beginnings of a word formed, Krahe willed Barzai to set upon her. He revealed himself, screeching with the voice of some bird that definitely wasn't a raven, and attacked the trafficker-woman's face, tearing into her wards with his beak, reddish flame spilling out. She wildly fired off her thaumaturgy, but Krahe had already preformed a dive, and before the boy could be hurt, she had the woman in a simplistic grapple. She had surfaced and simply wrapped her left arm around the trafficker from behind, pinning her arms to her body.

The trafficker-woman's strength faltered against hers, despite the fact she was stronger than a civilian man. Thanks to consistent physical training, Krahe's Force had grown to E2, but that alone would not have produced this result. The Left Arm of Chernobog grew in strength alongside all of her attributes, including even the Shardkey's benefits. This all coalesced into a crushingly powerful bearhug that squeezed the air out of the trafficker-woman's lungs and forced her to let go of the boy. Despite all this, the trafficker regained her bearings and fought back, summoning up ghostly hands that snatched Barzai, grabbed at Krahe's hair, and attempted to fight her off in any possible way to break free. Quickly realizing that it wasn't working, the trafficker gathered all but one at Krahe's arm and attempted to pry it loose while her only free arm continued fighting with Barzai. These ghostly limbs were all just as strong as the trafficker, four of them managing to weaken Krahe's grasp enough for the woman to slip out. Krahe couldn't help but wonder whether she was a trafficker because of this ability, or vice versa.

Either way, it didn't matter. She was a corpse that didn't know it was dead yet.

Originally, Krahe had planned to immobilize and interrogate the woman, then *maybe* give her a chance at survival by turning her over to the church. It would have depended on how she came across during the interrogation—whether she was just a broken person in a bad situation who was capable of redemption, and so on. There was no longer space for such nuance; not with the trafficker lunging for the child in an attempt to take a human shield. A simple skim forward, followed by a left straight punch into the trafficker's stomach, or rather—given how she was turned—her liver. The force of that punch alone was enough to send the fifty-something kilo woman to the ground. Despite having made an effort to avoid subjecting the boy to needless trauma, Krahe's anger got the better of her, and she held out her hand.

Furious redness illuminated the underpass.

An equally furious electric buzz accompanied the glow. It waned, then began again, doing so a total of three times. The child *tried* to look at first, but Krahe blocked his sight with a thin sheet of jade. Only a steaming, greasy silhouette remained upon the flagstones.

Krahe killed the fusion reaction for the final time, holding her hand to her face, somewhat dumbfounded. While the shardkey didn't strengthen her tolerance much more than the Twin Serpent Key, the dissipation rate was a total game changer.

"I did not know that Barzai could detect lies," Casus remarked as he approached, having emerged from hiding moments earlier.

"He can't; it was just a distraction." She shrugged. "I could just tell, both that she was a trafficker and that she was lying."

The boy, confused and terrified in equal measure, had walked out from under the underpass, bawling his eyes out. The child's panic and terror mingled with a sense of awe as he noticed Casus. He craned his neck to look up at the two-meter-tall living holy relic.

"Get the kid out of here. I'll go on ahead. Don't worry, I'll leave a few of them for you."

Despite her desire to save the child, Krahe strongly disliked dealing with kids, because she didn't know how.

"Are you certain?" Casus asked, though the question rang hollow. He was already kneeling over the child as he spoke. Looking back, Krahe reached up to her head and started pulling on her voidkey.

"I'll be fine," she said. "There's a shrine not too far from here, just take him there and come back."

Visibly conflicted, Casus sighed, picking up the child while keeping him from looking at the corpse.

"Five minutes. I shall return in five minutes," he uttered before sprinting off. The boy remained silent, too shaken to scream.

Before long, she had the key out of her head and slotted into the Black Sun Coupler. It was just her and Barzai now.

The underpass fell silent.

As for the hidden passage, there were a few loose bricks throughout the underpass, but only one that hid an actual lever. The others were supposedly a mix of duds and fakes that would send an alarm when removed. Casus had also noted Seer's claim that the alarms were usually ignored because of how often they were tripped on accident. The section of wall seamlessly swung open, revealing a heavy vault door behind the stone facade. She closed it behind herself, since Casus knew how to open it.

Inside, it really was just a tunnel. She continued deeper, keeping her senses sharp and her hand on the transformation dial. On and on, through the empty tunnel, twisting and turning with the only sound being her footsteps. Basic lights were strung up along the left wall. The air was dry, but not stale, but gradually, an unpleasant, dampness crept in. As she walked, she glimpsed a few side rooms, most being either empty or filled with random trash, boxes, and so on. A few were caved in, and several more contained recognizable items. Within one particular room, an articulated chair stood, bolted to the ground in the middle; next to it, a table, a bucket, and a tub. Everything was stained a crusty, dark brown. Then she noted several teeth littering the ground.

A second chamber of the same type waited a few steps further, entirely missing a door, with deep gashes in the stone and the chair clearly having been ripped out of the ground and thrown against the wall with inhuman force. This room too was stained. Further signs of carnage continued through the tunnel for some time, until at some point, they stopped at a repaired section, where the tunnel had clearly been severely damaged, likely by an explosion.

A handful of makeshift jail cells followed, clean save for a thick layer of dust, with three being clean enough to suggest recent use. They were empty with the exception of mattresses and shit-filled buckets. She couldn't tell in the dark, but the mattresses looked stained in spots that did not suggest an adult source, nor any sort of *natural* incontinence. She knew what it meant, and fostered the ember of rage as she continued onward.

The sound of footsteps splashing through the ankle-deep water could be heard.

Without much thought, she turned the dial and gave herself over to the Black Sun Coupler. The suit had slightly changed from its previous form, incorporating the Trinity Composite into its armor, creating an even larger, more ominous silhouette than before. Its plating, though still matte and utilitarian, was shaped subtly differently, influenced by the shardkey's fragmentary memory of its original form as the armor of a legendary warlord. The plates now bore additional minute details, as well as cuneiform inscriptions along the edges. Some were words of protection, others were proclamations of rebuke. The Forming Toroid incorporated seamlessly into the right arm's gauntlet, and the same went for her gun holster.

As her swift metamorphosis completed and her senses returned, the bird flew over to her and perched on her shoulder. He opened his beak, replaying a horribly garbled mess of noise that vaguely resembled a snippet out of a doom metal song. Monumental, ominous guitars and gigantic drums underlined demonic, bassy vocals, spoken more than they were sung. They surely conveyed what Barzai wanted to express.

"None can save your souls, none escape the wrath. Nowhere to run, nowhere to hide. No life is spared, renounce the cries for help!"

With her exhalation, Viridaimon's crow-like gas mask released long threads of smoke. Krahe raised her left arm, holding it straight to get a feel for the suit's stabilization. Then, she dived, just to dial-in any impact Viridaimon might have had upon the Liminal Coil's functions. The relative time distortion felt a bit weaker, but the dive worked fine otherwise. She began forming a burster in her right hand as she continued further, sending Barzai ahead.

CHAPTER 23

SEWER WARS

Achmed smoked a cigarette, lazily ambling out of the subterranean loading bay and into the flooded tunnel that led into it. He balanced atop one of the cart rails to avoid wading through water. His tendrils writhed inside his lungs as the smoke spread through them. But then, something felt off; one of his tendrils was caught, and he stopped dead, leaning slightly as he mentally commanded the tendril, dragging up a clump of tarry mucus before he spat it out and put the tendril back in place.

Meanwhile, the two hideous *things* assigned to him waded through the water, oily patches spreading out around their legs.

They were insectile, Evoy-like creatures, but wrong in countless ways.

To start with, their morphs were malformed, with emaciated, human-like torsos and lanky limbs, almost like dried-out corpses with chitin plates haphazardly stuck to them willy-nilly. Black tubes and cables snaked in and out of them, and fully artificial organ enclosures bulged their stomachs or protruded out of them in various ways. Heavy-duty, helmet-like sensor array grafts covered their heads. The one to his right had several large, circular graft eyes set into its head graft in a scattershot pattern, and as a result it had a habit of constantly looking around. A decal was sloppily airbrushed onto the side of its head. It read, "SB-55C-143." The other one had no visible eyes, but it constantly emitted a low buzzing and it seemed to *see* just fine. This one's decal read, "SB-55C-82."

Both of them had one functional arm, with clawed, knobby, dysgenic fingers, and one weaponized arm. One-four-three's leftie was a muscular limb with a bulbous, mace-like head, sectioned off into five petal-like parts that could open to reveal an array of six silver membranes, one at the center and five around it. As for 82, its left arm retained a hand, but it was distorted and partially split down the middle to fit a weapon graft onto the underside of its forearm. It looked like one of the Blasting Clusters that had been mounted on the Foreman's Hounds, but smaller, clearly accommodating for the unit's more limited power output and weaker build. A primitive, cheap, but effective "shotgun."

"Lotta good the operation at Slaughterhouse 9 did for those rich fucks if you lot're all that came out of it," he muttered derisively, taking another toke of his cigarette. Less human than even stitched-together hobo corpses, these things were supposedly failed Evoy molts that had been "recycled." Even lesser than corpses reanimated with heavy grafting; never even alive to begin with. They were in the same realm as the artificial bodies offered by the church. Suitable vessels only for the Gor'ah in their heads that gave them motion; they certainly took to these shells better than natural humanoid meat suits. It was obvious something about these "stillborns" was explicitly designed to accommodate Gor'ah and thus compensate for their sorely lacking intellect. The nature of that compensation was far beyond Achmed's station, but he was sure it was something extremely fucking heretical given the Benefactors' involvement.

Slowly, lazily, taking his sweet time, he continued his patrol. Being only one of many guarding the mansion, he didn't actually have a great deal of responsibility. His purpose here was threefold. The first task was to act as a minder for the stillborns, and the second was to receive a delivery that was to come through here. Some kid. He didn't think twice about the purpose or origin of that delivery, having long numbed himself to far worse cruelties than human trafficking. If it wasn't happening in front of his face, he could easily act as if it didn't exist at all. The third and perhaps most crucial task was to keep an eye on blasting charges planted along a section of the tunnel and to set them off if *any* intruder came through and managed to reach the area where they were planted. The stillborns were there to keep the trafficker honest and to act as a barrier between any would-be intruders and Achmed for long enough to set off the charges.

He soon got to the section with the charges. They were nothing like any explosives he had seen before. Occult-looking tetrahedrons made of brass, with long, three-sided black rods emerging from their apexes, ominous symbols glowing orange down the rods' sides. He couldn't read them, but they didn't look like any human alphabet, and Achmed was abnormally well-read for his current career path. Tetrahedral spikes emerged from the tunnel wall around each charge, seemingly "growing" out of the bricks. Achmed guessed it was some sort of geomancy. Feeling no need to hurry, Achmed took his time checking them over, eventually stepping onto the tunnel wall and walking up it. A petty trick learned from a Saurian he had inhabited in the past, but terribly useful. Sure, he had a fancy detonator built specifically for these things, but it was never bad to be double and triple certain that explosives wouldn't misfire.

Footsteps approached from afar, sloshing in the grimy water. Achmed perked up, anticipating the trafficker. He finished his checks and retreated a short distance outside the remote charges' blast zone. It was at a turn in the tunnel, this spot chosen specifically to allow him to look down the other side or to take cover.

It wasn't anyone he had been told to expect. He knew that the moment 82 became agitated, both in body language and sound. Its quiet buzzing took on a deeper tone and became *far* louder with inaudible frequencies sending ripples through the water underfoot and reverberating up through Achmed's body.

The stillborn, 82, surged forward, sprinting past the corner, its buzzing rising to a scream-like fever pitch as it raised its left arm and began firing. With a repeating sequence of whirring charge-up and thumping release, its weapon's focused shockwaves tore up the water surface with their mere passage.

But the distant footsteps only became quicker, accompanied by the unsettling caw of a raven and followed by a sequence of cannon-like, thumping explosions. They sounded not quite like gunshots, but close to it. What came from beyond the corner were not bullets, however. Achmed barely got a glimpse as he was busy retreating and preparing the detonator; they were comets of swirling blackness, zipping through the air like swift arrows, their trajectories bending to all strike 82. A greenish glow lit up inside the stillborn's chest as glassy wards of the same color revealed themselves around it, and these defenses held for a moment, only to be torn apart soon after.

The creature continued firing back for a moment longer while its body held up. Soon, 82 was shaking in place as countless explosions tore open the stillborn's exoskeleton, spilling its oily inner fluids into the water and painting the walls with the iridescent rainbow of their puke-like hues. A pretentious sort might interpret those stains as a veritable work of abstract art commenting on the traces left by those who are consumed by an opposing force's overwhelming violence.

Without needing to be commanded, 143 quickly prepared itself to face the enemy, ducking to the wall as its left arm split open to expose the emitter nodules. A black blur zipped past the corner, trailing black smoke and red light as it flew. It was a raven, or at least something in the shape of one. Opening its beak, the thing screamed with the banshee tone of a woman being murdered. Its eyes flashed, and the section of wall Achmed was hanging from exploded. Though not enough to make him fall, his right foot was left hanging onto a chunk of loosened stone, forcing him to release it and right himself, moving even further up the wall until he was nearly hanging upside-down.

Just as he got his bearings, Achmed saw it—a human shape in black armor, with an unfamiliar device on its waist. It didn't even cross his mind that it was a Mamon Coupler; he was not particularly familiar with those devices and only had passing knowledge of common models that his fellow gang members used.

A beaked mask concealed the shape's face. Its eyes were two impassive, circular lenses within which green fire burned, trailing light in a near perfect line as it moved. Its left arm bore a heavy, gun-like catalyst, spewing smoke and flames from its muzzle, while the right was concealed by a shield-like bracer-and-pauldron combination.

It walked as quickly as any normal person would run, gliding through the ankle-deep water with an unsettling, mechanical smoothness. Even its arms remained unnaturally stable as it leveled its weapon at him. In Achmed's mind, that *thing* had to be some kind of graft-beast, maybe meant to compete with or replace the Red Hoods. Its mask certainly looked Zaveshian.

A swarm of smoke-missiles spewed forth in Achmed's direction, and the shape threw a reflective, black sphere towards 143. Neither fighting back nor setting off the charges crossed his mind—only escape, and escape he did, raising his unique barrier. A pair of ghostly green wings formed on his back, contorting to cover him as he jumped from the ceiling to the ground.

Meanwhile, the smoke-missiles' trajectories curved in an effort to strike him, but they only ended up tracing a line of holes along the wall in front of where he landed, passing through the water and kicking up a cloud of foul mist. A spark of hope—their homing was limited.

Achmed spun around, continuing to run backwards as he watched and waited. That black sphere exploded, throwing 143 across the tunnel and into a wall, blowing off the stillborn's legs below the knees, and leaving ominous black smoke eating away at the stumps, almost like a smoldering alchemical flame. Achmed continued retreating, dodging, and blocking the missiles with his Wing Barrier. Each one struck with terrifying force, making it no wonder why the stillborns didn't hold up so well against the intruder. Their firepower was truly monstrous.

Even wounded, 143 fought back, raising its arm to the intruder. A barrage of pinpoint-focused shockwaves bombarded the invader, each punctuated by a high-pitched sound, but the shape neither slowed in its march nor showed any other signs of being affected. The only indication that the weapon was even hitting was the deformations in the armor. With each shot, a dent the size of a coin appeared on the green-eyed demon's monolithic chestplate, but each time, the armor's eldritch runes pulsed with light, and the metal simply buckled back into shape. Without slowing down or even turning its head, the matte-black monstrosity turned its left arm to 143 and recorded the end of the stillborn's struggle in oily splatters upon the wall.

Feverishly clicking the detonator, Achmed realized he had forgotten to make sure it was set to detonate all paired charges at once. With each click, one of the charges came alive, its respective rod slamming into the wall as the surrounding spikes grew out at odd angles, creating obstacles and preceding the true detonation.

Somehow, someway, the shape simply stepped out of the way of the spikes, as if it knew exactly where they would go just by looking at them *before* they grew. In a rapid sequence, numerous such stone spikes grew, dense enough to skewer or entrap the invader. The main charges were then consumed by forceful vibrations, their tetrahedral shells resonating. They were not mere pyramids full of gunpowder; instead, they sequentially released enormously powerful shockwaves with a range precisely confined to the tunnel's inner volume. The first shockwave traveled down the tunnel, forcing Achmed to stop moving and cover his ears.

"No collateral damage, fucking bullshit," he seethed inwardly. Each shockwave that came rattled his bones and made his tendrils shake, immobilizing him and disrupting his focus. The tunnel *was* indeed untouched, however.

When the shaking subsided and Achmed looked towards the killzone, he saw nothing—only a brownish cloud formed from the powderized stone spikes and vaporized water.

But then, as the cloud of dust and mist started to clear, he saw *it*. Completely unharmed. In fact, it looked like the shape had bypassed the killzone entirely, maybe even before the charges had gone off. An unearthly aura of pitch-black smoke rose from the invader's armor, as if it was some cursed ghost that had just walked straight through solid stone. Achmed raised his Wing Barrier without even thinking.

Some thirty meters downrange, it stopped. Somehow, he felt that it knew firing would be pointless, that he could effectively defend against its missiles while retreating too quickly for it to catch him before he got back to the mansion.

But then, the green-eyed demon adjusted its stance, turning side-on and leaning forward on its right leg to the extreme, with the left leg stretched backwards. It tucked in its right arm in a tackling stance, resting the left hand on its belt. With the turn of a dial, an ominous aura of dense smoke and embers enveloped the figure, and it pointed its left arm's casting catalyst backwards.

For a moment, Achmed was confused. To add to his confusion, that raven spirit from before appeared once more, simply coming into his awareness as if it had been invisible until now. It flew over him, strangely not attacking, only to stop dead-still, hovering near a wall while looking further down the tunnel.

This moment of confusion was, inevitably, broken. With an enormous rumbling noise, the green-eyed demon went flying down the tunnel straight at him, riding a pillar of smoke and flame like some sort of giant firework.

COUPLER CHARGE
BLACK SUN COMET

Achmed fearfully ran up the wall, hoping to avoid the charge to save his life. This job was just that, a job. He would not offer up his life for the mafia. The demon glared at him but passed him by as it went tearing down the tunnel. The raven, however, was different. It suddenly spoke to him with a demonic voice full of accusation. **"Filth."**

Achmed turned just in time to hear the spirit speak again. **"None can save your soul. None escape the wrath. Repent."**

And just like that, the bird vanished into a puff of smoke.

* * *

Krahe had fully intended to turn that wall-walker into a greasy smear, but she had severely underestimated the difficulty of controlling the coupler charge. Though the strain of harnessing the Black Sun Coupler's full power was substantially reduced by her strengthened body and the Viridaimon Armor's unique design, it was nonetheless severe enough that she had no choice but to focus solely on maneuvering through the tunnel's curves. She didn't feel any particular regret about leaving the gangster alive; Casus would get to him.

The rocket-charge didn't last nearly long enough to cover the full distance to the mansion's basements, but that was a mercy; immediately following the coupler charge's end, the Viridaimon Armor lost power. Without proper training and lacking typical safeguards, the coupler charge had dumped every iota of power output. The light in the armor's eyes sputtered out, and its full weight bore down on her.

It was so suffocatingly heavy she could only walk, stumbling over to the wall. Over the course of a few seconds, the armor returned to life, and the burden eased, but the belt had not been spared. It was still functional but drawing on it for combat-level power output, let alone further coupler charges, would inevitably destroy the belt's internals. She wanted to make it last, given the enormous power and durability it afforded her, but she knew better than to rely on a self-destructive prototype, let alone assume that it would last the full length of a combat operation.

Krahe checked if the wall-walker was following her, feeling a pang of disappointment when she found he wasn't. She continued onward and before long reached the entrance to the mansion's basement complex. It was a whole cargo loading dock, with three branches spreading out. The frames of great bulkheads yawned empty, and the loading area was deserted at first glance. In reality, there were indeed people here; she learned that the hard way from a multicolored hail of magic and bullets erupting from several spots. Some were behind pillars, another on an elevated walkway, and a pair beyond a corner, inside a storeroom filled with a maze of containers. A quartet of those borged-out *things* dropped down from the ceiling where they had been hanging, screeching and weeping as they charged headlong towards her on all fours.

And so, the first true battle began. Even as she was, armored and armed to a degree sufficient to take on mid-rankers, Krahe was still at a disadvantage. A direct battle was a foolish idea even with the Viridaimon Armor.

Striding sideways through the awkward layout of the loading dock, Krahe immediately began forming a smoke grenade before Astro Diving. Just this act was enough to damage the enemy's morale, with screams of possessed ancient armor abounding, while the few who retained their full composure hollered orders at the so-called "stillborns." Meanwhile, Krahe circled them like the ghost she appeared to be, ducking into the storage room before surfacing and tossing the smoke grenade. As she entered, she raised a jade wall to block off the entrance, leaving only one other. She sent Barzai to watch over that entryway as she cleared the rest of the storeroom. There were only two people here, huddled together in the corner—a man and woman, or more appropriately, a boy and a girl. Cowards with no killing instinct and auras about as strong as Mohawk, and dressed in a similarly threatening biker-esque style. Given the situation, it made them appear even less threatening. She openly walked between the rows of crates towards them, and the boy whimpered as he fired off a purplish buzzsaw crackling with electricity.

The electric saw flew by Krahe's head, not for lack of accuracy, but because the boy's intended aim was so obvious. As such, Krahe simply tilted her head out of the way. The saw bit into the ceiling and traveled some distance before it sputtered out.

As she looked down at the two, Krahe decided she didn't care to kill them. They barely looked like adults; their eyes lacked any sort of hardened shine. They didn't belong here; they reminded her of stupid kids back in Megacity Gamma. Stupid kids who joined gangs, thinking it was a glamorous lifestyle, only to get shot like dogs to protect the bastards who actually deserved those bullets.

With a gesture, she raised a slab of smoky jade, entrapping the two of them in the corner, but only pushed it to chest-height so she could easily peer over it. The Viridaimon Armor made her a head taller, granting her a truly towering presence at over 200cm. Fully exploiting the ominous size and stillness of motion granted by the armor, Krahe leaned forward to look down at the pair.

"You won't be this lucky next time," she said, her voice distorted and deepened by the mask. **"Get your shit together. Perhaps go to one of the churches or join a proper agency. You don't have what it takes to traffic children for man-eating flymen."**

The boy had gathered his wits, standing as tall as he could, staring back at Krahe with a defiant, but fearful gaze. She leaned in further until she was eye-to-eye with him, then willed Viridaimon to uncloud the lenses as she conjured a handful of CRC Rings into her hand. They totaled 5000 DDs in value, including four of a 1000 DD and two of a 500 DD denomination so they could be split evenly.

Sprinkling them onto the moron's head, she added, **"That's a good thing. Stay still and be quiet. The panels don't last long."**

At that moment, Barzai alerted her to an approaching person. She was surprised it had taken them this long to muster the courage to try and suss her out. Turning on a bootheel, she raised her left hand and formed yet another smoke grenade in her right. Before she moved on, she added, **"And avoid the Silversword Agency."**

She had barely interacted with them whatsoever, but those interactions, combined with what she had heard and read about, had sown the seeds of distrust and dislike. Out of every group in Audunpoint, they reeked the most like a typical black company.

Krahe approached the storeroom's entryway, raising a few more barriers as she went to prepare the field, leaving the Forming Toroid at roughly half charge. That default 2m x 1m x 30cm, 10-charge slab was really too much for most uses.

In these close quarters, using Tracers wasn't ideal. She directed the belt's output to the catalyst, building up a charge while embedding it with the mental pattern of Deathsmoke Spray.

As the first man stepped into the storeroom, Krahe was already waiting. At that instant, she released the smoke burster, letting it burst at her feet. She released the charge, and instead of a stream, the casting catalyst expelled a burst of black and red that smashed through the man's wards and sent him flying like a ragdoll. He trailed blood as he flew, crashing into the edge of a crate and smashing his head against it, both of which his wards absorbed. He was left wheezing in shock, a fist-sized chunk of meat missing from his stomach which grew larger with each passing moment as the deathsmoke ate away at his flesh like a smoldering flame spreading through steel wool.

This was the exact "shotgun" effect she had envisioned when she first conceived of Deathsmoke Spray. It was just a shame it was locked away behind a high-performance prototype Mamon Coupler. Knowing how these things went, even if she eventually bought a production model, it wouldn't come close to this.

She let a few more of them come for her but didn't just hole up in the storeroom expecting to win by holding that position. They were on the defensive here and could easily call in more reinforcements from above. Time was key. And so, Krahe formed a monstrously powerful burster with a long fuse, having Barzai carry it near the doorway. Meanwhile, she crossed the storeroom, stepping over a mangled corpse and a whimpering soon-to-be corpse on her way to a solid wall. This particular spot was perfect, as when she skimmed to the other side, she ended up covered on both flanks.

What she couldn't have predicted was that the two stillborns were still sniffing around the blocked-off door, as if even their own allies didn't want to interact with them. The one that lacked visible eyes emitted a loud click, then whipped around to face Krahe.

And so, she was forced into a melee with this monstrous thing, and Sector 7 Style's close-quarters methodology kicked in once more. That is to say, Krahe tackled the creature, shoved her left fist into its chest, and blasted its ward generator apart with two shots. Once it was on the ground, a downward punch with her right hand half-severed its weapon arm, leaving the joint ruined and black veins whipping about, gushing oily hemolymph.

The next abomination was already upon her before the first died, and so she rose up, stomping on the first one's neck as she threw the second like it was a ragdoll. While far heavier than its frame suggested, the thing was still skeletal, and the left arm was already strong enough to lift a hundred kilos without issue. With the Viridaimon Armor's extra strength and weight, this feral borg-zombie was more dangerous at range than up close, and she had just given it that beneficial distance. That was a problem; it started firing on her before it even landed, its sonic weapon pounding her armor like a jackhammer. Thankfully, the problem was easily solved with a prolonged burst of tracers, shattering the bioweapon's wards, tearing off its arm, and continuing through the hole into its chest cavity, thanks to Krahe circling the thing. True, this exposed her to direct fire from the actual people, but she pulled her arm slightly upwards and tossed a smoke grenade.

Over and over again, Krahe shamelessly threw filthy, isotope-infused smoke grenades, skimmed through walls, and simply rendered herself untouchable whenever the enemy's numbers and knowledge of their home turf proved superior to her tactical planning.

The slaughter continued like this for several minutes.

There were survivors, ones who reached the ground level before she did. One was in shock and unable to utter anything other than the words, "Smoke. Black armor. Ghost."

The other swore up and down that it had to be "Blackhand's Big Brother."

* * *

Casus carried the boy a short distance from the underpass before setting him down. He understood that Blackhand wanted to prevent the child from witnessing the gruesome reality of things, and he was in agreement. Right afterwards, he pressed the eye of his belt, initiating the transformation. His body was consumed by a surge of golden flame from the belt, a projection of its star-shaped pupil emerging, rising to Casus' head height. A silhouette wrought of silver flame followed, and the full phantom simply stepped back into his frame, silver flame momentarily overtaking gold before being consumed. In that instant, all the light and flame vanished, leaving behind only his armored shape. Despite its increased complexity, the transformation only took moments; it was so quick it almost felt wrong, sped up, incomplete. That last part was true.

The Silberblut Coupler spoke, its tone resolute and melancholy at once. **"Divine crusader, hero of justice, reforged in flame."**

This "Tarnished Silberblut" was not the new armor which Casus had manifested at the end of his training. Instead, it was born from the "Crusader of Black and Gold" boon as Heroic Subjugation's effect on the

Silberblut Armor in its base state, forcing the armor to better suit Casus' own preferences rather than forcing Casus to adjust his fighting style. He found it to be substantially more resilient and physically stronger, but less agile, not for lack of agility or speed, but because of its increased bulk. He also found that the strain on his body was vastly reduced, as he was not undergoing excess change with each transformation to compensate for a lack of compatibility.

He scooped up the child as if he weighed nothing, put him on his back, and took off running. Faster than his motorbike, he shot through the streets like a matte-black bullet, the child holding on for dear life.

* * *

The sound of rapid, heavy footfalls approached the shrine. A dark silhouette sprinted through the entrance, golden light spilling from every crevice of the stranger's form like flame from a ramshackle furnace. Lucia froze mid-turn as she beheld the tall man set a run-ragged child before her. He said something about keeping the boy safe and that he had been rescued from a human trafficker, but only the vague contents of his words and the tone of his voice registered to her in her shocked state.

At first, she had not recognized him, but this was definitely *him*. The belt, the voice, the armor—all wrong in some way, yet all too familiar. In an agonizing few seconds, Lucia unthinkingly took the child into her arms as she took in the familiar Mamon Knight's armor.

A single, stone eye stared down at her, an azure abyss overlaid by a four-spoked star of burning orange, and this same pattern now reigned within his belt's eye.

The Silberblut Armor's previously gleaming silver had tarnished to a matte-black shade, and the suit now bore significantly bulkier armor on the forelimbs. The golden crown upon his brow had grown substantially, forming horizontal, quarter-circular horns to either side alongside a third, dull-ended vertical horn, which ever so faintly resembled that of a stag beetle. Four peculiar motes of golden flame circled above his head.

In place of a closed vertical eye, his chest now bore two horizontal ones. To compliment the eyes, the lower torso plates were shaped to imply the presence of a face's lower half just below the surface.

The left gauntlet was even bulkier than the right, possessing an additional closed eye. His arm-blade was the largest change, clearly attached to his arm as a separate weapon rather than seamlessly incorporated into the armor. It was shaped like a four-pointed star with one of the points "stretched out" to form the blade.

His aura of cold, steely imposition was gone, replaced by a numinous warmth spilling out of him like he was the sun itself. It was not physical heat; the shrine's interior was as cold as it always was at night, yet the warmth was real all the same.

"Casus Aristedes? What happened to you? Need I report your condition to the Inner Wheel?" she blurted out without thinking.

"There is no need. Safeguard the child and perhaps prime the shrine guardian for tonight. I must go. Once tonight is over, you will know why."

With that, he was gone, not a phantom, but a matte-black bullet leaving a trail of golden flame.

Sometime later, after making sure the boy was uninjured and settling him in the back of the shrine, Lucia acted on Casus' advice. Behind the shrine's altar, a shape of gleaming metal sat, shrouded in a heavy robe, sitting on its pedestal in a relaxed pose with its head bowed too deeply for anyone to more than glimpse its face. It was a statue to all but the most well-read adherents, but to the shrine maiden and others who knew, it was a far more immediate promise of safety than the Banishment Veil. It was also a far more immediate threat of violence to those who would foolishly think this small shrine was unguarded.

Lucia carried out a ritual of offering up sacrificial liquor, burning incense, and performing an elaborate dance whilst chanting a specific sutra. It was not a sutra from any scripture, but one written particularly for this idol, embedded within its body and known only by vanishingly few besides Lucia.

By the time the ritual was over, the boy had come out just in time to witness the shrine guardian lurch upward. Its mouth creaked open, and it drew in every iota of incense smoke in the vicinity. The guardian thumped its staff against its altar, and a seven-spoked wheel of golden flame blazed to life behind it. Another thump, and the wheel turned by a full revolution. The shrine was enveloped in golden light, and the doors slammed shut.

Another thump. Another revolution. Reams of blessed paper sprung forth from the guardian's sleeves, flying upwards into the rafters and out of sight, circling the shrine. Thereafter, the guardian went silent, the wheel projection behind it fading until it was barely visible. The next morning, four known Hashem Family members would be found in the vicinity, bound by these same reams of sacred paper.

Meanwhile, Casus shot through the city streets even faster than before, his maximum speed no longer limited by the presence of a small, fragile passenger. He took sharp alleyway turns one after the next without slowing, sometimes running along walls and other times tilting his body as if he himself were a high-speed motorbike, tearing up the flagstones with his arm-blade to help him steer. He only stopped at the hidden door, and then it was back to full speed from a standstill.

Even the small loss of maneuverability really stung, but somehow, Casus liked this better. A man-shaped battering ram.

CHAPTER 24

THEY JUST VANISHED

Mirzaii 2. The ballroom. A chamber of refined luxury stained by ongoing debauchery. The air inside was thick with a miasma of smoke, alcohol, and a rainbow of fumes from drugs of all kinds, covering the full spectrum from the natural to the synthetic. The number of guests was nearly equal to the number of entertainers, and in turn, to the number of guards. A band of nervous musicians played an eclectic set of their greatest hits, songs that hadn't done so well, and hastily prepared covers, all picked out by their employer. They had, of course, not known ahead of time that this employer was Semzar Hashem, but the enormous paycheck and equally generous tips had sufficed to encourage them. It wasn't as if they could run at this point.

At the other side of the ballroom, a woman clad in naught but translucent silks and jewelry danced on a hexagonal stage that was slick with blood and viscera. The intermingling of human and Saurian blood colored her bare feet a strange shade of purplish scarlet, effectively concealing the talismans that safeguarded her from slipping.

"The patrols are gone, sir. All of them. The same is true for the men we sent out to assess what happened to the patrols."

The man speaking was an abnormally large baneworm hidden inside a mountain of muscle, which in turn was hidden by a mountain of fat; such bodies made it easier to conceal his possession of them, and his preference had earned him such names as, Strongman, Big Guy, Fatman, and so on. He, the baneworm, didn't actually have a personal name, simply making one up each time he took a new body. Even as he was riding in a two-meter meat mountain, he was in the submissive position here. He looked up from where he knelt to see the disdainful facade of Semzar Hashem, the heir's irritation distorting his meatsuit's handsome features.

"Gone? The fuck you mean gone?!" Semzar barked, throwing a glass of atrociously expensive liquor. Instantaneously, a nearby manservant cleaned it up, tendrils of azure magic extending from the jewels on his glove's knuckles to lift the mess into a trash chute.

Semzar proceeded with a multi-minute rant which involved drinking and spilling three more glasses of that liquor. While this went on, Strongman tuned out most of the heir's inane tirade and carefully took in his surroundings.

To Semzar's left and right, a small harem of women had been gathered. In Strongman's experience, such groups were usually made up of three sorts: self-employed women of the night, those with more ambition than reason, and those who had no choice in the matter—illegally owned or otherwise coerced by a third party. He wondered what the ratios were in this case. They didn't seem *particularly* dead in the eyes, at least. He supposed Semzar's choice of skinsuit must've helped.

Behind Semzar's opulent seat, there towered an enormous, two-and-a-half meter tall Evoy. He exuded a stoic threat of violence at any perceived aggression, his compound eyes perpetually twitching in place as he observed his surroundings. He looked unlike any other Evoy, unlike even the rare war-morphs; in short, he looked *wrong*. His left arm particularly stood out, being so engorged that its chitin plates bulged apart, revealing the musculature underneath. Its base shape even diverged from the Evoy's other arm. To the giant's sides, four further guards were posted. Their forms were mostly Evoy-like, but twisted and misshapen, each more heavily grafted than the next. These graft-beast abominations were scattered all throughout the mansion.

Finally, after calming down somewhat, Semzar leaned forward and asked, "Explain what you mean by 'gone.' As I recall, I spent a great deal on communications *specifically to prevent this.*"

With each word, the mask of calm cracked, tendrils and veins showing through as anger crept into his voice again. "We haven't received any calls, good or bad, in the last twenty minutes. Somehow, all of them seem to have just disappeared into the astral. The same thing happened to those we sent to check, and..." Strongman said, partially repeating himself.

Before Semzar could speak again, explosions sounded in the distance.

A wave of tension swept over the ballroom. Even that giant Evoy turned his head in that direction, ever so subtly. He leaned down to Semzar, uttering something in his ear. The heir listened with rapt attention, then barked out a series of commands, some of which pertained to Strongman himself. In effect, he was calling for the mansion's security contingent to go on high alert. It made sense, but Strongman instinctively filtered out the brat's actual words, coming away only with the general meaning.

However, before Strongman could actually get to doing his job, one of the ballroom's doors swung open, and a shell of a man stumbled through. His hair was burnt off in places, one of his eyes had burst open, and fist-sized chunks were missing from his left side.

"T-the basement, it's... it's Blackhand's big brother..."

* * *

Initially, Yazata wasn't particularly fond of these "Red Hoods." Battle-automata that they were, they mimicked human behavior far too closely, without the cognitive capacity to be held accountable. They lacked the token animalism of graft-beasts and bore no esoteric spark to imply the presence of an eidolon intelligence; they were animated wholly by artifice and were just as unsettlingly cold as that implied. Faceless things, yet at once their steel-silver bodies had the shapes of young girls, and each possessed hair of a subtly different color, hidden under the titular hooded cloak of scarlet fabric.

On the way to the Mirzaii Subdistrict, Yazata and her force of freakish silver maidens encountered some expected resistance. Even spread out as they were, Yazata was still obviously an inquisitor, and the Red Hoods were an even more immediate bogeyman to the city's miscreants than her. As they moved towards their goal, they identified and subdued nearly twenty patrolling Hashem Family foot soldiers.

And so, it came to be that she found herself bombarded with a rapid-fire barrage of Red Reapers from a first-floor window. It was inevitable, fully expected. This was no ambush—it was the path of least resistance.

She simply stepped to the side of one red comet, drawing her bar-mace with her right hand and holding out her left. Her eyes burned with purple light as she poured power into both the bar-mace and the Black Bindings that enveloped her body. Five reams of Black Binding sprung forth from her sleeve, capturing an encroaching reaper, and with a simple gesture, she sent it flying back. She hopped between two further reapers that had reached her in the intervening second, which appeared to be pushed away from her onto wildly divergent trajectories, debris and crimson energy coloring the space behind her as she calmly walked towards her adversaries.

All it took was a glance; she merely had to meet their eyes to get them in her snare. Sheer mental focus, honed to a razor point, set loose as a torpedo just beneath the skin of reality. A petty hex, but enough to make the trio freeze up on the spot. It lasted all of a second and a half, but that was more than enough.

Finally, she felt her mace come alive, and she chanted under her breath, "Oh, Black Trapezohedron, sound forth from the spires of Zor'Aguhastra..."

The black metal of its blade began thrumming with an unearthly sound, a thick distortion dripping from it, only upwards; it was like a heat-haze, if a heat-haze was as thick as pouring blood, and if it twisted the world itself rather than the air.

With a simple horizontal swing, an invisible force carved a gash across the wall, its existence only betrayed by a wake of the same distortion that enveloped Yazata's bar mace. The windows exploded out of their frames, and the brickwork crumbled. One of the men had his skull cleaved open, while the two others were sent flying back like ragdolls.

Two steps forward and a moment later, the light finally reached the ends of Yazata's Black Bindings. They shot out as if alive and mercilessly dragged the trio out of the building, slamming the one with a cleft-open face into the cobbles while restraining the other two. Yazata let out a sigh through her nose as she willed her bindings to envelop the survivors' heads, the bindings' sigils forming complex curse-seals in the process. In this manner, she sealed their awareness, rendering them into vegetables for the next several hours. Yazata honestly wished it were always this easy to place mental restraints.

Following this negligible obstacle, Yazata regrouped with her contingent of Red Hoods and directly approached the Gate of Mirzaii which was the main entrance to the gated slice of decadence that included the target building. The address numbers only went up to five, yet it took up an enormous swath of land, with anything and everything the owners could want on their properties. It made perfect sense; Audunpoint had never lacked for space, and according to intel, this place had been well outside the living city's bounds at the time of its original construction. In short, the city's expansion had only caught up to this location in recent years. The walls were like those of a small fortress, ten meters tall and shimmering with reinforcing runes and translucent barriers extending further upwards. The Mirzaii Subdistrict was, by all means, excessively well-defended. Yazata decided to investigate the owners of these properties after this was over and done with.

Gathering in front of the Gate of Mirzaii, they found it closed with a guard in well-wrought silver Mamon Armor standing in front, contrary to their intel. It was clear he had been stationed here specifically as another layer of defense.

Covered in fluting and elaborate inlays from head to toe, the wide-shouldered man possessed a truly baroque countenance befitting of the place he guarded. A large sword of equally complex design floated behind him. He lacked a typical belt; instead, attached to his left arm was an enormous tower shield which incorporated the Mamon Coupler into itself, constantly projecting a barrier and its surface shimmering with the implication of warding. Despite the thickly layered imagery, Yazata could identify no outward sign of the guard's affiliation to an agency.

"Halt. What is your purpose here?" he asked in a stern monotone.

Yazata simply poured a wisp of thauma into her pendant. The golden, seven-spoked wheel floated a hand's length from her chest, shining with golden flame. The wheel then shrunk inward, transforming the symbol into a spiky, seven-pointed star with the wheel in the innermost third.

"I am Yazata Heptaxia, Inquisitor of the Inner Wheel. By the authority vested in me by the Seven Spokes, I demand you allow my contingent and I to pass unimpeded. Our purpose in the Mirzaii Subdistrict is the detainment of Semzar Hashem, son of the mafioso Damrus Hashem, whom I have good reason to believe currently resides within the mansion on Mirzaii Two."

The gate guardian stared her down, motionless, faceless, for a solid five seconds.

"Unfortunate. I was not aware," he stated, retrieving a large key and touching it to the gate. As its enormous wings swung open, the guard walked off to the side. "I will see to it that my handler conveys my contract to the church. I would request that I be compensated for the loss of income from any goods confiscated as a result of your investigation. I am sure the Seven Spokes will understand."

Yazata very nearly raised her eyebrows at the man's temerity, but she let it go. It was not her problem. She led the Red Hoods into the Mirzaii Subdistrict, quickly approaching the mansion. They encountered no great resistance on the approach, easily subduing enemy patrols before they could use their glorified consumer-grade communication artifacts. Yazata continually observed the maidens' behavior as they followed her commands, noting that, unlike most automata, their adaptability was just as good as the technical documents suggested. With each encounter, the Red Hoods grew less stiff, requiring fewer direct instructions.

Before the final approach, she took a moment to look over each of them, adjusting the Black Bindings she had attached beneath their shells.

No erosion, good... Sympathetic transfer efficiency will be quite poor, but I will accept what is given freely, she thought.

It was time. The Red Hoods encircled the mansion, forming an enormous heptagram. At this point, the mansion's windows swung open, and its protective barrier flared, being tightly contoured to its walls. A deluge of hostile magic and gunfire poured out, but at this range, it posed little danger. Yazata captured the occasional would-be hits with her Black Bindings and sent them flying right back at the source.

The ritual proceeded without delay. She uttered a word, and it rang with the sound of a hollow, bronze bell.

The eye-like glyphs covering her hair vanished in a burst of purple light, reappearing suspended before the face of each Red Hood.

A second word, and she outstretched her arms. Black Bindings once more sprang forth from her sleeves, joining her with the Red Hoods and surrounding the mansion.

A third word, and the Red Hoods mimicked it, her bindings flaring with power and strain as these unliving things conducted such a profound force.

"The strain is too great; it shan't work at this rate."

The base cost was already enormous. With the added resistance of using these dolls as the other participants, Yazata had no way to power the ritual under her own strength.

With some remorse, she sent out several more Black Bindings, connecting them back to fourteen restrained foot-soldiers in the general vicinity. Onerous though it was, she crossed one of her many lines and used them to power the ritual, hijacking their Soul Furnaces for the moment.

Like the supplicants of an unkind god, the small crowd rose up and stumbled towards her, but she had gotten what she needed long before they could reach her.

The final, fourth word rang out, and the world ruptured. There came a ceaseless scream of unearthly pitch. The Red Hoods were consumed by Black Bindings, growing out from inside their shells, liquid distortion spilling out as their silhouettes twisted, overlaid by something else, yet undeniably under their control. At the same moment, all of her extended Black Bindings were drawn back towards Yazata, gathering into a sphere before her. The sphere of empowered bindings exploded, instantaneously filled by the shape of a chthonic monstrosity visible to the naked eye only as distortion.

HIGH THAUMATURGY
SIGN OF THE PRETENDER-ARCHON
WITCHCRAFT HEPTAGRAM: DREDGING THE DEEP GULF

The screaming ceased. From beneath Yazata's stoic mask, a cackling laugh escaped.

Seven seals undone, seven beasts from the deep astral called forth and bound to the material, dragged along like caught fish just beneath the surface.

"In accordance with the Third Tower's ancient accords, heed my shining words, o children of the fathomless deep! Go forth and eat your fill, o hounds of the Nameless Roaring One!" she invoked, still cackling as she drew the Black Trapezohedron.

This was Yazata's personal definition of *witchcraft*. Understanding and wielding the truly esoteric and forgotten in order to gain strength far beyond one's raw talent, using knowledge and craft to subvert the limits of nature. The method had a dozen restrictions, and all of them, she had solved.

* * *

The mansion shook, and the shouts of men carried through its halls. An immense force struck against its barriers, hammering on without reproach. The outside world laid out of sight, shutters having long since slammed into place over the windows.

Thus, Krahe made her way into enemy territory, checking corners and pushing deeper.

Unfortunately, the building was designed with several chokepoints, and it seemed the defenders had expected an intrusion from below. Perhaps they had even learned of her invasion somehow; she hadn't enough time to count the corpses.

A phalanx of three gun-armed stillborns blocked the hall, and behind them, four men stood. Three looked fairly typical for gangsters—of these three, two appeared on edge, while one was downright panicked, his eyes wildly darting around. The fourth seemed to have his wits about him and, by Krahe's guess, looked to be the controller of the three stillborns. His eye sockets were like bottomless pits, the skin around them colored black, and small yellow-glowing gemstones sat within them, far too small for his face. A pretentious, curled mustache sat beneath his swollen, bloodshot nose. His eyes swiveled Krahe's way the moment she came into view, and she felt appraisal wash over her, seeping into the Viridaimon Armor.

"Ah. Blackhand's older brother, is it? You've made a real mess of things, you know. No matter how good you are, you can't beat the odds. I know what you are. "

Older brother? she thought.

The man's eyes flared. Something vaguely akin to appraisal washed over Krahe, but it didn't try to intrude the way direct appraisal did.

"A fourth-order voidkey! Fourth!" the small-eyed man exclaimed, as if that would save him. Distant footsteps signaled the approach of enemy reinforcements, so she had to act quickly, but she also needed to buy time

before she could break through decisively. And so, she willed the Black Sun
Coupler to ready another Coupler Charge.

* * *

"Odds? You want to talk about the odds?!" the green-eyed demon
scoffed through its mask. It waved its left hand about, gesturing with its
catalyst like a conductor's wand while its right hand remained clenched
tightly to its chest, hidden by the shield on its forearm. The raven on the
figure's shoulder emitted a cackling laugh. Someone threw a chair. The
raven's eyes flashed, and the chair exploded into a hundred pieces mid-
flight.

"I've seen a full squad of armored killers get wiped out by a myopic car
nerd and an overweight alcoholic armed with two-shot pipe guns. These
are downright great odds!"

It threw something.

The hallway erupted into a cloud of choking smoke and razor-sharp
glass glitter.

Chaos usurped the reins, and any semblance of the enemy's team
cohesion shattered. They all started acting according to their own whims,
following whatever plan they had agreed to in only the vaguest sense.

Wooden arms exploded from the walls, grabbing at a silhouette that
was not the green-eyed demon, but one of the stillborns. Flammable liquid
sprayed throughout the hallway, soon blazing forth with green fire. The
shapes of three canine beasts rose from a carpet, only to instantly succumb
to the flames.

Of the group, the small-eyed man reacted the fastest, barking an attack
order to the stillborns as he manifested a spear and shield of cyan-glowing,
glassy arcane force. He thrust it forth and a beam of force erupted from it.
Wherever it touched, the hardwood floor exploded as if it was being ripped
open, subject to enormous tearing force. It even managed to nick Krahe's
leg, yanking her forwards into a wide, low stance.

The small-eyed man let out a sound of triumph as if he could feel that he had gotten a hit, and bashed with his shield, sending an explosion of reflective shards tumbling through the smoke cloud. Krahe was already out of the way by that point, having closed the distance. Another beam shot from the spear, reflecting and multiplying, bouncing around in the field of shards and diffusing through Krahe's smoke cloud, illuminating it in its entirety. The beams converged at a seemingly arbitrary point and tore out the chest of the panicking gangster, whom Krahe had shoved into the same spot where she had stood when she was hit. Just by looking at it, she could tell diffusion in her smoke had robbed around a third of the beam's strength. It was less than she had predicted, but then, it was pure magic, not light.

Despite the varied abilities presented by her foes, the borged-out abominations were her main concern. A person she could suppress, and that's the tactic she went with, firing recklessly down the hallway. But these things had no self-preservation, yet possessed the wherewithal to make that actually mean something. Their implanted ward generators were far stronger than the inax surgeon's version, and their pure physicality easily surpassed that of someone wearing a Dregsteamer belt. Combined with their built-in weapons and the fact pain or shock wouldn't stop them from fighting, they were the real threat here.

* * *

A force composed specifically to forestall intruders fell apart into panic and incidental infighting, while the lone trained professional struggled to stay alive. Siavash set off two more refracted beams from his spear before a mass of sparks and smoke ripped into his wards and sent him stumbling back a step, falling to one knee. At that point, he instinctively called his shield back, the shards reverting to one whole.

Decision paralysis took hold. Vague silhouettes whirled through the smoke, intermingling and briefly becoming illuminated by bursts of orange and green. The intruder's footsteps mixed with thunderous thumping and the incessant, *obnoxious* calls of that raven. Siavash glimpsed the intruder's form as it tackled one of his men against a wall, burying its fist into his stomach. Thump. Thump. Two flashes of orange, two gusts of dense ash and smoke racing out of the otherwise stagnant cloud. His lower body slid down, and the upper half soon followed with it, tumbling down. The small-eyed man took a shot, but it flew forward unimpeded, the armored juggernaut gone like a ghost. Just as the smoke seemed to be thinning out, a black sphere rolled out of the cloud and transformed the world into a choking limbo all over again.

* * *

Before long, only Krahe and the small-eyed man were left. He was breathing heavily, leaning against the wall with his shield held up, looking Krahe's way as she kicked the head of a stillborn against the wall. *Thump. Thump. Thump. Crack.* They both pointed their weapons at one another in an uneasy standoff, both waiting for reinforcements.

"You ae too good for your readings. What are you doing, skinwalking as a low mid-ranker? Somehow lost your *real* gear, hm?"

Krahe didn't answer. The stillborn's wards finally gave under her boot, and the lower half of its head followed soon after. She turned her gaze towards the small-eyed man, causing him to shrink back a bit, the grip on his spear tightening as a flare of power built at the weapon's tip.

"Look, I don't much feel like dying here," he said, attempting to negotiate. "That's way above my pay grade. I'm not with the Hashems; I'm just one of the contractors they brought in for today. What'd you say I just get out of your path, and we go our separate ways?"

"Your voidkey. Pull it. Then you can go."

She could see the reluctance in his gaze, but that resistance suddenly gave way when she took a step towards him. His eyes flickered back and forth, and then, a ray of death screamed forth from his spear, flying right by Krahe's head, passing left to right in front of her eyes. It had never been intended to hit her, but to obscure her vision as the small-eyed man fled—

even if only for a split second. Despite instinctively letting rip a prolonged burst of tracers in his direction, he disappeared around a corner.

Krahe gave chase, not to kill him, but to pass the chokepoint. From there, she picked out a room, cleared it, and set up shop inside, waiting while Barzai perched on a wall sconce just outside. She had never planned to push particularly deep into the mansion on her own, and this seemed a good point to wait for Casus. This was also a good opportunity to give the Black Sun Coupler a rest, as Krahe had felt it straining during that last fight. She didn't expect it to hold out much longer.

A small group ran through the corridor just outside, but no one checked inside. Their attention was pointed entirely outward at the *things* besieging the mansion.

Indeed, the mansion shook, and a wave of discordant magic washed through the floor with blackened lines showing through the carpet as the stench of burning fabric filled the room. Through Barzai's eyes, Krahe saw a similar backlash taking place in the hallway, spreading from one particular window. At its precipice, the walls burst open with the force of rupturing arcane circuitry, the phenomenon she had observed being just the waning aftershocks.

In the next moment, an indistinct distortion clawed its way through that window's shutter, outlined only by black wrappings. Within the silhouette floated a Red Hood, seemingly controlling the form. It sprinted down the corridor, broke into a room, and dragged out a screaming, thrashing Bane-Saurian. The distorted monster bit into his head, but he remained physically unharmed. He screeched in a rather bird-like manner as *something* flowed out of him into the manifestation, and he went limp, soon discarded like an empty soft drink can.

As far as she had been briefed, she should have had no fear of being attacked by what was obviously a result of the witch-inquisitor's skills.

Her gut told her otherwise. She still preferred to stay away from esoteric, unknown, and extremely dangerous combat vectors, even if they were allies. After all, even if it had no intention of harming her, she might get caught in the crossfire.

The possessed Red Hood made its way deeper into the mansion. Krahe waited until it was gone, then decided to follow in its wake. A small part of her regretted not laying eyes on it directly. That same part was thoroughly convinced that the distortion-creature was familiar, somehow, not in terms of having met or seen it before, but in terms of its fundamental nature.

Before long, Barzai saw a pair of familiar faces running for their lives— gangsters who had run down the way they were now running from, towards the basement. One of them, unfortunately for him, barged into the room she was hiding in. A prolonged burst of tracers did just the trick, sending the man stumbling back out the door in a seizing, gore-spraying dance. His half-pulped corpse soon slumped against the outer wall.

A third, fourth, and fifth came running from that same direction, but long before they could even reach the now-open door of Krahe's hideaway, a matte-black blur bulldozed through them, leaving one missing his head and the other writhing on the ground, legs broken. Now that he had stopped, she could see; it was Casus. He squatted down next to the survivor, said something to him, and moved on, with the survivor crawling towards another room.

Krahe willed Barzai to reveal himself, making sure Casus saw him before calling the eidolon back to herself. The Banisher followed as expected.

"Took you long enough. Close the door," she said.

"How long have you been in this room? Is the suit locked up?" he asked, approaching her where she sat, immediately kneeling to inspect her belt.

"Not long. The belt seemed to be struggling, so I decided to give it a rest and wait for you to get here. Didn't think it had enough juice left to get me to the upper floor."

"A correct assessment," he said, standing back up. "Perhaps half a minute of combat output. Perhaps finish it off with a ranged coupler charge. If you give the mental command, the armor should self-destruct as part of the charge. It will be more potent that way and spare you from the aftermath. However, the coupler will likely not survive. The inserted voidkey will be at risk as well."

"Can't worry about that. I'll just implant the Atomica; won't have the time to pull the shardkey out of a busted belt anyway," Krahe replied, holding out a hand. Casus pulled her up without wasting a moment.

"It will take me some time to go through with the implant, so it will be up to you to cover me," she added.

A simple nod.

"Let us go," said Casus.

Despite expectations, they encountered minimal resistance on their way to the foyer. Krahe sent Barzai ahead to do a quick fly-through. The first thing she noted was the state of the foyer. Signs of combat were widespread, with five or six corpses strewn about. She wasn't sure, as some were torn apart while others lay dead with no visible wounds.

At the top of the stairs, the defenders had set up a barricade using furniture and a pair of small thaumine-fired barrier generators. There were eleven human defenders—eight male and two female gangsters, all in cheap suits—the glaringly obvious commander and four stillborns. The man was giant, with a bear-like build, and was dressed far too well to be a foot soldier, wearing a properly fitted, real suit that heroically contained his bulging gut. The stillborns were arrayed behind the barricade, not in a good position to readily spring into action against an attack from the stairs. One of them—an abnormally lanky man with a third eye crudely implanted in his forehead—pointed in Barzai's direction as he flew through, calling down an ill-aimed outburst of bullets and magic that didn't even come close to hitting the eidolon.

Krahe immediately decided that spending her last coupler charge on breaking the barricade was the best choice. She reached for her belt, twisted its dial, and honed her mental focus as she did so. Shivers ran down her back as the belt began creaking under strain. The only reason the defenders didn't hear it being that they were making far more noise.

It would be nothing complex—a projectile that flies a certain distance and detonates in mid-air. A glorified Six Trees Killer. She had considered constructing a giant one with the casting medium as an ad-hoc thruster, but the armor dashed that idea by resolving her mental command with a much simpler response of what it could do.

The power would be an order of magnitude below the Daemon Core, but Krahe was certain it would at bare minimum smash apart the barricade, disable most of the defenders, and seriously wound the commander.

Smoke, ash, and cinders began pouring out of every crevice of the Viridaimon suit, enveloping her in a swirling maelstrom. It resembled a swarm of insects more than anything else. Her casting medium, meanwhile, formed a small bead of sputtering, flame, an ember more than anything else, and yet, its radiance grew. As if being fed with pure oxygen, the Black Sun Coupler roused an ember to the intensity of raging fire. She began walking through the short intermediary room separating this wing from the foyer, raising her arm above her head.

Streams of pyroclast gathered there, swarming like moths around a candle, casting a dark kaleidoscope of unsettling shadows over the foyer as countless shouts rang out and magic began raining down. All was consumed in the storm of pyroclast; in its self-destructive final flare, the Black Sun Coupler brutishly devoured hostile magic and converted it into yet further power for its final attack, its core blazing with the final flare of a dying star. Two Red Reapers, a Yellow Atropal, and four independent, albeit decently potent thaumaturgies struck her. With each one, the ember burned brighter, and cracks spider-webbed across the plates of her armor. A fifth thaumaturgy came, a ghostly fist wrought of stone-gray energy. It landed with such force as to send her stumbling back, caving in her chestplate and knocking the wind out of her. It was that bear-like man, and his other hand was already encased in another ghostly fist just like the first. Even as her body screamed for air, Krahe leveled her arm at her point of aim, above the defenders' heads.

At some point, Barzai manifested without being prompted and began circling around her, screaming and laughing. Krahe could barely move now, her thoughts wholly focused on firing this off and then immediately diving.

"Hahahahaha! Burn them under the fallen sun! We know what must be done!" the eidolon cawed in a manic tone.

With a low roar, a column of flame came pouring out of the casting medium, simultaneously propelling the sphere of ash and cinders whilst pushing Krahe back. Not the Viridaimon Armor, but Krahe herself. The recoil impulse coincided with the Viridaimon Armor's final and total structural failure, pushing her out through the suit's back, which crumbled under her weight with barely any resistance.

Her dive was instant. The moment she felt the air on her own skin, she dove into the astral *other*, and briefly beheld the aftermath of the Red Hood's rampage within the foyer. The traces were everywhere, almost painting a picture of how it had slaughtered those gangsters. Krahe's visual calculus did not have the time to even begin working out the puzzle. There came a high-pitched squeal, a brilliant flash of light, and the air caught fire. The room fell victim to a pyroclastic flow worthy of an actual volcano— not in scale, but in intensity. Krahe couldn't discern how the effect operated—certainly not through the mess, doubly so not from her side of the astral gulf.

FINAL COUPLER CHARGE
BLACK SUN NOVA BURSTER

In her state, she couldn't remain submerged for long; she barely managed to escape the foyer back the way she came and was left with a nearly bottomed-out entropy tolerance at the other side. Casus glanced down, nodded, and turned the corner in her wake, shutting the door behind himself, but not before Barzai slipped through to be the lookout, of course. Last she saw of him through her own eyes, the four stars above his head began revolving so quickly as to form a contiguous halo. A moment later, she both heard and felt his explosive take-off towards his opponent, with Barzai's sightline becoming obscured by a cloud of dust.

Krahe unbuttoned her back pocket and pulled out the Twin Serpent Key, shoving it into place behind her ear. Already, she could feel her wards crumbling, and the Twin Serpent Key's re-implantation only slowed that decay—it couldn't hold them together properly. The labor of wrenching open a window to her Kenoma Sack began as the sounds of superhuman violence played out just next door. Rapid footsteps came from the other side, the wing of the mansion they had entered through, and Krahe's instinctive reaction at that moment was *wall*.

Without a moment's hesitation, she dragged a 10-charge slab of smoky jade from the ground, stretching it out to obstruct the double-winged door. She heard it open moments later, and bewildered profanity followed. The people on the other side banged on it, even shot it, and then ran off. Fifteen centimeters of magically reinforced stone would stop a fair bit—a couple reapers, even—but Krahe had no illusions of true safety. She pushed harder and harder, painstakingly dragging the box out of Kenoma's grasp as Casus fought in the other room. Tremors from his clashes with the head of security reverberated through the floor and walls, and set the overhead chandelier swaying ever so slightly.

* * *

Casus beheld the aftermath of Lady Blackhand's final coupler charge. He instantly deduced it to have been some variant of a burster, or perhaps an empowered variant of the Six Trees Killer—a "Sixty Trees Killer." He chuckled at his own wordplay.

Only the backless, one-armed husk of the Viridaimon Armor remained in the sanded-down foyer, and a layer of ash covered everything. The barricade had been torn asunder, one barrier generator still heroically soldiering on as thaumine dripped from its cracked fuel tank, projecting a garbled wall into the air.

Two of the defenders had survived the blast, alongside what seemed to be one of their graft-beasts.

One of the survivors was an enormous man in an unmistakable suit—the militarist-fusion work of Kharim Bayat, or a truly faithful, high-quality imitation. He stood at the top of the stairs, his suit only slightly charred, clearly having faced the blast head-on. Two giant forearms of translucent gray force rose before him as he held up a boxer's guard.

Despite blocking it entirely from the front, Lady Blackhand's coupler charge had clearly bypassed that defense, based on the fizzling and flickering wards around the man's sides and back.

As for the other human survivor, it was a three-eyed man, currently stumbling away as he coughed up globs of copper-green sludge. He had hidden himself behind his commander, likely using a high-coverage barrier to shield himself from the secondary element of the attack. The graft-beast was at his heel, scuttling behind him until the larger man called for it, causing it to join him instead.

The sizable man stared down at Casus, gray force coalescing around his fists and continuing further up his arms. The telltale tendrils of a baneworm twitched under his skin, concealed somewhat under a generous layer of fat.

A gray fist came flying at him. Casus shifted to the side and came running after his foe right away, closing the distance.

The man was impressive—his strength rivaled Casus', and despite his size, he was no lumbering brute. It was true that his bulk limited his mobility, what movement took place was both calculated and explosive. His technique was equally impressive—a mixture of common bare-knuckle boxing techniques elevated through understanding and adjusted to fit the user's nonstandard anatomy. It wasn't every day one met a man built like a hippo, that is to say, a mountain of solid muscle disguised by far less fat than there seems to be. On top of that, he seamlessly weaved thaumaturgy with boxing, using only simple but rock-solid techniques to enhance his comparatively far more advanced martial arts.

Casus matched the giant blow for blow, sensing something unsettlingly familiar in him. He wondered what exactly it was, and during their second exchange, he realized it. Tsetse. This was astonishingly similar to Tsetse's style but focused near-exclusively on the arms.

Right hook. Casus blocked it, ducked right, and drove a flame-wreathed uppercut into his foe's armpit. A left hook came flying in, but Casus willed his arm-blade to spin, its force throwing the punch off-course, cutting through the wards, and biting into flesh. Without time to spin up in advance, it didn't get much further than a shallow cut.

He immediately hopped back, landing across from the giant. To his right, the stairs and the rest of the foyer. To his left, a scorched, ash-encrusted double door, beyond it a hallway across which awaited the door to the ballroom. The graft-beast was banging on the door beyond which Lady Blackhand was, but Casus held no doubt in her ability to deal with just one of those things. Still, he shouted a warning—he couldn't afford to do much more.

Though he had not noticed it, a fifth star had joined the four revolving above his head, and with it, his strength had grown in all aspects.

Casus had decided—this battle would end with the next exchange.

"My name is Casus Aristedes. Return the flesh you have stolen and go unto Kenoma," he recited as he pressed in the eye of his belt, expecting no reply.

"Some call me Strongman," his foe replied, not divulging his true name.

The third exchange came and went, a dance of violence. Casus took some hits, but compared to Tsetse, Strongman was a manageable opponent. Merely applying what he had learned from his fights with Tsetse was enough to start pressuring the giant.

Such was his thought process: How could he ever become something more than a mere shadow of Silberblut if he couldn't even best someone objectively weaker than Tsetse, let alone Tsetse himself?

To any reasonable individual, of course, this was an absurd mindset, but it was the epitome of reason for Casus Aristedes.

His heroic aspirations demanded him to surpass himself, and with hope and anger in his heart, that was what he did.

* * *

Strongman didn't understand what was happening.

With every passing moment, that black-armored Mamon Knight grew stronger and stronger. He called himself Casus Aristedes, and sure, his suit resembled descriptions of the Silberblut Armor, but it clearly wasn't the Silberblut Armor. The eye on his belt was all wrong, and the outer rim was the color of copper instead of gold.

And yet, somehow, he would have preferred to be fighting Silberblut right now.

He had sent out his emergency ping before that explosion, but no help had arrived yet. Even that stillborn had left his side, bashing at a random door on the lower floor for some forsaken reason. Strongman hated this but he still put up his fists and summoned his strength.

CHAPTER 25

IT SCUTTLED LIKE THAT ONE SCENE IN THE EXORCIST

Moments earlier...

The moment it was out of the box, Atomica's seals sloughed off, revealing a gleaming mass of opaque, red crystal. Despite its far weaker physical glow, it still seethed with an immense aura, noticeably less intense than it had been right after transmutation, but far more solid. Tendrils of crimson energy reached out for Krahe, and the key floated towards her hand, hovering near it. Only one talisman stayed in place—it stated the voidkey's system readout.

[ATOMICA REFULGENT, FRACTURED SOLOMONIC KEY]

Tags

Fourth-order

Voidkey

Incomplete

Imprinted (Brunhilde "Blackhand" Krahe)

Details

*Thaumic Throughput +C1^*

*Entropy Tolerance +D3^^*

*Entropy Dissipation +D3^*

*Thaumic Fusion Efficiency +18%^^^*

*Isotope Tolerance +D1^^*

*Isotope Dissipation +D2^*

It curiously showed which aspects had grown during its stabilization period, with small upward arrows next to each attribute signifying growth. *A side effect of the seals?* she wondered, recalling Yao's mention of the possibility. She peeled it off, stowing the box back in her Kenoma Sack. The readout continued onto the other side—there was one new line, a reiteration of the warning Yao had given her about possible collateral damage.

First-time implantation of this voidkey will reshape the holder's Soul Furnace, permanently conferring the following Boon: "Astral Implosion Furnace"
This voidkey may be safely implanted only by the Imprinted individual. Implantation by any other individual will result in catastrophic Soul Furnace rupture (as with simultaneous implantation of two voidkeys).
First-time implantation may cause volatile thaumetic phenomena. Conduct in a safe place free of fragile objects and/or people.

Stowing the paper in her Kenoma Pocket, she quickly formed a Tar-tendril, grasping her gun with it. The loaded clip held six mescalt bullets. After that, she extracted the Twin Serpent Key, her unenhanced dissipation more than enough to maintain that one tendril. At the instant the Twin Serpent Key was out, her thoughts of implanting Atomica triggered something. With a pulse of red light from the hexagonal voidkey, Krahe felt a searing hot sensation race up her right arm, quickly spreading throughout her entire body, settling in her chest where she felt the flame of thaumaturgy when channeling. Her spine and ribcage thrummed with a strange vibration, a dull headache took hold, and then, she *knew*.

The Atomica was preparing her Soul Furnace for the reshaping it would undergo during actual implantation. She was stuck like this for now. As she wondered how long it would take, a new HUD element manifested, a simple percentage bar. It readily faded out of view, but Krahe remained aware—*agonizingly aware*—of its wavering rise, slowly going up and down by half-percent increments, totaling out to a gradual rise.

She suppressed a groan—one of frustration, pain, but worst of all, pressure. With each percent, Atomica shone brighter with both light and power, and so did the flame of thaumaturgy within Krahe's chest. A ceaseless deluge of power roiled inside her, flowing back and forth through the voidkey. Withstanding it was one thing, she could do that, but she was deathly certain that proper thaumaturgy was beyond her. She had the one Tar-tendril, and that was it; all else would be theurgy or crude energy expulsion.

As far as facts went, she could see herself just sitting here for a minute or however long the process took, hiding.

But she felt that was not possible. The Atomica burned too brightly.

Casus shouted a warning through the thunderous noise of his battle with the chief of security, but Krahe had already seen what he was warning her of through Barzai's eyes. All the borged abominations had snapped in her direction, one already rushing towards her. She knew with certainty that she could not dive as she was—it would be catastrophic for what was taking place between her and Atomica. But a skim? She could afford that.

The abomination scuttled up to the door, smashing and wrenching. Soon, one of the hinges bent and broke, and the stillborn leapt in through the hole, flying perfectly towards Krahe. She adjusted her position, waiting. At the last moment, she wrenched control of the enormous flow, forcing it into her left arm. With a flash of red, she sprung upward from the ground, arm cocked back. She unleashed the punch at the last instant, sending the stillborn hurtling up towards the vaulted ceiling. The pressure in her Soul Furnace waned—she would have to let it build up before doing something like this again. A silver lining was that it appeared that the flow readily scoured away all impurity, be it entropy or Isotope, meaning her dissipation was currently comparable to how it would be with the Atomica fully implanted. It was not a particularly thick or lustrous lining—in effect, it only meant that as long as the process continued, she was effectively operating on a cooldown system.

Before that *thing* could fall and possibly become a problem again, Krahe jumped through the half-busted door and went running. The floor under her feet shook, and thunderous impacts reverberated as Casus did battle with that strongman-looking guy in a nice suit. He parried flying fists of gray force with his arm-blade, deflecting them towards the walls as if they didn't carry the force of two Yellow Atropals each.

Strongman took note of her between clashes, throwing a flying fist her way. Krahe skimmed out of its path rather than risk a physical dodge and immediately regretted her decision. As she emerged, in that instant of extreme time dilation that allowed her to reorient herself, it felt as though the Liminal Coil had been struck with a tuning fork-shaped sledgehammer. The enormous flow of energy going through her roiled and whirled about in an unstable manner, forcing her to lean against the wall as she ran across the foyer.

That one moment of distraction sufficed for Casus to push his already obvious advantage even further, carving gashes into Strongman's wards with a flurry of flame-wreathed slashes of his arm-blade. Krahe didn't have the luxury to sit back and watch as two more stillborns crawled out of the woodwork to come after her, one of which was familiar and had a gaping hole in its chest. Somehow, by some stroke of luck, that punch hadn't hit anything critical to that abomination's functionality. She could see its ward generator peering out through the ruined flesh. It took her two shots to hit the cabling and send the creature tumbling head-over-heels. Her aim just wasn't that good using a tendril instead of her own hand.

Atop the foyer's stairs, Strongman reared back for a desperate strike, holding both fists together as he struck out, placing his enormous body weight behind the punch. A giant, meter wide, gray fist flew forth. He instantaneously began melting down when the thaumaturgy came out, and it seemed as if Casus would be hit for certain.

This was true. Casus didn't dodge.

At the instant of impact, the eyes on his chest shot open, marked with the same exact pattern as his belt.

In a blaze of gold-silver flame, his armor devoured the thaumaturgy. Another mote of flame flickered to life above his head, and he approached his foe.

"Ah, so you *are* Silberblut!" Strongman wheezed, his form stiffened and rendered monochrome by his ongoing meltdown. A coughing laugh sounded from him—Strongman had already come to terms with his own impending death.

That death came to him just as he expected. Casus skewered him with an uppercut, running his blade under Strongman's ribcage and up through his skull. The baneworm tried to burst out of his body's eyes, but the golden flame consumed his true body all the same.

As Casus wound down and spread out his focus once more, he noticed Lady Blackhand running from one of the stillborn. Just as he was about to aid her, she turned in place, and with her palm turned towards the graft-beast, a red flame exploded from her hand. It was far too violent, far too unfocused to be called thaumaturgy. Nonetheless, the discharge of raw power sent her flying through the foyer and in turn obliterated the stillborn's upper half.

Casus nonetheless aided Lady Blackhand. She shouted, "Catch me!" as she flew, and he complied. He then immediately dropped her, for his instincts *screamed* when he touched her. The energies coursing through Blackhand made her seem like a roiling furnace to his sight.

"Are... Are you alright?" Casus asked.

Krahe gave a nod, raising her right hand. The Atomica floated in her grasp.

"Pre-implantation attunement. Can't use thaumaturgy properly until it's done. One-third of the way there."

She glanced at the stillborn's toppled lower half.

"Something tells me those won't be the last freaks to blindly chase after me in the meanwhile."

"Of course. You are a walking beacon," Casus agreed, walking up to Strongman's corpse. He took the keyring from his belt and moved to unlock the doors that stood between them and the rest of the upper floor. "Do you think it may be better for you to hide until you are in a more combat-ready state?"

"As it stands, I am... *somewhat* more combat-capable than with the Twin Serpent Key. My wards will hold out a bit longer, and you've seen what my unrefined energy output can do. Tactically speaking, it would be best for me to purposely draw the graft-beasts away from the ballroom, and thus away from Semzar. I will be able to outmaneuver them, possibly barricade them all out of the way with the last of the Forming Toroid's charges."

"Moreover, humoring Semzar with a face-to-face confrontation would likely work, given his personality," Casus thought aloud. Clack. Clack. The circuits of the door's warding flared for a moment, and then it slid open.

"A bulkhead disguised as a swing-out door? How tasteless," he remarked.

As it slid open, they beheld... nothing. At first. The hallway was deserted, with neither guards, stillborns, nor barricades waiting for them. In fact, it was suspiciously calm. Then, the door across slid open just as the first one had, revealing the ballroom, and right through the precipice, Semzar upon a sofa, surrounded by women and guards—a throne of debauchery.

Casus could see him pressing something on an unassuming remote control. Looking closer, it was emblazoned with a "closing door" glyph, but he didn't have any time to warn Krahe. Both doors began closing, only for Krahe to summon short walls as she passed through, jamming their mechanisms open.

Krahe, despite being undeniably the more vulnerable of the two, walked right into the midst of the enemy, adjusting her stride to radiate an aura of piss and vinegar to match her very real aura of writhing, seething magic. She was in a weakened state, but she also exuded the single brightest aura in the building, making it impossible for anyone to perceive her condition as anything other than a power-up—certainly not with any of the half-dozen appraisal attempts that feebly washed over her.

Behind Semzar, Tsetse stood, calm and motionless—entirely in contrast with how Krahe remembered him. It felt like a different person piloting the same battle body. Countless performers and lower-ranked gangsters were clustered throughout the ballroom, but only a vanishingly tiny minority seemed ready to fight, even among those who seemed competent at a glance. The majority of Semzar's security force consisted of stillborns and their handlers with about sixteen stillborns in total, three to a handler. Only one in three stillborns had visible weapons, and less than half had ward generators. Most of them were also sonar-types, with domed "helmets" that lacked visible eyes. Their heads immediately snapped towards Krahe, and some of them began approaching her, only for their handlers to pull them back—some with commands, others using physical leashes.

"Zavesh, spare me," Krahe sneered. "And here I thought I was ready to meet you in person. Is your face rejecting you, or is that what you consider *handsome*? Is your venom gland perhaps atrophying?" The mafioso's visage was nearly identical to how he had looked when she first saw him at the smokery, but his jawline and cheekbones were even more pronounced. He resembled a plastic surgery addict who got lucky and ended up looking only somewhat grotesque.

"So speaks the half-burnt anathemist. I expected you to be more cowardly in your approach. To think you would have a sense of decorum about coming after the boss of a rival gang," he replied, visibly trying to put on an air of composure. The panic behind his eyes nor the twitching of his tendrils could be denied, even as he smugly raised a cocktail from the table and poured it into his gaping maw, exhaling a puff of bluish mist.

"Rival gang?" she balked. "The bounty you put on my head was one thing. I was almost flattered, really. Then, you sent Crescent Jezail after me—*twice*—and even paid him for a custom shot just for me the second time! Didn't work; I can tell you that much! But the last straw, what made me decide to tear you out of that stolen skinsuit with my own bare hands— was that you had a street vendor killed just because I bought my breakfast from him. And what, did you think I wouldn't find out it was you? Or that I wouldn't come after you? I liked that food cart, Semzar. He made good foldovers, Semzar! I *really* miss that fucking food cart, *you half-Gor'ah trust fund fuckboy!*"

The mafia heir shrunk back at that last phrase as if he'd been struck.

Krahe felt Casus' cold, firm hand on her shoulder, snapping her out of her tirade. Despite its physical chill, an ephemeral warmth spread out from the spot he touched. Krahe had to gather herself. She realized she was *far* angrier about Imraal's death than she had thought. Her anger had shown itself in her tendril gesturing wildly with the Pattner, randomly aiming it at the members of Semzar's retinue. She hadn't noticed herself giving into all her built-up rage, so busy was she trying to wrangle the flow of thauma within herself. She masked it by fishing a cigarette out of her pocket and lighting it up. Then, she immediately went back to pushing, unwilling to let up an advantage of psychological pressure.

"*You wish this was just a gang war. That leaves room for politics.* This is both a personal and a church matter—and would you look at that, both of your victims are right here!"

She finally took a drag.

"Casus, if you would."

Casus stepped forward.

A dozen men aimed their guns and thaumaturgies at the black-armored Banisher. At least three unique iterations of Mohawk's "bladed chains" motif sprung up among them. Pandemonium unfolded, but the distance between Silberblut and his foes was simply too great. None could strike him, let alone harm him.

"What are you waiting for?! Kill them!" Semzar barked as the women swarmed away from him and he raised his barrier. It formed instantly as a flat wall of purple force, letting off mist and electric sparks, before bending to wrap around Semzar's personal space. The instinctive ease with which he wielded it betrayed that it was stolen from his current host, the body acting before the worm's mind realized what he was doing. After realizing he had raised a defense, his head whipped to and fro as he called out, "Cabral? Cabral!"

Tsetse looked down at Semzar in silence. Almost resigned, he stepped forward to interpose himself between his employer and Casus. At this point, Casus felt the geyser of power swirling around Lady Blackhand intensify even further. Through the eye on his back, he saw her holding that voidkey above her head as she ran, power visibly bursting from her arm. Were it anyone else, Casus would have expected them to explode at any moment.

"Your name is Cabral?" Casus asked matter-of-factly, in his hand grasped a battered corpse. The mass of flesh shuddered as a bullet tore into it. A Red Reaper followed right after, shredding what was left of the dead man's rapidly dissipating wards and tearing off a third of his torso alongside his left leg. Casus dropped the body, but the shooter was already fleeing.

In the same manner, Tsetse answered, "Cabral Khan. You will not find me in your church's registry."

The true battle began only then. Those with half a brain and a will to live had already cleared out from the middle of the room, and many had scurried away, with guards quietly opening other doors in an effort to facilitate evacuation.

The two warriors faced off—tremors carrying through the floor as thunderous impacts rang in people's ears. The alien whirring and bassy thumping of Tsetse's sonic weapons played the percussion, whereas Silberblut seemed to fight in an almost restrained manner, avoiding coupler charges in favor of trying to feel out his opponent.

It seemed, at first, that Silberblut might even keep up—at first. Within two exchanges, it became clear that Tsetse still had the upper hand. Within three exchanges, Silberblut was obviously on the back foot and Blackhand was soaring overhead, riding on a scarlet pillar of high-energy thauma.

* * *

As she felt the tides of chaos surging, Krahe raised her right arm, purposely stoking the flow of power between herself and the Atomica. Many pairs of eyes immediately turned her way. The Atomica responded instantaneously, and as the intensity of the current grew, so did the intensity of the Liminal Coil's resonance, until the pain was nearly unbearable. In turn, the glow of her left arm also intensified, narrow geysers of crimson energy erupting from the cracks as a constant blowtorch-like flare vented from her palm. A second and third tendril inadvertently emerged from her back due to the sheer energy output, their nascent silhouettes writhing under her suit the same way her muscles twitched and seized.

Bullets and thaumaturgies were loosed her way, but the power writhing about her swept them aside. Bolts of power went careening wildly in other directions, while bullets were simply obliterated. Nearly every stillborn in the ballroom immediately began doing everything in its power to reach her, some dragging their handlers along. Others responded to their handlers' attempts at control by turning on them. Two packs slew their handlers, and in turn, their heads exploded, adding further to the chaos. Only one handler managed to retain control of his beasts—another man with an implanted third eye. He did so by dragging them over to Tsetse, who exhaled a mist of what had to be pheromones onto the creatures.

Having achieved her goal and not wanting to risk it any longer, Krahe disposed of the excess energy as best she could—by expelling it directly. The only problem was that the mere thought of doing it was enough to set it off before she could properly align herself. She went flying through the ballroom, leaving a gaping, seething hole burned straight through the floor, rampant magic eating away at its edges even as she flew. On one hand, the pain abated immediately. On the other, she had no way to reorient herself mid-flight. Skimming was her only choice, and something told her the backlash would be an order of magnitude worse this time around.

In the span of moments, she did several things. First, she ripped a pen-type autoinjector kicking and screaming from her Kenoma Pocket, despite the item's audible creaking and the scraping of otherworldly fangs against her skin. One out of many she had looted from dead bodies, it was loaded with Class 3 Pain Inhibitor. Second, she willed her tendril to squeeze the Pattner's trigger just as the pistol happened to be pointing in the right direction. The bullet struck Semzar's back. Not nearly enough to penetrate his wards, but he certainly felt it.

The landing was just as rough as she had feared. She skimmed at the last moment with the intention to shunt all her momentum, landed perfectly on the ground, and immediately doubled over in pain as the people around her stumbled back, visibly being pushed away as the carpet under her feet unraveled and burned. The painkiller, somehow, made it worse. As it spread through her bloodstream, the secondary effects of pain fell away, and even the nature of her pain changed, but it remained, and alongside it, all other sensations were altered in turn. Her insides felt like a wriggling sack of serpents, her eyeballs throbbed in their sockets, and that was just the start of it.

Nonetheless, she could move again, and that she did. She wove through the mass of panicking bodies and was provided ample cover by the half-stampeding crowd that had formed around the ballroom's outer perimeter. Such was the threat of collateral damage that even numerous gangsters, despite being able to harm Silberblut and especially Krahe, had been cowed into inaction.

The small comfort of using a crowd for cover didn't last long—Krahe's aura still pushed people away, and they readily scattered from her even without its encouragement. The stillborns were hot on her trail. She just needed to drag the abominations out of here, and until then, she was glad to let Casus and Tsetse take center stage. She certainly wouldn't grace that flyman with his preferred name, even in thought.

As she made her way to one of the ballroom's staff exits, she caught sight of a Saurian guard waiting there. Countless scales swarmed out of his sleeves as he channeled his magic, swarming towards Krahe. She sent herself flying through that door with a short burst from her arm, her wards gaining numerous new gashes as she flew into the corridor. A handful were only impeded partially, leaving cuts on her trousers and the back of her bodysuit. No follow-up attacks came—the guard was too busy avoiding the stillborns.

And so, Krahe went tearing down the mansion's corridors, playing a lethal game of cat and mouse with a gaggle of bioweapons. In this matter, Barzai, once more, proved himself invaluable, as Krahe had him always flying ahead, purposely leaving him visible. The sight and sound of him sent people running well before Krahe would arrive. The eidolon took quite readily to the command to scare off the chaff, harassing stragglers with explosions as he cackled and foretold her coming as if she was an inhuman calamity.

"DEATH! DEATH COMES! FLEE NOW IN TERROR OR STAND AND FIGHT, NOTHING CAN SAVE YOU! THE GREEN-EYED DEMON COMES, AND ALL SHALL MEET THEIR ENDS! WHO PILES CORPSES AT HER FEET, DISEMBOWELER, BEHEADER, SCOURER OF LIFE AND HOPE FROM ALL WHO STAND IN HER WAY! SHE COMES AND NONE SHALL BE SPARED!"

The raven rambled on and on in this manner, and Krahe tuned it out before long. Gradually, the stillborns closed the distance, most of them sprinting on all fours like feral beasts. She couldn't help but grin as she blasted down the length of a hallway, the air whipping past her face. A few pulled ahead of the pack, standing out as particularly quick on their feet. To her surprise they exhibited a degree of tactical thinking, overtaking her in a clear effort to box her in. Krahe couldn't help but grin as she pointed her left arm right into the face of the stillborn behind her, releasing her built-up pressure and sending herself flying down the corridor. One of the stillborns that had overtaken her tried lunging at her as she passed it, but she sent it staggering back with a well-placed shot to the chest.

CHAPTER 26

FLIGHT OF THE CROW

Yazata wasn't sure what was going on.

It was not a matter of lacking eyes inside the building. She could see through the possessed Red Hoods—or rather, through the *things* possessing them. The problem was they *refused* to go to the upper floor. From what they saw through the floor, she couldn't blame them.

The entity's shape and damascened pattern suggested the astral body of a human Greater Pilgrim, and even carried with it something sacred. But somehow, it was *wrong*. Terribly, ominously wrong. A shroud of pitch-black smoke swirled about the shape, obscuring details normally unseen without appraisal, exuding an implicit threat at all times. It was as if it were *daring* her to try and look closer, to see what would happen if she did.

As the creatures they were, who supped upon the astral bodies of their victims, it was the ultimate form of aposematism. Yazata would have understood disobedience if she had tried to command her hounds to consume such a being, but they refused to even come into its vicinity.

Nonetheless, she continued playing her part, commanding the Red Hoods to patrol the ground floor.

It was not as if she had nothing better to do than watch from afar. She was here not just to keep them *in,* but also to counter any possible reinforcements from the outside. Going by the group of four rather ominously dressed individuals speeding towards the mansion at this very moment, that prediction was correct.

She struck the Black Trapezohedron against her leg, its blade reverberating with deep pitch. Distortion bled upwards as she spun around to face the newcomers.

"Hear my shining words..."

Yazata spoke, and lo, they heard, but neither their ears nor minds were spared the mercy of human language.

* * *

The sound of thunder carried through the ballroom as two armored figures clashed, darting back and forth with inhuman speed. Bursts of gold-silver flame and shockwaves of sound tore into the floor, forestalled only by the mansion's abnormally durable construction.

With each clash, Casus grew to understand the rift between himself and Cabral, or rather, the rift between Tarnished Silberblut and Tsetse. While he now knew that the individual's name was Cabral, in the absence of a known name for his transformed state, Casus simply shifted his perception of Tsetse from the entity as a whole to the transformation specifically. Even as he was now, it was undeniable that he couldn't match the might of "Abara Morph Tsetse." He could keep pace in physical terms, and his increased durability allowed him to weather direct blows, but once Tsetse brought out his sonic weaponry, the scales tilted steeply in the Abara Morph's favor.

He could read most of them, of course. Most. But Tsetse hadn't simply stopped evolving since their last battle. In their short battle, in three mere exchanges, Casus had faced three distinct attacks incorporating the sonic blaster in Tsetse's left palm. It was a horrible, wretched thing, adaptable beyond compare, as Casus painfully learned during the third exchange. Both of them had landed blows on the other, but neither had caused any serious damage—not until the third exchange.

Tsetse threw a quick jab, one which he had thrown several times before as a normal strike, and without anything to hint at its altered nature. He imbued it with an insidious vibration at the last split-second. It couldn't be more than one-tenth of a second before impact, else Casus would have sensed it coming. His fist smashed into Casus and speared him through with the same concentrated force as that which had defeated him back in the lab.

The shockwave continued through him, blowing fist-sized holes through three men before it shattered a window and dented its shutter. Casus followed, thrown backwards into that same shutter. He would have flown right out of the mansion had it not been there.

Falling to the ground, he picked himself up, uttering prayers to Zavesh. The pain was manageable, and his armor could withstand the damage just the same. He wasn't the same Silberblut as back then.

He prayed because he had learned what he required and felt the pain he needed to feel. A small part of him was relieved that Tarnished Silberblut didn't suffice against Tsetse.

"Stronger. Not strong enough," Tsetse remarked with a faint disappointment in his deadpan tone.

"You speak the truth," Silberblut agreed. "I must thank you for reminding me that mere imitation of my predecessor would only doom me on my path. That my reason to wear this belt was just as important as my ability to do so."

He reached for his waist, as if to press the eye of his belt for a coupler charge, only to detransform. To those who knew what to look for, it was obvious that this was not some kind of sudden failure, but an intentional act. Strangest of all, he didn't *just* detransform—he pulled the belt right from his waist. At that instant his armor burned off of him, consumed by silver fire. As Casus retreated a few more steps, the burning ghost of his armor charged ahead to meet Tsetse, clashing with the insectile giant for a moment before disappearing.

Semzar shouted, and the three-eyed stillborn-handler to his left sicced two of his creatures on the Banisher—one with clawed hands, the other with two gun-arms. Despite being stripped of his armor, Casus's arm shot out with the force and speed of a cannonball, hints of golden flame flaring between the exposed muscle fibers. He shattered the charging stillborn's chitin with one punch and set it off balance. Without wasting a moment, he tore into the same spot, his fingers digging into flesh and bathing in leaking hemolymph as he braced his foot against its chest. With a single motion, he tore out not just its side, but also a vital cable. Oily blue sprayed onto the tile as the graft-beast toppled down.

"No ward generator?" Casus asked as he threw the fistful of flesh aside.

"My employer expressed dislike for the sound they made. Those with ward generators were assigned elsewhere," Tsetse remarked, pointedly tilting his head as he glanced at Semzar. "Your specifications surpass my data. Your compatibility must be excellent to channel the coupler's power so readily untransformed. Two questions. How, and why? I sense no new relics. No new catalyst. No new voidkey. The change was you. How, and why?"

Tsetse's tone was full of curiosity, entirely unconcerned by the destruction of his toy. His attention was fully on the conundrum of Silberblut's sudden growth.

Driven to a near speechless fury by the implication that something was his fault, Semzar shouted for the onerous intruder to be struck down. Tsetse didn't move, but those surrounding him did. His silhouette was completely consumed by the assault, tearing apart the floor and engulfing him in a clashing blender of magic, but it was too late—he had donned his belt once again.

The shape of his armored form, of Tarnished Silberblut, had formed from silver flame, overlaying him without actually becoming the solid armor. Five stars of golden flame burned above his head.

"I am a warrior of justice, not because I have been chosen, but because that is the path I chose!"

A sixth star ignited. Their revolutions accelerated.

"In my past life I fought for what is just, and in all lives that follow, so too shall it be!"

A seventh joined the six.

"Should the shadows grow darker than black, so be it! I need only burn more brightly than the sun, even if it leaves my armor charred black!"

Seven became one—a flaming halo with seven notches. It widened, descending to the ground, and with it, the armor of Tarnished Silberblut took form, pristine and gleaming for just this brief moment.

"Igaria steel my spirit and Zavesh guide my hand, so I pray!"

Then, from the halo, a fiery inferno erupted—at once, it consumed Casus Aristedes whole, and a projection of the seven-notched halo emerged in front of him, as tall as he was. One by one, bursts of golden flame flowed out of the flame-vortex and into each spoke, forming the shapes of additional armor components.

From the midst of the golden inferno, an enormous voice bellowed, one that did not belong to Casus, yet also slightly differed from how the Silberblut Coupler normally sounded. It was distorted in a manner that, to Krahe's ears, resembled a disrupted or otherwise incomplete signal.

"The son of ho-pe, broth-er to anger and cou-ou-ourage! Mamon Knight Eisenretter!"

In rapid succession, the new armor flew into the pillar of flame, joining with Casus' silhouette.

The swirling inferno tore itself apart, and the burning wheel that had given it shape rose up, shrinking to now revolve around Eisenretter's head. His previously horn-like crown had expanded even further, completing a physical halo. The lower half of his left arm twisted into a gigantic, disproportionate thing, with spherical joints and clawed fingers, an extra cross-pupiled eye adorning the back of the gauntlet. By contrast, his right arm only possessed a minimal gauntlet, a curved blade attached to it and sweeping forward over his hand. The blade looked as though it had been melted in the transformation's flame. Neither its star-shaped form nor elegant attachment joint were anywhere to be seen. The closed-eye face on the suit's chest was a mismatched blend of the robotic and the demonic, with large golden fangs. Similarly, curved golden spikes protruded over the knees, and the boots had short claws of the same color.

It was crude and incomplete, yet the sheer, unrefined power pouring out of Casus at this moment truly felt as if he were the sun.

THE SON OF HOPE
BROTHER TO ANGER AND COURAGE
MAMON KNIGHT EISENRETTER
-IMPERFECT MANIFESTATION-

"Lucky," Tsetse remarked, a tinge of unease creeping into his voice.

Seeing Semzar's look of panicked confusion, he added, "Catalyst Resonance Evolution. All old-style speaking couplers could do it. Some modern models still can. Enormous performance increases through resonance with the catalyst. This one is incomplete. He forced it. Got lucky. Hence the detransformation and the excessively complex transformation sequence. Can't do it *properly*."

"Why did you not interrupt him, then?!" Semzar demanded.

Tsetse scoffed.

"Foolishness," he said. "In seven thousand years, do you think none have thought of that? Even the oldest couplers have countermeasures."

"Do you mean to tell me you cannot handle him? Did I pay you for *nothing?!*" Semzar hissed, trying to project the mask of an indignant, angered employer. It was a poor mask, all but see-through. His eyes trembled, his tendrils bulged under his skin, and his tone veered into pleading in the second sentence.

Tsetse, calmly, reassured his employer. "I can keep him busy. Any more is beyond me as I am now. Unless you would prefer I go after Blackhand?"

It was clear that, in truth, Semzar still considered Blackhand the bigger threat, if for no other reason than because there was a good chance that Aristedes would try to capture him alive. Still, Aristedes was the more immediate threat, while Blackhand had run off elsewhere, somehow drawing away the vast majority of the stillborns.

* * *

As Casus Aristedes, Mamon Knight Eisenretter, took his heroic stand against Cabral Khan, Abara Morph Tsetse in the ballroom, and as Yazata Heptaxia took her own stand outside the mansion, so too did Brunhilde Krahe take a stand of her own.

It was not quite as glamorous as the other two, as her foes could not be said to possess the mental faculties to comprehend what "taking a stand" even meant. They were, nonetheless, numerous and mighty, a writhing mass of grafted flesh and metal armed to the teeth with heretical technology.

The corridor was being torn apart around her, and her wards weren't spared that fate, each grazing hit another step towards an injury she wouldn't be able to walk off. The only thing keeping her in the fight was her vastly superior mobility and tactical sense. Time and again, she had eluded the stillborns thanks to a well-timed screen of smoke, their senses dulled, and bodies impaired by the toxicity Arrha held to the Evoy.

Yes, it was Arrha that had become her lifeline at this moment. It was this property that she imbued into her smoke eruptions after she had run out of Isotope to thicken her smoke with—or rather, she still had *some* Isotope, but she kept that bare minimum for forming tar.

But even this wouldn't last. Arrha-imbued magical smoke dispersed even faster than that which she didn't imbue with any extra properties at all. She burned through a dozen cigarettes at a pace comparable to her expenditure of bullets, and at this point, her lungs *burned*. She couldn't tell whether the unearthly terribleness of that sensation was natural or if it ought to be blamed on the Class 3 painkiller.

It's like my airways are full of menthol oil and glass dust, she thought, wheezing against a corner after barely slipping past the jabbering swarm for the Nth time. Barzai spotted them catching up to her all over again, but she was in no state to continue fleeing. She thought to blast herself out of harm's way once more, but the energy pressure just wasn't building like it used to. The power she could bleed off for her own use was quickly waning as the attunement process continued—the threshold where it felt as if she would explode became ever tighter.

And so, Krahe purposely cornered herself by heading for the end of the corridor. The door to a bedroom awaited her there, but it was locked, and so, left with no other options, she burned up every remaining charge in the Forming Toroid to put up a barricade. It wasn't pretty and it wouldn't actually keep the stillborns out, but it would have to do.

They crashed into her maze of jade like a tidal wave, but soon enough, the smarter and lither among them began weaving their way through, while others scaled the rods to climb over.

She shot down two as they reached her side of the barrier. A third withstood her last bullet, and she had to chop it in the side of the head. That staggered it enough for her to knock it to the ground, its willowy, unarmed frame proving to be the graft-beast's undoing as Krahe caved in its chest cavity with a full body weight jumping stomp-kick.

In the time it took her to achieve this small victory, two more abominations had made their way through, and both were armed. The first had a Blasting Cluster, the second a sonic weapon-arm as well as a ward generator graft.

It was at this point that she made a judgment call and plunged the Atomica straight into her own chest. The sensation lay somewhere between connecting to a bitey nerve-interface and plugging in an overvolted charging cable. Krahe found relief in it, in the knowledge she hadn't just killed herself. Rather than refuse to go in, or worse, rather than tear her open from the inside out, the Atomica resisted for a moment, only to finally enter right through her biosuit. An alien, thrumming pulse resonated in her chest, carrying through her spine. She felt herself collapse inward, her awareness of the world detaching from presence, time appearing to slow to a near-halt even as the stillborn swarmed towards her. It felt unsettlingly similar to the Rite of Dho-hna, combined with the dream-like quality of her visions during the Liminal Coil's implantation.

As she gathered her bearings, she came to the undeniable conclusion that she was inside her own Soul Furnace. She could only make out a few details, including the vaguely spheroid shape and the presence of the Atomica, now as an enormous obelisk reaching the center of the chamber. At the Atomica's end, in the chamber's center, there floated a swirling mass of black tendrils, within it glowing the unlight of Kenoma. It resembled the Daemon Core, but it was obviously just a closest-equivalent representation for something she couldn't mentally parse in its true form.

The enormous flow of energy that had been coursing through her and building up suddenly gathered within her Soul Furnace, rousing the Atomica to glow ever brighter, surpassing even its radiance when it had just been transmuted. Six spotlights erupted from it, one for each side, burning the inner walls of Krahe's Soul Furnace. The initial pain crossed over into the realm of a sensation that she couldn't even interpret, registering as an itch perpetually being scratched and irritated in an endless cycle, combined with the hellish burn of menthol and capsaicin.

Spotlights narrowed down to laser-like pinpoints, and at once began a wild dance, carving an eye-crossingly complex pattern in the span of seconds before ending at their starting point, where they carved out six hexagonal empty spaces.

The Atomica resonated with a soundless tone, and she instantly knew what she needed: words. The same sort of *words* she had used to give form to the Daemon Core.

One would suffice. The others could come later. But she would need all six. She couldn't afford to take things slowly—she had already felt hopelessly outgunned after losing the Viridaimon armor. How could she keep up if she didn't grasp every iota of power in her reach, and then dislocate her own arm to reach for even more? How could she strike at the people behind Damrus Hashem if she struggled with the meager forces that Semzar could muster?

And so, she spoke the first word, and its emblem was carved onto the inside of her Soul

Furnace.

WILL TO MIGHT

Might, not power—in the sense of strength obtained through great effort and will, rather than the strength one possessed naturally. Such had been her modus operandi in her past life, and so it was in this one, despite the powers bestowed upon her by her status as Deiphage. Even the fact she had usurped something of Chernobog, infinitesimal as it was, had resulted from Krahe's enormous will, grasping for strength even as a disembodied spirit, rejecting death in the face of the void.

The moment the sigil was completed, the hexagon erupted with gleaming obsidian, forming a control rod of sorts. She instantly understood—it had to be the influence of her incantation during the ritual. A later version of the Solomon reactor used such "control rods" to precisely manipulate the fusion transmutation, allowing larger reaction masses and more complex target results with the same energy input. This, then, was clearly a similar adjustment mechanism for the Astral Implosion Furnace.

One after the next, the words came naturally. It was no more than self-definition. From the matter of the self, Krahe wrought the rods with which she would control the vast and terrible power of thaumaturgy.

The second could still be vaguely put into words with some effort.

HATRED OF EVIL

It was simple. Straightforward.

However, though she had already formed the base material that were these unspeakable maxims, she nonetheless spent strength to dredge them up and give them form in her Soul Furnace. With each maxim, it felt as though the resistance grew greater. The first came like nothing. The second took effort. The third was an ordeal, encompassing her abiding, melancholic love for the ideal of her hometown—the idea of a "better world."

The fourth, she could barely finish, spending every iota of mental strength she had. She couldn't comprehend it in terms of language, and wasn't entirely sure of its exact meaning, but it was what came into her mind's hand, nonetheless. She was deathly certain it defined a core aspect of who she was, but she couldn't mentally process it to the extent of breaking it down into simple, expressible concepts.

She couldn't even start on the fifth, let alone consider the sixth.

Four.

That was her limit.

With that acknowledgement, everything settled into place.

ASTRAL BODY RESHAPING
FOURFOLD ASTRAL IMPLOSION FURNACE

Awareness of the physical world suddenly pushed back into the forefront. Her body floated half a meter off the ground, scarlet light shining from her chest where she had implanted the Atomica, diffusing through her flesh and out of her mouth. The pressure of time began to return with one subjective second after the next. The hideous faces of the stillborn resumed their approach.

Atomica Refulgent came alive once more at her command, piercing into the beyond, and her Soul Furnace flooded with power—thauma waiting to be set alight, the substance of Kenoma itself. One after the next, the control rods receded, only to slam forward, compressing it all into a spot the size of a hairpin.

At the instant of ignition, Krahe's awareness returned to the physical. The same could not be said for full control of herself. She remained in place for some time as an uncontrollable deluge of pyroclast erupted from her being. The red-orange death-swarm flooded the corridor, shredding and burning everything that wasn't its source. Outside, the shutters of several windows visibly began to glow, only to be torn out moments later. A solid flow of glowing embers poured out of each window, gathering up against the mansion's barriers and forming a waterfall, its color rapidly shifting to red and then black as it moved down.

Krahe finally returned to full presence in the here-and-now to a scene that evoked déjà vu.

Everything was sanded down and charred. The windows had blown out; the shutters melted from the inside. Her smoky jade barricade had become an abstract art piece, and the stillborn transformed into macabre statues of compacted pyroclast. Boiled gore had sprayed out of them in places, painting the floors and pillars in oily hues.

They were left frozen in poses of reaching towards her.

The mansion shuddered as an explosion carried from the ballroom.

Krahe opened and closed her fist, then picked up her gun. Its lanyard had been severed, but the weapon itself was unharmed. A spark of will, and thauma surged in. With its ignition, searing-hot power coursed through and tendrils emerged from her back. The intoxicating sense of newfound power was somewhat dulled by how *off-kilter* everything felt due to the Class 3 Pain Inhibitor's persisting effects. There was something different in *how* things felt *off-kilter*, but Krahe wrote it off as the Atomica settling in.

I'll get used to it. Once this shit wears off...

With a spark of anathema and a burst of red light, she sent herself flying to the top of her own barricade, landing atop a pair of narrow pillars. With some trepidation, she skimmed to the next pillar over. Feeling no backlash, she readily initiated an Astro Dive and hurried to the ballroom.

A scattered handful of survivors would later tell of a devil of living smoke flowing through the mansion's halls.

The mansion was enormous—too large to traverse from one end to the ballroom in a single Astro Dive. Krahe surfaced intermittently to recover, continuing her advance as she did.

From a few tentative tests between dives, it instantly became evident that this was *nothing* like anathema. More than being transformed, it felt as if every aspect of her natural thaumaturgy had been amplified—the smoke was thicker, the embers burned brighter, the pyroclast came out visibly superheated. Besides being more intense and coherent, it was also *livelier*, for lack of a better term.

As Krahe rapidly approached the ballroom, so too did resistance rapidly increase—from none to some. Enough to be noted, to have been a problem not long ago. Now, Krahe saw the brave few who stuck around as target practice. She surfaced just as one of the guards finished an impressive burst of thaumaturgy that really tore up the wall right next to her.

To start with, she wore down his barrier with a few shots from the Pattner before hitting him with a Tar-tendril empowered punch, sending him into meltdown. Out of everything, they had changed the least, gaining increased responsiveness and strength, but little else.

As the quickly formed tendril crumbled, Krahe formed a tracer, but even a mere tracer wasn't a tracer anymore. Its elongated shape remained the same, but the first one came out significantly larger than normal. It flew as quickly as the Viridaimon Armor's tracers even without a bullet to carry it, and it visibly curved to strike its target as it flew. The man was thrown backwards by the blast, a hole blown clean through his chest cavity.

Two gangsters later, Krahe had settled on a modified casting procedure. Instead of one at a time, she would spew out bursts of tracers. Their homing was very limited—inferior to even the Viridaimon version. It was little better than the cheapest piece of shit smart-guns with the cheapest piece of shit ammo, but even that much was a godsend.

The Viridaimon similarity made her curious as to whether Deathsmoke Spray could now produce a shotgun-blast effect. She poured in some Isotope for good measure, hoping to improve its coherence with a tiny bit of tar. It erupted out of her palm less like a burst-beam and more like a whip, lashing one of Semzar's goons nearly in half before it fell apart. Hair-thin, gossamer-like threads of tar bound together rapidly disintegrating slivers of red-hot glass. At that instant, her mind shifted, and she lost any desire to replicate the Viridaimon version. Memories from before she had obtained her radiation blasters came to the surface. Wolf and Raven ZT-8, Model 32 "Tactical Monowire Dispenser."

With this in mind, she pushed onward, intending to refine this current "Death-Tar Whip" into something using numerous, separate strands. There was no time to do it now—she had to back up Casus as soon as possible, and, as it happened, four surviving guards had just turned the corner coming her way. Her current toolkit just had to do. Forming bursters still worked the same, the only major difference was that they felt heavier by almost half and she could tell their shells would hold up to slightly higher pressure. The first one she formed was a smoke burster, intending to just pass them by, given that a fight against four at once could end up going on longer than she could afford.

"It's her!" an observant man cried.

The four readied themselves for combat, or rather, two of them did; the other two looked for escape routes.

A gunshot rang out, the bullet carrying the burster along.

Not quite a Six Trees Killer. Six Trees Vanisher, maybe... Krahe thought, already entering Astro Dive before it even reached them. Following its firework-like explosion, shrapnel scattered with about enough force to inflict a nasty bruise and a writhing wall of gray expanded to fill the hallway.

Krahe was gone in moments, a black blur.

The four gangsters ended up stumbling around and blindly lashing out in the smoke for a full half-minute as the cloud shifted around, actively trying to envelop them. The terror of having their vision cut off was only intensified by the manner in which the smoke writhed around them, becoming so dense it almost felt solid in places. Worst of all, it actively tried to shove itself down their throats, halted only by their wards. One man, a man whose wards had been compromised, emitted stomach-turning wheezes as he writhed on the ground, grasping for his neck.

CHAPTER 27

FLESH-THIEF'S HEX

A short time earlier...

The Inquisitor's attention snapped towards one end of the mansion's upper floor, as her bound servants broke their orders to flee from the source of the outburst. Even she could sense it, despite the barrier. It easily compared to the immense flare of transformation energy she had sensed from Silberblut earlier. Unlike the Silberblut Coupler, this outburst's signature seemed thaumetic in nature, albeit far too intense, teetering on the output of advanced burning techniques. Yazata didn't think this was plausible, given that such techniques weren't common even among mid-rankers, but she didn't have time to dwell on it.

Her opponents were good. *Too good.* Their coordination was impeccable, their movements twitchy and unpredictable, and their barriers held up better than most physical walls—against the blunt impact force of her distortions, no less. Their offense, too, was equally potent and treacherous, manifesting as invisible sonic blasts strong enough to tear up the front garden and register to the mansion's barriers. Every so often she glimpsed the source—silver membranes and chitinous armatures darting out of her foes' trench coat sleeves. It was in line with the briefing that warned of a new type of artifact weapon. She was certain now. Certain of what they were. There was no room for guesses with the measure she was about to take, given how vulnerable it would leave her, but Yazata hadn't gotten this far by hesitating and being unsure.

"Om, Zavyarana sowaka, behold the heretics and set their stolen flesh against them! Om, Zavyarana sowaka! Sear the mark of their sin upon their souls!" Yazata chanted, pulling her church signet from her neck. She held it up as she hopped back and forth in the desperate attempt to keep all three of them in her line of sight. Her eyes burned in their sockets, her hair floated weightlessly behind her, and her gaze was briefly filled by a numinous light that scorched the grass. At that moment, she went blind.

Yazata's sight returned to a blurry shadow of what it was normally as the surge of divine power faded. She could see well enough to be certain—she could see them writhing, twitching, wringing their hands together, their cheeks splitting as their faces opened with mandibles, and the contents of their stomachs poured out. At a glance it resembled coffee grains—it was half-digested blood. Though not visible physically, their astral bodies had been branded, the curse sigil a modified, refined version of one which had once been used to brand body thieves in a far-off land, trapping them within bodies that rejected them.

"Th-the Flesh-thief's Hex, but ah, it reeks of self-righteousness! What have you done with it, you church harlot?! I shall pluck the eyes from your skull!" one of the three Evoy seethed, visibly regaining self-control quicker than the two others.

"Good guess," she admitted as she struck the Trapezohedron against her leg once again. "My version is better. My *Plunderer's Branding* never goes away."

The Plunderer's Branding was a reconstruction from the ground up, making it impossible to dispel using the methods that worked on its lesser counterpart. She had even embedded traps that would agitate the brand under specific conditions, and a targeting mark for the purposes of her other abilities. One such trap was in place to prevent the victim from using Mamon Couplers—terribly convenient and justified within the brand's purview by the fact some Couplers could be modified to temporarily suppress rejection symptoms by overriding them with the transformation.

One after another, the three Evoy burst out of their skins in a manner Yazata had never seen. A wave of heat and rancid stench washed over her, fluid gushing onto the ground near them. In moments, the three transformed, growing to easily two and a half meters tall, into forms clearly intended to resemble war-morphs—the so-called "Abara Morphs" Aristedes had mentioned.

Yazata couldn't help smiling, and then, she began cackling.

They were huge, hulking, but also completely malformed. One couldn't breathe properly. Another's legs were comically tiny in contrast with gigantic, oversized, clumsy arms. The third—the one who had recognized the curse—was the only to transform mostly successfully. In fact, his malformations increased his offensive power, silver sonic blaster membranes gleaming across him from head to toe.

He would've been a problem had Yazata spent the past few seconds doing nothing, but she knew better. While she couldn't use her eyes as a casting medium for the next several hours, she had backups. This whole time, she had been striking the Black Trapezohedron against her leg, modulating its frequency towards a desired pitch.

The blaster-covered Abara Morph joined Yazata in laughter, shockwaves of sound blasting out with each cackle, shattering the stones underfoot and throwing them out like pebbles, forcing Yazata to focus every bit of her remaining strength towards deflection. Her eardrums would have surely burst, were she unwarded. She weathered the storm for a few moments more, finally reciting an invocation, covered by the noise. "Ring out from the spires of Zor'Aguhastra, and sing…"

At once, distortion flooded out of the Black Trapezohedron, flowing through the air and swirling around the three Evoy. Their chitin began to crumple in on itself, as if submerged far underwater, and quickly being dragged deeper.

"Sing, o Great One chained in the deep!"

With the passing of a breath, the three Evoy's bodies burst under the pressure.

Yazata let out a satisfied sigh. Each time one of her coworkers questioned how she could put up with so many limitations on her magic, she wished she could show them this.

* * *

Dozens of blows exchanged in moments. Hundreds of meters traversed in seconds. Tracks carved, burned, and torn into the flooring, shards of polished stone shifting and sparking with crimson magic as the ballroom floor struggled to pull itself back together.

He had to finish this quickly. To say he didn't have much time was a generous understatement—he had *no* time. With each passing second, Casus could feel his brute-force-evolved transformation eating away at him—*consuming* him. He just wasn't strong enough to hold it together, neither in physical nor in astral body, not to mention where he lacked spiritually. It had been purely this moment, this context, that had allowed him to transform into Eisenretter.

Had it been anyone else, anywhere else, at any other time, he could not have done it.

But it was Tsetse, right here, right now. That, alone, had been the permitting factor. This sword on his arm—this twisted, malformed thing—had been forged solely to cut down this Abara Morph. A part of Casus knew his armor would burn straight off of him if he turned it against Semzar.

As he sprinted, Casus used his left arm as a counterweight, drifting at a 270-degree angle, nearly flat against the floor, in order to get under one of Tsetse's kicks. Its blastwave removed the heads of eight or nine fleeing people and shattered numerous pieces of glassware, sending a small tidal wave of razor-sharp dust roiling through the ballroom.

From his near-prone position, Silberblut pushed off of the floor with his left hand. The blade of his right arm trailed a gold-burning arc through the air, intended to sever the Abara Morph's left arm. Tsetse dodged, of course, but the wound had been struck—oily blood gushed forth from a flesh-ravine that now ran the entire length of his torso on the left side. His left arm visibly lost some volume.

Tsetse emitted a grunt of pain and frustration, but he was neither deterred nor thrown off-kilter. The fly-man twisted himself like a humanoid spring in order to deliver a kick from an entirely bewildering angle, sending Silberblut flying into the ceiling. Rather than smash into it, Silberblut tucked in his legs and outstretched his left arm past them. The eye upon it shone with a silver brilliance, and a strange force of the same shade flowed out of it, bracing against the stone. It vanished as quickly as it appeared, but nonetheless slowed his flight enough that he could comfortably bounce off the heretofore immaculate fresco. A face upon that fresco was turned to rocky gore once he used it as a jump-off point. Spinning through the air, the Mamon Knight stabilized himself in a flying-kick position whilst Tsetse dug in his heels—literally. The Abara Morph's feet and heels unfolded and anchored into the stone underfoot.

Pulling open his own chestplate, Tsetse revealed an immense array of sonic membranes. In the same motion, he tucked his arms close to his body, even now concealing his left-hand palm-blaster with his fingers and holding his right hand in the same gesture to not give it away. After all, even if the Evoy was fairly sure Casus knew of the palm-blaster, he wasn't sure that he knew which hand concealed it.

The ground shook, and soon the furniture followed. Glasses and bottles began resonating and cracking.

All sound cut out as it was overtaken by a thunderous bass, louder than thunder. To whomever might have the eyes to see, the distortion wave would be plainly visible as it flowed through the air towards Casus. As he met it, the face upon his chest opened its eyes and mouth. His flight slowed for but an instant, as in the next moment, the entire shockwave vanished. In turn, the brightness of his halo grew, and his armor seemed to grow darker in turn—or was that a mere play of the light?

The true blow, of course, had yet to come. Tsetse set loose a sonic kick as if it were the gotcha, nestling the killer strike within the motion's end. It was awkward, and that was the point, to go against reasonable expectations, reducing the likelihood it would be noticed or countered. Silberblut slipped past the kick's shockwave, holding his left hand out as a shield.

At the very next moment, Tsetse's trump card struck. The eye of his left hand came alive, locking not onto Tsetse, but onto the trajectory of his strike, all in a singular instant. Silberblut's halo turned clockwise by a one-seventh increment. A burst of light from the eye met Tsetse's shockwave and dispersed it.

Immediately upon landing, Silberblut transitioned his momentum into an unnatural, zigzagging rush, tearing up the floor as he combined his raw physicality with his left arm's exceedingly monstrous strength and strange powers to forcibly change his trajectory time after time. Tsetse let off another barrage of kicks accompanied by shockwaves from his chest-mounted array, slipping in two precision strikes, but even those which would have struck had no effect. It was as if they were all devoured by the face on Eisenretter's chest or shot down by the eye on his left arm.

Before Tsetse knew it, his left arm had been severed from his body, and the blade which did it had trailed a half-moon of empyrean refulgence through the air. He stared Silberblut—Eisenretter—Casus Aristedes—in the eye and felt that Silberblut's left hand was pressed closely against his chest's exposed sonic membranes. But so was his right hand against Silberblut's side, and if he still held any advantage over the Mamon Knight, it was in how quickly his trump card came out.

The wave passed through the black-armored warrior, punching a hole in a nearby table. It merely sent Silberblut stumbling to the side, but at this moment, putting him out of position mattered more than the cumulative damage. In that forced stumble, Silberblut's clawed hand grasped with its monstrous strength, and Cabral found the entire front of his meatsuit all but torn off. The cold air met his real chitin, revealing a many-jointed, lanky form designed specifically to fit inside Abara Morph Tsetse.

If anything would undo Silberblut, it would not be Tsetse's own combat power. It would be time. His incomplete Eisenretter form, though frighteningly powerful, could not last.

Still, Tsetse was cautious, and he strongly considered creating distance and turning this into a stalling game, even as Silberblut approached him.

"Unlucky. You have new defenses," the Abara Morph remarked matter-of-factly. It was clear to him that the left hand had been devised specifically to counter his trump card. He was already considering how he might alter his form to work around Silberblut's defenses.

"The Visage of Judgment and the Left Hand of Anger," the righteous warrior announced, openly naming two of his tools. "I would have been a fool to not forge a Mamon Armor that could counter your strength and more. And now, with the Right Hand of Courage, I shall excise your tumorous existence from the world!"

But at that moment, as Mamon Knight Silberblut held out his right hand and golden flame enveloped its curved blade once more, his arm, too, was severed from his body. A sudden flash of dark light, leaving behind a fading blackness alien to the mundane world, ripped through the ballroom. Everything between its source and fading point was cleft in twain.

The hiss of frustration pointed to its origin: Semzar Hashem.

* * *

Moments earlier…

Semzar had not been idly cowering in place. He had spent the entire battle clutching a jambiya dagger which rested at his waist, for the dagger's blade was a potent artifact for resolving tense negotiations. Its sheath, in turn, was an artifact of the same grade, capable of concealing the transfer and buildup of power within the blade. As Semzar poured his own thauma into the weapon, it flowed through its handle and reacted with the thaumstone jewels set into it, creating an enormous buildup of arcane power. The efficiency was nearly miraculous, the only downside was how long it took to fully power the artifact.

But as he drew the blade, the sheath's effect was lost, and the swing veered wildly off course. It was akin to trying to steer the force of a tsunami. Semzar did not have even a tenth of the strength required to control it properly. Nonetheless, he managed to strike his target.

In a flash, reams of black runes sprung forth from the dagger, and all before them was parted. Even one of the mansion's mighty barriers was split in twain, and it only shattered a second later.

BROKEN RELIC OF A FORGOTTEN LAND
FAINT REMEMBRANCE OF A GLORIOUS PAST
TAINTED BY THE HANDS OF A COWARD

With Silberblut's focus entirely directed towards Tsetse, he was caught off-guard even by this attack that originated in plain sight. Under different circumstances, he could have dodged in advance based on Semzar's body tells. Moreover, even the Left Hand of Anger didn't react, despite the fact automatic defense was its core functionality. Tsetse was the only target permitted to Eisenretter's nascent form.

And so, the dismembered Mamon Knight fell to one knee, holding himself up by his remaining arm. In moments, his halo sputtered out, and his armor burned right off of him. With a loud thud, the severed limb fell to the ground, its armor burning away, musculature wildly spasming. A horrific creaking resounded as the limb's panicked throes bent its own elbow backwards and twisted its metal bones out of shape.

The attack seemed to shock even Tsetse, enough that he recoiled for a moment and glanced in Semzar's direction. However, he quickly regained his composure, approaching Casus as he drew back his fist in preparation for the killing blow.

Right then, a blurry form of black smoke flowed into the ballroom through the backmost door on the left.

"C-C-Cabral! *She's back!* Finish him off already!" Semzar called out, panicking as he shoved the jambiya back into its sheath and grasped for something else inside his jacket—doubtlessly another artifact.

The flyman froze mid-step, for but a split second, only to spin on his heel. With a forward stomp followed by an upward knee with the same leg, he sent out a shockwave that toppled the couch and threw the mafioso into the air. His barrier took the brunt of it, and Semzar cried out in outraged disbelief rather than pain.

With a stomp, he rebuked the mafioso. "Honorless cur. First, you failed to deliver the full shipment of thirty. Now, you've poisoned my combat data. Our arrangement is void. You can use your own strength to save your own hide."

Lady Blackhand emerged from her dive a few dozen meters away. She began pelting Semzar with bullets and tracers astonishingly similar to those she had wielded as Viridaimon, while Barzai flew overhead. Soon enough, she started throwing bursters and clouds of supernaturally thick, near-sentient smoke cropped up. Strangely, the raven split from his master and made his way to the stage, upon which half of the band was still to be found, including a drummer, a singer-guitarist, a bassist, and a keyboardist with a thaumatech piano. They would have better fit a bar than a ballroom. Barzai perched atop a notation stand.

"Play," the demonic bird ordered in the same baritone he had used to demand meat from his master. He glanced at the notations, then at the cowering musicians. *"Crest of Z. Can you?"*

Confused looks and hesitantly shaken heads were the response.

"Soul for the Sword?"

Again, the same response.

"Steel Messiah?"

Once more, nothing.

Then, almost jokingly, **"Mad Machine?"**

This time, they nodded.

Bobbing up and down in return, Barzai reaffirmed. **"Play."**

Once the rattled musicians got in position, he abruptly stopped, spreading his wings.

"Play. Or else."

With that, he flew off to aid his master.

A bass chord riff filled the ballroom, pulling the various melodies in as Tsetse picked up and carried through the mostly empty ballroom. Tsetse turned towards the dismembered Banisher, offering clemency. "Run. Leave. Get stronger. I will let you."

With blood leaking and golden flame bursting out of Casus' eyes and the seams between his skin-plates, he choked out these words, "You can make that choice. I have no such liberty."

He reached out for his severed arm, nearly falling over in the effort. Nonetheless, he picked up the limb and pressed it back into its socket. Wires leapt out from both his stump and the arm, lashing around the ends of the severed bone, pulling them together, winding and tangling around the joint into a knot. As this took place, the arm's grafted musculature rejoined in a similar manner, forming an unseemly, swollen connection, but one that would hold. The hiss of boiling blood filled the room with the stench of carbonized flesh as the wires superheated and soldered together. The graft's internal tubing, too, had been severed and reconnected with a gruesome sound and the leaking of blood between muscle bundles where the arm had been rejoined. Golden light erupted from between every muscle fiber of the limb, and with the gruesome sounds of metal scraping, it twisted itself back into shape.

The process only took a few seconds, but they felt like the better part of a minute due to how closely Tsetse observed it. Meanwhile, Semzar was scrambling in total panic as he tried to create as much distance as possible between himself as a rapidly approaching Blackhand. The ballroom was, nonetheless, huge, and it would take her a few moments more to get within range.

Casus tried to gather the strength to stand, but he could barely breathe. Everything hurt. Even the shallow breaths he managed sent brilliant, burning pain shooting through his body, piercing through the all-encompassing agony like flares lashing out from the surface of the sun. He wasn't sure where the pain of injuries ended and where the pain of isotope sickness began.

"Please... Just once more..." Casus pleaded. *"Just for a moment... Om, Zavyarana sowaka..."*

There, in the depths of a flesh-stripping blizzard of despair, Casus found a golden ember of fierce will, burning ever brighter in defiance. But just as he grasped that ember, consciousness slipped away from him.

That the Banisher lost consciousness, however, would not be known to the world just yet. His body stiffened for a moment, and he rose to his feet with a steadiness that did not hint at even the slightest injury or exhaustion.

The three claws holding the Silberblut Coupler's eye inside the socket suddenly sprung open. Once more, golden flame engulfed him, and out of the fire burst a figure of ebon-black, blacker than the blackest night. Its only distinguishable features were its blindingly bright halo of golden flame, a golden blade upon its right arm, and *six* seething eyes with seven-pointed stars for pupils—one on its head, one on its waist, one on its back, one on its giant left arm, and lastly, the two eyes upon its chest. All else of the figure was so dark as to be more of a three-dimensional shadow than a person. The Face of Judgment, its eyes wide open, screamed a soundless word.

That word reached Tsetse faster than sound would permit, permeating through him, and in that instant, the Evoy knew he was doomed.

"BE CLEANSED FROM THE WORLD."

He couldn't dodge. He couldn't block. The matter of even trying never crossed his thoughts. At this instant, he felt as if he were facing a saint from millennia past, and all will to fight left him.

This wasn't an attack. This was the blade of a guillotine speeding towards his neck.

FINAL COUPLER CHARGE
CLEANSING BLADE OF COURAGE

The shadowy shape of Eisenretter, blackened by the radiance of his own light, passed unimpeded through Tsetse. His passage and shining blade cleft a vertical split through the monstrous flyman three-quarters of the way up his chest. Miraculously, Tsetse remained standing. Even as gold-silver flame scoured his flesh from the inside, widening the wound, as Cabral's internal organs spilled out, and as both the Abara Morph's and the Host's blood ran freely down Tsetse's legs, pooling at his feet, he calmly looked down at himself.

"Unlucky... me. Hoist by my own petard. Heh. I shall see how you do... against my next self."

Tsetse went limp, toppling backwards with a fleshy thud. However, the same could not be said for whomever was inside. Cabral's lanky, mutilated upper half wrenched its way out of the Abara Morph's rapidly decaying flesh, confusion evident on his face. Various connection ports stretched between him and his meatsuit, tearing in half as he emerged, propping himself up by his arms.

"Where... Who... How?"

The Evoy clutched his head. He then toppled over forward, and the umbilicus connected to the back of his head snapped.

At that instant, he went limp like a puppet with its strings cut.

Meanwhile, "Shadow Eisenretter" melted away, leaving Casus barely standing in his place, his right arm hanging limply at his side. Frayed muscle peeled away from it. With each labored step the Banisher took towards Semzar's sofa, blood and other fluids ran down his arm's length and trailed across the ground. The Silberblut Coupler wasn't in a much better state. Its outer casement had cracked, and its trio of securing claws had been welded open. Casus was somehow certain that the Mamon System's relic components had purposely taken on the brunt of the strain to spare his life.

Casus, of course, was already unconscious by this point. Nonetheless, his body walked to Semzar's sofa of its own accord and sat down, holding vigil over Tsetse and Cabral's rapidly disintegrating forms.

CHAPTER 28

VS. SEMZAR

Whilst rushing to reach the ballroom, Krahe had encountered several more of Semzar's subordinates. To call them defenders would have been a stretch—they were either fleeing or just frozen in panic when she encountered them, and only some of them turned to fight. Those stupid, *stupid* few served as further target practice for her heretofore unnamed tar-whip thaumaturgy, each a new attempt to refine it without slowing down. It would have been terribly convenient if she had just so happened to perfect the thaumaturgy by the time she arrived at the ballroom, but alas, no such thing came to pass.

Oh, she felt close. So, *so damnably close.* Its true, ideal form was within her grasp, she just knew it. But she had to start fighting Semzar without it.

Furthermore, as she approached the ballroom, another thing became patently evident—something *far* less positive. That *something* was that quite a bit of her pain stemmed from the Atomica, or perhaps even from her altered Soul Furnace. She couldn't discern the exact nature and extent of it, but one thing becoming clear was that burning thauma was somehow causing her body to break down. As to the nature and extent of the damage, she wasn't sure, but this was certainly the polar opposite of what she had hoped for with the Atomica. A part of her feared that Yao might have purposely sabotaged the key, but a much larger part was certain this had to do with implanting it prematurely, or perhaps some other factor external to the key itself. Perhaps she hadn't let it cool off long enough after the transmutation, or it was something as simple as her body not being physically tough enough to stand the power, even if such a possibility was counterintuitive given her frequent use of anathema without issue.

The silver lining was that she was certain the damage wouldn't catch up with her before she killed Semzar and dragged Casus to safety. Half of this certainty stemmed from her possession of the Calbian Molting Tonic—the ultimate contingency from Razem himself, an elixir that would by his description allow her to survive beyond-lethal injuries if she injected it into her heart. Another quarter of it came from the fact Thaumic Fusion still worked normally, allowing her to mitigate the damage to some extent. The rest was just self-confidence, bravado perhaps. It would all come down to how good Semzar was and how long it would take her to off him.

All considerations aside, it wasn't as if she had much choice in the matter. That much she knew the instant she entered the ballroom. She had arrived, as it seemed, just in time to witness Casus carry out a heroic and undoubtedly self-destructive final attack against Tsetse. The enormous gash in the floor and the *seething* dagger in Semzar's hand told the rest of the story. She was certain that, had she arrived later, she would have found Semzar leering towards Casus with the intent to take the Banisher's body for his own. If everything went wrong, she would at least try to get Casus out of there and rendezvous with the inquisitor, whom she knew to be stationed outside the property. At least, she hoped she was still in position, and still alive.

Despite her dicey-at-best position, when she surfaced from her dive and set loose that first salvo of tracers in Semzar's direction, Krahe couldn't help but let a grin push its way onto her face.

A body breaking down from an experimental power source, one high-grade drug keeping her going and another in the back pocket to pull her through the final stretch. An opponent—no, a target—such as Semzar, one with bought and stolen power that he didn't know how to use properly, relying on the muscle memory of his body's previous unfortunate inhabitant. The one unfamiliar variable was Casus. A wounded comrade whose life, for once, was a higher priority than the death of her target.

All in all, she felt more clear-headed, more focused, more confident than ever.

Nothing she had experienced on the face of Zastreon had brought her back as much as this. Her mind raced with countless possibilities and past operations to draw on. Every moment stretched on and on like a distended synthetic tendon. The pain burned through every inch, turned sideways by Class-3 painkillers, suddenly feeding into a razor-sharp bodily awareness.

Hopping backwards and scrambling to keep distance from her, the mafioso babbled something under his breath whilst rummaging through his inner jacket pockets. Krahe wasn't sure if it was an incantation of some kind or just a nervous tic. His physique began stretching his suit, tendrils bulging out from under his skin, which itself turned an unseemly shade of bluish purple. He became faster and faster, his apparent physicality now equal to a Mamon Knight using a High-Pressure type Dregsteam cartridge—only, with none of the finesse. More than anything, he resembled an ape in the manner he bounded from spot to spot.

Between barrages of tracers and Cinder Gatling rays, Krahe threw in a Six Trees Killer—but one of a different kind. Semzar's movements were too erratic for a timed fuse, and as she understood the evolution of her thaumaturgy, she thought remote detonation ought to finally be within her reach. The mechanism was a simple pulse of thauma keyed to a particular thought-impulse, much like a real radio detonator would work. She couldn't just release thauma in all directions at any reasonable range, so she still had to keep the burster in her sightline, but that was an acceptable limitation.

A satisfied chuckle rose from Krahe's throat when the bullet-propelled grenade zipped over Semzar's head, and the shockwave nearly knocked him off his feet a moment later. He quickly regained his bearings, and with an angered gesture, stood his ground, stomping with a great release of thauma. The floor cracked under his foot, the fissure racing forward as great gouts of blue flame sprung forth. It was a display of power to be sure, but a mere decoy. The real danger was a double-barreled pistol he pulled with his free hand, and from it set forth two Bloody Reapers in quick succession.

Krahe halted in her tracks and performed a dive, letting them pass through her as she made mocking gestures towards the mafioso. Immediately after emerging, she whipped a burster his way, and while his attention was on it, she peppered his side with a few Cinder Gatling beams. And so, the struggle continued.

As the two played cat-and-mouse through the nearly deserted ballroom, Krahe scattered a great deal of smoke across the field, and it was not *just* smoke. Within the smoke, under tables, and even in plain sight, she dropped fuseless bursters. By slightly reducing the internal pressure, she ensured they would last without maintenance for a little while.

It could not be said that Semzar was so gutless as to just take her onslaught whilst trying to run away. When she managed to slip a handful of tracers past his barrier, Semzar responded with a mighty flex, and a second pair of arms burst free from his trapezoid muscles. These arms were not of flesh but of the same translucent purple force that formed his barrier. Their fists were enveloped in dark-blue flame, with long wisps of it trailing off. Out of the four tracers that made it past his defenses, only one managed to hit—the other three were punched out of the air by these newly formed arms. In the process, they fully detached from Semzar's body, now floating above his shoulders. As for the single tracer that struck home, it smashed right into the side of his face. Its scarlet-black explosion elicited a counter-burst of blue flame and a smattering of purple shards akin to explosive reactive armor.

The obvious answer to the question these arms posed was an attack that could not be shot down—Cinder Flash or Wandrei Faust. As things stood, she couldn't get close enough to land a Cinder Flash. Barzai, though not able to inflict serious damage, aided in herding the bastard away from Casus and towards one of the bursters which she had quietly dropped earlier.

However, before she could lure him to one of her traps, Semzar finally found what he had been looking for inside his jacket—a silver ring, with a faceplate wide enough to cover the entire lowest segment of a finger and a four-pointed star of deep red gemstone as the centerpiece. It was none other than his father's "Crimson Star" ring! The mafioso slipped it on his right-hand ring finger, his flesh deforming hideously before the band expanded to fit him. Then, he began a reckless counterattack. It was a barrage of superhumanly fast, yet also amateurishly telegraphed punches, his fists wreathed in blue flame. With each punch he sent flying a fist-shaped construct, each taking with it only thin ribbons of that blue fire. They were fast, to be sure, but not the speed of bullets—between the volume of fire and size of projectiles, dodging them was much like dodging particularly pretty fertilizer rockets. It was as if, with the ring on, he felt safe enough to finally stop running. Krahe deduced it had to be a defensive artifact of some kind.

Nonetheless, dodging Semzar's rocket punches meant she wasn't attacking, and eventually, he might get lucky. Unlike him, she couldn't afford even one unlucky hit, and she had to keep pressuring him. The only solution that came to mind was smaller movements and closer dodges, though it would bring her closer to danger. Whether one dodged by a meter or by a centimeter didn't matter, so long as one didn't get hit. Less time spent dodging. Thus, more time for counterattacks.

"Sharper."

Thirty centimeters.

"Sharper."

Fifteen centimeters.

"Even sharper!"

Five centimeters.

The fire licked her skin and left the sensation of hot water behind—like going into a sauna from the freezing cold. It wasn't even hot enough to cause a surface burn.

She slipped into a state of absolute focus and perfect efficiency of motion, a pinnacle of clarity that warriors from eras past had spent their lives training to achieve and maintain for short bursts. It was something she had taken for granted, considering it one of the absolute basics thanks to neural implants, cognitive conditioning, and hormone controllers. Krahe had slipped into that familiar place a few times since her rebirth, always in the midst of battle, but never to this extent. Never fully. She had never managed to *truly* snap into the zone until now, only ever veering in and out for moments at a time. The reflexes, the muscle memory, the cognitive conditioning—it was all still there. She just had to get into the right physical state to set it off.

ZERO HESITATION
MAXIMUM FOCUS
ACCELERATED COGNITION
TACTICAL SUPREMACY
A LONE OPERATIVE
PREVAILS AGAINST ALL ODDS
RAZORMIND

"You stole that thaumaturgy, didn't you?!" she mocked him. "The flames are barely warm! Could you not simply adjust it to remove the fire element? Could you not even go to the effort of stealing a fire affinity to go with your stolen thaumaturgy?!"

No verbal response came, but Semzar's flames visibly grew, both in size and brightness, and so did the number of punches he sent flying her and Barzai's way. In turn, they became even sloppier, as did his positioning. Frankly, he didn't seem to be thinking about positioning at all, which was itself a problem. No thought meant that it would be harder to manipulate him into standing near a trap-burster. Nonetheless, Krahe managed it, more by pure luck than her own efforts. With a snap of her fingers, the burster went off right at Semzar's feet as he was standing atop a table. He was consumed by a great burst of pyroclast and splinters, which in turn was dispersed by the reactive outburst of his wards.

Then, Semzar did something unexpected, if only because it was too logical. He closed the distance, and not with a careless lunge, but with a steady, yet quick approach while keeping up his offense. If he closed the distance, Krahe would have less time to dodge his flying fists, his barrier would take up more of her field of view, and she wouldn't so readily detonate any given trap-burster lest she herself be caught in the blast. Even if she were to do such a thing and, say, dive beforehand or skim just out of the blast radius, Semzar could read that as a tell. This was all assuming that Semzar was thinking tactically rather than rushing in like a frustrated moron.

Krahe did what she could to manage the spacing, but even Astro Diving and Skimming could only go so far against someone who could bound around like a suited-up cyber-ape. Not wanting to dump a Cinder Flash or even Cinder Strobe straight into his barrier, Krahe decided to simultaneously mix him up and refine her Tar-whip thaumaturgy by employing it at this close-mid range. Right now, in this razor-like mindset, centimeters from death and burning up from inside, she knew she could grasp it, much like a self-destructive artist could grasp his best work whilst overdosing on hallucinogenic toad saliva.

And indeed, right there, in the refulgent moments between engagements when the world seemed to pause, there her answer was. Refining the lash's thinness and velocity only got her so far—the final step was hidden in plain sight, being the simple incorporation of her fingers as an additional layer of casting. By quickly opening her hand to act as a triggering gesture, the thaumaturgy came out as five separate threads centered on her palm, and each connected to the tip of one finger. They sprung forth with the speed of a bullet, lashed at their target, and then disintegrated into smoke. A fair portion of the lash's quickness and the velocity of its filaments stemmed from the left arm's increasingly superhuman characteristics, fed both by Krahe's physical attribute growth and by the Atomica's monstrous Throughput. Thaumaturgy and the filaments' whip-like motion did the rest of the work.

The combined velocity and gossamer-like thinness of each thread created the illusion of Krahe cutting things through sheer force of will with the mere gesture of her arm.

With a slight adjustment, she could detach the filaments from her palm early, allowing her to use them for a more traditional swiping attack. Forming a single, stronger cutting filament was still an option, especially if she wished to, for some reason, dust off monowire martial arts.

And so, after a monowire she had named it "Black Lasher," or just *Lasher* for short.

The original had been a legendary armament in its own time, the first "true" monofilament whip capable of cutting straight through the most advanced hard armor composites. Her version was perhaps not so universally effective, but it had an undeniable point of appeal in the form of overwhelming cutting power that allowed it to be effective even against barriers and wards, despite being predominantly lacerative in nature. In terms of efficiency, it didn't even remotely hold up to Cinder Flash or Tar-tendrils in their intended roles, but that didn't matter. One couldn't expect to always have the exact right tool for the job. Black Lasher came out faster than Cinder Flash and had a range somewhere between it and Tar-tendrils, allowing it to fill in where the other two fell short, not to mention its ideal use-case for cutting through flesh, which Krahe dearly hoped she would get to demonstrate against Semzar.

For now, she was satisfied with seeing his disconcerted look when the filaments ripped into his barrier and his hard entropy spiked much like it would with a purposeful kinetic attack. In concert with a hail of mescalt bullets, it was only a matter of time before he would have to drop his barrier or go into meltdown. Semzar, knowing this, turned to the logical answer and spent his entropy on trying to either kill Krahe or stop her from hitting his barrier.

One fist passed by her arm, close enough to agitate her wards, yet nothing happened. Another passed near her leg, tearing a yawning gash into her trousers and leaving the edges smoldering. Another, still, ripped her bodysuit on the left side, the gel already closing over the superficial burn it left behind.

Semzar realized that she had no wards. Whether they had collapsed from damage or from implanting this new voidkey, it didn't matter. To him, that realization was a shining ray of hope; it was victory within easy reach. He just had to get one, maybe two good hits in. How hard could that be?

* * *

As the battle carried on, Krahe felt time rapidly catching up to her. Even if she instantly stored any generated Isotope inside her arm, its presence within her body nonetheless caused damage—negligible damage, at first, but it gradually built up. Eventually, despite burning away as much Isotope as she could by generously tainting each and every one of her thaumaturgies with it, she exceeded the left arm's capacity.

Each use of Thaumic Fusion poisoned her, yet in turn, each Implosion-Burn set rampant thaumic power coursing through. Only 95% of the power generated by Implosion-Burning went where it was supposed to. The remaining 5% was tearing her apart from within, and now the damage was starting to show. Her skin began to split open, scarlet light shining through.

The more she deteriorated, the more Semzar's terror grew, and the more his already fragile grasp on focus slipped from his bloodied fingers.

To Semzar's gaze, which instinctively understood anatomy for the purpose of assessing a would-be host's suitability, she was worse than a rotting corpse. She was poison. Death on two legs in more ways than one. No... not death. Murder on two legs.

"Why? Why? Why won't you die already?! Whywhywhywhywhy—"

Each "why" was accompanied by a flaming fist, a machine-gun cadence of thaumaturgic strikes potent enough to strike down their target, each ripping apart furniture and flooring when it inevitably missed. Dust and debris wildly scattered into the air all around her.

Each fist flew mere centimeters from its intended target. Krahe swayed as she walked, moving no more than necessary to avoid each fist's generously telegraphed trajectory. With every movement, minute bursts of flame sprung forth from the many glowing fissures that split her skin. The wild currents of magic that leaked from her being set her hair billowing in all possible directions, and the dark smoke of entropy shrouded her. Semzar could swear she initiated a purge every ten seconds, as if mocking him, and all the more infuriating still, he never managed to hit her during one. Even while devoid of magic, she denied him at every turn. Each time he got close, she would simply vanish in a plume of smoke and appear elsewhere nearby—sometimes less than a single step's distance, other times a full three meters, and everywhere in between. It was Astro Skimming, that much he knew, but he didn't know the maximum range. It had to be something like five meters; it couldn't be more, but he wasn't even certain of that much at this point.

There wasn't a person behind those eyes, which swirled and flickered with green light. Indeed, through their apertures peered not a human but a demonic being of murder. A single-minded obsession, a whirling madness, spilling out with such pure hate and revulsion that Semzar thought, perhaps, she was employing an ocular curse. He had felt it before, having been the subject of curses, and he recognized that curse-like will flowing in abundance from her gaze. Only, she was staring not *at* Semzar but *through* him. For a moment, he genuinely considered if Blackhand intended to use his corpse as a medium to directly strike at his father or at the Benefactors. He well and truly came to think that this was the true reason she was after him—such was his coping mechanism for the reality that his own actions had directly led to this.

And the music. Why was the band playing? What was this trite love song?!

"Mad machine—I chase down my prey on a speeding bike! Mad machine—this fire burning in my chest defies logic! Time flies, chasing us, like a suffering, wounded beast. My burgeoning ferocity has me in its grasp—"

Another line came, but Semzar didn't hear it. That infernal bird screamed over it, **"The more masks I remove, the less human I become!"**

Then, wasting not a moment, the red-eyed thing bombarded Semzar's barrier with explosions and began orating, for lack of a better term. It spoke in a man's booming voice, the volume perfectly synchronized with the music, creating a confusing and frightening cacophony. Perhaps the most frightening aspect of the tirade was twofold; the plethora of alien words used and the fact that Semzar, somehow, understood all of them, their meaning imbued into the sound itself.

Thus spoke the raven.

"AT AGE TWENTY-ONE I SLEW THIRTY MEN WITH MY BARE HANDS I STRANGLED SEVEN WITH THEIR OWN PLASTIC INTESTINES I STRUNG THE HEADS OF THEIR KINDRED FROM THE RAFTERS AND DROWNED THREE MORE IN WHITE BLOOD. BY MY OWN HANDS I FORCED OPEN A STEEL BULKHEAD AND HAVING THUSLY BEEN CRIPPLED I BIT OUT THE TENDONS AND THROATS OF THREE WHO SOUGHT TO VIOLATE MY FLESH, AND TOOK THEIR LIMBS FOR MYSELF."

Blackhand rapidly closed the distance in the form of a flittering smoke-demon, emerging only momentarily to lash at Semzar's barrier, cutting gashes into the floor with each flash, gusts of flame erupting from her palm each time she opened it to cast the thaumaturgy. He couldn't comprehend how it worked—it appeared to simply *cut*, but it was such an outlier. Why would she have only this one arcane thaumaturgy when everything else was either energetic or construct-reliant? He glimpsed the glittering remnants, thread-like in appearance, but they were so short-lived that he assumed them to be the bare minimum to which she could reduce the thaumaturgy's visibility.

A dense mass of smoke erupted from her mouth, writhing forth like a swarm of ravenous insects moving to envelop him. Semzar's fists, both those he set forth and those which defended him, scattered it handily, his own thauma neutralizing Blackhand's. Even still, what remained of the cloud swiftly moved in to fill the gaps and obscure his sight as best as it could.

"I HAD THE BUNKERS OF THE CITY OF ANGELS UTTERLY DESTROYED AND I COUNTED THEIR OWNERS AND SPONSORS AS DIGITAL GHOSTS I TOPPLED THEIR SPIRES OF STEEL AND GLASS I TOOK THEIR BRAINS FROM THEIR DATA TOMBS AND DAMNED THEM TO THE NERVE LATHE. I LEARNED FROM THEIR DYING SCREAMS THE NAMES AND HOMES OF THOSE THEY SERVED AND HUNTED THEM IN THE SAME MANNER."

Despite the fact his eyes could somewhat see through the smoke, it added to the numerous elements acting to overwhelm his mind. He didn't even know it, but he had already been driven on the back foot—even as he lashed out and forced Blackhand to back off, Semzar didn't *think*. He didn't make plans or consider how he would finish her off. He was just reacting.

She appeared from the smoke, far too close for comfort, and Semzar's first reaction was not to strike—it was to pour his will into the Crimson Star ring. The artifact replied with the cruel knowledge that it wouldn't be ready for some time.

At first, it seemed as if she was punching into thin air from several meters away, but as she reared her fist back, a row of fanged mouths opened down the length of her arm. In perfect concert with the punch, great black tendrils erupted from these maws, and Semzar's entropy surged—the impact was more than twice the strength of a Yellow Atropal. His vastly superior reaction speed and physicality, driven by muscle memory and instinct not his own, allowed his body to counterattack instantly whilst Semzar was still reeling from the impact, despite the fact he had not actually weathered a strike himself. As he set loose a barrage of lightning-fast punches, she was already gone, and that damnable raven had returned, resuming its tirade.

It mockingly danced between his punches, moving in an erratic manner only ever so vaguely connected to the flapping of its wings.

"ANCIENT ARMS OF NUCLEAR FIRE I UNEARTHED FROM AN AGE LONG PAST AND WITH THEM PUT TO THE TORCH ALL THE WORKS OF THOSE WHO WRONGED ME. ON A QUEST OF TWO MONTHS AND THREE DAYS I DEVASTATED THE DOMED VILLAS OF XIAOSHENG AND SCATTERED COBALT-60 AND NERVE POISON OVER THEM I TURNED THE NOBLES WHO LIVED WITHIN TO SHADOWS UPON THE STONE AND OPENED THE BELLIES AND SEVERED THE LIMBS OF ALL WHO SERVED THEM. THEIR WALLS I CAST DOWN AND LET THE BEASTS OF THE WASTE FEED UPON THEIR FLESH."

Spinning in place, now entirely disoriented, Semzar released a guttural scream of frustration as he hunted for Blackhand. He glimpsed her shape at last! But he was merely reacting, and he had glimpsed her in the midst of executing a premeditated attack. Before he could even chamber a punch, let alone release it, a singular tendril with a mace-like head whipped around him and buried itself into his left side. An explosion of fire and razors followed, tearing away a vast swath of his wards. The shockwave smashed into his barrier from the inside, and the pure kinetic force, having caught him off guard, sent him tumbling head-over-heels. Swarming pyroclast followed in his wake, sticking to him and shredding away. Semzar had no choice but to shroud himself in fire, burning an enormous deal of thauma just to cleanse the lingering deathsmoke from his body.

But it never stopped.

She continued her onslaught without relent, and so too did her familiar's tirade. It just went on, and on, and on, fading into background noise. In the brief moments of mental clarity, the tirade somehow pushed itself into the empty space. Atrocity after atrocity. A life of endless murder and conquest. Within the last minute, the raven had recounted the merciless extermination of six mafia families, each dwarfing the Hashem Family by far.

* * *

Time after time, Krahe lashed at Semzar, dumping atrocious sums in mescalt ammunition into his barrier all the while lashing at him and herding him around the ballroom. Finally, she spent the final bullet in the clip on a Six Trees Killer, timing it to precede a nearby burster's detonation as the real attack. The moment she pulled the trigger, Krahe had already conjured a clip of dregshot alternated with mescalt and was moving to slam it into place. The grenade approached the space above Semzar's head, the new clip pushed the old one out, and a rapid sequence of events took place. First, he dropped his barrier. Second, a bright-red flash issued from his hand. Third, a shockwave of swirling scarlet force burst out of his being, spreading out in a spherical shape. It cracked the floor tiles, swept up a violent gust of wind, and flung furniture across the room as if it were weightless—and much in the same way, Krahe's bursters were flung aside as well.

Krahe hoped it was a one-time consumable, but knew it was unlikely. Were that the case, the form factor would have betrayed it. If she was unlucky, the ring could perform that feat on demand. She theorized that the ring either guzzled thauma to recharge, or at least had a cooldown between uses. That could not be confirmed, so she had to continue as before, keeping the ring in mind as yet another factor. Semzar had so graciously brought out one tool after the next, it was only right for her to do the same.

She shot the Pattner at her left arm, the empowered talisman plastering across her blackened muscle. In a mere moment, with a single mighty eruption of power from the Implosion Furnace, a mass of red-black pyroclast enveloped her left arm and solidified into the form of a monstrous appendage.

"Wandrei Faust!"

GRUDGE-FILLED GRASP
DEATH BORNE UPON CLAWS OF HATE
BLACK HAND OF DESOLATION: WANDREI FAUST

The monstrous claw ripped free, careening headlong towards its prey with the command to reach optimal standoff range outside his barrier's effective angle before firing. As it flew, Krahe wasted no time and unleashed a prolonged burst of Cinder Gatling beams, taking the opportunity to tear away at the mafioso's wards. It took him a second and a half of their angry strobing to get his barrier back up, and by then, his wards' reactive flaring had grown feeble indeed. His wards now had a gaping hole in the right side of his chest, about 20cm across. The Wandrei Faust, having reached overhead, flared with theurgic fury and spewed forth a screech of yellow killing light. Despite all expectations, Semzar ate nearly the full brunt of it. The flesh scoured from his side so far one could see his organs. Clutching his side, Semzar leapt backwards with a howl of pain. An angry fist scattered the nearly spent Wandrei Faust into a puff of glassy ash.

That injury, despite its grisly nature, was not a disabling one. It presented an ideal weak point to aim for, but the baneworm shifted his tendrils and used them to restrain his meatsuit's organs at the expense of his left arm, which lost much volume. That loss of volume and pure physical power didn't impact the performance of his ranged attacks. If anything, it made them harder to deal with by altering their timing.

Once more, the battle settled into a back-and-forth. Krahe still questioned why he had used the ring so early instead of waiting until he could affect the Wandrei Faust, whose Standoff-mode range was shorter than the ring's maximum effective range. Did it not work on attacks and constructs of Theurgic nature? Besides being rather generous, that explanation assumed that Semzar knew the nature of Wandrei Faust. The much more likely reason was that Semzar had been holding his mental trigger finger on the ring all along and ended up pulling it on instinct without deeper consideration.

Her second Wandrei Faust met its end swiftly, shot down by such an overkill barrage that Krahe was still happy with the outcome thanks to the opening Semzar had given her. Disappointingly, she had to use that opening to purge entropy instead of ripping into him, but she planted another bullet in his barrier to not let him off easy. Krahe allowed a few moments to pass without making any significant moves, half to test whether the ring had a cooldown, and half because she was struggling to keep up. As drugged as she was, the pain of her body breaking down didn't impede her, but the increasing loss of mobility could not be denied. She increasingly had to rely more and more on diving and skimming to compensate, cutting into her ability to mount assaults of sufficient intensity to pressure Semzar.

She sacrificed a third Wandrei Faust alongside a burster and a Six Trees Killer to keep the bastard occupied. He shot down this Faust too, whilst leaping out of the range of the two others before they could detonate. While that took place, he clenched his fist twice, accompanied by flashes of red from the Crimson Star Ring. They were much dimmer than before, bright enough to see, and Krahe observed no tangible shockwave emission.

From this, she inferred that he was mentally smashing the button while the ring was still recharging, having both seen and done similar things in the past.

Krahe considered using the Calbian Molting Tonic, but the problem was she would need time to do so, and it would likely require more time after that to take effect. Storing it in the Kenoma Pocket had cost her a significant chunk of entropy, so retrieval would be the same, and she would have to line it up just right to get between the Liminal Coil's abnormally shaped ribs, exactly into her heart. In short, the same opening needed to inject it would also be wide enough to finish Semzar off.

It wasn't long before Krahe lined up another decisive strike, blasting herself through the air and using a fourth Wandrei Faust as a distraction. She rendered her landing abnormally smooth by astro diving, but as she slid away from him, she skimmed into the floor—just far enough to trigger the kinetic rebound. In the blink of an eye, she was suddenly sliding towards him, fusion-forming a Tar-tendril with a burster in its tip as she transitioned from sliding to a low sprint.

He shot down the Wandrei Faust as expected, but before her explosive tendril could reach him, there came another flash from that ring. From this close, she could clearly see its two shockwaves spreading out, tearing at the flooring and tossing aside furniture as they went. She immediately realized she had made a severe mistake—she couldn't adjust her course quickly enough to avoid the shockwave altogether.

Thus, the answer was to skim *through* it. Spanning no more than thirty centimeters in thickness, surpassing the twin shockwave would be possible, so Krahe committed to that course of action. She released her hold on her burster-tendril, honing her focus to the absolute extreme of Razormind. When the world felt as if it would come to a halt, she dipped her feet into the astral gulf, set her target destination, and initiated the skim.

A moving wall of force halted her, throwing her aside like a ragdoll. She had just enough time to realize that, somehow, the Crimson Star Ring's shockwave could negate Astro Skimming, and presumably Astro Diving. The sole reason she got the time to consider this was that despite her skim being halted halfway, she still experienced a moment of extreme time dilation when she resurfaced—thus leaving her suspended in mid-air for a stretched-out split-second, locking eyes with an unaware Semzar. Before she could hit the ground, a pair of flaming fists smashed into her ribcage and decisively sent her flying into the wall.

* * *

Victorious laughter erupted from Semzar's throat, resembling the cackle of a rabid animal due to how hard he had pushed his meatsuit. He didn't know how or why that demon had been thrown back; he had acted purely on reflex, and it had taken him a few moments to realize what he had just done. But now that he knew, Semzar's immediate response was to bask in a victory he perceived to be rightly his, even as his body tensed in alarm, setting off cascades of bodily memory that the baneworm himself did not fully comprehend.

Another source of laughter rang out. It was the raven, cackling as it flew towards its master, its persistent presence a hint as to what was to come. A few seconds passed, and, for some reason, Semzar found himself unable to act or move. Those green pinpricks flared to life from the cloud of dust and smoke, and soon she emerged once more. Her skin was decimated, bare flesh showing through in countless places, and the shape of an unnatural rib cage was impressed upon her bodysuit from the inside, lit by a red-orange glow. Her trousers were reduced to rags, yet miraculously retained some vague notion of their original shape as they billowed about her legs. Above her left hand floated a hemispherical tangle of black tendrils, and within that nest, the laughing raven roosted.

"W-What are you?!"

The green-eyed demon gave no answer. Instead, the raven ceased its cackling to speak once more.

"AT THE END OF MY LIFE, CUT DOWN BY A BETRAYER, I, BLACKHAND, THE MONSTER, DIED. EONS HENCE, LIKE RAZGRIZ, I, BLACKHAND, THE HERO, HAVE BEEN BORN ANEW. MILLIONS HAVE BURNED BY MY HAND BEFORE YOU AND MILLIONS WILL BURN ERE I PERMIT THIS WORLD TO BE OVERRUN BY YOUR KIND. THIS IS THE CLEANSING OF YOUR SIN. PREPARE TO DIE."

In concert with her familiar, Blackhand spat at him, ***"YOU ARE A TAPEWORM. THAT BODY IS NOT YOURS. RETURN IT TO ZAVESH."***

* * *

Krahe's side of that exchange was significantly uglier and more painful. That double-fisted punch had not only scorched her lungs, bursting one of them, it had also bruised her heart. Her impact with the wall didn't do her any favors, either. As she slumped to the ground and slipped out of consciousness, Barzai's shrieking call inside her own skull dragged her back into the world of pain. Groaning on the inside for lack of strength to do so vocally, Krahe mobilized a monumental force of will, ripping open a wound-like grin within the palm of her left hand. She used a tendril of tar as thin as one finger to reach inside, and by the power of Thaumic Fusion, she brought out the silver-cased injector—but she couldn't raise it up to drive it into her own heart. Her left arm gripped the implement, but she could barely raise her wrist. Once more, Krahe summoned a monumental force of will, gritting her teeth such that she felt a molar crack under the pressure. A strained groan rose from her throat. Blood began leaking from her nostrils, steaming as it ran down her face, and her vision was dyed crimson a moment later.

Feeling as if its weight were comparable to a mountain, Krahe raised her arm and pushed the injector's monolithic needle into her chest. It scraped against one of her ribs, and with a sensation of icy heat, it pierced her heart. That same sensation soon flooded her, and pain returned as an ocean of clarion clarity. At once, the serum refused to let her ignore her state, yet also clarified her thoughts. While she had been burning herself alive from within, now she very much also felt that way.

What had felt like a protracted struggle had, in fact, taken a few seconds. So short, in fact, that the cloud of dust her impact with the wall had created was still yet to dissipate.

She nonetheless got back up, feeling her own insides writhe as they rearranged and pulled back together. Layers of skin, ravaged and baked to coal, sloughed off, revealing bare flesh underneath, threads of new dermal tissue already growing to cover the gap. It was then that Barzai returned to her, perching sideways on her left forearm.

And so, she raised her hand and once more ignited a flame, collapsing it into the light of anathema.

Tendrils of blackest black, suffused with glass and dark jade, twisted together from her wrist to form a nest. Within it Barzai perched, cackling, and as Krahe emerged from the cloud of dust, the raven began screaming the final stanza to its tirade. Though the sound reached her ears, her mind was so focused on moving forward and *not* collapsing that she didn't process what he was saying. She only noticed that at some point he stopped.

At the sight of Semzar, still staring at her in disbelief from behind his barrier, a deep, guttural disgust cut through it all, through the pain and exhaustion. It perfectly matched just how sick she felt. From the boundless well of vitriol she had refined and distilled throughout her life, a rebuke bubbled, and Barzai spoke it alongside her in perfect synchronicity.

"YOU ARE A TAPEWORM. THAT BODY IS NOT YOURS. RETURN IT TO ZAVESH."

Around the framework of black tendrils, solid panels began forming an icosahedron. Semzar snapped out of his daze and once more began sloppily losing flaming fists Krahe's way, but even as wrecked as she was, it took minimal movement to dodge them. He wasn't even putting the bare-minimum thought into them as he had done before—by now, Semzar was lashing out in pure panic, his ring flashing a dim light that spoke clearly of just how doomed its fool of a wielder was. There was not a chance in hell it would be ready before the Daemon Core was.

But... just in case.

Krahe opened three more mouths along her arm.

And spoke the Words. She knew not whether there was any point or benefit, but she did it regardless.

With the first Word, three flaming fists closest to her were cast aside, tinged in red and black, and sent flying back at Semzar, changing shape mid-air into the clawed talons of Wandrei Faust.

With the second Word, several chairs and tables were sent flying.

With the third Word, the windows blew out.

With each Word, the Daemon Core's formation sped up.

With each Word, the ember at its core burned ever brighter, with ever more wretched hatred for its victim.

THREE KEYS TO SWING WIDE THE GATES OF BLACKEST BLACKNESS
THREE WORDS SO MIGHTY NO MORTAL MIND CAN HOLD THEM
THREE BREATHLESS MOUTHS WITH WHICH TO SPEAK THEM

At the moment of completion, as Krahe gestured forth to sic the Daemon Core upon Semzar, the baneworm had the good judgment to strike, rightly thinking that she was not in an ideal state to evade. Krahe, without even thinking, raised an unassisted barrier, a swirling, undulating mass of smoke and sparks, almost alive in appearance. It didn't matter how much entropy it cost her, and it would not have mattered even if that impact had sent her into meltdown. Without hesitation, Semzar feverishly looked around, and when his gaze fell upon the couch where he had sat, or rather upon the unconscious body of Casus Aristedes, he thought he might still have a chance. But by the time he began moving in that direction, the Daemon Core had, with unsettling swiftness, caught up to him, floating ominously overhead. One of the shell's panels cracked.

In the next moment, screaming death poured forth and obliterated everything below his meatsuit's head, burning a farcical silhouette into the floor tiles. Crimson light filled the ballroom and poured out of all available openings. In every way that mattered, Semzar was already dead. Only an anathema-poisoned, mutilated, dying baneworm remained, writhing impotently within its skull in a vain effort to escape. His ring and dagger clattered to the ground. It was the only possession of his to survive the blast.

AN EYE OF CRIMSON IMPRISONED IN BLACKNESS
ITS GAZE ERUPTS FORTH TO SCOUR AWAY THE
UNWORTHY
BLACK HAND OF DESOLATION: DAEMON CORE

Krahe, with every ounce of will left to her, stumbled over to Semzar's head, leaning on furniture along the way. Slowly, with great effort, she stomped and stomped until the skull cracked open and Semzar flopped out. He was severely discolored, veins bulging beneath his slimy skin, and blackened anathema burns covered a third of what remained of his body. He didn't even try to escape, twitching in her grasp. She brought out a souldreg extractor and jabbed it into the dying worm. A multicolored mass of souldregs filled the vial halfway, the natural pearlescence marred by black and purple threads and specks. After stowing it away, Krahe struggled back to her feet and ambled over to the couch, sitting down next to Casus.

Every screaming muscle in her body insisted it would be fine to fall asleep, that the Inquisitor would arrive any time now. Krahe didn't trust that instinct and forced herself back up. Lacking the strength to do anything so glamorous as carrying her unconscious comrade out of the mansion, she dragged him along instead.

* * *

Having already entered the mansion, Yazata was in no position to witness the light show. However, out of anyone, she was particularly well-suited to hearing the Words, to feeling the reverberations of a high theurgy being carried out to the utmost extent. Sensing the abrupt dimming of Blackhand's magical signature that followed the theurgy, the Inquisitor continued making her way into the mansion with renewed urgency.

With her pack of Red Hoods in tow, she came across the two of them at the foot of the staircase leading to the ballroom's main door. To say they were in a sorry state would have been an enormous understatement. Casus bore numerous wounds; his right arm was wrecked, as was the Silberblut Coupler. He was unconscious, but besides the filth, he would be fine. Blackhand, who was dragging him along, resembled the burnt-out husk of a dead anathemist more than any living thing. The left side of her face was completely overtaken by anathema burns, as was a significant portion of the rest of her body. Trails of blood crusted her face, yet somehow, her bodysuit was pristine. Then, a chunk of burned skin sloughed off, and fresh skin made itself known underneath. Calbian Molting Tonic. Unmistakable. That she still lived was no longer a surprise—the question became how she was able to walk in her state given the tonic's clarifying, painkiller-neutralizing side effects.

Yazata didn't get to ask any of the many questions swirling in her mind. Blackhand locked eyes with her, smirked, and uttered with a death-like whisper, "Ah. Good. You must be the Inquisitor."

With those words, she collapsed.

Afterword

Brunhilde Krahe's adventure isn't over yet. The third installment of *Cherno Caster* will hit digital shelves Summer of 2025.

Don't want to wait to get your fix? Check out *Corpo Age*, a LitRPG Sci-Fi Isekai.

Rollo believed that money ruled the world. Then his world came crashing down.

Now, Rollo finds himself in a dystopian, corporate-ruled world where greed and exploitation are the norm. Armed with a mysterious system, he must navigate a high-tech yet unforgiving society where survival means leveraging every advantage. Rising to the top won't be easy, but it's the only way to thrive.

To rise, he will need more than cunning—he'll need to outmaneuver those who would see him fail. What kind of mark will he leave as he climbs the ranks of this new world?

Follow Rollo in this sci-fi adventure as he uses stealth, cybernetic upgrades, and system progression to rebuild his power and wealth.

Read it on Kindle Unlimited today!

Thank you for reading a MoonQuill original novel. More exciting stories can be found at www.moonquill.com.

We would greatly appreciate it if you would take a moment to leave a review. Every review helps the author and supports their ability to continue writing fantastic books for everyone to enjoy!

If you're looking for more great books to read, join our mailing list by scanning the QR code below. You'll get 4 books for free!